THE FINAL COLLAPSE

WILLIAM ODAY

ISBN-13: 978-1-942472-12-4

Cover by Christian Bentulan

Note that this book was originally titled *The Darwin Collapse* in *The Last Peak* series.

WANT BOOKS FOR FREE?

Join the Readers Group to get a free copy of The Last Day, Sole Prey, and Saint John. One novel, one novella and one short story, all for free. You'll also receive exclusive discounts on new releases, other freebies, and lots more.

Go to WWW.WILLIAMODAY.COM to find out more.

READERS ARE SAYING

EDGE OF SURVIVAL SERIES

THE LAST DAY, Book 1

THE FINAL COLLAPSE, Book 2

THE FRAGILE HOPE, Book 3

THE DESPERATE FIGHT, Book 4

1

November 1963
Brooklyn, New York

A BOY grimaced in disgust as he squeezed into the crowd surrounding the newspaper stand on the corner of Union and Fourth. Cries of dismay echoed through the air. The people pushed and shoved against each other, always jockeying for better position while never realizing the underlying truth.

Their lives were so full of wealth and yet so empty of value.

If things went according to plan, one of them would soon find a small portion of that wealth missing. The boy drifted with the moving currents, repulsed and yet grateful for the warmth of so many bodies. He wasn't trying to get to the front of the line because he had no money with which to purchase a newspaper. Besides, he had no interest in news. That was for these rich people.

People with food in their bellies.

The passing thought of food made his stomach twist on

itself in agony. The sudden pain made him dizzy and he might've fallen over if it weren't for the people pressing in on all sides.

Rough, wool coats scratched his cheeks and arms. A woman passed by and her perfume momentarily masked the stench in his nose. His own stench. The relentless stink of life in the gutter.

He hated winters in the big city. His bare hands and feet had been tingling numb for days. The heat of the crowd was all he could afford. But the warmth of this tight squeeze wasn't the only benefit. Mixing with the masses had another advantage.

It made pinching a wallet easier.

And he needed all the help he could get. While he was a better pickpocket than most of the other urchins he'd come across, winter always made the profession a challenge.

It was the freezing wind that did it. It made his hands feel thick and clumsy—two things that made the job almost impossible. Add to that the fact that his bare feet felt like blocks of ice and he couldn't trust them to run right if a mark caught on and got physical or whistled for the cops.

The boy bumped through the crowd looking for the right opportunity. Long, dark wool jackets surrounded him. There would be an opening if he just kept moving, kept waiting for it. He couldn't afford a mistake.

Even if his feet weren't half-frozen, he couldn't have run. He just didn't have the energy. A mistake would mean getting collared. And getting collared would mean a beating.

Or worse.

New York City's finest took a dim view of street rats like him. And they used every opportunity to make their feelings known. A week ago, they'd beaten a kid to death for trying to steal carrots from the local grocer. There were supposed to be laws against that kind of thing, but laws only protected rich people. Street rats protected themselves or they didn't live long.

The boy had survived many winters, but the emaciated limbs hanging from his bony torso suggested that streak wasn't likely to last much longer.

He needed food.

Something more than the rotten scraps he occasionally found in trash bins. Something more than the infrequent feasts when he landed a decent score.

And so he'd moved to a new street. One with more people and possibilities. Of course, there were always dangers entering new turf, but he'd run out of options. He wasn't inclined to take unnecessary risks when simple survival already required so many necessary ones. He'd been holed up for days and would've stayed put, but the clawing beast in his gut drove him half-mad with hunger.

There came a point when the possibility of death by beating was better than the certainty by starvation.

He'd already reached that point many times this winter and he would again if this attempt didn't kill him.

Weaving through the crowd, he patted coat pockets with fingers that burned like fire now that feeling had returned. He patted another and the pocket contained something. Something promising. But the flap was buttoned down and his stiff fingers weren't all that useful yet.

He was considering how to approach the job when the burly man turned and spotted him. The man looked down at the boy and both knew the score in an instant.

The boy tried to dodge into a gap but the burly man caught him with a hammer blow to the head before he could get away.

The thump sent a jolt of pain through the boy's

shoulders and back. His legs almost gave out but he managed to dive between two dark coats and leave the burly man behind. In a daze, he hurried through more coats, trying to put distance between himself and another crippling punch.

He pushed through a gap and stumbled into an open pocket at the front of the crowd. The newsstand owner took money with one hand and handed out copies of *The New York Times* with the other. The edition pinned to the stand had a big headline in black ink.

KENNEDY IS KILLED BY SNIPER
AS HE RIDES IN CAR IN DALLAS

It had a picture of the president and the story below.

The boy couldn't have cared less. The president had never done anything for him. The president had never put food in his hands or boots on his feet. He was just another rich person in a far off land called Washington who made laws for other rich people and talked about even more far off lands like the moon.

If this country could spend so much money trying to put a man on the moon, why couldn't it spend a few cents to put a sandwich in his hand?

New York City was like that. Too many people all trying to grab their share and more before someone else could get it. They were rats fighting to chew off an ever-larger piece of the cheese.

The arriving and departing eddy of bodies swept him sideways to the next spot in line. A magazine with Elvis on the front captured his attention. The king of rock and roll had glorious sideburns. Perhaps they were the mark of a king.

The crowd shifted him over in front of the newspaper seller.

"Hey, kid!"

The boy looked up.

"You buying?"

The boy shook his head.

"Big surprise. Get lost, or else!"

The boy didn't have to guess at what the *or else* might mean. He slipped back into the crowd, rubbing his hands together and blowing warmer air from his lungs over them.

If he didn't score something solid today, he was certain he wouldn't make it through another freezing night.

2

He stumbled through the crowd a while longer, letting the press of bodies move him where it might, trusting to fate that the right opportunity would present itself eventually. As he drifted, he curled and uncurled his fingers hoping to get more feeling back into them before that moment arrived.

Something soft brushed by. It tickled the fine hairs on his bare arm. A black coat. Finer and softer than the usual rough wool. An understated sign of wealth that shone like a spotlight for people in his profession. He gently bumped a shoulder against the man's coat pocket and felt a distinct bulge.

A magical bulge that promised an end to the agony of his body eating itself.

He winced as his stomach clenched tighter, anticipating the meal that was not yet assured. The boy followed the mark through the crowd, but never too closely. Now that the target was set, he didn't want to blow it by tripping on the mark's heels. A successful pick was as much about timing as technique. And both were required if you wanted to walk away with your head intact.

Between two dark coats, he caught a glimpse of another filthy, young face. One not so different from his own. He'd seen the older boy around a number of times and had thus far managed to avoid him. And that was the way he intended to keep it. The older boy was a good foot taller than him and, while skinny, had a lean frame that hinted at a dangerous strength.

It wasn't uncommon for fights to break out between kids living on the street. Over resources. Over turf. Over pride. Over nothing. And, as often as not, one of the parties involved ended up dead.

The boy avoided other urchins wherever possible. He simply didn't have the size or strength to defend himself. Running was the only option. It had worked thus far.

He ducked and lost sight of the taller boy as he continued trailing behind the rich man. Trailing and waiting for the right moment.

The rich man bought a paper and then began pushing his way out of the crowd.

The boy followed.

The rich man neared the edge of the crowd.

The boy knew all would be lost the instant the man broke free of the mass. It was the chaos of the accidental jostling that covered the execution of the intended one.

It was now or never.

He dodged between two coats and bumped into the rich man. As their bodies collided, the boy slipped a hand inside the long coat. He trailed down the silky lining and parted the interior pocket.

His fingers dipped lower and pinched around a soft,

leather wallet. He lifted his hand. His heart pounded in his ears as the wallet pulled free.

He had it.

Who knew how much money a man like that carried around? It might be enough to eat for a month!

The boy completed the pick with the wallet gripped tightly in his hand. He turned to disappear into the crowd when plush wool fabric wrapped around his neck and drew tight. The arm inside the fabric bulged with muscle. A large hand wrapped over his hand holding the wallet. The grip closed tight, crushing his fingers into a ball.

The boy panicked and kicked out but his limbs were so weak and the choking arm so strong.

A breathy voice whispered in his ear.

"Thinking I'm an easy mark, eh? I'll show you easy."

The man dragged the boy free of the crowd. The boy struggled to break loose but it was no use. The man pulled him into a nearby alley and deeper into its darkness. He slammed the boy against the brick wall and then slammed a fist into his gut.

The boy doubled over, crying out to anyone that would listen.

No one did.

"You filthy scum! Try to pinch me?"

Blows rained down on the boy until he collapsed into a stream of sewage. He couldn't smell it through the blood filling his nose. He curled into a ball and covered up as the man continued to kick and stomp.

Eventually, the beating stopped.

The boy peeked out, wondering if he'd died. But while the beating had stopped, the agony had not. He was still alive.

The man bent over, holding his knees, breathing hard.

He caught the boy's gaze and grinned wickedly. His eyes lit up.

"We're not done yet, boy. You're not going to leave this alley."

The boy noticed movement behind the rich man. It looked like a flickering shadow at first.

The shadow emerged behind the rich man. The older boy. The dangerous looking one he'd succeeded in avoiding.

Well, it was over. Perhaps they would take turns beating him to death. Maybe that would make it end faster, at least.

The tall boy gazed down at him, at the bloodied mess curled on the ground. There was no softness in his eyes. No pity. He drew a long, thin shadow from inside his shabby coat. The razor edge glinted as it caught the light.

The rich man spat on the injured boy and snarled. "What say we finish this?"

It wasn't a question.

The tall boy stepped to his side and the long, thin shadow in his hand pierced the rich man's neck. The shadow sliced sideways and parted the neck into a grisly smile.

Blood spilled down the man's coat as he clutched at the gaping wound in shock. He collapsed in a heap. Blood poured out of his neck, pooling first and then running through the cracks between the uneven cobblestones.

The tall boy kicked the man over onto his back. He rifled through the man's pockets and found the wallet. He opened it and pulled out a huge wad of bills. He snapped through the stack and grinned. He stepped on the dying man's chest, pulled the boy up to a sit and leaned him against the brick wall.

"This is my street. I should kill you to send a message."

The boy's head hung low, because it was too painful to

lift. Breathing was agony. Maybe death would be better. Probably.

"Do you want to die?"

The tall boy lifted his chin, not gently, and gazed hard into his eyes.

"Do you want to die?"

As easy as it would've been, as preferable to the unending misery that was all he could remember, yet he wanted to live. Something inside raged to take one more breath.

He shook his head.

"Then you work for me now. Do you understand?"

The boy nodded.

The tall boy slipped the razor shadow under the boy's neck. The blade pressed a hard line into his throat.

"I have only one rule. Absolute loyalty. Break that and you'll wish this suit killed you."

The boy nodded.

The tall boy sifted through the wallet and pulled out a coin. He turned it from side to side.

"Must be foreign. Keep it."

He flipped the coin into the boy's lap and then dropped the empty wallet on the sputtering man's chest. He wiped the steel shadow clean on the rich man's fine wool coat. He stood and gazed down at the boy.

"Loyalty. Unquestioned and absolute."

He turned and strode away.

3

The Present Day
A Week After the Outbreak
Los Angeles, California

DR. ANTON RESHENKO gazed out of the floor-to-ceiling windows on the seventy-third floor of the Milagro Tower. He barely registered the startling changes of the City of Angels. Urban centers around the world had undergone similar transformations. Movies had once been the region's most famous export.

No longer.

The virus had spread with astonishing speed, killing off most of the world's population. He couldn't have been a prouder father.

Like a modern Mount Olympus, the cylinder of glass and white concrete raised him into the heavens. The crown of the building had the Milagro name in big, block letters that shone at night, even now when few had power.

It truly was a miracle.

Rather, *he* was the miracle.

Like Jesus with the merchants and the moneylenders, Anton had swept the disease from the temple and laid the foundation for a glorious future.

His thoughts soared above the inconsequential happenings and struggles of those bound to the surface below. All of them but one. The one that tethered him to mortality. He abhorred weakness in others and he found it no less offensive in himself. She was the single off flavor in his grand achievement.

How he longed to pluck her out and, at last, be free of petty emotion. But he could not. She was too much like her mother.

He gazed out over the Pacific Ocean to the west and experienced a certain kinship, a soulful resonance, with explorers from bygone days.

Surely, they felt both fear and delight at the prospect of sailing into the unknown, into a future of unlimited potential.

He felt the same way.

After centuries of increasingly imbecilic decision-making, after a continual weakening of the human mind through dependence and distraction, profound change had finally arrived. And he was the spark that had lit the fire from which a new and better world would emerge.

To wield such power was gratifying.

In the left pocket of his rumpled pants, Anton rubbed the silver Dirham of Genghis Khan between his thumb and index finger. So deep was his reverie that the pain of the blistered and bleeding flesh went unnoticed.

Objectively, he grasped that some might think his actions were those of a delusional megalomaniac. A villain with a soul so black that archetypal historical villains seemed a shade of gray in comparison.

People regularly cited the evils of Hitler and his campaign that ended the lives of over forty million people. And yet few recalled Genghis Khan, a conqueror who dispatched a similar number. And gallingly, even fewer factored in the period in which each man lived. Khan made his name when the earth held just four-hundred million people. He wiped away ten percent of the planet's population, whereas Hitler claimed less than two percent.

And Khan did so with the crude and laborious implements of his day. His genius was as breathtaking as it was under-appreciated.

Anton felt a close kinship with the ancient Khan. He often wondered if the infamous Mongol somehow felt the same connection through the ages. As magnificent as Genghis Khan's achievements were, they were nothing to the changes Anton himself had wrought.

He suspected even the great Khan would sink to his knees in supplication. The knowledge warmed him.

Like no conqueror ever before, Anton had changed the course of humanity's evolution forever. His bravery and intellect set a new course into a great unknown, one where mankind might reach the greatness that was its birthright.

The same potential it had let drown in an ocean of satisfied complacency.

A voice from behind startled him.

"Do you expect me to just stand here all day?"

The senator's voice sounded infinitely more weary than it had just a week ago before the change began. It sounded infinitely more *pathetic*.

Anton turned away from his thoughts as his right hand subconsciously scratched at the growing bald spot in his formerly glorious sideburns. His nose curled as a whiff of old age and frailty wafted from the elderly man. His stomach churned as it always did after he'd been thinking of her.

Iridia. His daughter.

The source of his worry.

Her absence was the crack in his heart and mind. The fault line disgusted him. His words flicked like a whip in the senator's direction.

"What I expect you to do is retrieve my daughter!"

Senator Charles Rawlings pushed his thick-lensed glasses up the bridge of his nose and shook his head.

"I got us here from D.C. And with all the chaos, that was no small feat. Let me remind you!"

"That was four days ago," Anton answered and then looked around theatrically, "and yet I still do not see my daughter standing next to me." His cheek itched like fire. He scratched at it for a measure of fleeting relief.

"From what little communications we've received," Rawlings replied, "the command and control structure of the United States of America is a shambles. I'm the Chairman of the Senate Armed Services Committee, and even I can't call up a rescue team from nothing."

Anton rounded the elegant desk of glass and air and confronted the elderly senator. He leaned forward until their eyes were inches apart.

"You *were* the chairman. *Now*, you are a useless old man. One for which I have fewer and fewer reasons to keep alive."

"How dare you!" the old man said. "I brought you on board. Without me, you would be nothing!"

Anton slapped the senator across the face with all of his might. It, perhaps, offended good taste to hit a man of such advanced years, but Anton was in no mood to be challenged just now.

The senator dabbed a crooked finger to his bleeding lip

and stared at the small patch of black marble floor that separated them. "We don't know that she's still alive. Or, if so, that she's still like she was."

Anton's palm connected again with the slack skin of the senator's face almost before he considered the act. "Never say that! She's with a resourceful colleague of Mr. Pike's."

He turned to the tall bodyguard standing by the door, stoically looking ahead. "Mr. Pike, what do you say?"

The bodyguard broke into an easy grin. "Sarge could keep a penguin alive in the Sahara. I reckon if anyone can survive out there, it's him."

The towering Texan's enthusiasm wasn't one of Anton's favorite qualities. Fortunately for him, he had other skills of greater import. He was deadly. He was efficient. But most important of all, he was loyal.

Anton returned his attention to the sniveling goat before him. "She's out there and *you* need to get her for me."

"I'm doing everything I can with limited communications and limited connections to other areas of organized activity."

"Mr. Pike, please leave the office and close the door. The senator and I have classified information to discuss."

"Yes, sir," the beefy man replied with a nod and then did as he was told.

Anton smiled. He appreciated unquestioning obedience. Casimiro Pike knew his place in life and he performed his role. An important role considering the changes. A bodyguard was no longer a luxury of the rich. It was a necessity of the living.

The door clicked shut.

Anton turned to Senator Rawlings. He grabbed the old man's collar and curled it in his fist.

"The problem is you lack sufficient motivation."

The broken politician quailed in terror.

Anton tore open the senator's oxford shirt and raised a syringe in his other hand. He slammed it down and buried the long silver needle into paper-thin, crinkled flesh. He pressed the plunger and delivered the death sentence.

Anton stepped back, leaving the syringe stuck in Rawlings' chest.

The old man yanked it free and flung it away in horror. "What have you done?"

Anton smiled with genuine pleasure. "I injected you with the Delta Virus."

It still bothered him that *Delta Virus* had somehow caught on in the popular media, before said media went dark and thankfully stopped broadcasting its repetitive puke.

He informally thought of MT-1 as the Darwin Virus. The name had a poet's truth. But even using the name repeatedly in those first interviews streamed around the world didn't anchor it sufficiently in the public consciousness.

The *Delta Virus* caught on instead. Delta in science meaning *the change* in something. People began to witness the incredible effects of the virus and The Change Virus was all they could come up with. Though he appreciated the scientific angle, as any man of intellect would, it was still unimaginative and inferior to his version.

Who knew how such viral movements took shape? It would be a fascinating topic for later research.

The change was a rather rudimentary description of an infinitely complex set of chemical and neurological processes that, in the end, resulted in the way forward that Anton had envisioned so long ago.

The senator's knees buckled and he collapsed onto a

svelte black office chair. "No! No! No!" His head dropped so low it looked like his neck had surrendered.

"Yes."

Anton grabbed his chin and lifted it so their eyes met. "You will get the resources to retrieve my daughter or you will die horribly. Or, worst yet, wish you had."

The senator's eyes went wide and white. "How long do I have?"

"You've seen the pathology. Somewhere between twenty-four and seventy-two hours." Anton turned to the closed office door. "Mr. Pike!"

The door opened and Anton's bodyguard entered. "Yes, sir?" His eyes darted around the room searching for signs of danger.

He would find none visible, the danger was only beginning to flourish in Senator Rawlings' blood stream.

"Escort Charles to the comms station. He has vital business to attend to."

4

MASON WEST checked the time on his watch. One minute to noon. He reached over the kitchen sink and grabbed the small emergency radio from the windowsill. The solar panel on the top warmed his palm. He clicked it on and stared out into the backyard, waiting for the broadcast to begin.

Cold thoughts began to creep in when warm arms encircled his waist and an equally warm body hugged his backside. He knew the feel of Elizabeth's body on an instinctual level. Over fifteen years of marriage could do that.

And that was just it.

It *could* do that.

There were no guarantees. The passage of time didn't require that closeness. Quite the opposite, in fact. It seemed the passage of time often induced distance; a growing apart as the years sped by.

A couple of those years had torn them apart and pushed them away to opposite cliffs separated by a bottomless abyss.

But they hadn't surrendered. They hadn't given up on each other, on their shared life together. To be fair, it was Beth's bottomless well of compassion that pulled them through. But they did it.

They survived.

Together.

As warm and welcoming as Beth's hug was, it was also a reminder of a question he'd been asking himself more and more.

Could they survive in the world they now faced?

Not for a day or two. Not for a month or two. Not for a year or two. But for a lifetime?

And even if they could, what kind of life would it be?

"Have you seen Mr. Piddles?" Beth said.

The cat they'd been forced to inherit after their neighbors passed away from the outbreak. He was named Mr. Piddles for a reason. Mason had no use for a cat in the first place, much less one that squirted its nasty urine indoors.

Not in a cat box indoors.

"No, but my pillow reeks. I'm pretty sure it peed on it. Can we get rid of it?"

"The pillow? Sure."

"I'm talking about the cat, although the pillow might have to go too."

"Mr. Piddles is a *he*. And no, we're not getting rid of him. He's just expressing his sadness. Can you imagine how upset he must be?"

"I try not to. But he'd better not express on my pillow again."

"Anything yet?" Beth asked, wisely deciding to change the subject.

"Nope, should be any second now."

"Do you think anything will be different? Any updates?"

"It's been the same for seven days now," Mason replied. "I don't know."

The message always played three times in a row starting exactly at noon. It had done that for the last seven days. Mason didn't want to think about what the static, daily repetition might mean. No possibility that came to mind was a good one.

"We'll find out soon," Beth said as she rested her cheek against his back. "How's the calculating going?"

Mason surveyed the long gray granite countertop. Every bit of food in the house lay stacked and sorted on it. Cans of beans, vegetables, and fruit stood four high. A large block of boxes contained an assortment of pasta shapes and sizes. An unopened bag of dog food for their recently deceased Bullmastiff, Max, was at the end.

He hoped it wouldn't come to dog chow.

At least it was organic.

"I still have to count—"

The tiny speaker in the emergency radio chirped to life as an unwavering tone indicated the transmission had begun.

This is a message from the Emergency Broadcast System. This is not a test. Repeat. This is not a test.

For the protection and safekeeping of all citizens, the President of the United States has declared martial law. Anyone not engaged in official business of the state is required to stay indoors at all times. Anyone violating this restriction is knowingly placing him or herself in extreme danger and will be dealt with accordingly.

The President, along with the surviving legislative branch, is taking all prudent action to resolve the crisis as soon as possible.

The best course of action for the citizen is to stay indoors, keep you and your family safe, and wait for further instructions. Tune in at noon tomorrow for the latest news on the state of the emergency.

This concludes the message from the Emergency Broadcast System.

The radio was silent for ten seconds, and then the tone and message repeated. The cycle began again, and nothing seemed out of the ordinary (if that could mean anything anymore), until the transmission cut out early.

...The best course of action for the citizen is to...

And the radio went silent.

It wasn't supposed to go silent. It was supposed to finish the message.

Mason checked the volume knob. He cranked it all the way over and the static grew louder. He checked the red dial on the frequency band to see if it had somehow slipped away from the correct frequency.

Nope. Right on the nose.

Beth came around to his side. "Why did it stop?"

"I don't know," he said as he met her warm amber eyes. "But I think their guidance is no longer the best approach, if it ever was. We need to get out and assess the situation for ourselves. We've been dug in like gophers for the last week. All of the regular media channels blinked out days ago. We need intel."

"Slow down, Sergeant Mason. How are you feeling?" Mason stretched the tender muscles in his left calf and flexed the muscles in his back. The wounds he'd acquired in rescuing his daughter and Elio from that crazed gang were healing well.

"Sore, but good, Dr. West," he said as he winked at her.

"Why are you winking? I *am* a doctor. A veterinary doctor, I'll give you that. But I'm your best shot right now."

Mason grinned and kissed her lips and then her forehead. "It's your bedside manner that keeps me coming back."

Another voice intruded on their private moment.

"Ewww, gross. Aren't things bad enough already without you two going max PDA in my face all the time?"

The other most important person in Mason's life, his daughter Theresa. Maybe *the* most important. He and Beth had had conversations over the years about the hierarchy of deepest love and, by mutual and inoffensive consent, they agreed Theresa came first. That was just what being a parent meant.

She was a carbon copy of his wife in so many ways. Long, wavy black hair framing amber eyes. An easy smile both coming and going. A sharp tongue when the situation suited her. A tenderness forever hidden beneath.

His heart ached for the world she'd inherited.

She deserved better.

Beth pushed up on her tippy toes while pulling Mason's head down to hers. She slipped her tongue between his lips and flicked at his teeth until they gave way.

"NO! NO!" Theresa yelled. "I'm scarred for life. That unholy image is burned into my retinas!" She held her arms out and cast her eyes around the room like a cat following a laser light. "It's everywhere! Everywhere!"

Elio Lopez flew into the kitchen and jolted to a stop behind Theresa. He held her shoulders. "Are you okay? What's wrong?" His eyes darted back and forth from person to person. He narrowed them. "Wait. Am I missing something here?"

Theresa giggled. "No, nothing you should be subjected

to seeing. I just walked in on these two making the kitchen into a love shack. And the kitchen is *not* where it's at."

Elio scrunched his brows together in confusion.

Theresa turned to him, "That gives me an idea." She leaned in to Elio, their lips drawing ever closer.

Mason's heart leapt into his throat. He jumped over and lowered a hand between their faces. He eyeballed Elio. "Back up, hero. I'd hate for you to get injured right when you're getting better."

Theresa tried to slap his arm away, but it held firm. "Dad, we weren't going to actually kiss!"

Elio's eyebrows jumped and he stumbled back. "Uhh, no. No, sir. I mean—"

"Yeah," Mason said, "I was seventeen once. I know what you mean."

Elio shook his head. "It's not like that, sir. It's not—"

Theresa whirled on him, her hands anchored to her hips and a dangerous glint in her eye. "It's not like *that*? So, we're not like *that*, huh?"

She had her mother's fire. The same ability to flit from humor to anger and back again in heartbeats. It occasionally terrified Mason, but it always captivated him.

"No, it's not like that. I mean, yes! Yes, it is with us!"

Mason's mood darkened. "So it is?"

Elio looked between Mason and Theresa, caught in a trap from which he couldn't escape.

Beth cut smoothly between the opposing forces and swept her arm around Elio and led him away. "Come help set the table while her father adjusts to his daughter's growing independence."

"Yes, ma'am," he said with clear relief in his voice as they disappeared into the dining room.

"Dad," Theresa said, "don't scare him."

Mason shrugged. "Isn't that my job?"

Theresa arched a brow at him. "I thought you were a bodyguard."

"I am."

5

The sizes of the portions on each plate were exacting and unavoidably meager. Mason ensured that each plate got a cup of Cajun rice and beans, a slice of bread, and a slice of apple. His mouth watered tasting the spicy scent in the air. His belly grumbled. It would get one of the plates even though three or four were needed. He surveyed each one and shook his head. This was going to be considered feast before too long.

Theresa had left to go check on her blossoming love interest. His mind almost gagged on the words. She was fifteen. That was too young. Back when she was five, fifteen had seemed like a reasonable age to start this kind of thing. But now?

No. Too soon. Way too soon.

Maybe the lack of calories would suppress their teenage hormones. Maybe that was the one up side. Rationing was a clear necessity. But that wouldn't make things last forever. Which brought up the question of what to do next.

There was no way to know without more intel first. It

was just that he wasn't looking forward to confirming what he already knew in his gut.

Things were bad.

Really bad.

It wasn't the inconvenience of rolling blackouts in the middle of the day that had become common in recent summers.

It wasn't the widespread power outage that took down most of the Northeast for a week in August of 2003.

It wasn't even the abject failure of local, state, and federal government in the response to the Hurricane Katrina disaster.

Those were problems.

They had solutions, even if the powers that be were slow to implement them.

This was a predicament.

There were no solutions, per se. Only adjustments. Only hard choices that burned in the kiln of an unforgiving new world. And every choice was another round in the fire.

Another chance to crack apart and fall to ruin.

The apple slices came up a plate short. He'd go without. In another time and country, he'd lived on far worse and far less.

Iridia Reshenko sidled up next to him. She eyed a plate and Mason gritted his teeth, willing himself to be calm while she registered her complaint.

"I can't eat that many carbs!" she said.

That wasn't the complaint he expected.

Though he should have. A Ukrainian supermodel that had appeared multiple times in Sports Illustrated's swimsuit issue (if he could believe Miro, at least) had somehow ended up in his care, in his house, in his space.

She was the job that never ended. The one that wouldn't die. And it was his job to keep her that way. But, it had gone way beyond a job. Over the last week, she had done her best (which was generally terrible) to integrate into the West household.

Mason appreciated that she tried to be helpful, which for a supermodel accustomed to the world waiting on her every whim, meant she tried not to whine and complain every time Beth asked her to do something around the house.

This new reality wasn't easy for any of them. But it was probably the hardest for Iridia. She'd had the furthest to fall.

Still, Mason wished she'd fallen onto that plane that would've taken her out of his life. But, it wasn't meant to be.

He'd done his best to do the job as directed. But factors beyond his control ended up making that impossible. The federal government closing down the airspace above Los Angeles was one thing. His daughter's life in danger yet another.

It should've been simple. Get her on a plane back to her father, some genius scientist. It was the first job he'd ever not completed. The first in almost a decade as a close protection officer.

He didn't like it.

But the world didn't turn according to his preferences.

He scraped away half a cup of rice and beans and put the recovered half back into the lidded glass bowl.

Iridia picked up the slice of bread from her plate and peered at it. "Is this gluten-free bread?"

Mason rolled his eyes. "It's packed with glutens. I specifically picked up the one with extra-gluten."

She tilted her head away like the inert slice of baked flour might bite her.

"Eat it," Mason said. "You're too skinny."

Iridia lifted the long, loose-fitting shirt that she'd borrowed from Beth, exposing her waist and lack of clothing to cover her minimally functional underwear. She twisted around and her sandy blonde hair trailed across her shoulder. She patted and squeezed an exposed butt cheek.

"*This* is a disaster," she said.

"Tell me something I don't know," Mason replied as he stared off into the backyard thinking of what might be beyond.

She turned back to Mason as if stricken. Her crystal green eyes wide and worried. "You see it, don't you?"

"What?"

"Just say it. It's there."

"What are you talking about?"

Iridia squeezed the butt cheek again and a sob welled up in her chest. "I have butt fat."

Mason pinched his eyes shut and shook his head. He forcibly returned his attention to something less infuriating, like the fact that he was providing his family fewer calories than their bodies required, and yet, here was this person complaining about the tone of her butt cheeks.

"Hello," Beth's voice said from the doorway to the dining room. "Iridia, you were supposed to be getting lunch for everyone, not showing your half-naked body to my husband."

Iridia whimpered and dropped the shirt which still ended mid-thigh. "This is terrible. The worst."

"What is—"

"Don't ask," Mason said hoping to save her the grief.

"What is terrible?" Beth asked anyway.

"I should've expected it. I mean, I've missed my daily workout with Esteban for over a week. And I eat any old garbage you put in front of me..."

She said a few other things but Mason's brain had stopped listening. She was complaining about eating into his family's dwindling resources? How could she be so clueless?

"What are you talking about, Iridia?" Beth cut into Iridia's ongoing complaining.

Iridia spun around and hiked the shirt up again to show Beth her bare butt cheeks. She really needed some underwear that consisted of more than a cord up the crack. "I have butt fat."

Beth waved her off. "Pffft! Talk to me when you're thirty-four and you can tell me how perfect your twenty-five-year-old butt used to be. Now, stop flashing your flesh under this roof and take those plates to the table."

Iridia's full lips looked even more pouty than usual. Mason wondered which way she was going to go. Typical Iridia flameout or one of those few instances of reasonable responsibility? Iridia grabbed two plates off the counter and marched them into the dining room.

Beth shook her head. "I swear to God. I bet you've seen her butt more times than mine in the last week."

Mason decided to poke the bear.

"Hey, who's counting?"

"I am. That's who. And the balance better lean towards my column."

"I'm just the cook here. I only recently realized I was working in a strip joint."

"Very funny... not."

"Grab a couple plates and I'll get the rest," Mason said.

"We need to discuss the food and water situation with everyone."

Beth bit her lip and led the way back to the dining room. Together they brought enough food on each plate to ensure that, today at least, no one would starve.

Mason wondered how long they'd be able to say that.

6

The small round table in the breakfast nook of the kitchen wasn't big enough to accommodate everyone, so the larger rectangular dining room table had become the gathering spot where they shared food, touched base, and did their best to keep each other sane.

That was the idea anyway.

Everyone sat down and eyed the noticeably undersized portions. Before anyone could take a bite, Beth spoke. "We should say a blessing. Does anyone want to lead it?"

"I do!" Iridia said before anyone else could volunteer.

"Okay," Beth replied through pursed lips.

"Dear God," Iridia began, "I know you're, like, amazing and can do anything you want with all of your powers. And I know you see and know everything happening to everyone down here. So you can totally see the disaster."

Mason nodded as he stared out a window at the clear blue, summer sky. He agreed. May as well pray for heavenly help. Couldn't hurt at this point.

"So, I'm begging, praying I guess, for your help. Please make my butt fat go away."

Theresa laughed so hard she snorted. Elio did his best to suppress it, but laughter had him in choking convulsions. It was too much. Or maybe just enough.

Beth and Mason broke into laughter as well and the entire table laughed themselves silly while Iridia looked on in confusion.

"What? I know it sounds stupid. But if anyone can fix it, it's got to be him, right?"

Beth forced herself into a semblance of composure and replied, "Yes, please help Iridia's butt first, and then, if you happen to have any time left over, maybe take a crack at the lesser needs of the rest of the world."

"Exactly," Iridia said, "I figured he knew all about the big problems we face. It's the little problems that sometimes escape notice."

The laughter resumed and it took a full two minutes before it died down again. Mason took a big breath. The suffocating weight on his chest felt one ounce lighter.

Laughter.

They needed it.

A light to resist the clawing darkness.

"Thank you, Iridia," Mason said.

"For what?"

"Never mind, let's eat," Mason said. "And go slow. This isn't the Sizzler all-you-can-eat buffet." He took a spoonful of rice and beans and chewed it slowly. His body buzzed at the incoming caloric delivery. Food became sacred, a sacrament, when the end of its abundance was in sight.

A wet rasping cough came from the hallway leading to the bedrooms.

"Where's Clyde?" Mason asked.

Beth had saved the week-old Bili chimpanzee from dying inside his mother's womb. If Iridia was an odd addition to his household (and she was), Clyde was stranger yet. But Beth wouldn't have it any other way. She was as committed to his future as she was her own. Mason didn't think the extra burden was a wise choice considering the state of things, but Beth had made it clear the topic wasn't open for discussion.

Mason understood.

Clyde's mother had been like another daughter to Beth. Her death still very much a tragedy Beth was working through. Besides, Clyde was good for Theresa, too. The gruesome deaths of their dog Max and her best friend Holly had punched a hole in Theresa's heart. Caring for Clyde distracted and focused her attention at the same time.

Caring for another was a powerful means of caring for yourself.

"He's snuggling Lambchops in my bed," Theresa replied.

That was a surprise considering how attached she was to the old stuffie that had been her nightly companion over the last fourteen years.

"Didn't he chew off the remaining eye button yesterday?" Mason asked.

Theresa's jaw twitched. "Yes, he did. But he needs Lambchops more than I do right now. So, I'm sharing for the time being."

Elio giggled under his breath.

Theresa smacked his shoulder, but not too hard as he was still recovering from the gun shot wound to his left side. He'd gotten lucky. It had torn out a chunk of flesh on his left side below the ribs, but no bones or vital organs had been involved. "Don't laugh at me!"

"I'm not! I mean, a little maybe. You're fifteen years old and you still have a woobie."

"Elio Lopez! He is *not* a woobie. He is Lambchops. And he'll be around longer than you will at this rate."

Mason laughed. So like her mother.

"Sorry," Elio replied. "Baby stuffies are A-okay with me."

Theresa pinched her face tighter and frowned.

Beth grinned. "That hole keeps getting deeper."

Elio stared hard at his plate. "I'm going to eat now."

"Smart choice, for once," Theresa said in an icy tone.

Everyone ate in silence for a few minutes, each in the shadow of their own thoughts, as if the blazing sun outside couldn't reach them. Elio broke the spell.

"Mason?"

Mason blinked his eyes back into their shared reality. "Yep?"

"I'm not trying to be a problem, but I can't wait any longer. I have to go check on my mom."

Mason had stalled the kid for days on the decision of when to go check on Maria. She lived at their apartment in Inglewood. The first few days had been easy as neither of them were in shape to do anything more than rest and recuperate. But now that they were both growing stronger, it was likewise growing more difficult to keep him contained.

The danger involved in traversing eight miles of dense urban jungle in its current condition was incalculable. It was incalculable simply because none of them had ventured further than the front yard in a week.

"Elio, we have no idea what the situation is in the larger city. We can expect that it's not safe. You and I have healed enough to move around, but we're in no condition for a lengthy expedition into danger."

"I know," he replied, "but it's my mother. And she's got no one else in the world but me." Elio's eyes lifted to connect with Mason's.

A dull pain stabbed at Mason's chest. Elio knew the truth now. The boy's eyes didn't accuse or blame him. They simply stated the truth. She was alone.

"I agree we need to check on her," Mason said, "but we need another day or two to get stronger and shore up our situation here. A shorter expedition is the way to start."

Elio breathed out heavily and shook his head. "I can't wait much longer. She may already be in trouble and need me."

"You going out and getting yourself in trouble isn't going to help your mother. Give me another day or two here and I promise we'll go together."

"Whatever. You just want to sit around here until we all die," Elio said as he dropped his eyes to the last bite on his plate.

Mason didn't like the delay either, but he knew better than most that recklessly putting yourself in danger in order to save another usually ended up with both people dead. He'd seen how quickly death could come for you when you lived at the boundaries; out on the edge where seemingly simple decisions could unleash devastating consequences.

Death lingered just beyond the edge.

And the virus had thrust all of humanity closer to an unexpected rendezvous.

7

"Theresa and I will go on a supply run tonight," Mason said.

Theresa looked to Beth for confirmation.

She nodded. "Your father and I discussed it this morning. We don't have a choice."

"Can I go?" Iridia asked.

"No," Mason and Beth answered in unison.

He sometimes wondered how they somehow ended up with three teenagers under their roof. Iridia was technically twenty-five, but her immaturity and selfishness brought her emotional intelligence right in line with the other two actual teenagers sitting at the table.

"I've rationed out our food and, plus or minus a day, we have eighteen days remaining."

Mason chewed the inside of his lip as his words settled into the minds of everyone present. Two additional unexpected mouths to feed didn't help the situation, but still, he was furious with himself for not laying in a larger reserve. They had the resources. He always knew it was a good idea. The options were there. But he never had time. It never quite made it high enough on the priority list.

It wasn't that he was totally unprepared.

They had a reasonable amount of canned and dried goods in the pantry and even had a month's worth of freeze-dried Mountain House #10 cans. Drinking water wasn't a problem in the near future as he'd drained the old eighty gallon hot water tank in the first twenty-four hours of the emergency. They'd been waffling on about tearing it out and replacing it with a modern tankless system for years and never got around to it. Thank God they hadn't.

Who knew being lazy could be so productive?

He also filled a WaterBOB collapsible bladder in the bathtub, which stored another hundred gallons. Add the four fifty-five gallon drums in the garage and a package of six sealed LifeStraws, and they were set for many months.

That was the drinking water. They gathered water for other uses from a neighbor's pool two houses down. Mason had torn down the two backyard fence lines in between and created a path that kept them from being visible from the street. Things had gone quiet over the last few days and he had no intention of attracting unwanted attention.

They'd done their best to keep their bodies, clothes, and house clean. So far, it was generally working. It helped that the Mrs., Dr. West, reminded everybody about the importance of hygiene. A small cut could quickly turn into something much worse with their stress-weakened immune systems.

"We need to find more food," Mason said.

"And we need medical supplies," Beth said, "specifically antibiotics. Mason finished his course yesterday and Elio will finish the last of it tonight. We need more. Clyde's respiratory infection is getting worse. And who knows when the next time one of us will need help getting over an infection."

She swallowed hard and stared at her fork.

Mason reached across the table and grasped her hand. "We'll get more. Don't worry."

She pursed her lips and nodded. "That's not my biggest worry, Mason. What if you two get hurt?"

"Beth, we discussed and settled this. We'll be careful."

She shook her head and looked out the window. "I know you'll try."

"Dad, where are we going tonight?"

"We'll check out the CVS by Whole Foods and the Rite-Aid by Ralphs. Looters have probably hit them by now, but we'll see what we can find."

"Won't that make us looters, too?"

"Maybe. We wouldn't take anything by force, but if there are supplies to be had, we'll need them."

The people surrounding the table went quiet.

And then the sound of a gunshot jolted them into action.

Mason shoved the seat back and drew the holstered Glock 19 tucked inside his waistband in one fluid motion. He was headed for the front window before the others at the table had managed to stand. "Beth, you're armed."

It was a statement, not a question. He'd convinced her of the necessity. The statement was more a reminder of the severity of the situation.

"Get everyone in the kitchen."

A chair squealed across the wood floor as Beth dragged someone to their feet, probably Iridia. "Let's go," she said.

Mason chamber-checked his pistol and verified it was hot as he edged up next to the large front window. He inched the heavy curtains open enough to get a view of the yard and beyond.

Across the street, half a dozen armed men stood on Mr.

Raybury's porch. The front door was open and they all yelled over each other into the darkened interior. Mason had no doubts about what this ragged band was up to.

Looters.

A man with a thick beard appeared in the doorway dragging the elderly Mr. Raybury behind him and then shoved him onto the grass. Before Mason could formulate a plan to help, the bearded man drew a pistol from behind his back, placed the muzzle to Mr. Raybury's forehead, and squeezed the trigger.

A sick feeling slammed Mason in the gut.

All the men circled around the body and laughed, pumping extra rounds into the corpse.

Mason ached to hurt them. To make them feel what they made others feel. His mind warred with itself, the desire for action wrestling with the need to protect those in his charge.

The bearded man screamed something lost in the hail of gunfire. He shouted again and the men stopped firing.

"Save your bullets, you idiots! They don't grow on trees!" He pointed toward the house and three men disappeared inside. They returned a few minutes later with bags filled with whatever goods they'd deemed worth stealing. One of the bigger men grabbed for a bag and tried to yank it away from an exiting invader. The smaller man charged his assailant and both men ended up rolling around on the ground, throwing wild punches and swearing to kill each other.

The other men that had surrounded Mr. Raybury's body now circled around the fight in progress. They hooted and hollered and called out bets like it was a dog fight.

CRACK.

The leader shot a round into the air.

"Enough! Get up and stop messing around, or I'll kill

you both myself." He aimed the pistol at the two fighters. They rolled apart and got to their feet in a hurry.

"Sorry, boss."

A loud, screeching sound came from the hallway at Mason's back.

Clyde.

His call for attention wasn't insanely loud. It was just that almost any sound was loud in the newly muffled world.

Mason heard Beth's footfalls as she sprinted for Theresa's bedroom. She spoke to the chimp in a calming, reassuring tone.

Another screech.

The men across the street all turned as one. The leader tilted his head like a dog trying to understand something. He waved his pistol at Mason's house. "Go check it out."

8

Four rough-looking men sauntered across the street pushing and shoving at each other like they were all just out for another Saturday night with the boys.

Idiots.

But four of them. All armed. At least they'd split their forces. Mason would have to handle the first four quickly before the other three got involved. He wasn't in the Marine Corps anymore. His family members weren't trained soldiers. They weren't ready for a large number of deadly aggressors.

His wife carried a Glock 19 identical to his own. It was a good idea for parts redundancy and caliber commonality. She was trained well beyond what the average citizen achieved, but still, she was not and never had been a soldier.

She'd never killed anyone. She'd never lost someone in battle. How she might react was a wildcard in a situation with too many variables already.

And so that left him.

One against many.

The odds were not in his favor. Not that it mattered. His

family was in danger. When your back was against the wall, you did what you had to do. Not because you were a hero. Not because you were cut from a more formidable cloth than mere mortals.

You did it because it had to be done and nobody else was going to do it for you.

You did it, or you died trying. Such was life out on the edge.

Mason narrowed the curtain opening to a sliver as the four men crossed his front yard. The first two bounded up the porch steps. The second one planted a boot on the loose second step and it collapsed to the side. He tumbled over, arms wheeling. He went down hard on the pavement.

CRACK.

A round discharged and hit the guy in front. The shot tore into his leg. He screamed and collapsed forward. The shooter on the ground looked around in a daze.

The loose step had been a result of domestic laziness rather than a premeditated trap, but it worked nonetheless. He'd reset it if they made it through this encounter.

The bearded man ran across the street hurling threats and insults. His face turned beet red as spittle flew from his lips. His pants slipped down under his protruding belly and he yanked them up with one hand while waving the pistol with the other.

He kicked the shooter in the gut before bounding up onto the porch. With his pants situated, the bearded man helped his wounded friend to his feet. "Bunch a idiots! Think we're just gonna head over to the ER and get you fixed up?" He shook his head in disgust.

Now only inches away beyond the plate glass, Mason could see just how filthy and disheveled these people were. The boss' beard was encrusted with what looked like dark mud. Bright red droplets covered his face. His jeans were ripped at the knees and as much brown as their original blue. His short-sleeve button-up hung open and a sizable belly spilled out. Bright blood created a new pattern on the gray shirt. Older patterns showed a history of his misdeeds.

Mason aimed the front sight of the Glock at the man's chest. Two shots and he'd be down. Maybe the rest would panic and run. Brave men could fall to fear when their anchor was torn away.

The leader waved to the two men standing dumbfounded in the front yard. "You two, check out the house! And do your best not to kill each other!"

"You got it, boss," one said.

The leader helped the injured man down the steps and landed another hard kick on the shooter as they passed.

The front door knob jiggled.

It jiggled harder.

"It's locked, boss."

"Then kick it down!"

THUD.

A boot slammed into the wooden door. The frame shuddered but held fast.

THUD. THUD.

The noise stopped and the door didn't budge. Mason silently thanked the builder for choosing solid oak.

"Not budging, boss."

"Lord help me! I'm dealing with idiots! Shoot the stupid lock out!"

Mason pivoted away from the door as a handgun's report rang in his ears.

"Missed it, boss."

"Jesus H. Christ! I should kill you myself! Forget the door! Kick the window in!"

"Yeah, okay. Good idea."

Mason's pointer finger slid inside the guard and gently rested on the trigger. Three men were now in his immediate field of fire. He was confident in dispatching them, but the remaining three and the wounded guy were less certain.

Less certain sank a cold stone into the depths of his belly. He swallowed hard and found no saliva to help.

It was time to do his job.

But failure meant his entire family would die.

The would-be invader squared up to the window that Mason was next to. Mason backed up, still keeping the window at an angle, and aimed his weapon where the man's chest would be behind the heavy curtains.

SMASH.

The plate glass caved in and pushed into the closed curtain. Fragments clattered to the wood floor.

As soon as the curtain parted...

Any second now...

A keening shriek from outside caught Mason off guard. The primal fury of it jolted him. It wasn't human. But it wasn't an animal he recognized either.

A voice from further away shouted, "Boss! It's them! We gotta get outta here!"

"Yeah, I know! Let's go!"

"What about me? I can't run with a bullet in my leg!"

The bearded man answered in a flat tone. "You know where to find us if you make it."

"Don't leave me!"

Mason peeked through the curtains. The injured man hobbled down the street after his fleeing companions.

Leaving an injured man behind.

Scumbags.

They all deserved no better than whatever befell their

injured brother. And he didn't deserve any good turns either.

"What was that sound?"

"Beth," he whispered, "you're supposed to be in the kitchen!"

"Barefoot and pregnant, I know," she said with grim humor.

Leave it to his wife to stay cucumber cool, even in situations she had no experience with. Part of it came from operating on sick animals. She'd had her share of unwelcome surprises in surgery. But losing her head would achieve nothing more than losing her patient.

That was part of it.

But the other part was just who she was. He was blessed beyond words.

"What was that?" she whispered.

"Don't know. But it set a gang of seven armed looters running scared like the devil himself was at their heels."

9

Mason stood guard by the window for the next two hours waiting for the source of the noise to show itself, or waiting for the looters to return to finish their business. His legs alternated tingling numbness, but nothing else came to pass.

The quiet minutes wore on, oblivious to the distance they accumulated between the present and the last breath of his neighbor lying across the street.

"I'll keep watch," Beth said as she squeezed his shoulder. "You need to get ready for tonight."

He held her eyes and she simply nodded.

What did he ever do to deserve her?

She understood the risk, but she also knew that holing up with dwindling supplies was a plan with a very definite end, and that end was no better than what might happen out there tonight.

"You're not the boss of me," Mason replied with a lopsided grin. The levity was forced, but it was better than lumbering around filled with morose dread.

"Not as far as you know. But a woman has her ways."

"Duly noted," Mason replied as he hugged her tight.

He checked in on everyone else and found the household in a more relaxed, if still concerned, posture.

Elio watched Theresa feed Clyde formula. The tender look in his eye was something Mason filed away for future consideration.

Iridia was in what used to be his and Beth's shared office. She'd overtaken it completely, which was saying something considering she'd arrived at his house with little more than a backless dress and a pair of high heels.

He brushed through the rainbow of tapestries that draped across the doorway.

Mr. Piddles turned sideways, arching his back and hissing like a leaking tire.

"So this is where it's been hanging out."

"*It* is a *him*. And you're upsetting him," Iridia said as she rolled off a yoga mat and stroked the cat's back to calm it down.

"Well, cat pee on my pillow is upsetting to me. So we're even."

Iridia rubbed under its neck. "Don't listen to him, honey. You're a sweetie." She kissed its whiskered snout.

Mason noticed the office didn't stink. Mr. Piddles must've chosen him to be the lucky recipient of its expressive nature.

Iridia rolled back to the mat and bent up like a pretzel, supporting her body weight balanced on her hands. She didn't weigh that much, but still, it was impressive.

"Yoga," she said. "Good for staying calm. Stress can make your body store more fat, and it can also cause premature wrinkles. Want to join?"

"Nah, thanks," Mason said. "I've earned my wrinkles."

He went around the house, verifying that all points of

entry were secured. They were, in so far as being locked. But a large number of plate glass windows, including the shattered one by the front door, made the house utterly insecure on a practical level. They'd have to board up everything, starting with the broken window, if he could scrounge up enough plywood.

Should've done it days ago but between being beat up and not really believing it could all fall apart so fast, fortifying their position hadn't gotten done. He'd have to get on it tomorrow. Tonight's supply run came first. His attention was required there first. Besides, they might learn something tonight that would affect their planning tomorrow.

Mason headed to the master bedroom and closed the door. He pulled off his shirt and recoiled at the stink emanating from it. He'd missed the window of afternoon warmth that made bathing in the backyard reasonably bearable. What passed for bathing these days... half a gallon of increasingly stale pool water and a single squirt of body soap.

The pool water from two houses down was no doubt a godsend, but it wouldn't be that way forever. At first, the chlorine made their skin itchy. Now that most of the chlorine had broken down, the water no longer dried out their skin, but it did leave a musty odor. And the odor was growing. He'd have to dig through the neighbor's shed and figure out how to dose the pool with more chlorine.

He settled for a quick minute scrubbing a wet wipe over his stinkiest parts.

Relatively refreshed, he donned black pants, belt, and a black sweatshirt. He reverently laid out the tools of his trade on the bedroom dresser. He looked forward to preparing for the evening's excursion, to the ritual he'd performed countless times in his years as a close protection officer.

Gearing up. A ritual preparation he'd learned in the Corps and carried over to civilian life.

A sanctuary of ordered progress in a broken world.

Something to keep him grounded and sane.

Though his gear no longer occupied the hood of a Humvee, it gave him the same sense of mental preparation.

Preparing for battle.

For the unknown.

He picked up the 9mm Glock 19 and checked the chamber. Empty. He slammed in a fifteen round magazine, racked the slide, and checked the chamber. Hot. He holstered it inside his waistband. Next, a ten round magazine clipped to his belt. Next, the Glock 26. Same process. Hot. Into the ankle holster on his right leg. The Bonowi 26" collapsible baton clipped to his hip. In less than a second, he could wield a big, and very hard, stick. The Cold Steel Recon one-handed tactical knife clipped to his belt. Finally, four pairs of disposable handcuffs clipped to the belt at the small of his back.

No tie this evening.

That part was unusual, not that he missed it. He never understood why hanging a cloth noose around your neck made you more respectable.

He remembered the last time he'd geared up, tie and all, and ended up meeting Iridia at her hotel room. Him praying she didn't turn out to be crazy. Her opening the door completely naked but for the towel wrapped around her head.

If only the insanity had stopped there.

Unfortunately, that was just the beginning.

He checked himself in the mirror and laughed when he

realized he was staring. He looked suspicious. Made sense. He wouldn't trust anyone dressed like he was. But the dark color made situational sense. They were going out at dusk and darker clothes drew less attention.

Above all things, they wanted to avoid attention.

He grabbed a black LA Galaxy cap on his way out of the bedroom.

Time to check on Theresa and load up the Bronco. He didn't relish the thought of what she might be exposed to this evening.

But shielding her from the new world was no longer an option.

10

ELIZABETH WEST carried a stuffed backpack out to the Bronco in the backyard. Her hands trembled, not from the weight of the pack but from the weight on her heart. The two people she loved most in the world were about to risk a supply run. She understood the need, but it didn't make it any easier to accept. Her tongue felt fat and useless in her mouth. Her thoughts veered toward mad despair, and she fought to rein them in.

Borrowing future grief wasn't a useful propensity in a world where the present had plenty of its own.

A cool evening breeze tickled her nose with the welcome scent of lavender. She'd taken to plucking a few leaves from the overgrown bush in the backyard each morning, and then rubbing them on her wrists and neck. She'd never been the princess type, but she still liked to smell nice. And that was getting more and more difficult as the days ticked by.

She recognized the dim outline of the giant Ford truck. The old beast didn't have a single edge that wasn't rough, but that just made her appreciate it more. Mason claimed to love it like a fourth family member, and she could understand the attachment. You invested a part of yourself into fixing something, into keeping it alive. Whether it was healing sick animals or fixing Spock, her old Kawasaki Vulcan 750, Beth knew more than most about not giving up on things.

Spock had all the badges of old age and failing faculties. It hadn't been treated well before she adopted it. The bucket of bolts should've given up the ghost long ago. But Beth didn't give up on a patient, whether made of flesh or metal. She'd nursed the blown bike back to health and it now rode as good as ever.

Her persistence didn't always pay off so wonderfully. Jane hadn't pulled through despite Beth's best efforts. Beth shook off the dark memory as a light flashed across her chest.

Mason stood at the open door with a headlamp around his head. Light from the fading sky bathed the backyard in soft contrast. He accepted the backpack and unzipped it.

"Gloves, dust masks, cloth bags, extra flashlights..." he said as he rifled through the contents. He finished and zipped the pack shut. He tossed it up onto the front seat— the ginormous tires put the Bronco a few feet above most other vehicles on the road.

The things she'd seen while riding in the passenger seat.

The things she'd *done* while riding in the passenger seat.

Riding being the operative word.

She grabbed Mason's waist and looked up into blue eyes that appeared a shade darker than usual in this light. He was as devastatingly handsome as the day they met, if a little more lined with experience.

"You look positively nefarious," she said with a forced smile. A joke was better than what she longed to say.

Stay here!

Don't go!

There's danger out there!

I need you!

I can't lose you!

And so she told a joke to keep the fear at bay.

"I feel positively nefarious," he said as he gathered her up in a hug that she could've sunk into forever. His embrace made the world feel safe again, if only until it ended.

He tilted her chin up and stared quietly into her eyes. Her heart thumped against his firm chest. "We're going to be fine, honey." He dipped down and kissed her softly. He pulled back and captured her eyes. "Don't worry."

"I'm a mother. It's my job to worry."

"And it's my job to keep people safe. Our daughter more than anyone else."

"Not just Theresa. *You*," she said as she tapped his chest. " You keep *you* safe too."

"I will. I promise."

Theresa bounded out of the back door with a backpack slung over her shoulder. As requested, she was dressed in generally dark colors. She saw them and rolled her eyes. "Is there anything I could do to see less of this?"

Beth shrugged. "Sure, close your eyes."

"Very funny."

Mason looked up at the darkening sky. "We need to get going." He reached up to the driver's seat and pulled down three walkie-talkies, the Motorola Talkabouts that they used for camping. He handed one to Beth and one to Theresa.

"I solar charged them up to capacity this afternoon. Keep it on your hip at all times. You'll probably lose us when we get enough buildings and houses in between, but it's the best we've got. Theresa, we shouldn't need one each, but it's backup if we somehow get separated."

He looked at Beth. "Which we won't."

Each of them clicked on their walkie-talkie and took turns verifying they were sending and receiving correctly. They got the volumes right and then stowed the devices.

Mason lifted his sweatshirt and unclipped a holstered pistol from his belt. "This is for you, Theresa."

Theresa's eyes opened wide.

Beth stepped back to give them room. This wasn't something they'd discussed, but she trusted Mason implicitly. This was his expertise, from a career as a Marine to a career as a bodyguard... or close protection officer as he preferred to call it.

"You should carry for tonight. Again, redundancy. This isn't the call I'd make in a sane world, but we no longer live in one."

They'd all gone to indoor and outdoor shooting ranges over the years. They didn't do it every month and they weren't what your average person would call gun nuts, but Mason had made certain that Theresa was both comfortable with a handgun and also respectful of the damage it could do. He pulled the Glock 26 out of the holster, making sure to keep it pointed down in a safe direction.

Beth knew it was identical to the one he carried on his ankle. Yet another redundancy thing. She also knew he used cartridges for Theresa that didn't kick as hard. Whatever they were, their daughter had never expressed any serious discomfort at firing the gun.

Mason reversed the grip and wrapped Theresa's hand around it, making sure to keep the barrel pointed at the ground. He held her hand in place. "What are the four rules of gun safety?"

Theresa rolled her eyes.

"I'm waiting," Mason said, not releasing the pistol.

"One, treat all guns as if they are always loaded. Two, never point a gun at something you aren't willing to destroy. Three, keep your finger off the trigger until your aim is on the target and you have decided to fire. Four, be aware of what is around and behind the target."

Mason glanced at Beth. "She's good."

"She is."

"Holster your weapon and attach it to your belt," Mason said as he released the firearm. He watched closely as Theresa did as instructed. "Last reminder. I'll handle security tonight. You are backup. Backup like I'm in big trouble and you're our last hope. Otherwise, keep it holstered."

He was expecting big trouble?

Mason turned to Beth. "And no, I'm not expecting big trouble."

Theresa gave a theatrical salute. "Yes, sir, Sergeant West!"

Mason rolled his eyes at her. "One, you don't call an enlisted man 'Sir' and a Sergeant is an enlisted man. And two, I haven't been an active duty soldier in more years than I'd like to count. Dad is fine."

Theresa struck her sneaker heels together with a dull click. "Yes, sir, Sergeant Dad!"

"Get in the Bronco, Private."

Elio appeared at the back door. "You guys about to leave?"

Theresa bounded over and wrapped an arm around him. "Yep. Someone's got to do the manly work."

"Hey, I'm on the injured reserve."

Theresa pinched his cheek. "Don't make excuses! It only makes it sound worse."

Elio pulled her close. Their arms created a bubble that sucked the air out of the rest of the world. "I'm serious. Be safe."

The space between them shrank and Beth waited to see what might happen. She was genuinely curious and saw no harm in it.

"We'll be fine," Mason replied in a flat tone. "Private Theresa, Bronco."

Elio seemed to snap back into confused reality. "Yeah, uhh, you should get going."

"Wait up for me?" Theresa asked.

"How could I not?"

Theresa smiled and pecked his cheek.

He was a good kid. His affection was both earnest and endearing. Beth hadn't said it explicitly yet, but he had her seal of approval. Mason was another matter altogether. He couldn't be blamed though. He was a father, and he'd eventually come around.

He would if he knew what was good for him.

Theresa tilted her head and kissed Elio before dashing to the Bronco's passenger door.

Elio's mouth gaped open.

Beth's heart warmed to see the two in their first stumbling steps toward romance. It was sweet. It was natural. She glanced at Mason. His eyes nearly bugged out of his head.

He didn't share her opinion. He needed time. A lot of it by the look of the bulging veins in his neck.

"Easy, tiger," she said as she patted his chest. "Don't push her away just because you're afraid to let her go. She's growing up."

His eyes settled back into his head. "You're right."

"I know," Beth replied with a smirk. "I thought you knew that by now."

Mason kissed her lips and then hopped up into the Bronco. "You're right about half as much as you think you are, and twice as much as I'd like you to be." He slammed the door shut.

Be safe.

The words choked in her throat.

Mason nodded. "We'll be safe."

Beth didn't doubt Mason's intention. She doubted what could happen when that intention encountered the chaos in the wider world.

11

As much as she might not like to admit it, watching Iridia clean the toilet gave her a certain smug pleasure. The model's gloved hand squeaked as she scrubbed at the stain ringing the bowl. A lock of hair fell out of her ponytail and dipped into the water. She jerked it out and flung droplets on her cheek.

"Disgusting! I need scissors! Where are some scissors?"

"Calm down," Beth said. "It'll wash clean."

Iridia looked up at her in horror. "Clean? It just took a deep dive in toilet water! It's contaminated!" She held it at arm's length like it might try to bite her.

Beth laughed. As annoying as Iridia was, she also brought much-needed humor into the household. She was a real *look on the bright side* kind of deal.

The impossibly skinny and aggravatingly immodest supermodel wore a pair of Beth's shorts and a tank top. She'd taken to wearing her clothes after Beth put a stop to her wearing Theresa's undersized garments. Unfortunately, Iridia had almost no clothes of her own. On second thought, maybe it was a good thing she didn't have more of her own clothes on hand.

She'd worn one of Mason's old UCLA sweatshirts one time and one time only. After enduring the gorgeous bimbo blabbering on and on about how yummy and manly it smelled, Beth forbade her wearing any more of his clothing.

It wasn't that she felt threatened.

It wasn't that.

Okay, it was a little of that.

Not that she thought Mason would ever do anything in a million years. It was just that Iridia was a freaking-for-real-in-life supermodel. It was hard not feeling a scooch inadequate in her objectively stunning presence.

It would've been impossible not to be intimidated were it not for Iridia's knack for sounding like a selfish idiot. That tended to put her whole package into perspective.

"Ack," Iridia said as her body spasmed. "I'm going to vomit. I'm not kidding." She convulsed again. "It's in my throat. It's literally in my throat."

"If you puke, you'll have to clean that up, too."

Iridia held up a soapy sponge with a grimace on her face. A curly, black hair was stuck to the frothy white bubbles. "A pube." She gagged again. "I mean, seriously. This is why I have weekly visits with my esthetician."

"You *used* to have weekly visits," Beth corrected her.

Iridia glanced down between her legs. "Don't remind me. The horror."

"Wash your sponge off in the bucket," Beth said.

Iridia grimaced. "But then it'll be in there... somewhere... waiting to stick to my fingers the next time I rinse the sponge."

Beth rolled her eyes and continued wiping down the sink. "Occupational hazard, sister. Get to it because we've got three loads of clean laundry that aren't going to hang themselves."

Much to Beth's surprise, Iridia finished helping her clean the bathroom with no more than the occasional muttered comment and the infrequent theatrical gagging. "Please put everything away while I get the laundry together."

"Joy," Iridia said as Beth headed to the living room, which had also become their makeshift laundry room because it was the biggest place to hang a cord to dry clothes. Beth made sure to dim the battery LED lantern to the minimum as she entered the living room. The heavy curtains blocked any light from escaping, but it was easy to miss a tiny open fold or crevice.

One oversight and a spotlight would pour out advertising to the world that they were a juicy target. That there was more than a looted house of decomposing bodies to be had by those bold enough to enter.

Elio brought out a tub stacked high with wet, clean clothes from the kitchen. "I squeezed them out the best I could."

Beth finished securing the cord across the room and joined Elio in draping sheets and clothing over the taut line. A few minutes into the task and Iridia joined them on the other side of the line. She knew the drill. Beth had walked her through it a couple of times already.

Five people in a house that all worked hard and didn't take showers like they used to. Clothes got stinky fast. But Beth was determined not to live in a sty, even if the world was collapsing around their ears. Perhaps even more so then.

"I hate doing laundry," Iridia said as she hung a sock

that looked like it needed another soak. "Does it really happen, like, every few days?"

"Do you wear clothes everyday?" Beth asked.

"Yes."

"Well, then you make dirty clothes everyday. Times that by five people and that turns out to be a lot to do by hand."

"Fine, then," Iridia said. "I'll fix that."

Beth laughed. "Yeah, that would be great. Fix the electricity so I can have my washer and dryer back. Do that and I'll take bathrooms for a month."

"In my dreams," she replied.

"Mine too," Beth agreed.

Elio continued to hang up things in a daze. His mind was clearly elsewhere... with her daughter.

They finished hanging everything and they all paused to admire their effort. Looking over a hanging sheet, Beth saw Iridia cradling her hand and peering closely at it like it was injured.

"Something wrong with your hand?" Beth asked as her doctor instincts kicked into gear. What medicines did she have on hand? Not much. What gear? Did she have a splint?

"Yes," Iridia said, "my cuticles are growing in!"

Beth's doctor mind dropped into annoyed pseudo-parent mode. "Did you know your cuticles are there to prevent fungus and bacteria from getting in?"

Iridia stared blankly. She looked back at her hand. "They're hideous!"

Elio slipped under the sheet with the empty tub and then froze in his tracks. His eyes went wide as dinner plates. They were locked to Iridia, to somewhere below her eyes.

Beth dipped under the laundry line and came out face to crotch with Iridia's naked body. Not believing her eyes, she did a double take. Yes, naked. And she did have hair growing in. "Why are you naked?"

"Laundry is too much trouble. I'd rather go naked."

Elio didn't move.

"That wasn't the solution I asked for!" Beth said.

"I know," Iridia replied. "But I'm creative like that."

Beth grabbed her shoulders and turned her around. She marched her out of the living room and noticed Elio frozen like a statue the whole way. They arrived at her room and she guided Iridia inside.

"You are not to leave this room without clothes covering your body. Do you understand me?"

Oh.

Em.

Gee.

She was such a parent! She was being forced to parent a twenty-five-year-old supermodel! How screwed up was that? One daughter was hard enough to handle.

"So, you're saying I can hang out in *here* naked, right?"

12

THERESA WEST peered out the passenger window of the Bronco as they slowly wound through a maze of abandoned vehicles, discarded furniture, decomposing bodies, and random junk that littered the street. Her dad drove with the Bronco lights off, but the last tendrils of twilight still revealed more than she wanted to see.

Her heart pounded in her eyes. At first, it was from the burning touch of Elio's lips on hers. But over the last few blocks, it had shifted much darker. Lost was the warmth in her belly after their brief kiss. Lost was the giddy glow of his reflected desire.

She felt cold now. Deathly cold.

It was the evidence of suffering that surrounded them. How odd that some blocks could seem almost normal where others were like this one.

The faint scent of smoke reminded her of weekends at Tito and Mamaw's house. Of how Tito would work up a roaring fire in the stone pit he'd built decades ago. Of how the flames would spit out little glowing fireflies that would shoot up and twirl away into the black sky. She always wondered if any of them made it to wherever it was they were going.

Or if every last one was sooner or later snuffed out and forgotten.

She looked down and noticed a bloated body lying face down next to the curb. A woman. More than that was hard to tell. Maybe it was a trick of the gathering darkness or maybe it was a simple defense mechanism, but none of it seemed real.

It felt fake.

Like it was a huge set in a Hollywood movie, maybe *Death Before Life*. She could almost see Ryan in his leading role step out of the shadows after defeating the enemy once and for all. His shirt torn off. Carved chest and abs throwing off sex appeal like nothing else in the world mattered.

But Ryan didn't appear.

And this reality didn't have an upbeat, sexy ending. One where she and Holly could clap and hoot like crazy, finish off the last kernels of popcorn, and then head home going over every second of a totally kickass two hours.

Because Holly was gone. Her best friend since third grade.

Buried in the ground in the Crayfords' backyard.

Gone.

It couldn't be real.

Her dad said something from the driver's seat.

"Hmmm?" she said.

"Are you okay?"

"I don't think so."

He squeezed her knee and didn't say a word. He saw exactly what she saw. What could he say? If this wasn't a movie, what could he do to change what had already happened?

"Dad?"

"Yes?"

"I'd like to visit Holly's house. See if her parents are alive. It's on the way to Rite-Aid."

He didn't answer and so Theresa prepared herself to battle over it.

"Okay."

That was a surprise.

"Thanks."

She really did want to check on them. Maybe they'd survived. But she also wanted to be in Holly's room. Just *be* for a minute. She longed to feel connected to her best friend again, if only through the things she'd left behind.

They cut over a block and headed up Holly's street. It wasn't as chaotic as the last one was. That one looked like a war zone. This one looked like the morning after a block party. They stopped in front and Theresa saw a large red triangle sloppily painted on the front door, the sign that the house had been touched by the Delta Virus.

In the first days of the outbreak, an attempt at a coordinated response had been made. The national guard had rolled through Los Angeles marking and cordoning off infected zones, trying to impose order where none would take root.

She wondered if the Pearson's door was painted by a soldier as a warning to others to stay away, or, like their house, someone had painted it as a deterrent to looters. Like a sign in your yard of an alarm company that didn't exist. She looked at all the nearby houses and saw the same spray-painted, red triangle on each of the doors.

It didn't look like a trick.

Mason cut the engine and she grabbed the door handle to exit.

"Wait," he said. "Put on your respirator mask and latex gloves. A virus isn't supposed to be able to live for more than twenty four hours outside the body. Then again, the world has never seen a virus like this so we're going to play it safe. Got it?"

"Okay."

Theresa dug through her backpack and pulled out a white N95 respirator mask and secured it to her face. She pulled out blue latex gloves and stretched them over her hands.

Her dad checked the mask and tightened it a little. "Let's observe first."

She nodded. Made sense. If anyone or anything came after them, good luck messing with the Bronco. This old tank could probably bulldoze through a house in a pinch. They watched in silence for a few minutes. She watched how her father turned his head back and forth, constantly scanning in every direction.

"Seems quiet," he said in a hushed tone. "This is how we're going to do this. I want you right behind me at all times. If I stop, you stop. If I get down, you get down. If I run, you run."

He flicked a look at the holstered Glock at her hip. "You only draw that if I am unable to defend us. Understand?"

"Yes," she replied.

"Good. Get your headlamp and backpack on." He looked her over and blew out a deep breath. "Let's go."

He met her on the passenger side and they crept toward the house that held so many happy memories for her and, yet, now seemed so full of nightmares. Her dad moved with his gun drawn and pointed a few feet in front of him.

She watched him and marveled at the transformation. He was no longer the annoying father that snooped through her texts or shoved his overprotective nose in where it didn't belong.

He was an animal in his element.

He moved like a predator on the prowl. A creature of the night welcoming the end of day and the return to the shadows. It sent chills up her spine and set the hairs on the back of her neck on end.

He appeared deadly calm, which made the hammering in her chest all the more violent. He stopped at the door and dropped to a knee. She did the same. He held his finger to his lips while listening through the door.

They stayed there for a few moments. She started to wonder if maybe he'd forgotten what they were doing and was lost in thought or something.

He tapped her shoulder and brought her attention back to the present. He nodded and tried the doorknob. With the faintest click, it opened a sliver. He paused to listen again.

Nothing.

In a burst of speed, he swept inside, flicked on his headlamp and scanned the front room with his Glock following his eyes back and forth.

Empty.

He eased the door shut behind her and brought his mouth to her ear. "Leave your light off until we need it."

She nodded. She took a deep breath and immediately regretted it.

Even through the N95-rated filter, the air stank of rot and disease. The Pearson's didn't have a pet, so the most likely source of the stench wasn't hard to figure out.

Mason tapped her shoulder and waved for her to follow.

As they moved deeper into the darkened house, a wild scream bubbled up in her throat and threatened to tear free.

13

In the living room, cords hung out of the wall above the fireplace where a huge flat-panel TV once hung. All of the family pictures that had lined the mantle were now on the ground, images trampled and glass shattered. The cabinets on either side were either open or missing the doors altogether. Old VHS tapes and newer DVDs were scattered all over the carpet. A large, irregular patch of charred black in the middle evidence that a fire had briefly burned.

Mason motioned her on. She took a step.

CRUNCH.

A plastic DVD case cracked apart underfoot. The sound shattered the silence like the gunshot that starts a horse race. They both froze, expecting a response and thankfully not getting one.

They moved through the kitchen and on toward the back of the house. The stench grew stronger. They encountered nothing living through the remaining rooms and finally came to the closed door that was Holly's parent's room.

The odor was so thick Theresa could feel it on her skin.

Mason turned to her and whispered, "Stay out here. You don't need to see this."

She nodded. She had no desire to add some gruesome scene of decomposition to the material that already invaded her nightly dreams.

He opened the door just enough to slip through and disappeared inside. The light from his headlamp bounced dimly back into the hallway through the opening.

Theresa's chest started to hurt. A dull ache that squeezed tight, making it difficult to breathe. She sucked hard through the filtered mask that was beginning to feel like a plastic bag. Her fingers tingled and her head swam. Her pounding heart echoed in her ears. She leaned against the wall trying to catch her breath.

Mason appeared and shut the door behind him.

"Holly's parents are gone."

Theresa slumped to the floor. Tears cascaded down her cheeks and soaked into the cotton mask. She heard a low moaning and was only dimly aware that it was coming from her mouth.

Her father pulled her up with ease and wrapped his arms around her. "I'm sorry." He held her in place as her numb legs supported no weight.

Something inside Theresa broke free and the dam behind her eyes collapsed. A river of grief flowed from her soul and onto his chest. He held her tight until the torrent eased to a trickle. "I can't believe she's gone, Daddy."

"I know, honey. I know."

"I want my best friend back."

Another wellspring of anguish billowed up, but then sputtered when there was nothing below it to continue building the pressure.

"Can I go to her room?"

"I'll go with you," he said.

"Can I do it alone?"

Mason considered and then answered, "Yes. Just be careful. I'm going to look through the kitchen to see if anything useful might be left."

"Okay."

They walked together back to Holly's room. Theresa clicked her headlamp on to the dim setting.

"You sure you want to do this?" Mason asked.

"Yes."

"I'll check on you in a few minutes."

She stepped into the bedroom that was once occupied by her best friend in the world. The place was a total mess, which wasn't all that different from when Holly had lived here. She sat on the mattress on the floor and looked around. A torn *Death Before Life* movie poster hung from the wall above Holly's bed. Holly used to say she loved waking up with Ryan's hot body on top of her.

A choked giggle escaped Theresa's lips as she remembered Holly bragging about how she'd fall asleep gazing at the poster and then find Prince Charming in her dreams. Her very non-Disney, and shockingly explicit, dreams.

That was Holly.

And she was gone.

Theresa shone her headlamp around the room, as much in the present as in the past that dwelt more deeply in her heart.

A sparkle in the corner of the room caught her eye.

She swept across the area and there it was again. Probably a shard of broken glass. She got up and shoved aside filthy sheets and clothes that might've once been Holly's.

There.

Lodged in the corner where the carpet met the wall.

A fine silver chain.

She dug in with her fingernail and pulled it free.

A silver locket in the shape of a heart. The letters BFF engraved on the surface.

Her heart broke in two as she wedged a fingernail into the seam and popped it open. Each half contained a faded picture of each of them in third grade. Theresa remembered giving the locket to Holly for her ninth birthday like it was yesterday.

She pinched it closed and pressed it to her chest over her heart. Holly was gone. But Theresa would never forget her.

Never.

A noise from outside the bedroom made Theresa jump. She turned around and saw nothing. It sounded like a door opening or closing.

"Dad?" she said in a loud whisper.

There was no reply.

"Dad! Is that you?" she said a little louder.

Still no reply.

She stuffed the locket in her pocket and crept out of the room. A shuffling sound and then what was definitely a door shutting froze her in her tracks. Her hand went to the holstered Glock at her hip.

It had to be her dad. He just didn't hear her. That was all. No reason to freak out.

Her hand stayed glued to the pistol.

She quietly made her way into the kitchen and didn't see Mason. He said this was where he'd be, didn't he?

A strange sound raised the hairs on her arms. Like someone talking, but not using words she'd ever heard. She pivoted toward the sound and saw that the door to the garage was ajar. It had been closed when they came through earlier, hadn't it?

Had Mason gone in to check for anything else worth taking?

She listened for further movement. All she heard was the hurricane squall of her own breathing, like she had a stethoscope stuck to her nostrils.

She tiptoed to the door and still heard nothing. Maybe it was noth—

There it was again!

Her dad must be out there, probably looking for gas or tools. Stuff you'd find in a garage. She pulled the door open and stepped inside. She edged around Mr. Pearson's shiny black Land Rover and didn't see or hear anything.

Maybe she was imagining things.

Maybe she'd gone crazy. Who knew? Maybe she was actually napping in first period American History class because Holly had kept her up too late on yet another Sunday night.

She headed back for the kitchen feeling like an idiot and trying to forgive herself for acting crazy in an objectively insane situation.

She took a few steps and then an odd whimpering sound dumped ice water down her back. She flicked her headlamp to the far wall. There, nestled in a corner behind a deep freezer, was a woman crouched on all fours. Two young boys peeked out from behind her with terrified looks in their eyes.

The three looked like wild animals.

14

The woman wore a summer dress that had been torn to filthy rags. Twigs and other bits of debris poked out of a matted mess that once must've been beautiful dark hair. One full breast hung out where the cloth no longer covered. The ruined dress now revealed more than it hid. Scared but unyielding, she held the boys behind her. She blinked hard at the bright light in her face.

"Sorry," Theresa said as she angled the beam down a little. "We can help you. We have food and water, clothes for all of you. My mom's a doctor. A vet actually, but she's been doing fine working on people lately."

Theresa smiled awkwardly realizing her nerves were making her run at the mouth. She couldn't imagine what these three had been through. She only knew she needed to help them.

The woman stared with something between caution and curiosity in her eyes.

"Sorry," Theresa said, "I just didn't expect anyone to be out here. Was a shock is all. I'm not normally this jumpy.

Things out there have me a little on edge. Maybe a lot on edge. Anyway, we can help you."

She took a step toward them and the woman jerked like she'd been attacked. The muscles in her arms and legs coiled tight. She looked ready to spring.

"It's okay. I'm not going to hurt you."

Theresa took another step and the woman tilted her head back and screamed. The primal desperation in the wail sent Theresa backpedaling. Another scream sent her sprawling back into the Land Rover. Her headlamp swung wildly across the wall and ceiling and back again as she tumbled back. The side of the Land Rover kept her upright and she realized with a start that she was looking at the boards that held up the sloped roof.

More importantly, the woman was somewhere in the darkness below.

She whipped her head down and zeroed it back in on the spot beside the freezer.

It was empty.

The oval of light lingered as Theresa's brain tried to catch up to what her eyes were telling her.

They were right there!

That was the spot, right?

Were they real?

Theresa wheeled around the black void and the light found the trio again, now over beside a workbench. The woman held a hammer with the wrong end in her hand. She banged the wooden handle on the concrete floor. She drew her lips back to reveal a full set of teeth. She hissed a warning. They weren't vampire teeth. Just regular human teeth. But she bared them like a rabid beast.

Another cone of light appeared at the doorway to the kitchen.

"Put the hammer down!" Her father's gun fluidly tracked the woman as he bounded into the garage and landed in front of Theresa. "I said put it down!"

The mother howled at Mason but showed no signs of obeying. Of even understanding, really.

"Are you okay?" Mason asked.

"I'm fine. She hasn't tried to hurt me. Just protecting her kids I think."

"Please put the hammer down. I don't want to hurt you or your children."

The woman still showed no sign of understanding.

"Theresa, stay behind me and back up into the kitchen."

Theresa did as she was told and they made it through the door without further incident.

Mason slammed the door shut. He scanned the kitchen behind Theresa and then grabbed her hand. "Let's go!"

They jogged outside and jumped into the Bronco in record time. Mason fired up the throaty V8 and, unlike on their way in, gunned the engine and took off down the relatively clear street.

Theresa held on to the dash as they bumped over the curb and tore through someone's front lawn to avoid a snarl of cars at the end of the block. They turned right and broke clear onto Lincoln. The Rite-Aid pharmacy was a few blocks down, though not lit up at night like it usually was.

Like it used to be was more accurate now. Their short trip had shown her a completely changed world. A world that was a distorted, nightmarish reflection of what it used to be.

Mason slowed the Bronco and the roar of the engine subsided.

"Dad, what was wrong with her?"

"Stress can overwhelm the mind. Take away its reason.

Make you do things you'd never normally do. I've seen it happen."

15

MASON knew that pharmacies and other stores would already be looted, but the level of destruction still shocked him. The first stop at Rite Aid didn't last long when they discovered that it was nothing more than a burned out husk. It, along with the grocery store Ralph's next door, contained nothing but ash and melted amoebic structures that may have once been aisle shelves.

The next stop at CVS wasn't much better. There was no evidence of past fires, but the pharmacy had been stripped bare. They now sat in the Bronco considering what to do next. Clyde needed antibiotics and Mason didn't relish the idea of returning empty-handed. Another tragedy might be too much for Beth to handle.

"I don't think we're going to find a store that hasn't been destroyed or picked over," Mason said.

Theresa chewed on her lower lip and then paused. "What about Fernando's?"

"You mean that little neighborhood corner mart on Rose and Main?"

She nodded. "Yeah, it has a little pharmacy in the back."

Mason could've smacked himself. He didn't remember because he never went there for anything other than a quick gallon of milk or bag of chips. "That's my girl. Thinking outside the big box stores."

Mason fired up the Bronco and headed out, careful to avoid the tangles of overturned shopping carts and abandoned cars choking the parking lot.

He drove slowly down the street now that night had fallen. The road ahead was darker than seemed possible. Los Angeles usually had so much ambient light bouncing around on the ground and up into the sky that there was almost no need for headlights. Tonight was different.

Mason kept the headlights off because the high-powered lights in the sea of darkness would act like a lighthouse, a beacon to whoever and whatever lurked out there in the shadows.

He waved the small beam of a handheld flashlight back and forth across the road, identifying obstructions and navigating up around them.

"Dad, why did this happen? Is God punishing us?"

Mason didn't know if the *us* meant them in particular or mankind in general, but his answer would've been the same either way. "I'm probably not the best person to ask about God's motives or actions. That said, I don't think a creator would cause this much suffering."

"Well, then why did this happen?"

Mason could come up with a few theories. From the overuse of antibiotics that for decades had been creating more and more resistant superbugs. To the accelerating deforestation of the Amazon and other wild places which put mankind into direct contact with various viruses and bacteria that had been out of the evolutionary loop for millennia. The same dynamic decimated the Native Americans when Europeans arrived.

From there, he could go even more conspiratorial (and yet no less likely to be true) and consider how governments around the world secretly developed weapons of biological warfare. Genetically engineered microscopic strains that had the potential to wipe out all life on the planet.

"I hope someday we find out so we can make sure it never happens again."

They slowed to a stop at the corner next to Fernando's. They geared up and Mason led the way to the front door. In the light of his headlamp, he tested the wood panels that had replaced the busted out glass door. Nothing so much as creaked. Without making a whole lot of unwanted noise, they weren't going to get in that way.

"Let's check around the sides and back and hopefully find an easier way in."

They skirted around the corner to the right and saw the familiar mural of waves crashing on a beach that covered the brick wall. They kept moving towards the back of the building with Mason scanning his light back and forth and his Glock in the low ready position. Nothing drew his attention nor the front sight of the pistol.

Around the back they discovered a door partially ripped away from the frame and hanging on by the lower hinges. Through the open doorway, the interior was pitch black.

What he wouldn't give for some night vision goggles right now. He considered telling Theresa to turn on her headlamp but then decided against it. If they encountered anything, he wanted all the attention focused on him.

He whispered over his shoulder, "Stay close."

They crept into the silent tomb with nothing but Mason's

narrow cone of light guiding the way. He did a quick sweep as they entered and saw no one. Aside from the crazed mother and her children, they'd seen no other living being all night. They entered what must've been a small stockroom. Ripped sheets of cardboard and torn apart boxes intermingled with overturned wire shelves. The air reeked of rotten food.

He hoped it was food.

They moved slowly, stepping over and picking their way through debris. Making sure to test each foot placement before committing weight to it.

He rifled through a mound of black trash bags piled against the wall. He accidentally tore one open and gagged when a wave of rot billowed out. He reached in again to sweep more of the bags aside and his hand hit something firm. He pushed another bag aside and found an unopened cardboard box.

Could it be food?

Could they be that lucky?

He tore the flap open. No food. The box was mostly empty. But not completely. There were two bottles of vinegar and a bottle of rubbing alcohol.

Pay dirt!

Neither had a smell he was fond of, but both were miracles in their own right. Vinegar especially was a miracle solution. You could clean almost anything with it. It was crazy how successful Procter & Gamble and other mega corporations were in brainwashing people into believing they needed a thousand different cleaning products when they really just needed one. The all powerful and totally unpatentable vinegar. The latter aspect being why said corporations had no interest in selling it.

He grabbed the three bottles and secured them in his backpack.

"Score," Theresa whispered from behind him.

What a testament to how much the world had changed and his daughter along with it that their find excited her. Eight days ago, she wouldn't have cared if their entire house was stacked floor to ceiling with bottles of vinegar. Or maybe she would've cared only in so far as they blocked her from getting to her room.

Seeing her adapt so quickly made him proud.

Knowing that she had to broke his heart.

They approached another open doorway and Mason cleared them through into the front part of the store. The low shelves that used to hold a tempting assortment of snacks and household basics were kicked over and covered with a stirred rainbow of plastic wrappers, crushed aluminum cans, and broken bottles. Mason ground his teeth in frustration. He should've gotten out days ago, when supplies like these might've still been available. He blamed himself but the remaining tenderness in his left calf reminded him that it hadn't been a choice.

Besides, they were alive now because they'd been unable to get out in those first days. The highly contagious virus had apparently wiped out most of the world's population. Ironically, their injuries had probably saved their lives.

He slid the circle of light to the right along the floor and landed on the pharmacy section of the store. A wall of thick bulletproof glass stretched from chest high to the ceiling securing the area. The glass still stood, though it had acquired a large number of scrapes since the last time Mason had visited.

Nothing.

Struck out again. Where was he going to get ahold of some antibiotics now?

Through the glass, Mason saw the shelves were swept

clean. Sporadic piles of printer paper and glinting shards of glass were all that remained. He scanned further right and saw that the door to the area behind the pharmacy counter was open. The lock had clearly been pried apart.

Maybe they'd still find something useful. Never knew until you checked. He headed for the open door.

CREAK.

He froze and Theresa did the same behind him.

16

There was no way the sound came from either of them. What was it?

Metal on metal. Hinges maybe.

Mason swung his head around with the Glock raised and ready. The elevated beating of his heart thumped in his ears. He exhaled slow and deep to suppress the flood of chemicals in his system. Dangerous situations required a clarity of focus that a body soaked in adrenaline, cortisol, and norepinephrine made difficult to achieve. He blew out another calming breath and the racing tension in his chest slowed. Slowed but not stopped.

That was good.

The edge kept you sharp, helped you survive.

After listening another moment and hearing nothing, he continued through the pharmacy doorway.

"Turn your light on," Mason said. "Look through everything. Shelves, file cabinets, drawers, the floor. Everything. Who knows what might turn up."

"Okay," Theresa whispered.

Theresa's headlamp kicked on and added another

glowing oval to their dark world. The shadows swallowed the light so quickly that the room remained bathed in darkness just a few feet beyond the reflected light of their focus.

Mason didn't like it. Something didn't feel right.

It made sense. Practically everything was potentially dangerous. Mankind, or at least his little neighborhood of it, had returned to wandering the savannah at night with no fire to protect and warm them.

Living to see another day no longer had the sense of inevitability that it had artificially acquired in modern culture. We'd conquered so many things that the notion of vulnerability seemed antiquated.

Of course, the certainty was always an illusion. People died every day in every imaginable way.

Still, over time, the averages had improved dramatically. So it was no surprise that humanity got too comfortable, too self-assured in our position standing apart (and above) the natural world.

But that brief period of impressive mastery had passed.

We'd climbed too high too fast.

And so we'd been cast back down into the web of life with the warming blanket of technology torn away.

In the darkest night, our ancestors reminded us of whence we came. Of the terrible weight shouldered by every beast that instinctively knew it would be hunted. Technology and training could blunt the terror, shape it even.

The Marines had done that for him and his men.

But it was always there, underneath the bravado and bloodlust.

"Dad, found something."

Mason crept over and examined the nondescript, amber bottle filled with little capsules. He read the label.

Sildenafil citrate.

Take one thirty minutes to one hour before activity.

No idea. He stuffed it into his pack.

CREAK.

Mason turned, muzzle pointed at the open doorway to the main room of the store. Still nothing visible.

"What was that?" Theresa said in hissed whisper.

Mason touched his finger to his lips and kept the Glock on target.

Was it just an old building murmuring its age to whoever might listen? Was it just the odd sounds old structures made as they continuously settled and shifted in their slow motion slide toward entropy?

Maybe.

But that sound didn't have the same hollow feeling, like it came from down in the bones. It came from the surface, from the skin, from the place where people and things interacted.

He approached the open doorway from the side, his right shoulder to the transparent wall, making sure to keep his exposure to the fatal funnel to a sliced angle.

CREAK.

This time louder. Closer.

"What was that?" Theresa said, an edge of panic rising in her voice.

It was something. Mason knew that much. He looked right and shone his light through the glass to scan the interior of the small store.

There. Over by where the cash register used to be. A little eddy of plastic wrappers settled to the ground.

What had caused the disturbance?

Mason leaned closer to get more of the headlamp focused through the glass, rather than reflecting back into his face.

His eyes inches from the surface, he methodically scanned back and forth. Then paused.

What was it?

WHACK.

A disfigured face leapt out of the darkness and slammed into the clear barrier. Mason stumbled back and aimed his firearm at the attacker.

Theresa screamed.

The shrill edge in her voice curled his finger around the trigger and had it pulled halfway back before he could stop the involuntary reaction. He froze, a millimeter from where the trigger would break.

The thing outside the glass was a young man, probably in his mid-twenties. Their eyes didn't connect. His were feral and inhuman. His broad chest was bare and riddled with long scrapes and gouges. He wore no clothes at all. No pants. No shorts. No underwear.

His manhood swung freely as he slammed his fists into the barrier that separated them. His face twisted up as he growled at Mason.

He was human, but not human.

Blood from a busted lip smeared across the glass as he tried to bite into the smooth surface. He looked back into the darkness and howled.

A flood of movement swept in from the surrounding darkness and smashed into the safety glass like a wave crashing on the shore. The glass shook with the impact but held.

Mason lunged for the security door and got a trio of shots off as three bodies jumped through it and bowled him over. The first one absorbed the rounds and landed inertly on top of him. He rolled to the side and shoved it away.

One of the two remaining bit his leg and only the thick canvas pants kept the teeth from puncturing the skin. The other one jumped onto his chest and lunged for his throat with its mouth wide.

Mason fired two rounds into its mouth and through the back of its skull. Its head snapped back and it collapsed to the side. A jab of pain stabbed his inner ears as a high-pitched keen drowned out the howling shriek of the remaining attacker.

Another body landed on his chest knocking the wind out of him. It smashed a fist into his arm sending it arcing down to the side. His hand cracked into the concrete and the Glock skittered away. The flurry of movement with the light bouncing around erratically was almost hypnotic.

Almost.

Mason scrambled for the knife clipped to his belt. It was wedged under him a little and, before he could get it free, another frenzied body landed on top of him.

Time slowed.

Or maybe his perception of it sped up.

He thought of Theresa, somewhere near him. Who would save her when he was gone? How had it come to this?

He strained until his joints popped to shake free.

"No!" he spat out as he struggled.

Rage burned in his gut, fueled his limbs into action, but the onslaught was too much. Too fast. Too violent.

They weren't people.

They were animals.

17

His body pinned down and battered, he yet fought to break free. The terrible finality of the situation struck him.

And Theresa would be next.

BANG. BANG.

The sharp report of a Glock firing.

The attacker beating on his chest jerked to the side and then tumbled over.

BANG. BANG.

BANG. BANG.

He glanced over and, in a funnel of light, saw Theresa's shaking hands holding her Glock 26. The smoking barrel jumped as a flower of flame shot out.

The force subduing Mason's body ebbed as Theresa fired at another attacker. He broke free and recovered his weapon as their attackers paused, apparently unsure after a few of their number fell so quickly. Mason didn't waste the pause. He lunged forward and drove his shoulder into the chest of a man standing in the doorway. The man fell backwards into the press of bodies behind.

Now clear, Mason slammed the security door shut. He

threw the bolt just as they resumed the attack. The door shuddered. The frame showed cracks where it had separated from the surrounding wall.

Another impact and the cracks grew a few inches. It wouldn't keep them out much longer.

He looked back at Theresa who stood frozen with the Glock's slide locked back. He'd deal with her in a second. They needed something to barricade the door shut. He surveyed the interior of the pharmacy and saw nothing that looked like it would hold for more than a few minutes.

But a few minutes might make all the difference. He grabbed an overturned office chair and jammed it up under the door handle. The bodies outside smashed into the door again. It shivered and the metal chair groaned as it absorbed some of the blow. The cracks around the frame continued to grow.

They'd be lucky for a few extra minutes.

Pounding on the safety glass drew his attention and he swept his headlamp in that direction. What he saw swept a chill through his body. The surface was covered with frantic bodies clawing, biting, fighting to get through.

Ten or so of them. And more behind struggling to get closer.

Mason's hasty fortification seemed to be holding, so he checked on Theresa. Her face was pale and lax. He gently took the pistol and recharged it with the last full magazine from his backpack. He secured it in her holster and then squeezed her hands. They were cold and sweaty.

"Hey," he said.

He squinted as her headlamp tilted up and blinded him. He angled it up and caught her eyes.

"You did good," he said. "Stay with me. It's not over yet."

She nodded in dull agreement. Her eyes seemed distant

and disconnected. Shock. Not surprising for what just happened. But not a luxury they could afford either.

He squeezed her shoulders and stared into her eyes. "Theresa, look at me. Look at me!"

Her eyes finally focused.

"You have to stay with me here. Okay? Can you do that?"

She nodded again.

"I want you to say it."

She stammered out incomprehensible words.

"Focus your attention," he said as he locked his eyes to hers.

"I... I can... I can do it."

"I need you to cover the door while I look for another way out." Mason glanced back at the mass of bodies shouting and screaming behind the glass. There were no discernible words. It would've been less terrifying if there were. Just sounds. Incomprehensible sounds of fury and frustration.

He pivoted to the side of her. He needed to know she was together enough to watch their back. "Draw your weapon and cover the door."

Her motion was hesitant at first, but once her hand found the grip, it settled. She drew the pistol and aimed it at the closed door. Bodies intermittently slammed against it. The fault line around the frame inched forward with every impact.

How many more blows could it take?

Mason swept his light over the space. There were no other doors or windows. By design, the pharmacy was a secure area. Only it wasn't designed to indefinitely keep out a mass of insane humans. One or two until the police arrived, maybe. But they weren't facing one or two.

And the police weren't going to rescue them.

He looked around at a loss. They weren't going to be able to shoot their way out. They had insufficient firepower to gain superiority. If he had an M249 SAW, sure no problem. He'd mow them down like blades of grass. But a couple of handguns? And with the way Theresa looked, one of those handguns might not even make it into the fight.

No, that was the last resort. The long odds he didn't want to take.

So what else?

He gritted his teeth in frustration while staring at the bodies pressed against the safety glass. Their eyes shone with a simple, primal madness. A burning rage that an incomprehensible obstacle only fanned brighter.

An idea flickered in his mind.

It was something, at least.

18

The door shuddered again and the upper right area around the door frame tore free. It wouldn't hold much longer.

Mason rifled through his backpack and found the bottle of rubbing alcohol he'd found in the storeroom. He tore the lid off and splashed its contents on the safety glass. He dug out his lighter, lit a flame, and touched it to the vertical surface.

A sheet of blue and yellow flame ignited and cast the room in flickering light. A searing wave of heat sent Mason jumping backwards. The attackers on the other side fell back as well. Though not from the heat, as it couldn't have made it through the safety glass so quickly. They stared at it, cringing in terror. The flame dripped down to the counter and pooled in an expanding ring of fire.

The assailants on the other side of the glass kept their distance, looking at one another in confusion. None wanted to be the first to approach the conflagration. The wall of flame slowly diminished and began to wink out around the edges. The flame on the wall extinguished and only a small puddle on the counter remained.

It could work.

He yanked off his black hoodie and pulled his white t-shirt off as well. He cast about the area and found something that would work. A forgotten broom. He grabbed it and slammed the end on the counter. The plastic bristles snapped off the metal rod.

The door shuddered. The left side was nearly torn free from the wall. Arms reached around the door, waving and grabbing at air.

Only seconds before they got through.

He ripped the thin cotton shirt into strips and quickly tied each strip in knots around the end of the metal pole. That complete, he dumped half the bottle of rubbing alcohol on the lumpy ball of fabric. He tucked the bottle inside his belt.

SMASH.

The door shuddered again and the frame came free from the surrounding wall. It tumbled forward and slammed to the ground. Three of the animals fought to be first to get through the opening. A roar of excitement rippled through the others. They sensed the opportunity. That a shift had occurred in the chase, one that would soon bring victory. The attackers stumbled in, tripping over the fallen door and each other. More filled in behind them.

Theresa screamed.

Mason tugged at the lighter wedged sideways in his pants. He yanked again and the length caught on the lip of the pocket.

The lead assailant lunged for him. He powered a front kick through the man's stomach and sent him sprawling backwards. Several more parted around and then over their fallen brother.

He rotated the lighter and got it free. With a flick of the

thumb, metal struck flint and a spark ignited the alcohol-soaked ball of cloth on the end of the broom handle. The ball flared to life with a rush of heat and light. The effect was miraculous.

Mason shoved his makeshift torch into the face of the nearest attacker. The sizzle and stink of burning flesh filled the air. The man dropped like a stone holding his face in his hands. The rest broke for the door in a panic.

"Theresa! Holster your weapon!"

In a daze, she managed to do so.

He spun her around and stretched out an arm on each side of her. He put the torch in his left hand and drew her Glock with his right.

"We're going to walk out of here."

He tried to move forward and she shoved her back into his chest.

"We can't go out there! They'll kill us!"

"They're afraid of the fire. This is our best chance."

"I can't, Daddy! I can't!" The hysteria in her voice made him want to hurt them. Kill them. All of them.

"We have to go. Now. I don't know how long this thing is gonna last."

Mason started forward again and this time Theresa hesitantly went along. He waved the torch in a wide arc. The creatures climbed over each other scrambling away. They melted away as Mason guided Theresa towards the storeroom and the exit beyond.

He pivoted right and left covering the full arc of the circle with the lone point of crackling light. The fire proved an effective deterrent. However, each time the flame drove them away on one side the animals on the opposite side edged closer.

They made it into the storeroom from which they'd first

entered and found more of the creatures. Mason thrust the torch forward to wedge open a path towards the back door.

The hairs on the back of his neck stood on end. He whirled around and slammed the ball of flame into the face of a woman reaching for Theresa. The fire smashed into her cheek and some alcohol must've splashed off because the side of her cheek bubbled into a small sheet of flame. The others behind her immediately fell back, crouching and covering themselves.

Mason swung through the entire arc and reestablished their circumference of safety.

He thrust the torch toward the open door. A few creatures still ahead of them stumbled out into the night air. Now free of the cramped interior of the store, they fled together down the alley. Mason turned to face the doorway just as the leading edge following them made it to the threshold. He jabbed the torch forward. The edge shrank back into the mass of bodies behind.

"Dump the rest of the bottle in the doorway!"

Theresa tugged the bottle free and poured out the remaining half on the ground.

"Get back," Mason instructed. They cleared the puddle and he touched the end of the torch to the glistening surface. A flickering yellow and orange pyramid of flame leapt into the air. The flash of brilliance illuminated the terrified faces beyond.

Mason scanned the area and saw no additional threats. He grabbed Theresa's hand and took off for the safety of the Bronco.

They made it to the passenger door. Mason tossed the torch and hurried them both inside. He fired up the engine and slammed the pedal to the floor. The huge beast roared and its tires clawed at the pavement.

Theresa sat in the passenger seat with her knees up and her arms wrapped tightly around them. She mumbled something again and again as she stared blankly forward. The words were faint, but Mason caught it after a few repetitions.

"We're not safe."

19

ELIO LOPEZ sat on the couch in the living room quietly tapping his foot with nervous energy. Even in the near total darkness, he knew that Beth and Iridia were also seated in the room. Beth had checked the time a few minutes ago and it was almost midnight. Theresa and Mason should've been back hours ago.

"Do you think something happened?"

It was the hundredth time he'd asked the question and he knew Beth wouldn't have any better of an answer than the ninety-nine she'd offered before. But it wasn't about the answer. It was more an involuntary expression of his circling thoughts.

"Mason can take care of them," she replied.

He'd seen firsthand just how capable Mason was at protecting those he cared for. He also found out the truth.

That Mason didn't have a perfect record.

And that the one blemish that he knew about had resulted in the loss of his father.

He didn't hate Mason for it. He barely remembered his father. He wasn't even sure if the memories he did have were real or manufactured from old pictures and home videos. He went through a phase when he was younger of endlessly watching the videos, as if that would somehow bring him back.

They didn't.

While he didn't blame Mason, he also didn't forgive him. For his mother. Maybe his life would've been better having a father all those years. Probably. But for his mother, there was no doubt. He didn't know if he'd ever be able to forgive Mason for the suffering she'd endured. Even a decade after losing her husband, she awoke every morning and kissed his picture that sat on her bedside table.

No. For his mother, Elio didn't know if he could ever completely let it go.

It hadn't been easy for her. And he was honest enough to know that his poor choices sometimes added to her burden. Elio chewed the inside of his cheek and felt strings of flesh tear away.

Was she still alive? Was she right this minute waiting for him to come rescue her?

Maria Lopez had always been the strong one. The one who never let Elio give up. She had to be alive. He knew in his heart that, somehow, she was. She wouldn't leave him alone in this dark, new world. As close as he'd grown with the West family, and especially Theresa, over the last many days, they still weren't his family. His family consisted of one person.

And she was out there, alone and waiting for him.

One way or another, Elio had to find her. And despite what Mason might say, he wasn't going to wait much longer.

Where were they anyway?

"Do you think something happened?"

The words spilled out before he could stop them.

And so the thoughts chased each other in an endless circle of anxious distraction. He sat there with his muscles rigid and his foot tapping out the beat of his frantic mind.

Something interrupted the pattern and he froze to figure out what it was. He jumped up and ran to the front window when he recognized the low rumble of the Bronco approaching. He parted the curtain and watched the big truck creep toward the house with its lights off. He ran out into the backyard and opened the side gate so they could pull through. He secured the gate and then raced to the passenger door just as it opened and Theresa hopped down.

He grabbed her waist as she wobbled and fell into him. Her head dropped to his shoulder and she broke into tears.

Mason came around the bumper and pulled them toward the house as Beth ran into his arms. He hugged her tightly as she fought to control her emotions.

"I was so worried you wouldn't come back. That something had happened and I'd never see either of you again."

"We're okay," Mason said.

"Why are you so late then?"

"Something did happen. We'll talk about it inside."

Elio's heart swelled with his arm wrapped around Theresa's trembling body. The relief at finding her safe, but also something else. Something unfamiliar. He wanted to do something, to act, to release the surge within his chest.

He wanted to protect her.

Mason secured the kitchen door behind them while Elio guided Theresa into the living room.

Iridia kissed Theresa's cheek. "I told him there was nothing to worry about." The softness of her voice betrayed the uncertainty of her words. "I'll get you some water."

Elio helped Theresa sit on the couch and then took a

seat beside her. He pulled her close. Mason and Beth walked in with Iridia following behind. The LED lantern on the coffee table gave out just enough light so they could see who was who. He intertwined his fingers with Theresa's. She squeezed so tight it hurt.

Iridia handed the water over. "Here honey. Drink some. You need it."

Theresa accepted it and took a tentative sip. Then she took another drink which turned into her downing half the glass. She carefully set it on the table before leaning back into Elio's embrace.

"We ran into some surprises out there," Mason said. He said it so matter-of-factly that you'd think he was talking about what was for breakfast tomorrow morning. Mason launched into the story of what happened.

As Mason described how they escaped the store, Elio didn't know what to think. It sounded ridiculous. Like a big-budget Hollywood zombie movie. But he knew Mason wasn't given to exaggeration and he could feel the memory of terror emanating from Theresa's body.

However unlikely, Mason was telling the truth. He was describing their new world.

A world Elio's mother might've already encountered.

20

They sat around the coffee table quietly discussing what happened. Beth kept going back to the possibility that those people were desperate and mentally unhinged by what they'd experienced. Mason wasn't convinced. He and Theresa kept saying how their attackers somehow didn't feel human.

"The bottom line is," Mason said, "things are getting more dangerous. The looters this morning broke into the house across the street. It had a red triangle painted on the door. They're getting more desperate or more bold. Add to that there are people out there behaving in ways I've never seen. Both threats lead us to the same conclusion. We need a defensible position." He paused. "And this house isn't it."

Beth sucked in a sharp breath. "You want us to leave our home? Where would we go?"

"Not far, hopefully. I want to check out the house next door tomorrow morning. Two stories surrounded by a six foot concrete wall. Made of concrete blocks."

"What?" Beth said. "Are we just gonna bust in and kick out the family that lives there?"

"I haven't seen the father or the daughter in weeks," Mason said. "Not that we ever spoke, but I'd occasionally see them pulling in or out of the security gate." He looked from Beth to Theresa. "When was the last time you saw them?"

"Not recently," Beth said.

"I think you're right," Theresa said. "It's been a couple weeks, at least. Maybe they were on vacation when all this happened."

"Maybe," Mason replied. "I'm gonna find out tomorrow. That's my best idea for the short term. We don't have the supplies or manpower to defend our house against a determined assault."

Beth shook her head. "We're going to abandon our home?"

"I'd rather lose this house than lose one of you. Listen, it's late and we all need rest. Starting tonight, we're instituting night watch duty." He looked at the glowing watch on his wrist. "I'll take the first shift until four. Beth, can you take over from there?"

"Of course."

"Good. We'll continue this discussion in the morning. If anyone comes up with any better ideas, I'm all ears." He helped Beth up and escorted her to their bedroom. Iridia trailed behind to her room.

Elio pulled Theresa up. She leaned heavily into him. "Will you walk me to my room?"

"Uh, sure." Elio's heart skipped a beat. A longing ache in his chest drew him towards her like rare earth magnets. The kind that are the size of a pencil eraser and yet pull like a tractor beam.

He walked to her room in a trance with his arm around her shoulder. He prayed that somehow their steps would never end, that the future would always find her at his side. With Theresa beside him, Elio knew he'd have the courage to face anything.

All too soon, they arrived at her door. He squeezed her shoulder and desperately wanted to go in for a kiss, but the roiling in his gut and the knowledge that her parents' room was right down the hall kept him in check. "Good night, Theresa. I'm happy you made it back safely."

"Can we talk for a few minutes?"

The bubbling cauldron in his belly flared fire into his chest. His fingers tingled and he swallowed hard through the dryness in his throat. "Okay."

As they sat on the bed, the curled ball of black, fuzzy hair snuffled and coughed. Theresa leaned over and stroked Clyde's head with the softest touch imaginable. The cute little chimp settled and his breathing became regular. She sat up next to Elio and slipped her hand into his.

Elio sat quietly trying to think of something to say. The booming of his heart didn't leave space for ideas. His mind was blank. He literally couldn't think of a single thing. It was like his brain was unplugged from his body.

"Elio?"

He turned to respond and her lips touched his in the darkness. The soft contact blasted tingling echoes down to his toes. He stared in euphoric shock at her closed eyes. Tasted the salty sweetness on her lips. The tingling waves bouncing around his body concentrated lower and he felt his excitement stir.

She blinked her eyes open and paused mid kiss. She pulled back a fraction. Their lips smacked apart as the contact broke. "Are you just gonna stare at me?"

She smelled like summer sunshine. Her scent warmed

his lungs and added to the pressure building in his underwear.

Did she say something?

She giggled and it sounded like the refreshing burble of a waterfall washing over him. Another part of his brain recognized that she was giggling at him, which sent him into a blind panic.

"Hello?"

A sliver of air separated their lips. Her breath brushed across his skin sending shivers down his spine. He realized with a start he was still in a stupor. He had to say something! He was acting like a total idiot!

"Earth to Elio." She giggled again and it again splashed over him with equal parts ecstasy and terror. "Is this some new technique I haven't heard about?"

"What?" he managed to squeak out.

"You keeping your eyes open. If you ask me, it's a little creepy."

Her words finally filtered through the chemical haze.

He forced a laugh that sounded ten times more ridiculous than it should've. "No, sorry. I was just surprised."

"Good surprised or bad surprised?"

He leaned forward a fraction of an inch, closed his eyes, and returned a kiss that communicated a small part of the clawing need in his chest.

After a deep kiss, he pulled away and opened his eyes to see her reaction. Her eyes were still closed and her lips still waiting for his.

He realized at that moment that he wanted to be with Theresa forever. That he was meant to be with her forever. Like two halves of a whole. Two puzzle pieces shaped only for each other. He wanted to devote the rest of his life to taking care of her.

Only, he had responsibilities that required his attention first.

His mother.

Her welfare was always in his thoughts. How could it not?

Theresa opened her eyes and watched him. Her brows lowered and pinched together. "What are you thinking about?"

"Nothing."

"That's not true. Tell me."

Elio pulled away and turned to stare at the floor.

"Please, I want to know."

"My mother. She's all alone out there."

Theresa wrapped her arm around him and pulled him into her soft warmth.

"I have to get home to check on her. I'm her only hope."

"I understand."

"I know your dad doesn't want anyone leaving, especially not after what happened tonight. But I don't have a choice. I won't be able to live with myself if it turns out I could've helped but didn't."

"How far is it to your apartment?"

"I don't know. Seven miles maybe."

"How are you going to get there?"

"Steal a car I guess."

"I'll go with you," she said.

"I can't let you do that, Theresa. It's too dangerous."

"You're still healing, Elio. And even at a hundred percent, you're not some badass Rambo type."

"You mean like your dad?"

"Something like that."

"It doesn't matter. I have to do it. You don't."

"Elio Lopez, this is not a discussion." The words came

out hard and unassailable. "You will agree to my helping you or I will walk into my parents' room right this second and tell my dad what you're planning to do."

He had no doubt she would do exactly that. The tone of her voice offered no concession.

"Are we agreed?" she asked.

As much as he wanted to say no, two things made him say yes. One, he had to find his mother. And two, he never wanted to be apart from Theresa again.

A figure appeared in the doorway. "You're not on the injured reserve list anymore, Romeo," Mason said. "Back to the couch for you. And no middle of the night meetings either because I'll be watching all night."

"Dad, we're not doing anything."

"Good. I showed up in time then."

"Dad! You're embarrassing me!"

"Better that than grounding you, am I right?"

Elio rose still holding Theresa's hand. He squeezed it. "Yes," he said as he left the room under Mason's watchful eye.

He landed on the couch floating on air. It may as well have been a cloud. His lips tingled where hers had touched them. She liked him. She really liked him.

Right?

They kissed. People didn't kiss if they didn't like each other. A tiny voice tried to ask him why she would ever like him in a million years.

She kissed him. First!

His palm was still warm from her touch. He'd agreed to let her go with him. It was crazy. He was crazy for allowing it. Maybe she'd change her mind. Be too afraid to go back out and potentially run into more of those crazy people. He wouldn't blame her. For her sake, he hoped it turned out like that.

But whatever she ended up deciding, he knew one thing for certain.

He had to leave tomorrow.

21

MASON rolled onto his side and winced at the stabbing ache in his back. He forced an eyelid open and saw dim light slipping in around the edges of the heavy curtain covering the bedroom window. Beth was already up. He didn't have to look over to verify her absence. If she was still in bed, her warm body would be glued to his backside. He cracked open the other eye and stared at the ceiling. He'd had better mornings. His body complained from a hundred places at once. He pinched his eyes shut and rubbed life into the puffy lids. How long had he been asleep?

Not long enough.

He glanced at the digital clock on the bedside table. It hadn't had power in days but the habit of checking it yet remained. He checked his watch.

Half past six in the morning.

He pivoted around and dropped his feet to the floor. Feeling more like rising from the dead than getting out of bed, Mason levered himself up to a standing position.

Clyde broke into a hacking, coughing fit from somewhere in the house. The little Bili chimp sounded almost human. Beth was supposed to have slept last night while Mason took the first, and longest, watch but she was awake fussing over Clyde every time he came in and checked.

Mason slowly rotated each arm, feeling out the various aches to see if any required immediate attention. He did the same with his legs and torso. There was plenty of hurt, but nothing torn or broken.

The faint smell of roasted coffee tickled his nose. His body demanded he either fall back into bed and pass out or go investigate the scent. He lumbered into the kitchen and found Beth seated at the breakfast table holding Clyde in her arms. The cute, little ball of black fur snuggled deeper into her arms. He glanced over at Mason with large, brown eyes, and then broke into a silly, toothless grin.

"He likes you," Beth said.

Clyde reached out with tiny, slender fingers and then drew back quickly as another coughing spell hit him.

Beth turned to Mason with a worried look on her face. "Coffee should still be hot."

A camp stove hooked up to a five gallon propane tank was one of their emergency cooking methods. The other was the solar oven but it didn't work until the sun climbed high into the sky.

It was an old survival maxim. Two was one and one was none. And the important part of that credo was that the two duplicated capability, not SKU codes, meaning they had two different methods to achieve the same result.

He poured himself a steaming cup and took a slow, deep breath. The aroma alone reminded him the world wasn't a complete disaster. He took a sip and liquid heat poured into his belly. Yes, maybe today wouldn't be such a terrible day after all. "Did you sleep?"

Beth twisted her mouth up. "Not really."

"How's the little guy?"

"Worse." Her bottom lip trembled and she turned back to her week-old patient. She was a fierce mama bear. And, being the Chief Veterinarian at the LA Zoo, she was that way with every animal in her care. Mason wondered at the seemingly endless wellspring of love in her heart. She always had more to give. More care. More compassion. More space to love.

He wasn't the typical fifties father—the type that bottled up his feelings and then keeled over a week after a retirement party that earned him a gold-plated Timex. His emotional intelligence was more modern than that. Heck, he'd even read a book on how to raise a happy toddler way back to give him insight for Theresa.

That said, he wasn't on the same level as his wife.

"Mason, he needs antibiotics. The respiratory infection has progressed. His lungs are bubbling with fluid."

"We checked three different places and there was next to nothing. Totally cleaned out. Actually, we found something at Fernando's. Let me get it."

Mason retrieved the brown prescription bottle from his backpack and read the label. "Sildenafil citrate. That something that might help?"

Beth laughed. It was short and tight, and contained only shadows of the usual mirth. "To help you maintain an erection? Yes. To clear up an acute respiratory infection? No."

"It's Viagra?"

Iridia stumbled into the kitchen looking like this might've been the earliest she'd ever risen in her entire life. "Viagra? My old boyfriend took stuff to get bigger muscles but it did a number on his Johnson. Total wet noodle. He got on Viagra and whoa! Let me tell you."

She raised her arm straight into the air. "I'm talking Man of Steel. Hours and hours of pleasure. A real human dildo."

Beth's jaw dropped open.

"Good to know," Mason said. "Thanks for the personal history."

Iridia looked between him and Beth. She frowned. "Oh no! Are you two having a problem with Little Willy?"

Mason nearly blushed. "His name is not *Little Willy*."

"Little Jimmy?"

"He's not little! Why Little? He's not little."

"I saw you naked."

"What?" Beth said.

"After finding the neighbors." She trailed off and a distant look crept across her face.

"Oh, right," Beth said.

"You can't count that," Mason said. "That water was freezing cold!"

Iridia seemed to accept the excuse.

Not that it was an excuse. It was a reason. A biologically proven one. Why did he have to explain it?

"So what's the problem down there?" Iridia asked.

"There's no problem down there!" Mason replied.

"Oh, why are you taking Viagra then?"

Mason flung the bottle to the kitchen counter like it was a venomous snake. "I'm not taking Viagra. And can we please stop talking—"

"I'm not the one that brought it up," Iridia said.

Clyde broke into a desperate coughing spell and the topic thankfully died. Beth wiped the snot and saliva dripping from his nose and mouth. She turned back to

Mason when the spell subsided. "We have to get antibiotics today. *Today*."

"I understand. But how? I don't think we're going to find a pharmacy that isn't cleaned out."

A muscle in Beth's jaw rippled. "I have an idea, but you're not going to like it."

22

That wasn't the most reassuring way to pitch an idea. Mason didn't know whether to stop listening now or wait for her to actually say it and then stop listening.

"What?" he asked.

"The zoo," Beth replied.

"The Los Angeles Zoo?"

"No, the San Diego Zoo. Of course, the Los Angeles Zoo."

Iridia poured herself a cup of coffee. "I love the San Diego Zoo. We did a shoot there once. Have you ever had a fourteen foot snake wrapped around your shoulders?"

Mason and Beth ignored her hoping she might take the hint and enjoy her morning joe somewhere else.

She wasn't good with hints.

"No? Well, it's terrifying. My nipples were rock hard the entire time!" She took a sip of coffee and stared off into a past that only she cared anything about.

"Why the zoo?" Mason asked.

Iridia's brows knotted together in confusion. "Well, where else are you going to find a gigantic snake?"

Mason squeezed his eyes shut. "I'm talking to Beth."

"My lab," Beth said. "The medical wing is behind locked metal doors that only a few people have the keys for. And the medicine itself is locked in a security cabinet that only I have the key for. It's the one place that's guaranteed to still be stocked."

From the sound of it, she was probably right. There probably were antibiotics right where she said they'd be.

"Absolutely not," Mason said.

"Don't 'absolutely not' me," Beth said.

"It's too far. Too dangerous. No."

Beth raised an eyebrow at him. She wasn't the type that surrendered a position by force. It just made her dig in harder, even if she wouldn't have otherwise cared. He loved that about her, but it was also exasperating at times.

Mason held up a hand for parley. "Look, think about what you're saying. Theresa and I went less than two miles last night and ran into serious trouble. You're talking going all the way over to the east side. That's twenty miles!"

"Twenty-five miles. I rode it every day, each way."

"That's insane."

Iridia waved her hand in the air as she parted the space between them and headed for the dining room. "Your vibes are killing my morning cup. And it's bad enough already." She swept out of the room with vague annoyance, like royalty leaving behind squabbling commoners.

"Listen to me, Mason." Beth's tone softened. "I know it's dangerous. I know. But Clyde is going to die without antibiotics." Tears welled up in her eyes. "I can't let that happen. I promised Jane I'd protect him. Keep him safe."

Mason didn't want him to die either. And he knew how much Jane, Clyde's mother, had meant to both Beth and Theresa. But knowing that didn't equate to him agreeing with her ridiculous plan. Before he could reply, she continued.

"And it's not just about Clyde. It's about our family too. All of us. Elio will take the last of his round today. That's it. What happens the next time one of us gets an infected cut or scrape?"

Mason didn't know how to respond.

"We've done our best, but general hygiene is slipping. And that's saying nothing about the contaminants in the outside world. Sooner or later, and probably sooner, one of us is going to need them too."

Mason remembered the conditions he'd endured in Fallujah. Where the environment was so filled with poison that every single nick got infected in no time. The only reason any of them didn't instantly succumb was because they each took a massive daily dose of antibiotics as a matter of course. Even with the chemical assistance, some sores took weeks to heal.

"I'll go," he said.

"You can't go," she said. "I'm not being a martyr here. You're beat up. You limped in here this morning."

"I did?"

"Yes. Your calf is still healing. And after last night, you've got new bruises on top of old bruises."

She wasn't wrong about that.

"I can still do it," he said.

"I have no doubt you could, but you already have an urgent job to do."

He knew what she was going to say before the words came out.

"Like you said, we can't stay in this house. It's only a matter of time before looters or whatever attacked you comes after us. Whether it's next door or somewhere else, we need to make that move today."

She wasn't wrong about that either.

"I can't lose you, Beth."

"You won't."

"How can you know that?"

"How did you know that you'd return to me after your deployment?"

The truth was that he didn't. He assured her, of course, that it was some unwritten guarantee. But he knew better.

"I just knew that I'd do whatever it took to get back home to you and Theresa."

She nodded.

Mason sat in the chair next to her. "If you're going to do this, I need to have an open communication channel with you at all times."

"Mobile phones haven't worked for days. Our walkie-talkies are lucky to work more than a mile in the city. I don't know how we could do that."

A possibility flickered in Mason's mind. An old jarhead buddy. He wasn't a part of The Thundering Third, but Mason didn't hold it against him. He hadn't seen him in too long. Before the outbreak, life was too busy. After the outbreak, social calls weren't high on anybody's priorities.

But if anyone could help, Corporal Francis Knipplemier could. Juice as he preferred to be called. As much fun as it was to yank his chain about his given name, every knuckle dragger Mason had ever met called him Juice because the guy could perform miracles with anything that had electricity coursing through its veins.

Juice could figure it out. If he was still alive.

23

Mason pedaled the cargo bike south on Pacific Avenue letting the electric assist do most of the work. He'd opted for a slower, but near-silent mode of transportation. This wasn't a supply run and the Bronco's engine was like an air siren in the unsettling quiet that blanketed the new world.

It wasn't that it was silent.

Seagulls screeched and fought with the ravens perched atop bodies in the street picking at decomposing flesh. It struck him in an oddly removed way. The air stank of rotten meat, and then a fresh breeze would sweep through and all he'd smell was the briny scent of the ocean. And then the stink would settle back in and make him regret that last big breath.

The onshore breeze rattled palm tree leaves high above. It caught bits of trash, cartwheeling them across the street to pile up against the curb on the leeward side.

Despite the natural sounds, the sounds of city life were unsettlingly absent. The usual hum of cars driving, people talking, and music drifting from store fronts was missing.

Few things felt lonelier than being all alone in the middle of the city.

Juice lived over on the Venice Canals in one of the multimillion dollar homes that lined the waterways. He and Linda shared a sparkling modern construction that they designed themselves. Mason's old 1960s Craftsmen cost half as much and was a quarter as cool. That was west side real estate, before the outbreak. You could spend a million and a half dollars and live in a shack within a mile of the ocean. Or you could spend twice that and end up with something ten times nicer.

It seemed like a weird bifurcation of the market until you thought more about it. Your average, successful double-income Joe and Sally could pull a million dollar loan no problem in the sloshing easy money environment created by the Federal Reserve. That inflated the market and created an artificial floor above the million dollar mark. But Joe and Sally really stretched to make it happen. Whereas if you jumped up to two and a half to three million dollars, Joe and Sally were left behind by the truly wealthy.

The people that didn't need loans to purchase real estate. The competition at that level of the market was much, much lower. And therefore, those less contested square feet had to work much harder to earn a sale.

It was nonsense propagated by an institution that had done as much to harm the economy as to help it.

Maybe the outbreak did have an upside. Not since the days of Manifest Destiny had west side real estate been so cheap.

Mason didn't encounter any threats on the way over. The exertion of the trip loosened his muscles and took the edge off the innumerable pain signals coursing through his nervous system.

He headed down a concrete ramp to the canal level below. A row of expensive houses occupied each side of the small canal. A wide sidewalk ran along each side. Small docks with canoes and paddle boats dotted the shore. Just over a week ago, this was one of the hottest neighborhoods on the west side. Now, it was a ghost town without all the tumbleweeds.

Juice's house was two down on the right. He turned off the electric assist and coasted to a stop in front. What used to be large glass windows were now gaping holes edged in razor shards. A blood red triangle was painted on the exterior wall next to the missing front door. The painted delta symbol reminded him of the story of how the Israelites had painted lamb's blood above their doors so that death would pass them by.

Obviously lamb's blood and spray paint didn't offer the same level of protection.

Mason looked around. All of the surrounding houses were clearly looted. It made sense. When things fell apart, desperate people noticed those with the most. Juice was not the type to go quietly, but maybe the virus had already taken him by the time looters hit his house.

Mason hid the bike behind tall bushes that also artfully hid a water meter. Was probably an HOA regulation in this neighborhood. He drew his pistol, inched the slide back to verify a round was chambered—it was—and kept it in the low ready position while listening for clues. The small front yard was covered in a thin layer of decomposed granite and dotted with a variety of drought tolerant plants. It was the kind of yard that people who didn't like to think about yards had.

A flight of ducks glided in from the east. They lined up to the canal and splashed up small wakes skidding to a stop on the surface. He considered taking a shot at one to add to their protein reserves but refrained, knowing the shot would sound like a cannon in the canyon formed by the houses that lined both sides.

A careful step over the lip of a shattered window and he was inside. The place was gutted to the polished concrete floors. The open floor plan design made almost everything on the first floor visible. The expensive stainless steel kitchen appliances were gone.

Really?

Did someone think they needed a fancy dishwasher more than anything else while society fell apart around them?

A large, conspicuous hole showed where the fridge used to be. Even the sinks had been ripped out. Was someone building an HGTV dream home with all their stolen plunder? With no power or water service, those anachronisms of modern convenience were nothing more than shiny doorstops.

An elegant span of clear acrylic stairs led up to the bedrooms on the second floor. Mason went upstairs and cleared them one by one. Thankfully, he didn't find the bodies of Juice and Linda.

CLANG.

Someone grunted.

The hushed voice came from downstairs. Mason crept downstairs looking down through the steps as he went. The faint sound of an intentionally placed footfall to his left made him pause at the bottom of the stairs. He circled around the steel bannister and saw nothing in the living room, foyer, or kitchen. He hugged the wall on his left side with the Glock up and ready for action. With all of his senses switched on, he inched toward the back of the house. The wall ended and he paused at the corner.

What was around the corner? He remembered a dinner party he'd attended over a year ago. He'd gone looking for Beth when the conversation lulled. She'd been in a bathroom at the end of the hall. There were two more doors along the hall. The one on the right led to the garage. The one on the left had been closed and he didn't recall ever knowing what was behind it.

Now was as good a time as any to find out.

He backed up from the wall and pivoted around the corner, slicing the arc of the fatal funnel. Nothing. He sliced more of the arc. Still nothing.

SHUCK SHUCK.

The sawed-off barrel of a Remington 870 Tactical shotgun appeared from the yet hidden slice of the pie. "You picked a good day to die."

24

A cold knot clenched in Mason's stomach. He stared at the end of the barrel with the tunnel focus of a massive adrenaline dump. Through the crystal clear haze, he suddenly realized that he recognized the voice.

"Juice, you left a few burrs on the muzzle. That's an amateur night saw job."

Juice's face appeared from around the corner and he broke into a wide grin. "Sarge, I almost blew your head off!"

Mason swallowed hard and forced the feeling back into his legs. "Yeah, I'm really glad you didn't, though."

Juice slapped him hard on the shoulder. "You look terrible, bro!"

He was one to talk. The goatee he'd grown after returning to civilian life had once been a mere curiosity. Now it made him resemble a kung fu master without all the wrinkles.

"Did you know you had a horse tail growing out of your chin?"

He stroked it like it was a cat. "This? It's my pride and joy. Helps me think."

"It's good to see you're alive and well," Mason said. "How's Linda?"

The light in Juice's face sank beneath a cloud. "We're getting by. How is your family?"

"Tough times with no end in sight, but we're together and alive. Considering the state of things, that's something."

"Right you are, Sarge. Listen, this isn't the safest place to catch up. Follow me."

Juice spun on his heel and Mason followed. They walked into the guest bathroom at the end of the hall. Juice closed the door behind Mason and then stopped, waiting for something.

"Why are we hanging out in the bathroom?" Mason asked.

"Have you used this bathroom before?"

"Yeah, I remember wandering back here for relief at that Christmas party two years ago."

"And when you used the bathroom two years ago at the Christmas party, did you notice anything unusual about it?"

"No."

"How about now?"

Mason looked around. It was a fancy modern design. Flexible water tubes hung out of the wall where the sink had once been. It had been one of those faucets that spilled out like a waterfall into a clear glass sink. Apparently someone's HGTV home needed it too. Large holes in the wall showed where they'd ripped the anchors out.

"There's no place to wash your hands?"

"Very funny," he said. "Anything else?"

The toilet was still there. Apparently even a fancy one wasn't worth the average looter's time. The shower stall to the left was one of those that had no door and a wall to keep the spray in.

"I give up. Aside from it looking like it cost more than most kitchens, I don't see anything unusual."

"Exactly." Juice turned and reached into the shower stall over to the recessed shelf in the tile wall. His fingers curled up into the overhang searching for something. Mason heard a click and a muffled whirring sound, like gears turning. Juice stepped back and looked at Mason with a broad grin. "Open sesame."

With all that had happened, Mason didn't think he'd ever be surprised again. He was.

The tiled shower floor lifted. Sixty seconds later and the whole thing had rotated up revealing a set of stairs descending below.

Juice smacked his shoulder. "Didn't expect that, did you?"

"Can't say I did."

"I knew the world would crack at some point. So I created this little emergency refuge for Linda and me. Watch your head."

"Where is she?"

"Sleeping."

Mason followed him down the stairs making sure not to bump his head as he cleared the floor, now roof. They entered a large room with a couple of closed doors along the wall to the right. Juice tapped a button next to the stairs and the shower floor above slowly lowered into place. "Very secret agent. Very Juice Bond."

Juice laughed.

Mason glanced around. Emergency bunker? This was a prepper's palace. Six columns of heavy metal shelving units contained endless rows of supplies. Enough food, water, toilet paper, batteries, to last years. A long worktable covered with ordered piles of electrical equipment lined the left wall.

At the far corner under the worktable sat a row of shiny silver appliances. Dishwasher, front loading washer and dryer. The missing refrigerator was squeezed between the far wall and the end of the work table. The lights on its front panel glowed blue.

"Do those work?"

"Wouldn't be much of a refuge if they didn't," Juice replied.

Mason shook his head. Amazing. Everyone forgot how utterly transformative automation was until it stopped working. Less than a week without power, and Beth was already getting cranky about laundry. He knew he'd be recruited to the task as soon as their bigger projects were finished.

Juice walked over and picked up a crazy looking gizmo on the near end of the table. It had a spider web of wires looping in and out of circuit boards. A soldering gun sat next to it with the tip smoking.

"Was just working on something when I heard you bumbling around upstairs."

"I wasn't bumbling. I don't bumble."

"You bumbled."

Juice held up the device and Mason could tell he was about to launch into an extended explanation of whatever it was supposed to be. That would have to wait for another time.

"Hey bro, sorry to show up without an invitation, but I need your help with something."

Juice delicately set the device back on the worktable, obviously disappointed at not being able to dive into the details of his latest invention. "Anything, Sarge. You know that. I have what you call the life debt with you."

Mason almost groaned. He'd heard Juice say that before. And even more painfully, he'd endured the explanation of the cinematic reference.

"Don't go Star Wars on me now."

"I still can't believe you've never seen *A New Hope*."

"Was never my thing. And doesn't look like it'll ever get a chance to be now."

Juice's face brightened. "Banish the thought! I've got it on my laptop. We can send it over to the flatscreen." He pointed at an enormous TV on the wall. It was so big Mason hadn't noticed it wasn't the wall itself until now.

"Another time."

"Well, what can I do for you?"

"I was hoping you could help me with a long-range communication system."

"What do you need it for?"

Mason related the highlights of Beth's plan and the necessity of it. It sounded no less insane coming out of his mouth than when he tentatively agreed to it after coming out of hers.

Juice shrugged. "I would've given you some of my antibiotic stash, but I ended up having to use it all. Making that trip sounds dangerous."

Mason nodded. "Not many things aren't these days."

"Well," Juice said. "The zoo is what, twenty miles as the crow flies?"

"Near enough, yeah."

Juice looked up at nothing in particular, murmuring to himself, tilting his head back and forth. Mason waited quietly. He'd seen Juice like this countless times back in the sandbox. Another minute or two of waiting and Juice snapped back to the present.

"Yep, I think I can patch something together. I'm going to have to bounce it through a relay station here to pick up enough power, but it should work. It'll take a half hour or so. Want a cold beer while you wait?"

Cold.

Beer.

Mason wasn't a beer in the morning kind of guy, but this might be the last cold one he ever had. It wasn't even a choice, really.

25

Mason glanced at his watch. It was a quarter past eight in the morning. Yep, a cold beer sounded like the closest thing to heaven that he was likely to find on earth. "Cold?"

"Arctic."

"Yes," Mason said. "Like nothing else in the world."

Juice chuckled and retrieved two beers from the futuristic refrigerator. "All of this is solar powered from panels I have up on the roof." He handed one to Mason.

"Pliny the Elder?" Mason asked. "You're getting pretty cultured in your old age."

"An ice cold Schlitz may have tasted like liquid caviar back in the sandbox. But here in civilization, it tastes like the dirty water that it is."

"I'm not sure we qualify as civilization anymore."

Juice tapped the neck of his bottle against Mason's. "All the more reason to enjoy a fine microbrew while we still can."

Mason took a long, slow drink and enjoyed the bite of the hops as it slid over his tongue and down his throat. He finished the gulp and stared at the half-empty bottle. "Wow.

As long as a man can drink a cold beer, there's still hope in the world."

He looked over to see if Juice agreed but the eccentric tinkerer was already hard at work. The outside world had faded to black. Juice was like that. Artillery could be coming in danger close and Juice would only look up and swat it away like an annoying fly before returning to his work.

Realizing he was no longer needed, Mason wandered the aisles of stocked shelves amazed at what his friend had squirreled away. Cases of wine stacked six high and three deep with probably ten bottles per case. Further down, a portion of one shelf held enough batteries to power a thousand Energizer bunnies for a thousand years.

"Grab a bag and take whatever you want."

"You sure?"

"Absolutely, Linda and I won't use all this stuff in a hundred years."

Mason spotted an ordered pile of brown paper bags. "Thanks. We can definitely use it." He went about filling a number of bags, as much as he thought the cargo bike could hold in its saddle bags. As he shopped around, he noticed a surprising lack of drinking water. He looked through all six aisles and saw nothing more than a few cases of bottled water. There was no way that Juice had overlooked something so basic.

"Mason, come hold this together for me." Juice handed him a collapsible antenna with exposed wires coming out the end. He held the exposed ends to the contact points on a radio. "Keep them right there."

Mason took over while Juice retrieved a soldering gun and a roll of solder. "You could open up a Walmart with all the stuff you have in here."

Juice shook his head as he started to melt the wires into

place. "Don't think so. I don't sell at bargain-basement prices."

White wisps of smoke curled up into the air as he worked.

"One thing I don't see is enough water. Are you handling that?"

Juice pulled off his safety goggles and grinned. "Astute observation. We have a 10,000 gallon water catchment system underneath the house. Even with the drought of the past several years, it's never gone below half full. It's sitting at around 7500 gallons right now. You'd be surprised how much 2000 square feet of roof surface can gather."

"How much did that cost to install?"

Juice winked. "Wasn't cheap. Hold still now while that cools."

"Juice, tell me if I'm being nosy here, but... where'd you get the money for all this? I mean, I know you have a few patents. Is that what bought all this?"

Juice's eyes lit up."Yeah, for the most part. General Electric ended up licensing one of those patents for a manufacturing process. That paid millions."

Mason shook his head. "Looks like I went into the wrong line of business."

"Those patents are small potatoes compared to what I was working on before civilization decided to take a giant dump."

Mason laughed. "Tell me you were working on a giant roll of toilet paper."

"If only I'd had the foresight."

"What was it then?"

Juice rubbed his hands together. His eyes sparkled like a ten-year-old about to show off his favorite Christmas gift. "Personal aerial transport. PAT. It's a she."

"You mean like a flying car or something?"

"Not exactly. Smaller."

"A jet pack?"

Juice pinched his brows together and grimaced. "Jet pack? What am I? An idiot?"

"I think we both know that's not the case."

"Exactly," he said as he checked the soldered connections. "That's gonna take another few minutes to set. Come take a look."

They entered the second door on the right and entered a large room filled with a dizzying array of advanced electronic equipment. The stuff out on the workbench looked like Legos in comparison. If someone had told Mason a nuclear bomb was under construction, he wouldn't have ruled it out. In the center of the room, a large tan tarp covered what was presumably not a jet pack.

"Prepare to witness the future," Juice said as he grabbed a handful of the cloth. "Or what would've been the future." He tugged the tarp off. It tumbled to the floor revealing a steel-framed half-cage that hugged the form of the intended occupant, much like the bottom half of an Egyptian coffin. Behind that were two large turbines about three feet across each. Shiny black housings encircled each propeller. It sat on skids like a helicopter. Two metal arms extended out and ended in joysticks. The left one had a small digital screen at the end.

Juice stroked the smooth surface like it was his firstborn which, considering he didn't have kids, maybe it was. "This baby was gonna change the world." He looked down at the concrete floor and shook his head sadly. "And now it'll never see the light of day."

"Looks a lot heavier than a jet pack," Mason said.

"It is. But it's infinitely more reliable and has ten times

the range, too. The latest state-of-the-art fly by wire controls. Self stabilizing gyroscopic attitude mechanism."

"What does that mean in English?"

"It means even an idiot like you could fly it without killing himself."

"How did you plan on getting it out of here? I know it's not making it through that doorway."

Juice held up a finger without saying a word.

"You're going to blow a hole in the ceiling?"

"No need. See those controls on the wall over there?"

Mason nodded.

Juice then pointed to a fine line along the ceiling. "That seam is the edge of two panels that split apart and fully retract. That nearly featureless front yard you may have disparaged on the way in is for more than satisfying my distaste for lawn work."

"Makes for a nice skylight."

"Perhaps it's a little ahead of its time, but I had this bay built in anticipation of the technology making it mainstream. I bet every house would've had one of these within the next ten years."

Mason didn't reply. He'd heard the promise of flying cars from the age of four. And it was always just a few years away. But he didn't see a point in raining on his nonexistent parade. "I'm sure it would've changed the world."

A scream echoed in from another room.

Mason dropped his hand to his holster.

Juice bolted for the door. "Linda! It's okay. I'm coming!"

26

Mason hustled after him expecting trouble. He followed him back into the main room and then to the closed door to their left. Juice threw it open and hurried inside. The trouble that Mason found was not what he expected.

Linda cowered in a corner with her arms wrapped around her naked body. A bed sheet lay crumpled on the floor at her feet. She wept uncontrollably with a hand covering her face.

Juice knelt beside her, and she jumped at his touch. "It's okay, baby. I'm here. It's okay."

Mason's heart ached. He waited while Juice tried to calm and reassure her.

The room was a complete mess. A total juxtaposition to the extreme order of the rest of the bunker. He remembered that Juice sometimes complained about Linda's natural state of messiness, but this was a whole other thing.

A bed in the corner had sheets pulled off and piled on the floor. An open closet had a rack full of empty hangers and a pile of clothes underneath. A plastic cup lay next to a puddle of what looked like spilled milk on the floor.

Linda finally calmed down.

"She okay?" Mason asked.

His question drew her attention. She screamed and broke away from Juice and bounded into the closet on all fours. She cowered in a dark corner watching Mason with wide, unfamiliar eyes.

He'd seen eyes like those before. The last time he'd seen them, they were trying to kill him.

"Mason, get out!" Juice said. "Get out and shut the door!"

"Sorry," Mason replied as he hurried out. He waited by the workbench trying to think about anything other than what he knew to be true. After several minutes of failing effort, Juice emerged and closed the door behind him.

All the happiness had drained from his face. His skin was waxy and hollowed out. He stumbled to a chair and collapsed. "It's getting to the point where I'm not sure she recognizes me anymore."

"I'm sorry, brother."

Juice looked up, his words coming out in a stuttering rhythm. "Why her? She was the most generous soul I'd ever met. She was everything. And now she's turned into that." Tears welled in his eyes and he curled forward as his body convulsed.

Mason laid a hand on his back. "I'm so sorry."

Juice sniffed and wiped his eyes. He made an effort to straighten up and get his breathing under control. He plucked a tissue from a box on the table and blew his nose.

Mason waited for him to compose himself. Besides, he didn't know what else to say.

Juice cleared his throat a few times and then chugged the nearly full bottle of beer he'd left on the table.

"What happened?" Mason asked.

Juice shook his head. "She got infected and sick. I used

up every last bit of our antibiotics thinking they'd help. They didn't and she turned into a delta."

"A delta?"

Juice nodded. "It's what they call the people changed by the Delta Virus. Guess it's why they called it the Delta Virus in the first place. You've never seen one?"

Mason recalled the mother and her kids in Holly's garage and the close call at the neighborhood market. "Yeah, I have. A couple of times now, but I don't know much about them."

"Not a surprise if no one in the family has turned. The government didn't give out any useful information while it still functioned. I picked up bits and pieces from other ham radio operators around the country. Then, when Linda changed, I got a front row seat."

Mason chugged the last of his beer and set it next to Juice's empty bottle. "I'm completely in the dark on this one. I'd like to know more if you're up to sharing."

Juice nodded almost imperceptibly. "She'd been to Reagan Medical Center the day before the outbreak for her annual physical. All routine stuff. She checked out fine. But the next day, the day of the official outbreak, she started complaining about stomach cramps and nausea. She woke up in the morning with a burning fever. I did my best to keep her cool and she seemed to improve after a while."

He stood up and wandered away. "Want another beer?"

"Nah, thanks though."

He pulled a beer from the fridge and cracked it open. After a long pull, he continued.

"I thought she was getting better. That we'd beaten it. And there was nothing on the news or radio about people changing. But she didn't get better. Yeah, the fever and vomiting let up, but she seemed to sink away into herself as it did."

"What do you mean?"

He took another drink. "I don't know how to describe it. The Linda that I knew and loved, the personality that made her who she was. It just faded away."

He squeezed his temples with one hand and scrunched up his face like the memories were a migraine. Maybe they were.

"It was only later that stories started to leak out over the shortwave frequencies. People talking about seeing their loved ones change. Becoming deltas, as they started to call them. Some idiots were calling them zombies and screaming about the zombie apocalypse."

After the attack last night, Mason didn't think that sounded totally off base.

"They're not zombies," Juice said. "They're people, only changed."

"How do you mean?"

"Well, it's like they devolve. The unique thing that makes us human is stripped away."

"You mean our intelligence?"

"Yes, exactly." He turned and hurled the bottle across the room. It hit a concrete wall and exploded into a shower of foam and fragments. "It's like she's an animal. You saw her."

"I'm sorry I scared her."

"It's not you. It's anything and everything. She can't use a toilet. Can't take a shower. Can't drink out of a stupid plastic cup! She doesn't understand any of it!"

"Do you think she'll ever get better? Become the real Linda again?"

"God only knows. I'll never give up on her, though."

"I ran into a pack of deltas yesterday. Thirty or forty maybe. They attacked Theresa and me."

"Attacked you?"

"Yeah, we managed to get away. But I'm telling you, they wanted to kill us. No doubt about it."

"Linda's never acted like that. Why would they want to kill you?"

"I don't know."

"Maybe to defend their territory," Juice said.

Mason nodded. "Maybe." But the attack hadn't made him feel like an intruder. It had made him feel like prey. "Or maybe they were hungry."

27

BETH watched as Mason secured the two-way radio to her motorcycle. She hadn't ridden Spock in over a week. She imagined the wind rushing by as she and the old Kawasaki Vulcan carved through the air as one. Until this moment, she hadn't realized how much she missed it.

The average driver of a four-wheeled vehicle would never understand. And she couldn't blame them. The typical commute for them meant being trapped in a slow-moving inchworm. Part of the spine humped up and a section of cars raced forward. Then that part came back down and ground to a halt. Over and over again until the driver made it to work or home.

Talk about soul-crushing.

It was something else altogether for riders. Sure, it could be risky. It frequently was. Those same drivers would do bonehead moves like accidentally weave into the next lane as they slept through the interminable journey. Or they'd wake up and rage at the futility of their entrapment. And that inevitably resulted in the driver whipping into the next lane the instant half a car-length of space opened up. Of course, it achieved nothing. They got to wait in that lane, too.

What it did achieve though was putting her and other riders in instant and mortal danger. She'd be cruising along in the space between the lanes and a car would jerk across the dashed line. No signal. No declaration of intention. No effort toward even verifying anyone might be entering the space they were hell-bent on overtaking.

Then she'd slam on the brakes so hard her front fork nearly dug channels in the concrete. She'd had a few close calls, but always managed to avoid the sickening crunch of metal and bones.

She'd even had a few run-ins with bullies who thought it'd be fun to weave toward her with their three ton rides just to see her panic. Of course, she panicked. A six hundred pound bike was like putting a flyweight in the ring with a heavyweight. The knockout punch could only go in one direction.

That said, the last time a jackass tried that move, she dodged the weave, then accelerated by and kicked the guy's side mirror off before flipping the bird and leaving him in the dust.

It was a stupid move. One she'd never told Mason about because he would've flipped out. But it was satisfying. Eminently satisfying. All that said, she knew the ride she was about to take wasn't going to make the daily commute look like a cakewalk.

"I'll be careful," Beth said.

"I'm not worried about what you'll do," Mason said.

She smirked. He might be if he knew about the side mirror incident.

"What?" he asked.

"Doesn't matter. Different world. How's this radio work?"

"The distance to the zoo is too far for your portable unit or my handheld. So, Juice wired up a way to relay transmissions through his higher-powered setup. He'll basically be receiving your message and relaying to me and vice-versa."

"Good friend to have."

"The best."

Mason tightened the last strap and turned on the unit. He unclipped the microphone and pressed the side button.

"Juice, this is Mason. Over."

The speaker crackled.

"Sarge, Juice here. Transmission is five by five. Ready for relay. Over."

Mason handed the corded mic to Beth, and then clicked on his handheld unit. "Say who you're speaking to and then your name. *Over* lets the receiver know your transmission is finished and the channel is open for return communication."

Her husband loved his protocols.

"Moonbeam, this is Flowerchild. Can you hear me now?"

Mason slanted an eyebrow down at her. "Now is a great time to make jokes?"

She laughed and then cut it short when he didn't share her mirth.

"And you have to release the transmit button when you're finished speaking."

"I'm not an idiot." She pressed the button. "Mason, this is Beth. You look grouchy. Over." Her voice came out of the speaker of his handheld.

"Beth, this is Mason. I am. Over."

Juice's voice broke in, "Annoyingly cute married couple,

this is Juice. The relay looks good on my end. How is it on yours? Over."

"All good here. Over," Mason responded.

"Okay then," Juice said. "I'll be monitoring communications and tweaking the relay if needed to keep the signal strong. Otherwise, I'll be like Uncle Sam. It feels like you have privacy, but you don't. Over."

Mason chuckled despite his somber mood.

"So he gets a laugh, but I don't, huh?" She didn't really care. She was just happy to see a ray of light in the usual darkness of his blue eyes.

"Thanks for the warning, Sam. Over," Mason said as he checked Beth and her bike over. He'd set her up like she was going for a trip into the wilderness. Food, water, a tarp for shelter, extra ammo for the Glock holstered at her hip, fire starters and kindling, binoculars, and more. It should've been going overboard, but it wasn't.

He was right. She was about to ride into the wilderness. Alone.

The radios were crucial to making it happen. Mason wouldn't have let her go without them. However, they wouldn't make him magically appear if she ended up needing help. They'd gone over the back-up plan several times. If she got into trouble, she was to immediately transmit her location and then find a safe place to hole up and wait. Mason would jump in the Bronco and fight his way through heaven or hell to come get her.

It wasn't a great plan.

But it was the best they could come up with. Assuming things went fine, he'd have checked out the house next door and hopefully have them moved in by the time she returned in the afternoon. The sun would set with them having the meds they needed for Clyde and potential future injuries, and also having a solidly defensible position from which to get a good night's sleep.

Considering the circumstances, they had to make it work.

Mason pressed his forehead to hers. "Stay safe," he whispered.

"You're not the boss of me," she whispered back as his lips touched hers.

THE OCEAN BREEZE filled Beth's lungs with a pungent, lively scent. She rode south on the Venice Beach boardwalk heading down to Ballona Creek. From there, the plan was to cut in and head east. That would take her almost ten miles inland. She would then have to navigate a few miles of city streets before dropping into the LA River and following it the rest of the way to the zoo.

The rationale was to minimize her time on surface streets where she was more likely to run into others and where there was less space to maneuver in response. Riding a cruiser through creeks and rivers would've sounded like a fool's plan to most people. But the Ballona Creek and the LA River were not creeks or rivers as people in the rest of the country understood them.

Few things in LA were.

Both were actually wide concrete channels with vestigial waterways trickling down their centers. They were constructed to carry flood waters out of the city and into the ocean where they could disperse without threatening the ever more expensive real estate.

Through the padding of her helmet, Beth heard the muffled sound of the rushing wind. She'd never taken her bike on the boardwalk, much less ridden it at thirty miles per hour. It was thrilling and melancholic at the same time.

The boardwalk wasn't packed with its usual spread of eclectic citizens. There were no tourists with cameras pinned to their chests and white sun cream streaked on their cheeks. No young girls wearing skimpy bikinis lazily cruised down the path on longboard skateboards. No aging hippies in makeshift booths hawked homemade trinkets and visions for a better tomorrow. No muscled behemoths strutted around in loincloths showing off their enormous slabs of shredded beef. Why they were proud of that look, Beth never understood.

There were no crowds circled around dancers performing feats of physical prowess so astonishing you'd happily toss a dollar and maybe two into the hat.

Even the guitar-playing, inline-skating guy that rolled around wearing white robes and a turban was nowhere to be seen. She missed him most of all. He'd been a fixture on the boardwalk for so long that some thought he was a vampire. People assumed he'd been there long before everyone else arrived and he'd be there long after they'd gone.

But he wasn't there. He'd gone too.

Beth's heart ached remembering the time she'd paid the guy twenty bucks to serenade Mason with five straight Jimi Hendrix songs. She knew it would drive him crazy. It did, only not in the way she expected. By the end of the third song, he'd dragged her to her feet and made her join him dancing like hippies at Woodstock.

That was all gone.

Despite the evidence of human life scattered and gathered in piles everywhere she looked, the life that created that debris was missing. She didn't even see any bodies here like there'd been on some of the neighborhood streets. There were marks in the sand here and there that looked like something had been dragged across the pavement. But that could've just as easily been the ocean breeze blowing patterns into the sand.

The roar of the surf off to the right combined with the rumble of the motorcycle lulled her into a daze as she continued south through the once-expensive oceanfront properties of Marina Del Rey. The small community that had once been an elderly haven of the wealthy one percent. She used to wonder what they would've done if a tsunami came their way. They were trapped between an ocean of water and an ocean of humanity.

Apparently, she'd been concerned with the wrong apocalypse.

A small dog, a terrier of some kind, darted out from behind a corner and ran right across her path. She cranked the brakes down and the rear wheel locked up. It fishtailed out to the side as she fought to keep the bike upright. Despite her efforts, the tiny granules of sand drifting across the pavement won out. The bike crashed down to the side throwing her into a sand bank headfirst. She rolled into the impact and watched the bike skid off into the bank further down.

She dropped her head and tried to breathe. The impact had knocked the breath out of her. She knew what had actually happened was that the impact had temporarily paralyzed her diaphragm and that the condition would dissipate in a minute or two.

The knowledge only helped a little in fighting the panic that clawed at her mind. After a minute of ceding ground to the terror, a small breath trickled down her throat. Another few breaths and the thumping in her ears began to subside.

GRRRR.

Beth was going to kick that stupid dog. Did it seriously have the nerve to growl at her after knocking her down?

GRRRR.

The pitch wasn't right. It was a lower vocalization than a small terrier could make. A chill crept up her spine. She pushed herself up and scanned for the source.

A freakishly muscled pitbull had its flews curled up and its teeth clenched tight. It was crouched low to the ground and tensed for action.

GRRRR.

Beth jerked her Glock out and fired a round into the air. The dog bolted back between the buildings from where it had come. The terrier was nowhere to be seen. Which was a good thing since she wasn't sure if she wanted to help it or shoot it.

She struggled up and limped over to the fallen bike. It didn't feel like she'd broken anything, but she'd be sporting some serious bruises tomorrow.

Idiot dog. Both of them.

The radio Mason had strapped to the bike was busted on one side. She clicked the power on and off and got no response.

Great. So much for communication.

She kicked the kickstand out with more force than was strictly necessary. She then shoved her backside against the bike's frame dropped into a squat. She grunted and pushed with all her strength. Instead of the bike rotating upright, her boots sank down into the sand.

Nice. Fantastic spot to lay down a bike.

After her boots seemed to have settled enough to find harder ground, she heaved again and the old Kawasaki pushed over and settled upright on its kickstand. She blew out a big breath and jumped when the bike started to tip over to the other side.

The kickstand was slowly tunneling into the surface of the sand.

No!

She grabbed the handlebars and slung a leg over the seat and strained to get it back up. It hung in the air right where the force of the downward pull of gravity exactly equaled the force she exerted to bring it back up.

No!

Rage gave her the energy to tip the scale and the bike slowly came back up into balance.

GRRRR.

She pulled out her pistol and scanned for the pitbull. It wasn't going to get a warning shot this time. She glanced behind her. There it was about a hundred feet back.

Only it wasn't alone.

A pack of mangy dogs of equal or larger size surrounded it in a loose V like a flock of geese in the sky. They all growled and stared at her with unfriendly eyes. As one, they broke into a sprint like a whole quiver of arrows speeding toward their target.

Her.

She couldn't shoot them all. There were too many and she wasn't that good a shot. She holstered the Glock and fired up the Vulcan. She cranked the gas and the rear tire spun in place, spitting out a geyser of sand behind.

She let up and tried to duckwalk forward as she gave it a little gas. It edged forward and then the traction broke and more sand spewed out the back.

"Come on!"

She glanced back and the pack had closed half the distance. Only a few seconds before her legs would be shredded jerky. With the last bit of strength in her exhausted legs, she pushed off and hit the throttle.

The pitbull latched onto the heel of her right boot as the bike kicked forward and jumped back onto the pavement. She struggled with the front wheel and gunned it as soon as it pointed forward.

The bike roared and lunged ahead like a greyhound separating from the pack. The pitbull hung on dragging and bumping along the concrete. It rotated around and she caught its eyes as she glanced down.

"Let go!" Beth yelled as she slammed her heel into the engine casing.

Its broad, bony head smacked into the metal over and over. The monster was about to rip her leg off. She leaned down, careful to keep her balance, and tugged the zipper down the side of her calf. She wiggled her foot and the boot came free.

The pitbull smacked hard into a short, wood fence. It rolled to its feet and shook her boot wildly as if it wasn't dead yet.

Beth refocused on the path ahead. She was approaching the inlet where the Ballona Creek emptied into the ocean. The wind washed over her bootless foot, chilling the skin through the thick sock.

Great.

Hope that doesn't become a problem.

28

AHMED HASSAD didn't think his wife would ever forgive him. Perhaps he didn't deserve such a blessing. For the millionth time since she'd gone, he cursed the weakness in his heart. He cranked the can opener around and around until the sharp metal disk bit through the last of the ring sealing the can closed. He pried out the lid with a knife and began to assemble a lunch for his daughter as best he could.

He cursed himself for not being more prepared, for not taking the necessary action when such action was easy to take. Of course, he had an excuse. And that's exactly all he ever had. Excuses. Justifications for why he didn't do what he knew must be done.

He dipped the knife into the can and pulled out a dollop of thick, yellow paste. Hummus. Nalasif would've laughed in disdain. His wife made the best hummus in the world always from scratch from a recipe passed down through the generations. He spread a thick layer of what claimed to be hummus on a slice of wheat toast and laid it on a plate next to a few crackers.

Pathetic.

No more than ten days since the outbreak and already he was forced to feed them out of cans and their limited supply of dry goods. He poured out half a cup of water and eyed the nearly empty case of water bottles next to the kitchen sink.

He'd have to go out soon. He should've gone out already. But fear for his daughter kept him rooted in the security of their home. She couldn't go out into the madness. And how was he to leave her here in the house alone?

And so his every thought or action ended in despair. A few more days and their supplies would run out. He didn't expect that he'd have an answer by then, but then it would be too late to delay any longer.

He scratched at his oily beard and wished he could use one of the remaining bottles to rinse it clean. He hadn't bathed in over a week and the rank odor emanating from his body disgusted him.

The smell was starting to become so normal he sometimes went hours without noticing it. But then he'd notice a grimace on his daughter's face as he drew near and the desperate nature of their situation would crash back down upon his shoulders like an avalanche.

He carried the saucer bearing the meager meal upstairs and into the master bedroom. He turned the corner and his heart skipped a beat. His daughter stood across the room peeking through the curtains out the second story window.

"Noor! Get away from the window! It's not safe!"

She flinched at the sharpness in his voice and stumbled away from the window. Her long black hair swept gracefully around her shoulders just as her mother's had. Her dark eyes regarded him with a fear that instantly made him regret his response.

"I'm sorry, father. I just wanted to see the outside. To see if anything had changed."

Ahmed set the saucer down on a wood chest and gathered her up in his arms. "It is I who am sorry. I forget what it must be like at your age to endure such isolation. You deserve to be outside playing with friends."

"But I don't have any friends. And now, I will never have any friends."

He squeezed her tighter knowing the fault was his. Keeping up with his growing business over the years had required them to move internationally, with the latest move being to America. But it wasn't his business that drew them to this address. All the same, it was yet another move. Yet another occasion where Noor tearfully waved goodbye to the one or two dear friends that her shy manner managed to attract.

And now with the last move here several months ago, she had not had enough time yet to settle in at school and strike up a connection with one of her classmates. His heart broke for her. Not simply because of what she'd already suffered, but also because he had no way of making it end. He looked down and brushed a tear from her cheek with his thumb.

"We will survive, my daughter. Our family has survived times as dark as these. We have endured events even darker. And yet, we are here."

"And why are we here, father? If we are all going to die anyway, I would've rather not moved and died with my friends."

Ahmed grabbed her by the shoulders and held her tight. "Look at me."

She slowly looked up to meet his gaze.

"We will not die," he said. "I never want to hear you say that again. It would break your mother's heart."

He kissed her forehead and tucked a lock of hair behind her ear. He led her to a chair next to the wooden chest and sat her down. "You must eat. You need your strength."

She glanced at the plate and looked up. "Where is your lunch, father?"

"I've already had my share. Don't you worry about me."

The look she gave him spoke clearer than words that she knew he was lying. He'd been skipping meals for days to ensure that she had sufficient food. The decreased daily intake was already starting to show on his thin frame. He forced a sad laugh. Not that he forced it to be sad, but it came out that way. "It's my beard making me look skinny. It needs a good trimming."

She dropped her eyes to her lunch and took a bite of the bread.

A noise from outside startled him. He hurried to the window and parted the curtains a sliver. The neighbor, Mason West, had leaned a ladder up against his perimeter wall and was now peeking over it into the empty courtyard below. There was a man he could ask for help. For Noor's sake, he should ask this man for food and water.

But how could he request assistance from the man that had killed his wife?

29

His neighbor scanned the courtyard and then the house. Ahmed jumped as the man's eyes swept across the window. He flung the crowbar in his hand into the courtyard below, and then swung his leg over and lowered himself to the ground. The cretin meant to break into his house?

Ahmed hurried to the bedside table and pulled an old Beretta M 1951 out of the drawer. He'd acquired the old workhorse on the black market many years ago. He wouldn't claim to be an expert in using it because he wasn't. But he knew enough to make a bullet go where he wanted it to. He hurried to the window and peeked through the curtain again as Mason crossed the courtyard below and walked up to the front door.

KNOCK KNOCK KNOCK.

How thoughtful. He was a courteous looter.

"Father, who is that?" Noor asked.

"Get in the closet and stay quiet," he whispered.

"Should we answer it? Maybe it's someone who can help."

"Go! Do it now!" he hissed as he helped her up and pushed her toward the walk-in closet.

KNOCK KNOCK KNOCK.

Ahmed hurried out of the room and closed the door behind him. As he made his way down the staircase, he heard the front door squeak, crack, and then pop open. He reached the bottom and circled around into the kitchen.

"Hello?" Mason said.

Ahmed ducked down behind the wide island in the middle of the kitchen.

"Is anyone home?"

Someone was definitely home, but Ahmed had no intention of giving away the element of surprise.

He heard the shuffling of feet grow louder as the intruder approached the kitchen. Ahmed pressed his back into the side of the island and held the Beretta close to his chest with both hands. He strained his neck looking up and to each side. He'd put a bullet in Mason's head the moment it appeared.

The footsteps got louder, so close they had to be in the kitchen.

CLANG.

The abrupt noise almost caused Ahmed to cry out.

Mason must've set the crowbar on the granite island countertop. Something lighter clinked on the surface and, with a flash of terror, Ahmed realized that he'd left out all the evidence of the lunch he'd just made.

"Hello? I'm your neighbor, Mason West. I just came over to check on you. We have food and water next door if you need any."

The open can of hummus clinked as Mason set it down. Footsteps receded back to the foyer toward the living room. "Hello?"

Ahmed carefully got to his feet so as not to make a sound. He tiptoed over and stopped at the corner, listening intently.

Footsteps started up the staircase.

With a start, Ahmed realized Mason was headed upstairs to where his daughter was hidden. He crept around the corner and followed up as quietly as he could.

"You can come out," Mason said. "I'm not here to hurt you. We have food and water and medical supplies. If you're injured, we can help you."

Ahmed waited halfway up the stairs, his eyeline just below the highest stair, watching Mason creep down the hall. He could shoot him in the back right now. Shoot him dead and finally avenge his wife's murder. He could do it. He should do it.

Mason turned into Noor's bedroom on the left, across the hall from the master bedroom. Ahmed shook with rage thinking about how the intruder was violating his daughter's personal space.

Damn him to hell!

He regretted the blasphemy the instant his mind spoke it. But why should he worry about such trifles? Wasn't killing a man the greater sin? But was it sinful to right the wrong that had ruined his life? Was it sinful to mete out justice to a criminal who deserved it?

However Allah might weigh his actions, he still regretted the foul language. It achieved nothing but blemishing the soul.

Mason reappeared in the hallway and Ahmed ducked just in time to avoid being seen as the intruder looked in his direction.

Ahmed peeked back up as Mason disappeared into the master bedroom. He cursed himself for letting the murderer get that far, that close to his daughter. Ahmed crept up the last few stairs and tiptoed to the doorway of his bedroom. He peeked around the corner and saw Mason staring at the saucer with a half-eaten sandwich lying on the wooden chest.

"I can see that you're here. There's no reason to be afraid. You can come out."

A squeak from inside the closet got Mason's attention. With the murderer's back to him, Ahmed slunk into the room and aimed the gun dead center at his back.

Mason reached for the closet door handle to open it.

"Stop!" Ahmed shouted.

30

The condemned man froze and then slowly turned. Ahmed noticed his right hand going down to a pistol tucked into his waistband.

Ahmed thumbed the hammer back and it clicked into place. One pull on the trigger and it would slam forward, firing a bullet into Mason's chest.

Mason threw his hands up into the air. "Whoa, whoa, whoa. Easy there."

"Shut up!"

"You don't want to do that."

"You don't know what I want!"

Ahmed's heart pounded in his fingertips, especially in the one curled around the cold metal trigger. His mind screamed at him to do it. Just pull the trigger and bring closure to the horror that had ruled his life for so long.

Mason slowly shook his head. "You don't want to kill an innocent man."

"You?" Ahmed spat out. "You are no innocent man!"

"You mean breaking in? I only did that because no one answered."

"And so hearing no one you decided to break into my house and steal whatever you could!"

"Listen, I'll be honest with you. If there had been supplies in this house and no one around that needed them, then sure. I would've gathered them up for my family. But you're here. Alive. We can help each other. We've got food and water next door." He glanced at the sad excuse for a sandwich. "And it looks like you could use some help in that department."

"We need no help from you!"

Ahmed's blood boiled. How could this fiend be so calm when he faced his immediate execution?

The closet door burst open and Noor tumbled out. "That's not true! We do need help! Father? What are you doing?"

"Get back in the closet!" Ahmed braced his shoulders and arms to accept the recoil of the gun. This man had to die.

Instead of retreating to safety, Noor stepped closer to Mason. "Father, we must accept his help!"

"Back away, Noor!"

"I will not, father! Do you want us to die? Do you want me to die? Because without this man's help, we have no chance. If you kill him, you are killing me."

The truth in her words crumbled his wavering resolve. His chest caved in and he curled into the empty husk that his body had become. He lowered the pistol's aim to the floor and eased the hammer forward. He had failed his wife. He had failed himself and the pledge he'd made so long ago.

He broke into tears as the shame and disgust washed over him. Noor was right. As much as this man deserved to die, they needed his help even more.

For now.

They would not need him forever. And the closer Ahmed got to the unsuspecting villain, the easier it would be to eventually exact vengeance upon him.

"I'm sorry," Ahmed said. "I feared for my daughter's safety."

"Totally understandable. I have a daughter of my own. But if it's all the same to you, let's make sure you keep that Beretta pointed in a safe direction from now on, okay?"

"Yes, I understand."

Mason extended a hand in greeting. "I know you guys have been here for a few months but we've never actually had the opportunity for introductions. My name is Mason West. I'm your neighbor."

Ahmed shook his hand while trying to hide his disgust. "It is a pleasure to meet you. My name is Ahmed Hassad and this is my daughter, Noor."

"It's great to meet both of you. I meant what I said. We have loads of supplies next door and would be happy to share them."

Ahmed smiled and it wasn't completely forced. Knowing his daughter would have access to continued sustenance filled his heart with joy. "We very much appreciate that."

"I'm happy we can help. What we don't have next door is a defensible position."

"What?"

"What I mean to say is that I think we should combine forces and we'll both be stronger for it."

Ahmed didn't quite understand what the man was getting at. "What do you mean?"

"Your house has many defensive advantages that mine does not. I propose we move everyone in my house along with all our supplies into your house."

Ahmed's jaw dropped. He certainly hadn't been expecting the intruder to invite himself to stay.

"I know it sounds a little weird, but the times we're living in are weirder yet. If we band together, our families have a better chance of surviving."

Ahmed looked at Noor, at the pleading look on her face, and could find no counterargument of equal weighting. He nodded. "Yes, you are correct. How should we proceed?"

Mason slapped him on the shoulder like they were old friends. Nothing could've been further from the truth. "Fantastic. I'll go tell everyone next door. After introductions all around, you and I can set to fortifying this structure while everyone else brings our supplies over. Oh yeah, make sure to skip the second porch step on your way in."

Ahmed nodded. He would cooperate for now. For as long as the safety of his daughter required it.

But not forever.

31

BETH blew through dead stoplights heading east on Exposition Blvd. She'd splashed through a few unavoidable puddles making her way through Ballona Creek. Her soaked right sock leached the heat out of her foot, leaving it tingling toward numb. She considered stripping the sock off so her foot could dry, but she didn't relish the idea of bare skin getting hit by gravel or other road debris.

And there was a lot of debris.

Passage through Ballona Creek had been uneventful otherwise. She'd ridden it to the end and then made it a couple of miles on surface streets with no major problems. Assuming her frozen foot didn't turn into a major problem.

Exposition Park was a few blocks ahead on the right. She used to take Theresa to the Natural History Museum there when she was younger. Much younger. Back when petting a Desert Tortoise would be the unchallenged highlight of her daughter's day. She'd grown up so fast.

Too fast.

And now she would grow older in a world made almost

unrecognizable. One that no longer had the reassuring comforts and security that most people assumed was a God-given right. They weren't.

Society and all of its comfortable illusions were now swept away.

Theresa would be forced to survive in a way that mankind hadn't endured for hundreds of years. Maybe thousands. The descent hadn't been easy already and there was no reason to expect it would get any better. And so it was up to Beth and Mason to protect her and do everything possible to give her a fighting chance.

Beth would die, if necessary, to ensure she had the best chance possible. Retrieving antibiotics was one such necessary task.

If she did survive this task, she knew others just like it would arise in the future. Each and every one as essential, and potentially deadly, to their survival as the last. That was the cruel irony of the survival situation. The tasks were like tests and mother nature didn't grade on a curve. She gave only two grades: passing and failing. And it didn't matter how many times you passed, a single failing grade meant death.

Her own death didn't bother her overly much. But Mason losing his wife and, worse, Theresa losing her mother... she couldn't bear the thought of their suffering.

No.

She'd make it back. This time and the next. She'd survive anything and everything thrown at her so that her family would remain whole.

Would remain unbroken.

She approached another intersection with traffic lights just as dark and unnecessary as all the others. Here in the city, the rumble of Spock's engine bounced off houses and storefronts and generally made her anxious to get back down into the LA River where the sound could bounce harmlessly around with no one to hear it.

Not that she'd seen a single living human being, of whatever kind, yet. Aside from that pack of dogs, she'd run into no other threats. Hopefully, her luck would hold all the way to the zoo.

Out of habit, she glanced left and right as she approached the intersection. To the left, nothing unusual. Someday that phrase would make sense again. To the right, nothing—

A bright red Hummer H3 shot into the intersection to block her path.

She swerved to the left and managed to zip around it and keep going.

A loudspeaker squawked. "Hold up, honey! We want to help you! Slow down now!"

The Hummer's engine roared and tires squealed as it raced to catch up.

Good luck with that.

A metal fence ran along the left side of the road separating it from commuter train tracks. A fence on the other side secured an enormous parking lot. She was boxed in but fine because the Hummer was never going to catch up. She whizzed through another intersection and a part of her brain registered the dark metal statues on the corner of the Tyrannosaurus attacking the Triceratops, a fleshed out version of the larger skeleton one that occupied the main hall inside the museum.

A big black Jeep appeared in the intersection a hundred feet ahead. With fences on both sides and the Hummer behind, there was no obvious escape.

She slammed on the brakes and squealed to a stop, barely managing to keep her bike upright. She glanced back and saw the Hummer closing in fast.

The passenger door of the Jeep opened and a man stepped out carrying some kind of scoped rifle. He didn't point it at her, but he held it in both hands at the ready. "Hey darlin', shut your bike off and let's chat for a minute. Heck, it's a pleasure just getting to speak to a member of the fairer sex."

The loudspeaker boomed from behind her. "Baby, we just want to talk. It's dangerous out here and we want to make sure you're safe." The Hummer's tires chirped as it skidded to a stop twenty feet behind her.

Beth considered drawing the Glock at her hip, but she wasn't Mason and she had no doubt the man with the rifle would get the better of the exchange. So she kept her helmet down and scanned left and right looking for an escape path.

The man with the rifle raised it and aimed the long barrel at her. "Now don't go getting any crazy ideas. We don't want you to get hurt. Shut the bike off and step away from it. This is for your own safety. You have no idea how dangerous it is out here."

She definitely had an idea of what was out there and as bad as it could be, it was no worse than the vibe she got from these creepy jerks. The fence line on the right opened for the entrance to the Natural History Museum. She didn't want to get trapped inside the fenced grounds but she didn't have a better choice. She had to go for it. The rifle guy would probably shoot her down but there were worse fates for a captured woman.

Beth cranked the throttle and Spock's front tire lifted as the torque jerked her body forward. She popped up the curb and entered the museum's grounds.

Doors slammed behind her. "Go! Go! Go! We've got her now!"

32

She raced through the entrance and scanned left and right. How was she going to lose them in the multilevel terraced grounds? Her bike would quickly get mired down in the mulch and bushes whereas both of their vehicles would tear right through it. She glanced at the giant glass cube that was the entrance to the building on the north side. Looters had clearly paid a visit. The glass doors were missing. The evidence of their existence lay in the scattered shards around the gaping entrance. Whole sheets of glass in the surrounding windows were busted out like someone went crazy with a bag of rocks, or maybe bullets.

Light spilled into the interior through the remaining glass, or lack thereof. The interior darkened further in. Their vehicles might make it through the entrance but they definitely wouldn't be as maneuverable inside as her bike was. She gunned it, heading straight for the gaping hole that no longer required a member's sticker on your shirt to get in.

CRACK.

CRACK.

Rifle shots from behind shattered a sheet of glass above the entrance. Jagged shards rained down and bounced off her helmet as she flew through the entrance. She rode through the gift shop, narrowly avoiding overturned displays and cheap plastic dinosaurs that apparently even looters didn't consider worth stealing. She slowed down and wound her way through the tighter aisles and made it out into the exhibit hall.

She killed the headlight and popped her visor up to better see in the failing light.

Okay. Now what?

Had she escaped one trap only to flee into another?

CRACK.

A chunk of marble in the column two feet to her left exploded, showering her with fragments. She jerked right and almost dumped the bike as a result. She managed to hang on and rode through a large archway into the main hall.

In the near darkness, she saw even darker shapes hanging in the air ahead. She realized what they were and skidded to a stop before plowing straight into the gigantic skeletons of the Tyrannosaurus Rex battling it out with the Triceratops. They towered some thirty feet into the air. She'd nearly taken out the leg of the Tyrannosaurus. Take that out and the whole thing would've come down on her head.

"Straight ahead! She's in there!"

Beth looked back and saw three flashlights attached to rifles sweeping back and forth. All headed in her direction.

She had an idea. A way to turn this trap back on her pursuers. She shut her bike down and guided it behind a marble pillar in the far corner of the main hall.

The men appeared in the large room with their beams of light slicing this way and that.

"I know she came this way."

"Little lady? Come out, come out, wherever you are."

"Kenny, shut your mouth. You sound like an idiot."

Their flashlights landed on the skeleton dinosaurs. All three focused on the colossal display.

"Whoa! Will you look at that?"

"Big uns, weren't they?"

"Yeah, but they all died off. You know why?"

"Well, I read that a big asteroid hit sending up a huge pile of dust that covered the—"

"Kenny, shut your mouth with that science crap! They died because they weren't holding the guns like we are."

The men walked up to the exhibit stepping into the space between the ancient, motionless adversaries. They stared up at the towering carnivore. One pointed his rifle at its head.

"I'd shoot it dead if it was alive."

"There'd be a lot of meat on a beast that big. What do you figure it'd taste like?"

"I don't know. Chicken, probably."

"I read that chickens are actually descended from dinosaurs. Can you imagine?"

"Kenny, I'll shoot you if say another word."

"Be fun to hunt one of these, huh?"

"Be more fun to catch the prey we're after."

All the men laughed gruffly. Sickeningly.

"It's my turn to go first this time."

"No way! The last one didn't count. She was big as a cow. I did you both a favor going first."

"Shut up, the both of you! There will be plenty of time for each of us to get a turn. As many turns as we want."

"Now you're talking."

The hairs on the back of Beth's neck stood on end. Her belly squirmed with equal parts disgust and terror. How could they be so cavalier? As if raping her were no different than who got to pick what to watch next on TV.

What had mankind come to?

With the men still looking up at the skeleton beast above them, Beth lined up her bike like an arrow. She squeezed the brake and then fired it up. The headlight blinked on blinding the men as they turned in surprise. She cranked the throttle and then released the brake. The bike shot forward and tipped over as it reached them. It skidded across the marble floor and bulldozed through both ancient beasts.

The bones crashed down smashing the men below. They screamed and then went silent as they were either knocked unconscious or killed.

Beth drew the Glock and waited behind the column to see if anyone would crawl out of the jumbled pile of flesh and bones. They'd get a bullet if they did.

No one did.

She tiptoed out of cover and found Spock near the edge of the pile. It lay on its side pinned down by a number of large bones. She set the pistol on the floor and began clearing away the bones.

From somewhere inside the mess, one of the men groaned.

She grabbed the gun and waited, but no threat appeared. After waiting another minute, she returned to the task of digging the bike out. The bones were heavy, but much lighter than expected. It dawned on her that of course they weren't real bones. They were casts of the found specimens. Real bones weighed too much to use in a full body exhibit.

She pushed the last one off and then squatted Spock to an upright position. Her head throbbed and swam at the same time. She kicked out the kickstand and leaned on a handlebar to keep from passing out.

Lack of calories made intense exertion a brutal chore. It taxed her already overtaxed body.

Something grabbed her right ankle. Cold, hard fingers latched around the sock and yanked her to the ground. Her head smacked Spock's frame on the way down. Even with the padded helmet for protection, the impact dazed her. She scrambled for the pistol but couldn't find it.

Another hand grabbed her boot and pulled. The pile of bones shifted as one of the men began to pull himself out while also dragging her closer.

"You're mine now!"

His battered face emerged from the heap. The dim light reflecting from Spock's headlight made it a scary mask of shadows and gore. The man smiled and blood spilled out of his mouth.

"You're gonna pay for this."

She tried to kick free but his hands held her fast. "No! Let me go!"

The man pulled her closer. "Fighting will only make it worse for you."

She shook her right foot as hard as she could and felt the sock slip an inch lower. She whipped her leg hard and the iron grip slipped off, still clinging to her sock. With her leg now free, she aimed a kick at the man's face. Her heel caught him on the nose with a sickening crunch.

He yelped and let go of her boot. "You broke my nose!" The words came out wet and raspy. "My nose!"

Beth scrambled back and found the Glock under her bike. She grabbed it and aimed it at her would-be rapist.

"Go ahead and shoot me! Do it!" Blood flew from his mouth as he screamed.

She couldn't kill a man like this. As much as it might've been a public service to end his miserable life, she simply couldn't pull the trigger. Not when the threat had passed. She decided to leave him.

To live.

To die.

Whatever. He was no longer her problem.

He shouted insults as she mounted her bike and left them behind, letting the darkness swallow them whole.

She raced through the ruined glass entrance and out into the the bright sunshine beyond. She skidded to a stop next to their parked Hummer and Jeep. There was no chance she was going to let these vehicles be used to accost other innocent people.

She could shoot all their tires out, but that would be a huge waste of bullets.

How else to disable them?

Of course! She could shoot the gas tank and blow them up. She continued to a safe distance and then lined up the Glock on the Hummer's gas port figuring it had the larger tank.

BANG.

BANG.

Two holes ripped through the metal skin.

But no explosion.

What? It worked every single time in action movies.

She rode closer and smelled the gasoline before seeing it. A small stream leaked out from underneath. The liquid darkened the pavement as it streamed down the slope.

Mason had packed matches in her backpack in case she needed to start a fire. This probably wasn't the kind he had in mind, but whatever. She followed the direction of the stream and rode ahead a ways. She stopped and dug out the small orange bottle. She unscrewed the cap and grabbed a long wooden match.

Another minute and the leading edge of the tiny rivulet reached her. She sparked the match and dropped it.

A blue orange flame leapt into the air.

She cranked the throttle and didn't look back. The bike bounced down the curb and onto Exposition Boulevard just as the Hummer exploded. Another massive explosion signaled the Jeep had gone too.

Beth looked over her shoulder and smiled. A black column of smoke billowed up into the air. A smoke signal for anyone interested in investigating its source.

Yes, she didn't shoot those dirtbags, but that didn't mean they'd gotten lucky.

She cranked the throttle and headed east. A few more miles and she could drop down into the LA River. She prayed the road ahead didn't hold any more nasty surprises. She realized with a start that it wasn't a throwaway prayer. A thought tossed out like an empty bag of chips. It was more reverent than that. It was more honest.

It reminded her of the faith she'd learned as a child in the Catholic church. A past she thought she'd left behind.

33

THERESA stuttered out a greeting. The simple hello that coughed up her throat and tripped on her tongue came out sounding like an alien language. She shook her head and smiled in embarrassment. She never expected to see another normal human being again. Much less their mysterious neighbors. She shook hands with the girl that looked a couple years younger than herself.

"Hi, my name's Theresa. What's your name?"

"Noor Hassad. It's nice to meet you, Theresa."

"It's more than nice! It's amazing. I thought we were the only people left. Other than *them*."

Noor gave her a funny look. Did she know about them?

Elio extended his hand. "My name's Elio Lopez."

The dark-eyed girl tentatively extended her hand. "Noor Hassad. Nice to meet you."

They stood like idiots in awkward silence. Every second that passed made the membrane between silence and sound a little bit thicker.

Theresa wasn't a total dork at carrying a conversation, but she had nowhere near the flair for it that Holly had.

Maybe she would've been better at it, but with Holly around she'd never had to try. The memory of her best friend's easy smile made her chest ache.

Not being Holly, she stared at her shoes and chewed her lip.

"I hope everybody has had a chance to get acquainted," Mason said as he entered the living room. "We need to get to work now."

Her dad had returned a few minutes ago with news that the neighbors were still alive. Even more surprising was that they'd agreed to combine forces and live together. Before anyone had a chance to digest the information, the father and daughter had shown up at the front door like they were coming over for Sunday dinner.

Days of the week. Strange. She had no idea what day it was. Weekdays versus weekends didn't matter when you didn't have school structuring your life. It was like the endless blurred days of summer. Only ten times more terrible.

"Theresa, can you personally set Clyde up next door?"

"Sure."

Noor looked at her in confusion.

"Clyde is an infant Bili chimpanzee."

Noor's eyes opened wider.

"He's so cute. Big brown eyes and a goofy smile. You're gonna love him."

Noor smiled so wide it looked like her cheeks might explode.

"Also Theresa, I need you to lead the crew in getting our supplies packed up and moved over to the Hassad's house."

She didn't think Elio and Noor would be a problem, but she doubted Iridia would accept her as the boss. In the short time that she'd been a part of their household, she was already starting to feel like an older sister. Older sisters were sometimes fun and most times annoying. And they never went along with getting bossed around by a younger sibling.

"No problem, but I'm not sure where Iridia is."

Theresa congratulated herself on smoothly handling the situation. She'd passed off responsibility for finding Iridia, and more importantly, she'd passed off the responsibility of telling her what to do. Her dad would have no problem doing that.

"I'm sure she's hiding in her room," Mason said. "Go let her know it's time to work." He turned and began chatting with Ahmed.

Great.

He had just as smoothly dumped it all right back in her lap.

"Elio, can you show Noor where the cloth bags are so you guys can start packing up food?"

"Sure thing. Good luck with Iridia," he said with a wink.

Awesome.

She headed to Iridia's room and knocked on the wall next to the barricade of dangling tapestries. "Iridia, do you have clothes on?"

"Who wants to know? Is there more laundry to do? Because I did a ton yesterday and it's somebody else's turn."

"It's not that."

"What then?"

It was super annoying speaking through the fabric like a servant at the master's door.

"Can I come in?"

After a lengthy pause, a face parted the hanging tapestries. Iridia peered through with her gorgeous crystal-green eyes. They literally sparkled like freakin' emeralds! Whose eyes did that?

"What?" she said.

There was one thing worse than having an annoying older sister. It was having an annoying, supermodel older sister. One that the boy you liked occasionally stared at a little too long.

Theresa realized she was staring. How could she blame Elio when she did it too?

"What?" Iridia said again.

"We need help moving food and supplies next door."

"Don't you have a *boyfriend* for that?"

Boyfriend.

Did she?

And if so, why did it sound so horrible when Iridia said it?

Mr. Piddles strolled through the hanging fabric and wrapped around Theresa's legs purring loudly. For some reason, the Crayfords' cat had adopted Iridia as his new BFF. Mom was still a little jealous about it because she wasn't used to any animal ever liking anyone more than her.

Theresa knelt down and stroked Mr. Piddles' belly.

"Isn't he such a cutie wootie pootie?" Iridia said in the most irritating baby voice.

She really knew how to ruin a moment. Theresa stood and used her best bossy voice. "My dad wants us all to help out so it goes faster."

"Can you give me a couple of hours? I was about to start a yoga workout."

Her and her yoga workouts, *and* core workouts, *and* toning workouts. And the constant complaining about the changing shape of her butt. As far as Theresa could tell, her butt looked exactly the same as it did a week ago. And that wasn't blind guesswork either. She'd seen Iridia's naked backside more times than she could count with both hands.

"Dad?" she yelled down the hall.

"What's up, honey?" he said from the living room.

Iridia's eyes narrowed. "Fine. I'll work on my horribly flabby butt later."

Theresa flashed her best fake smile before Iridia's face disappeared behind the wall of tapestries. "See you in the kitchen." She waited. "You're coming soon, right?"

"I heard you the first time."

Theresa pivoted on her heels and headed back to the kitchen. A huge grin spread across her face as she turned the corner.

Elio saw her and raised a brow in question. "Oh no. What's that smile about?"

She shrugged. "Nothing."

Having an older sister could be awesome.

34

They'd been packing up and moving stuff for hours. Theresa's belly grumbled and sweat beaded on her upper lip. She looked around the kitchen and was amazed to see that they were almost finished. They had yet to touch their bedrooms because her dad said non-essential (as he called them) supplies would be handled later. Food, water, cooking equipment, and things like that were the priorities.

His priorities.

He didn't have the faintest clue of what essential supplies were for a fifteen-year-old girl. On second thought, she wasn't sure she did either. Not anymore.

A week ago, her iPhone would've made that list, but now it was just a thin brick of smudged glass and rainbow casing. A few things definitely made the list. Her yearbooks. Pictures of friends, especially Holly. Lambchops. Her purple sneakers. Her pillow. The silver locket around her neck.

If she could pick only one thing, it'd be an impossible choice between the locket and Lambchops. Leaving either behind would be like leaving a piece of herself.

Elio returned from dropping off a load. He dumped an

armful of empty bags on the counter. She was about to start filling one up for the hundredth time when he grabbed her wrist. "I need to talk to you."

"Okay, talk."

"Privately."

She looked around. "We're alone."

Her dad was at the neighbor's house working on making the place tougher to break into. Ahmed had a lot of leftover lumber stacked up in his garage. While the kids (plus her annoying older sister) hauled stuff over to their new home base, the two dads screwed plywood boards over all the windows on the ground floor.

Ahmed had objected at first as the house was brand new, but Mason's cold practicality won him over.

A new house wasn't worth much to a dead person.

Her dad didn't think she'd heard the comment, but she had. The grim honesty shocked her. She never really believed that it would come to that. They couldn't die, could they?

Many others had. Many of those that hadn't died changed into something worse than death, as far as she was concerned. She pledged to herself that she'd choose death over changing into a delta.

No thanks. Never.

But there was no reason to worry. That only happened to other people. She didn't know why that was true. But it was. They were the living proof. Hadn't they escaped the pharmacy last night?

"Noor will be back in a few minutes for another load."

"Then we're alone. I'm listening."

Elio looked around and listened to verify they were, in fact, alone. Satisfied, he turned back to her. "I'm leaving today."

Theresa's heart sank like a stone in a bottomless lake. She didn't think anything could happen to them, but taking off into the dangerous unknown tempted fate in a way that made her nervous.

"Why? We're getting totally set up next door. We'll be finished tomorrow. I'm sure my dad would be fine going after that."

Elio shook his head. "No, he won't. There will be something else to do. Always one more thing while my mother might be dying as we speak. I can't wait any longer. But..." He paused. "I think you should stay."

"I'm going," she said flatly. "We already discussed it and you *don't* want to test me."

Elio wrapped his arms around her. "You're an amazing person, Theresa West."

The warmth of his body stoked a fire inside her own. She grinned awkwardly. "I like to think so."

Elio leaned forward and she closed her eyes knowing what was coming next. Waiting for it. Longing for it.

A terrified scream from the living room jolted her awake just as his soft lips touched hers. Elio pulled away and then ran in to see what had happened.

"Put your hands on your head and have a seat on the couch!"

The voice wasn't one she recognized. She followed and found Elio standing in the living room with his hands on his head.

A man she'd never met had an arm wrapped around Noor, pinning her to his chest, while his other hand held a pistol pointed at Elio. He had a smooth carpet of short, grey hair. Like it was usually shaved but hadn't been in a couple of weeks. A big vein bulged in his forehead. He wore a black utility belt of gear like cops wore, before the outbreak.

"Sit."

The gun pointed at the couch and then returned to them. The gun was scary enough. His eyes were even scarier.

"Now."

The words chilled her to the core. Goosebumps popped up on her arms. She and Elio quietly sat down and stared at the intruder with wide, unblinking eyes.

Voices outside broke the spell. Her father and Ahmed discussing something. The man with the gun backed away from the door and turned to face it with Noor still glued to his front side.

Mason bounded up the front steps and skidded to a halt. He reached for the pistol under his shirt before his feet came to a stop.

"I'll kill her!" the man shouted as he pressed the end of his gun against Noor's head.

Her dad moved his hand away and remained motionless.

"Get on the ground with your fingers laced together behind your head!"

Ahmed walked in and froze when he saw the pistol pointed at his daughter's head.

"Don't move, Ahmed," Mason said as he held his hands out, to show they were empty. "Don't do this. Take whatever you want. But don't hurt her."

"You don't give the instructions! I'm the law!!"

Mason nodded. "Okay. Just don't hurt anyone."

35

The intruder pointed the gun at Mason and spit flew from his mouth as he shouted. "Tell me what to do one more time! One more!"

Her dad stood stone still.

"You!" the man yelled at Ahmed. "Get on the ground with your hands behind your head!"

Ahmed hesitated.

"Do it now or I blow a hole in this girl's skull!"

Ahmed dropped to the ground like his legs gave out. He laid on his belly and clasped his hands behind his head.

"You too, murderer!" he shouted at Mason.

Her dad knelt down and did as instructed.

The intruder dragged Noor over until he could reach down and strip away Mason's gun. The man patted her dad's body down and paused at his right calf. He yanked up the pant leg and found the smaller gun her dad kept there. The man patted Ahmed down next and found nothing.

He shoved Noor to the couch and waved his pistol at all three of them. "Any of you move, you're dead."

"Please don't hurt them," Mason said. "Please."

The man reared back and kicked Mason in the ribs. "You're begging? You worthless piece of filth."

He slammed another heavy boot into her father's side. "You have the right to remain silent. Anything you say doesn't matter one damn bit because you're guilty as charged. Before I spray your brains all over that floor, let me give you the courtesy of knowing why."

Mason grunted through the pain and looked up at the man. "Have we met?"

"No, but you did meet my partner, Raymond Cooper."

"I don't know that name."

The man crashed another hard kick into her dad's side, curling him over in pain.

"You don't know the name because you killed him in cold blood."

Mason shook his head. "You've got the wrong guy. I didn't kill anyone."

Theresa knew that wasn't technically true because she'd seen what he did to the gang members that had kidnapped her.

"You're lying! My partner was a month away from retirement and you walk in and put a bullet in his chest. And you thought you could just walk away free as bird? You're not so free now, are you?"

Mason rolled to his side and stared up at the man. "The Whole Foods shooting?"

"That's the one. You murdered my partner and messed up that pansy actor kid."

What was this guy talking about? Her dad wasn't involved in that shooting.

"One of our SWAT teams had you pinned down but then

some feds shot our guys up. It took a couple days, but we found you. We had an op set to take you down and then the city went to hell. The department fell apart as guys didn't show up."

"It wasn't me."

The intruder kicked her dad's head like a soccer ball and he collapsed. A busted lip leaked blood onto the floor.

"Don't lie to me!"

"I'm not lying," Mason said as he wiped blood out of his mouth. "I was there. I tried to stop it."

The man stood above Mason and leveled the pistol at her dad's head.

Theresa pinched her eyes shut. Her chest heaved in and out choking on air. This wasn't happening. It wasn't happening.

"Admit you did it and only you die. Otherwise, you'll watch while I kill every last person here."

"It was a gang leader named Cesar. The shotcaller for the Venice Ten. I tried to stop him, but he killed your partner."

Theresa peeked between her fingers as the intruder swung the pistol over at her.

"She dies first then," he said.

"No! No! Please no!" Mason screamed.

"Then admit your guilt!"

Her father slumped to the floor. "Okay. Okay. You're right. I did it."

What was her father saying? He was involved? He killed that guy? Theresa remembered the sketch she and Holly had seen on TV. She even remembered Holly joking about how it had looked so much like her father. At the time, it seemed laughable.

Theresa wasn't laughing now.

The intruder pointed the gun at her dad's head again. He spat on Mason's back. "Time for your execution."

"Wait!" Mason said. "Please. Not in front of my family! Do it outside. Please."

The man looked at Theresa and Noor, his face contorting as the urge for revenge battled with the decency that must've once been inside him. He shook his head. "Fine. Get up!"

Mason struggled to his feet, cradling his battered sides.

"Walk! And one wrong move and these kids are going to see what your brains look like!"

Mason winced with each step.

The man followed her dad out the front door with the gun pointed at his back.

This couldn't be happening. Her father about to be killed? No. No.

Elio pulled her into his arms.

BANG.

A shot fired and a body crashed to the pavement outside.

BANG.

BANG.

"No!" Theresa screamed as tears blurred her vision. She struggled out of Elio's embrace and raced for the door. "Daddy! Daddy!"

She made it outside and saw two bodies on the ground. The wood slat of the second porch step lay next to the body of the man who had killed her father. She jumped down clearing all three steps and knelt beside Mason's body.

Her shaking hand extended to touch his back. It froze in midair as he rolled to his side, wincing in pain.

Her dad looked up and forced a smile through the agony. "I'm okay. I'm okay." He tilted his head to the side and spat out a glob of blood.

Theresa collapsed into his outstretched arms. She should've felt bad when the impact of her weight made him grunt again.

But all she could feel was the euphoria of having him alive with his strong arms wrapped around her.

36

Theresa helped her dad wrap his middle with tape. She got him a glass of water while he sat on the couch in their neighbor's living room holding a rag to his lip. Elio and Noor were in the kitchen organizing all the supplies they'd brought over. Iridia was upstairs somewhere. Probably trying to take over Noor's bedroom.

Mason pulled the rag away and looked at it. A bright red cut split his lower lip but it didn't appear to be bleeding anymore. "He deserves to be buried."

Ahmed stood several feet away staring at him in disbelief. He shook his head. "He deserves to be dragged out on the street where the dogs can devour him. He put our daughters in danger. He wanted to kill you."

"He mistakenly thought I killed his partner. I understand the pain of losing someone like that." Mason looked at the ground and it seemed as if his eyes were focused on the center of the earth. "I've been in his situation and I wanted to kill the person who did it, too."

Theresa uncapped the tube of Neosporin and squeezed out a line of gel on her fingertip. "Hold still for a second."

As gently as she could, she wiped the ointment over his wound.

He winced but stayed still.

"The man was insane! We owe him nothing!"

Mason pushed up off the couch and looked Ahmed in the eye. "Losing someone close to you in such a violent way can unhinge the mind. I don't blame him for wanting revenge. He thought he knew what happened. That I was the killer. But he was wrong. And he died for the mistake. "

The fire in Ahmed's eyes snuffed out. The stiffness in his posture softened.

"I'm going to bury him," Mason said. "I'd appreciate your help because it'll be a lot of work and I'm not in the best shape."

Ahmed nodded. "Of course, I will help you."

"Theresa, we're going to be busy for a while. Can you make sure everything gets put away?"

"Sure, dad."

Mason grabbed a couple bottles of water from the coffee table and tossed one to Ahmed. "We can bury him in the Crayfords' backyard." They could do it near Holly's makeshift grave. He headed for the front door and Ahmed followed.

Elio walked in from the kitchen. "Where they going?"

"They're going to bury that guy in the Crayfords' backyard."

"Sounds like a lot of work for someone that was trying to kill you."

"My dad has an unyielding sense of honor."

Elio took her hands in his. He looked around to ensure they were alone. "It's time. I have to go."

Theresa didn't understand. "Now? After what just happened?"

"Yes, now. Don't you understand? My mother is alone. She doesn't have someone like your father to protect her. She only has me and I haven't been back since this outbreak began."

As much as Theresa wanted to argue, she understood. If her mom or dad were facing this alone, she'd want nothing more than to join them and face it together. "Okay. Let's go."

"Pack up a bag of food and water to take with us," Elio said. "I'll pull the cargo bike out of your garage." He squeezed her hands and nodded. "Meet you outside in two minutes. Okay?"

"Okay."

He released her hands and headed out the front door. Theresa returned to the kitchen and started stuffing a bag with supplies for Elio's mother. Elio had told her how they never had more than a couple days worth of groceries. If she was still alive, she had to be desperate.

Noor smiled shyly at her as she continued to stack cans of vegetables in a kitchen cabinet. She had each type lined up in a row with their labels perfectly centered. She probably would've just thrown them all in and slammed the door shut before the unstable mountain collapsed.

She finished filling the bag and decided to fill another with extra bottles of water. Her dad had drilled the rule of threes into her head at an early age.

You cannot survive for three minutes without air, three days without water, or three weeks without food.

The reality was that Elio's mother was probably already dead. Theresa didn't like to think about it like that but it was the truth. If she had somehow survived the fever that had killed so many, and hadn't changed into a delta, and didn't run into any insane people, then she had to be in desperate need of help. She finished packing the water and cinched both bags up tight.

"What are you doing with those?" Noor asked.

Theresa had almost forgotten she was there and she certainly hadn't anticipated being questioned. "I'm taking them next door."

"Why? I thought we wanted everything here."

"Well, my dad wants to have a few supplies in another location. For emergency backup." It was the first thing that popped into her head and she was surprised that it sounded fairly reasonable.

"Oh, okay." That seemed to satisfy Noor as she returned to the task of perfectly stacking cans in the cabinet.

"See you later," Theresa said. As soon as she said it, she realized it sounded a little off.

Noor stared at her silently for a second and then smiled before returning to her work.

Theresa hurried out of the kitchen and blew out a big breath realizing how close she'd come to ruining everything. She peeked out the front door and saw Elio waiting on the sidewalk. He had a backpack of supplies strapped to his back. She walked through the metal door in the concrete wall that surrounded the property.

"Hop on," Elio said pointing to a pillow he'd strapped to the cargo rack above the back wheel.

Theresa shook her head. "Nope."

Elio looked at her in confusion. "You changed your mind?"

"No. But you're going on the back because I'm healthier than you, so I can pedal and use less battery."

Elio struggled with the suggestion. Did he have a problem with a girl taking charge? If so, that was going to be a real problem for their future together. She wasn't going to be the type to sit back and wait for a man to do everything.

He nodded and grinned. "So you're kind of like my limo driver, right?"

She was happy to see he was the man she thought he was. "No, I'm kind of like your ambulance driver."

Elio laughed and held the bike steady while Theresa loaded her sacks, one in each saddle bag to keep the balance even. She swung her leg over the seat and grabbed the handlebars.

"Need a lift, stranger?"

He laughed again as he settled himself on the pillow.

Theresa was about to thumb on the power and pull away when a voice to her left startled her.

"What are you guys doing?" Noor asked standing in the open doorway.

Theresa froze. They were busted. She had no idea what to say.

"Mason wants us to go on a neighborhood patrol," Elio said. "To check things out so we have better situational awareness."

Nice use of the fancy bodyguard words!

Noor digested the information and then nodded. "Okay."

"Can you check on Clyde while we're out?" Theresa asked.

Noor nodded.

"Close the gate," Theresa said, knowing it locked automatically. "We'll be back later."

"Be careful," Noor said. "It's scary out there."

She had no idea. Unfortunately, Theresa did.

37

BETH rode through the Los Angeles Zoo parking lot and up to the entrance. The front gate stood open which was odd because there wasn't a car in sight in the vast, empty parking lot. Normally, she loved the throaty rumble of her old Kawasaki. Now was not normally. The burbling growl of the old 750cc engine was too loud. She'd never thought that before the outbreak. But now that ambient sound levels had fallen off a cliff, it stood out like a spotlight under a new moon.

Which wasn't good when attracting attention could get you killed.

She considered leaving it outside and sneaking in but she didn't want to be so removed from her getaway ride. She eased on the throttle and rode through the open gate. She snaked up the handicap ramp and headed toward the medical complex. On the left, the flamingos exhibit was conspicuously empty. Where would a flock of fifty hot pink and orange birds end up?

A flurry of movement caught the corner of her eye to the right.

She looked forward and hit the brakes as a small troop of monkeys darted across the path like they were between the lines in a school crosswalk. They all ignored her except for the last one. It paused in the middle of the path and then screeched at her before hurrying to join the others.

In the first several days of the outbreak, Beth had wondered what would happen to all of the animals at the zoo. At some point, there would be no one to feed them. And how did they manage to escape? Did one of the employees throw open the gates and wish them the best of luck? If someone did do that, which animals did they do it for?

Presumably not for the larger carnivores.

The zoo carried a wide variety of animals that mother nature never intended to be mixed together. The majority of them never would've encountered the other animals in their native habitat.

It didn't matter. The only thing that mattered was the age-old law of survival of the fittest. Predators and prey both hungered and so both struggled to survive. That most fundamental struggle didn't feel as removed as it once did.

She continued on with all of her senses attuned, listening for anything beyond the growl of her bike. She passed a concessions stand. The windows were closed. No customers were seated at the round tables or lined up at the windows complaining about how long it took to get a basket of fries and a soda. No children ran between the tables screaming with glee while parents relished being off their feet for a few minutes and so did nothing to rein them in.

For some reason, that vacant scene seemed sadder than the rest. And it was all sad.

The zoo had been Beth's life for over a decade. Many of the animals were as dear to her as her own family. The events that occurred the last time she was here flooded into her mind. How dear Jane, the Bili chimp she'd raised from an infant, had died on the operating table giving birth to her twins. One hadn't made it and the other was the reason she'd returned. As Jane died on the operating table, Beth had promised to take care of her surviving baby. Clyde would get the medicine he needed. Beth had bet her life on it.

A cacophony of clicking and stamping sounds caused her to hit the brakes. The sound thundered around the bend up ahead. The noise grew louder as she waited.

What could it be?

A large African Impala antelope raced around the curve. Its head dropped and it almost wiped out as its front hooves slipped on the pavement. Its back legs adjusted and the torso twisted to somehow right itself and continue on. A herd of a dozen or more followed behind the alpha. They rounded the curve and thundered toward her. They jostled shoulder to shoulder filling the width of the path completely.

For a second, Beth sat there confused by the spectacle. There just wasn't any reference for it. There was never a herd of anything sprinting along the circuitous paths that wound around the zoo. Well, there were herds of people. But they didn't run forty miles per hour and sport three foot, twisting horns on top of their heads.

The antelopes raced toward her.

She looked around for an escape, but it was too late. The herd was closing in fast. A blur of horns and hooves came at her. She dropped down low in her seat so that the bike would hopefully take the brunt of the impact.

The scraping and sliding and clicking of their hooves drowned out everything. The big male rushed by her on the right side. Another ripped off a side mirror as it passed. The mass of tan fur and taut muscles jostled her on both sides. A hoof stamped on her bare right foot and she screamed in pain.

And then they were gone.

Beth sucked in a slow breath and tried to swallow her heart back down into her chest. She checked her foot and was relieved to find a superficial cut that shouldn't require stitches. Now that her prefrontal cortex emerged from the primal ooze of the flight or fight response, she had one question about what just happened.

What were they running from?

She stared at the bend ahead. Her hands gripped the handlebars tightly, ready to whip the bike around and make for a quick escape. She waited. Nothing happened. Almost disappointed, she blew out a slow breath and then continued on to the medical buildings.

Maybe the herd got spooked by something silly like a branch creaking in the wind or one of the others in the herd passing gas. They were twitchy creatures and Beth couldn't blame them for it. In their natural habitat, they were always on the menu and that made for a necessarily nervous disposition.

38

The growl of the Vulcan couldn't die fast enough. Beth shut it off and coasted to a stop in front of the medical center. She stayed put for a minute, listening, waiting. For what exactly, she didn't know.

Nothing appeared.

She tried the front door and it silently swung open. The front gate open. Now this door unlocked, too. She wondered what it must've been like in the first few days of the outbreak. It would've begun in a sane and organized way. The security guys would've swept through the corridors and pathways to ensure that no customers remained inside. They would've gone through all the structures and facilities to verify everything was secured. They would've left a skeleton crew overnight to keep an eye on things until normal operations could resume.

It probably started that way.

But what happened on day two or three when people didn't show up? When no one arrived for the next shift rotation? What happened when whoever was left realized no one was coming back? What happened in the days after that, when the entire complex was completely abandoned? And finally, what happened when people living in surrounding areas started thinking of the animals not as entertainment and education, but as calories and nutrition?

And if they did, was it wrong?

Her heart said it was, but the grumble in her half-empty belly told it where to go. Maybe when she was finished here, she should track down those impalas and try to take one home. Surely a Glock with seventeen rounds of ammo could take one down. Couldn't it? But even if it could, could she? For her family?

Beth resolved to answer the question later. She'd come for medicine first. That was the most important thing. The thought of killing one of those beautiful animals could wait. Besides, she wasn't even sure she could safely strap a one hundred and fifty pound antelope to her bike and make it home.

Then again, the zoo had smaller animals. Some that weren't nearly as fast either.

Beth shuddered. It sickened her how quickly such insanity could become so sensible. It was her job to care for these animals and keep them alive. And now she was considering putting a bullet in their heads so her family could consume their calories. She shook her head.

Talk about messed up.

She clicked on her headlamp and entered the dark interior of the building. She tried the lights but there didn't seem to be any power. The interior security door was also unlocked. She followed the interior corridors—and they were creepy—and then took a left toward her old office and the lab. She arrived at the door to that wing and tried the handle. It jiggled but didn't open.

Locked. Thank God. She pulled the keys out of her

pocket and found the right one. The door opened like normal, just as it had thousands of times over the last decade.

She passed her old office and then arrived at the door to the lab. She almost snarled as she touched the door. The memory of Diana Richston firing her burned in her gut. She'd tried to stop Beth from taking Clyde home to care for him. She'd even tried to force a security guard to physically stop her.

Of course, Beth had then threatened to kill them both with a dart full of Etorphine, a synthetic opioid powerful enough to kill a human with a single drop. So, the hatred probably went both ways.

She entered the lab turning her head this way and that to illuminate portions of the expansive room. There in the center was the operating table where she'd lost Jane and saved Clyde. She'd occupied this room the day the world outside decided to stop making sense. The simple steel operating table was now empty. Jane's body had been removed and every surface sanitized.

Beth hurried to the security cabinet and rifled through her keys to find the right one. There. She rotated the handle and pulled the door open.

Yes!

Inside was a trove of priceless medicine. She quickly located several bottles of Cephalexin and Doxycycline capsules. Kept in a dual cool dark place, the antibiotics were known to store for up to a decade while retaining their efficacy. She shoved the bottles into a bag and then grabbed additional meds for other uses. She shuffled through the remaining bottles, ampules, and boxes determining which might prove useful.

"Take me with you."

Beth spun around ready to scream. The light of the headlamp came to rest on a disheveled, unrecognizable form. Tattered rags hung from limbs streaked with grime. A tangled mop of long black hair showed gray at the roots. The visual was bad but the smell was worse. The apparition reeked of feces and decay.

It took a minute before Beth recognized the revolting orange hue of her artificially-tanned skin.

"Diana?"

39

"Please take me with you," Diana said as she grasped Beth's arm. The days since their last encounter had not been kind. What may have once been a nice blouse was now little more than a tattered brown rag. The sleek material that was once suit pants now hung in patches that revealed more skin than it covered.

"Please Elizabeth," she said, "help me."

Despite never liking the woman, and at the end absolutely hating her, Beth was not the type to turn away another in need.

Diana faltered and Beth caught her hands before she collapsed.

"Come sit down." Beth led her to a chair and then helped her take a seat. "What happened to you?"

Diana stared at her hands as she rubbed at the coating of filth. She pinched her lips together and shook her head.

"Diana, tell me. How did you end up here, like this?"

She looked back up at Beth. Her eyes glistened with tears. "He left me here."

"Who is he?"

"Anton Reshenko." Her jaw twitched and her eyes grew hard. "After all I did for him! He left me to die!" Her back straightened as anger burned the tears away.

"Reshenko?" Beth said aloud even though she wasn't asking a question. That was Iridia's last name. Had Mason ever mentioned her father's name? She couldn't remember for certain. She just knew that he was some kind of high-level scientist working for the government.

"Yes, he's the Chief Virologist for Milagro Corporation. He's the reason we needed the Bili chimpanzees."

Beth froze. Her heart stopped. The blood in her veins turned to ice. The compassion she'd felt at Diana's condition vanished.

"What did you just say?"

"I don't care if you know. What does it matter now? Nothing matters now. Look at me! I may as well be dead!"

Beth grabbed her shoulders and would've been shocked by how bony they felt were it not for the crashing wave of fury in her gut. "What do you mean? Why did he want the chimps?"

Diana's eyes opened wide and she stared up at Beth, apparently realizing that maybe it did still matter to someone else. She sat there with her mouth hanging open.

Beth shook her violently. She wanted to wrap her hands around Diana's throat and choke the life out of her. Sadly, Diana was in no condition to resist for long so the pleasure wouldn't last.

"Don't hurt me! Please! It's not my fault!"

"Tell me what happened to the Bili chimps. You told me they were going to zoos in other countries. I wondered why I could never get ahold of them. That was a lie, wasn't it?"

Diana nodded her head.

Yes. Death by strangulation was the best this criminal could hope for.

"Then what actually happened to the chimps?" Beth leveled Arctic-cold eyes at Diana. They silently promised unspeakable violence if she refused to answer.

Diana crumbled to the concrete floor. "He demanded it. I couldn't say no. I wasn't involved in that part of the company, but I heard it was supposed to be a super vaccine. The last flu vaccine you'd ever need. I was never told what he needed the chimps for. I swear it!"

Beth's hand moved before she could stop it. Her closed fist hit Diana's mouth with a sickening crunch. Her old boss's lip split open and blood trickled down her chin.

"You stole animals from this zoo and illegally and immorally used them for medical research!" Beth hit her in the face again. She was going to beat her to death. Strangulation would've been too kind.

Diana cupped her mouth, watching the blood spill into her hand. "I had no choice. I was just following orders. I'm sorry it happened. Please, believe me. It was an impossible situation. One I couldn't escape."

As much as Beth wanted to hurt Diana, she wanted to hurt Anton more. "Why are you here now?"

Diana broke into tears. The moisture from her eyes mixed with the saliva and blood from her mouth. "Anton ordered me to stay here until an evacuation team could retrieve Jack. When they finally arrived, they took him but left me behind. They rescued an ape and left me to die!"

The pounding in Beth's ears urged her to finish Diana's misery. Her brain screamed for violent action. And yet, the boiling rage struggled against another part of her. A core much deeper. A quiet serenity and faith in greater things. Just as she was about to do something she'd never be able to take back, that core swept over the fury as the ocean swallows a lava flow.

This pathetic woman was no saint. She wasn't even a good person. Yet, she was a victim. Not in the way the chimps were, but a victim nonetheless. She was in desperate need and who was Beth to turn her away? Worse, who was she to judge and execute this woman?

The choice tasted foul in her mouth.

"Get up," Beth said as she helped her to her feet.

"You're taking me with you?"

Beth walked away before rage blackened the good deed. Before the dark thoughts defeated the light. She retrieved the bag of medicine on the counter.

"I haven't decided yet."

40

With the remaining stock of bandages, gauze pads, and other supplies stuffed into her bag, Beth turned and shined the headlamp at Diana. The rail thin woman stood there shaking like a leaf. As if an imaginary breeze would be enough to blow her over.

"When did you eat last?" Beth asked.

"I don't know... maybe two days ago."

"I've got some food for you. A few bags of nuts and dried fruit."

Diana nodded eagerly and then swallowed hard as her body reacted to the anticipated meal. The desperation nearly made Beth want to forgive her.

Nearly.

Beth led the way back outside. She secured the bag of precious supplies and then dug out a snack for Diana. The woman's hands shook as she reached for the Ziplock bag of almonds. In a rush to get it open, she ripped the plastic and nuts spilled out. The old Diana never would've touched a scrap of food off the ground. She would've yelled at the grounds crew to clean it up before a customer slipped and fell potentially causing a lawsuit.

This was not the old Diana.

The gaunt, haggard woman dropped to her knees and swept up the nuts along with a good amount of dirt. She shoved the handful into her mouth as quickly as she could.

Beth cracked open a water bottle and put it on the ground next to her. "Slow down. And drink some water as you go."

Diana nodded as she popped more nuts and dirt into her mouth. Wads of saliva and almond fragments clung to her chin.

Beth watched her in silence.

Was she really going to take this woman home? Going to give her food that would've otherwise contributed to keeping her family alive?

Insane.

Diana had made her choices and now she was paying for them. Beth couldn't save every sorry soul that suffered in the new world. Diana should be left to meet her own destiny. She should leave her boss to whatever fate she'd earned.

But she couldn't.

It had nothing to do with the resurgence of Catholic faith that she'd been noticing of late. It had nothing to do with a conscience that would feel guilty knowing it had chosen to leave Diana to die.

It was more direct than that. More positive.

It was seeing another human being suffering and simply wanting to help.

"You can go with me back to my house. We have shelter, food, and water. You'll be safe there."

Diana stopped scrambling for the fallen nuts and looked

up at Beth. Tears welled from her eyes and spilled down her cheeks. "Thank you... Thank you so much."

"Yeah."

She'd help her, but she still hated her. Beth waited as Diana gathered up the last of the almonds. She wasn't going to stop her from eating off the ground. Aside from enjoying the twisted spectacle, those really were valuable calories that something like a little dirt wasn't going to ruin. They were too precious now. You couldn't walk into a store and slurp down a Coca-Cola along with a pint of ice cream. The effects of consuming excessive calories were no longer a major public health crisis.

The world had changed.

Sustenance was no longer perpetually available and within reach. It was again arduous to obtain and quick to consume, as it had been for tens of thousands of years in the past. Beth tapped her big toe by one that had fallen out of Diana's search zone. "Missed one."

Diana snapped it up. She chewed and swallowed and then stared up at Beth. "Why are you only wearing one boot?"

"It's a long story. Get up. We have to go." She'd do the right thing, but she didn't have to be nice about it. She pulled Diana to her feet and then helped her settle onto the back portion of the seat. "Have you ever ridden a motorcycle?"

Diana shook her head. "No."

"Great. Just don't lean out to the sides or make any sudden movements. Can you do that?"

"Yes."

Beth checked all the straps and made sure everything was tightened down. She swung her leg over and fired up Spock. She eased on the throttle waiting to see if her passenger would do something stupid. After coasting a while without incident, she opened it up a little. They rode down the meandering path heading toward the exit. Beth did a double take at the empty elephant paddock as they passed. They were gone. It was impossible for the four thousand pound animals to hide. So where did they go?

The path curved around toward the administration building on the right.

"Wait! Please stop! Can I gather a few things? Personal things."

The absolute very last thing in the universe that Beth wanted to do for this woman was a favor. And a favor included anything not immediately related to her survival. Personal things fell very much inside the realm of favor.

"Please," Diana said.

Beth bit her lip and groaned.

"Fine."

41

She stopped her bike in the middle of the path, a good thirty feet from the entrance to the admin building. A favor sure didn't mean front door service!

Diana didn't move, apparently waiting for exactly that.

"Go!" Beth shouted.

Diana nearly fell as she scrambled off the bike and headed toward the entrance. She tried the door and it was locked. "It's locked. Can I use your keys?"

Beth turned off the bike and held them up. Diana waited at the door as if Beth was just slow in delivering them. The gall of this arrogant woman!

"Come get them," Beth said with thick agitation coating her voice. Maybe she could drop Diana off on the way home. Surely she had family that would be relieved to see her alive. Such relief was hard to imagine, but even the worst criminals had mothers that loved them.

Diana plodded over and accepted the keys. "Can you help me grab a few things?"

Beth gritted her teeth until she worried a molar would shatter. Was this woman purposely trying to push her buttons? "Fine." She swung off the bike and followed Diana back to the entrance. With every step, she fought the urge to turn right back around and take off with her load a hundred and twenty pounds lighter and infinitely less infuriating.

Diana jiggled the lock open and let them inside. She led them through the center hallway back to her office on the left.

How many times had Beth marched down this hallway to this office ready to set fire to Diana's desk? More than a few. And now, having heard the truth about what had happened to the Bili chimps? And more recently, to Jack, too? This time, she wanted to set fire to the woman herself.

The door to her office was open and the interior looked like a bomb had gone off. Her desk was overturned and framed pictures on the floor smashed to pieces. It seemed strange to Beth that only now did she notice the pictures. Every other time she'd visited, she'd been in such a rage that whatever personal affectations Diana may have had were unnoticed white noise. Beth stood by the door while Diana went around the room collecting whatever it was that she had come back for.

"You have one minute," Beth said.

Diana retrieved her purse from a filing cabinet and filled it with stuff Beth didn't care enough about to absorb. She filled another bag and handed that one to Beth. "Carry this one," she said.

The words stomped on Beth's last, raw nerve. Even in her desperate condition, Diana easily slipped into her old attitude of expected obedience. Maybe it was being in the office that did it. Whatever it was, she was no longer the boss.

Beth spun around and headed back down the hallway. "I'll be outside."

"I'll be another few minutes."

"Your ride leaves in t minus sixty seconds. Fifty-nine. Fifty-eight."

Beth kicked the front door open and walked over to Spock. She took a seat and stared at the darkening sky. Mason would be worried sick. Worried sick while she waited. And fumed. Fumed and waited.

No Diana.

Two minutes.

Three minutes.

Beth marched to the entrance and threw the door open. "Diana! Let's go! Now!"

Her voice echoed into silence.

She stomped inside ready to punch a hole in Diana's face. As she headed down the hall, the clicking of the front door locks caught her attention. She ran back to the front. Diana stood outside holding Beth's keys.

Beth shoved the door and it didn't budge.

"What are you doing, Diana?"

"I require your transportation. Mr. Cruz will want me to report in."

Beth pounded her fist on the glass. "Open the door!"

"I can't do that," she said as she turned and headed back to the motorcycle.

Beth drew her Glock and pointed it at the door. She was about to cover her eyes and fire when she heard a growing rumble.

Diana froze next to the bike.

The same thundering of hooves she'd heard earlier.

An instant later, the herd of impalas rushed toward Diana. She fell to her knees and curled into the fetal position. The male in the lead decided not to go around, but instead leaped high into the air and sailed over both the bike and Diana. A few of the herd followed suit while others darted around. They passed in a clattering rush and were gone.

Diana lay on the ground shaking. She lifted her head and stared back down the path, around the bend to where Beth couldn't see.

She screamed.

Diana struggled to her feet and ran toward the door.

Then Beth saw the reason for her terror.

Hubert. The zoo's fully grown African male lion. His black and tan mane trailed in the wind as he sprinted toward Diana. The powerful muscles in his back legs rippled as he quickly closed the distance between them.

Diana shoved a key into the lock and jiggled to get it open.

Hubert gracefully leaped through the air and smashed her to the ground. With one huge paw, he swept her over onto her back.

Beth stared. Her veins congealed with frozen shock.

The lion lunged and snapped Diana's neck between his jaws. He held her pinned down by the neck but she required no more killing. He looked up and spotted Beth mere inches through the glass on the other side. He let go of Diana and stared directly into Beth's eyes. He slammed a paw into the door and his nails scraped the glass like knives on a chalkboard. He opened his mouth wide. Dark lips curled back to reveal four huge canines dripping with blood.

His roar shook the glass. It shook Beth's reason. It promised death and the futility of resistance.

Hubert circled around his prize and then grabbed ahold of one of Diana's feet in his mouth. He bit down hard and headed away. Her head dragged and bumped along on the ground between his legs as he went. A red, brushed streak of blood was all that remained of Diana Richston after he disappeared around the bend in the path.

Beth's legs gave out and she fell back hard onto the desk behind her. The pistol clanked to the surface.

Did that just happen?

She sat in stunned silence while her brain digested the event. The ice in her veins slowly warmed. Another minute and rational thought began to seep through the primitive concoction of chemicals inundating her system.

Diana's death was her own fault. Her actions directly resulted in her own death. In a sick way, Beth was thankful for her old boss's treachery. If Diana hadn't tricked her, she probably would've ended up as Hubert's next meal.

She picked up the gun and waited to see if Hubert would return. She didn't like the odds of facing down an apex predator in his prime with a 9mm handgun. She waited a few minutes more but the growing darkness outside convinced her it was time to get moving.

Deciding to conserve ammo, she grabbed a metal chair from behind the office desk and slammed it into the glass window. A huge crack splintered out from the point of impact. She was about to take another swing when she realized her bare right foot was still exposed. Shatter the glass and she'd be hopping around like a pogo stick. She found a black scarf tucked in the desk drawer. She grabbed a few magazines off the table and wrapped them around her foot, making sure the bottom was the thickest. She then tied the scarf around the paper into a makeshift moccasin.

Terrible. But it would have to do.

Another couple of swings and the window fell away in large, jagged sheets. She poked a metal leg at the clinging shards that still hung over the opening.

No way was she going out like that bad guy in *Ghost*.

She cleared the upper rim and then stepped outside. After retrieving the keys from the door lock, she drew her pistol and hurried to her bike. She fired it up and noticed Diana's bags piled on the ground. She threw them in a saddle bag hoping they'd turn up something useful.

She holstered the Glock and hit the gas harder than she'd intended. The front wheel popped up a couple feet and nearly made her lose control. A little rear brake and it thumped back down. As the bike picked up speed, her mind screamed about the lion jumping at her back. But the only thing that roared was the old Vulcan as it sped down the last curving pathway and out the entrance, into the parking lot beyond.

A long sigh of relief escaped her lungs.

She had the antibiotics that Clyde needed, that any of them might need someday. Now she needed to get them home. Get herself home in one piece.

A sliver of moon peeked above the eastern horizon. She'd done this commute a thousand times. Oftentimes at this hour and later. In fact, the later the better.

That was then.

This was now.

The darkness was no longer the technological twilight of the old Los Angeles. It was now a truly shadowed world.

One that hid unimaginable horrors.

42

THERESA steered the cargo bike around a car and turned left onto Washington Boulevard. The setting sun burned the sky a dull orange color. They'd ridden south a few blocks on Lincoln and the entire time felt like something horrible was about to happen. There was too much evidence of humanity and yet none of the movement. They were like superheroes moving so fast that the rest of the world seemed to stand still. Only they were too slow to save it.

They wound through a maze of packed cars, and it felt fake like a movie set. Everything laid out for the big action scene but nobody showed up to shoot it.

Washington was just as freaky so they took the first right and cut into the residential streets of the Del Rey neighborhood. As they rode further south, they passed a kid's park on the right. She remembered attending birthday parties there as a kid. The place was always jam-packed full of people because it was one of the few open spaces in the area.

She stared at the vacant swings and sand pit, shivering at the silence. That wasn't the only weird thing though because she realized the giant, old maple tree was gone. She'd climbed it countless times back in the day. It broke her heart to think that other kids wouldn't get the chance to explore its upper branches. To feel the tickle of the wind on their faces. To look down with wide eyes, astonished at how high they'd climbed.

Then again, there weren't other kids around to miss it in the first place. Was there any hope at all?

They took a left and headed east through typical west side residential streets. Tiny houses on postage stamp lots with driveways that almost always had two cars because people used their garages for extra rooms.

Red triangles tagged most of the front doors—evidence The National Guard had swept through the area. Their hasty paint jobs had made the spray paint pool and run making it look way too much like blood.

Like Venice, the neighborhood was mostly gentrified. The infrequent run down old home contrasted sharply with the surrounding remodeled ones. Her dad told her these were refugees from areas further west that had been priced out by the ever- climbing price of real estate. He often complained about how crazy it was.

The changes of the last week or so put that whole thing into a new perspective.

"This is really not cool," Elio said from behind her.

"What's wrong? The pillow not enough cushion?"

"The pillow is fine. The problem is that I feel like your biker babe."

Theresa laughed at the unexpected comment. "Elio Lopez, are you a sexist pig?"

"No, not at all! It just feels a little weird is all."

"Oh, so it would be totally normal if you were in front and I was in the back?"

"Yeah, that'd be fine."

"Unbelievable. I thought I knew you. I suppose you'd expect your wife to cook all your meals, keep the house clean, and be beautiful when you got home from work."

"Hold up, now. Don't go fantasizing about being my wife already. I haven't agreed to marry you yet."

Something twisted in Theresa's belly. What started out as a joke was quickly turning into something else. "You're digging yourself into a hole. You might want to apologize before I shovel in more dirt on top of you."

"Two things," Elio said. "One, I apologize. And two, it's a little gross that you're making burying jokes considering what your father and the neighbor are doing."

Theresa thought about her father digging a grave in the Crayfords' backyard. He would finish the exhausting work and return to find her and Elio missing. He'd be worried sick. She felt terrible about it. But she couldn't let Elio go alone, and she couldn't betray his plan either. She'd chosen the only option that kept her and Elio together.

"You'd better start being a little bit more considerate or you might end up buried, too."

It was wrong to joke about something so serious. And yet, the humor helped deal with it. Helped to compartmentalize it so that she could carry on.

She glanced at the battery gauge and saw that it was still in the green at about three quarters full. With her peddling along to help extend the range, they should have enough to get back home.

"So, how long do I have to ride like this before I can get a bike of my own?"

Theresa laughed. "You could break into any garage on this street and get your own ride. The question is whether you could keep up."

"I could keep up."

"No, you couldn't. No way."

"Okay, I probably couldn't."

"Probably?"

"Fine. I couldn't. But that's only because I'm not a hundred percent and also because this bike has an electric battery boosting your speed."

"I didn't say it would be a fair race. I just said I'd win."

"You wouldn't win."

"How would I not? I'm the rabbit and you're the turtle. And this ain't no fairy tale."

"You don't know where I live."

He had her there. In order to win a race, you had to know where the finish line was. She was trying to come up with a snarky reply when a gunshot echoed down the street. The driver side window of the car to their right shattered.

CRACK.

Another gunshot and the windshield of the car ahead exploded into a thousand pieces.

Theresa weaved back and forth not so much as an evasive maneuver as it was just trying to keep the bike upright while shock numbed her sense of balance. She thumbed the battery power to the max and the long bike picked up speed. The acceleration and her wobbly balance nearly shot them right into the side of a big white truck. She steered away at the last second and the right handlebar smacked its side mirror forward. The driver side window exploded an instant after Elio's body passed by.

She turned right at the next cross street without slowing down. They rode another couple of blocks before she managed to swallow her heart back into her chest.

"Are you okay?" Elio said as he squeezed her shoulder.

"I'm fine. You?"

"A few bits of glass in my hair, but fine."

"That last one hit right behind you."

"Tell me about it. Listen, I don't like cruising down streets with houses lined up on both sides."

Theresa nodded as she looked at the apparently not totally vacant houses on each side. "I was thinking the same thing. It feels like we're in a shooting gallery just waiting for someone to win the prize."

"I've got an idea," Elio said. "There's an entrance to the four-oh-five a few blocks over. We can take it five miles south to Inglewood. My place is a half-mile east of the exit."

"You want to go up on the highway?"

"Yep. Should be safer. Just a road crammed with abandoned cars. You saw the news reports. Every major highway in the Los Angeles area was packed with cars going nowhere within twenty-four hours of the outbreak."

Theresa remembered the disturbing images on the news in those first few days. And how soon after that the technology to broadcast any news had begun to break down. For the millionth time since the outbreak began, she subconsciously reached toward her back pocket to pull out her iPhone to check something.

The something wasn't important. It was the act that was important. The security blanket of having instant access to information at your fingertips.

But the phone was no longer there. She'd stopped carrying it a few days ago when it became apparent power was not going to be restored. It was a photo album of the last year of her life because she was terrible at syncing it. She swiped through the pictures when Holly's absence threatened to drown her in sadness. The pictures and videos helped in a happy-sad way.

She dreaded the day when the battery died for good and

she lost those shared moments. They were proof that Holly had lived. That life had once been normal and fun and not terrible like it was now. The images reminded her of who she used to be.

"Hey," Elio said, "if you wanna continue testing our luck in the shooting gallery, we can do that too."

"No, you're right. Let's try the highway. It can't be worse than this."

43

They rode up the entrance ramp alongside abandoned vehicles. People had ignored the single lane and crowded two lanes onto the ramp. An open span about two feet wide ran along the right shoulder between the concrete barrier and the uneven line of cars on the left.

Theresa slowed a couple of times when that open space pinched in a little. They made it to the top of the ramp and she involuntarily sucked in a breath.

Cars went on *forever*.

As far as she could see.

A frozen river of vehicles with five lanes in each direction. Who knew there were so many?

She was surprised that for the most part, they were lined up between the dashed lines as they would've been on any normal evening. That was the only thing that resembled normal. The rest was a shock. Here was the symbol of the modern world. The symptom of it. And now, the end of it. All around in three dimensions.

The movie versions of the endless traffic jam didn't do the real thing justice. Maybe the details were off or maybe it was that a flat screen simply couldn't compare to the gut-punching reality.

Millions of cars carrying millions of people that all tried to escape at once and so blocked everyone from getting anywhere. She'd seen the stalled traffic on the news and it had seemed no different than a movie. It was nothing more than entertainment.

But now? Extending out in an endless swerving snake into the distance? It took her breath away.

"Why are we stopped?" Elio asked.

"What?"

"Do you want to turn back?"

"Oh, no. I just didn't realize it would be like this."

"Yeah."

Theresa thumbed back on the battery power and pedaled to help get the bike moving. She stuck to the right shoulder as that seemed to be the most reliable lane of open space. They cruised past about thirty cars with both of them staring into their empty interiors.

"I bet we could find some good stuff in these," Elio said.

"Want to stop and check a few out?"

"Let's do it on the way back."

Theresa nodded as she slowed down and was forced to cut in by a black Cadillac Escalade with its bumper touching the barrier. She clicked off the electric assist and carefully pedaled between cars trying to stay as equally far away on each side as possible.

She expected something to jump out at any second. They came up to some open space between cars on the right and she cut back over to the shoulder. The chill of the evening wind made her earlobes tingle. The setting sun was losing its warmth and she was glad she had brought a jacket to slip into later. The west side was like that. No matter how hot it got during the day, the evenings always ended up cool because of the air coming in off the Pacific Ocean.

Something seemed to move at the exit ramp up ahead, maybe a couple hundred yards away. Theresa squinted her eyes and stared to see if maybe she was just seeing things, expecting movement where there was none.

There was.

She eased off the electric assist and squeezed on the brakes. "Elio, do you see something up at the next exit?"

He leaned forward around her shoulder. "Yeah, something. What is it?"

They both stared and then spoke at the same time. "A dog."

They watched silently as it raced towards them at top speed. Theresa noticed movement further behind it and her jaw dropped open. "There's people chasing it!"

"Let's go back!" Elio said.

Theresa carefully maneuvered the bike around and was about to take off in the other direction when her thumb froze above the electric assist lever. "Elio, we have to hide."

"Why?" he asked.

"Now!"

They jumped off the bike and laid it on its side like it was just another failed escape plan. Elio threw open the door of an old suburban and a wave of stench washed over them.

Theresa gagged and swallowed hard to keep the contents of her stomach down. Rotten food. Rotten meat. Rotten human meat. Whatever it was made that spot a no-brainer, no thank you. She scanned the line of cars ahead and saw a big Ford truck. The body sat higher than the surrounding cars due to the huge tires it sported. They could get up there and the people passing by wouldn't see them as they passed.

She grabbed Elio's hand and took off. "Come on!"

They weaved back and forth between cars and made it to the truck. She jumped up on the sidebar and cracked the passenger door open. Aside from being stifling hot and stuffy, nothing disgusting made it a bad place to hide. She jumped across the passenger seat into the driver seat and Elio followed in behind her.

He closed the door and peeked above the dash. "Think they saw us?"

She peered over the steering wheel and saw the dog now maybe seventy yards away and still running in their direction. A group of five people pursued it. One paused and hurled a rock but missed.

Closer now, she realized her mistake. They weren't people. Some were completely naked. The others wore odd fragments of fabric that clearly had no purpose. It wasn't fashionable or functional. It was simply forgotten. Theresa spun around and looked back down the road from the direction they'd come. Another group of deltas, ten or so, headed their way from that direction.

How could they escape? The two groups were going to converge somewhere in their vicinity.

She looked at Elio and the resigned look in his eyes said he'd come to the same conclusion.

"What now?" she asked.

"Stay quiet. And hope they didn't see us."

44

They locked the doors and then slithered down onto the floorboard. After another minute of tense waiting wondering if she should peek out to see if maybe the two groups had turned back, the frantic sounds of the fleeing dog grew louder. His nails clicked the pavement and then skidded to a stop outside their door. Unintelligible shouting drew nearer from both directions.

The dog's paws smacked into the passenger door and it whined pitifully to be let in. It must've smelled them.

It jumped up again and smacked into Elio's door. The terror in its begging broke Theresa's heart. She had a good idea of what was going to happen to it if it was caught. With the wound from losing Max barely scabbed over, she yearned to pull it inside to safety.

Only there was no safety. If the deltas discovered them inside the truck, the dog wasn't the only one in trouble.

The poor thing whimpered and pleaded. Theresa had never heard a more pitiable sound.

Elio grabbed her wrist and shook his head.

She realized with a start that she was reaching across

him for the door latch. She nodded and pulled her hand back.

The inhuman screaming, hooting, and hollering arrived. The dog growled and barked viciously in a last ditch attempt to convince its pursuers that it wasn't worth the effort.

More shouting and scrambling bodies and then the sound that Theresa hoped to never hear chilled her to the bone. A long, high-pitched whine suddenly cut short with a gurgling choke. The deltas outside exploded into a frenzy of elated cries of victory. The celebration was cut short and the tone again turned dark. The voices moved toward the back of the truck.

Voices further behind, what must be the larger group arriving, answered in kind. Theresa crept up the seat and peeked out the back window.

The two groups of deltas stood about ten feet apart. Two men from the smaller group faced five men from the larger group. All of them waved their arms wildly, screaming, trying to intimidate the other group. The women and children stood behind their respective protectors watching to see how the encounter would play out. An older boy in the smaller group nearest the truck pulled against his mother to join the front line guarding his group. She clung to him struggling to keep him away from the danger.

Theresa had assumed they were part of the same group. That they'd split up to surround the dog. Either that was never the case, or now that the kill had to be shared, one of the groups had changed its mind about cooperation.

Competition got the meat.

A young girl at the back of the nearest group looked back and seemed to stare directly into Theresa's eyes.

Theresa froze, partly from fear and partly not to give

them away with sudden movement. The darkening sky made it unlikely the girl could see through the tinted window, she hoped.

The girl walked back to the truck and hooked a hand over the tailgate. The suspension shifted as she climbed up into the bed. She sniffed the air and crept toward the cab, totally ignoring the impending violence behind her.

Theresa slid down into the seat as slowly as she could.

The patter of the girl's bare feet drew closer and then her face mashed flat against the rear glass.

Theresa and Elio curled down into the floorboards trying to make themselves as small as possible.

The girl's eyes scanned back and forth and didn't seem to find them.

The shouting continued outside as each group tried to intimidate the other into retreat so their group could claim the dog's body.

The girl ignored it completely. She slid to the side still trying to see inside the cab. She backed away and Theresa let out a slow sigh of relief. Her lungs were half empty when the girl's face reappeared.

Theresa watched in terror as the girl's eyes swept over the interior and then connected with her own. They locked together in a frozen moment and, for a second, it seemed like nothing more would happen.

No such luck.

The girl clawed at the rear window and Theresa realized in a panic that while they'd locked the side doors, they hadn't thought to lock the sliding rear window.

Her fingers caught the edge of the window and it slid open an inch. She shoved it aside and poked her head in looking first at Theresa and then at Elio. She appeared more curious than afraid.

The feeling wasn't mutual.

Theresa waved at her to go away but the gesture was lost in translation. Or ignored.

The girl started hooting in excitement. She was going to draw the other's attention any second. And then it would be over.

"Go away!" Theresa whispered.

The girl poked her head back out and screamed for one of the others to come see what she'd found.

A chill settled deep in Theresa's belly. They were dead. They should've never run away. How could they have been such idiots?

Theresa wormed up to the seat and grabbed the girl's arm. The plan was to fling it outside, slam the window shut, and lock it. It wasn't a great plan but the alternative seemed worse.

The girl's speed caught Theresa off guard. She shrieked and bit Theresa's wrist.

Pain lanced up Theresa's arm and she let go.

The girl jumped away from the rear window howling like crazy.

Theresa slammed the window shut and locked it before sinking back down into the floorboard. She dabbed her shirt on the blood welling from the teeth marks in her left wrist. The wound burned like fire.

The confrontation outside exploded. The fight drowned out the pleas of the little girl. The truck shifted as a large body hopped up into the bed. A woman scooped up the little girl and bounded onto the roof and down over the hood before leaping off to the ground.

The sounds of the fighting outside did little to distract Theresa from the pain of the bite. She gritted her teeth and bore it because there wasn't much else she could do.

The conflict outside subsided and the patter of running feet replaced it. One side had apparently won.

Theresa crawled up the seat and peeked out the back window. The larger group remained. The largest of them picked up the dead dog and screamed at the losers fleeing south on the highway. He pounded his chest and shook his fist in the air.

The message couldn't have been clearer and yet no words were spoken.

The leader finished screaming at the losers and then turned back to his prize. He grabbed the dog's back leg and yanked. The dog moaned. It wasn't dead yet. The man bit into its rear leg and tore off a chunk of flesh. The dog whimpered as more of its blood spilled onto the concrete.

The man grabbed the rear leg and wrenched it off with a sickening, bone-cracking crunch. Gore dripped from the exposed red meat. He bit into the flesh and gnawed off a large, bloody bite. Red poured down his chin and onto his bare chest.

Theresa gagged. Her stomach pinched tight and yet she couldn't look away.

He was eating it alive. Like an animal.

The group circled around the body. Three children slipped from behind the women and kicked at the dead dog before darting away screaming.

"What's happening?" Elio whispered from the floorboard.

Theresa couldn't respond. The savagery shocked her to silence. A remote corner of her brain sensed Elio slide up the seat and peek out next to her.

The adults gathered around the carcass and began to tear off dripping chunks. A little boy wedged in and sunk his teeth into the dog's shoulder. He ripped and tore at it struggling to get through the layers of skin and fat. He finally tore off a piece and ran away before the other kids could steal it. The group sat down, huddling close around the body, each focusing on the meal in their hands.

Theresa and Elio sunk lower into the seats, their wide open eyes just inches apart. How long was this group going to linger right outside the truck? How long before they were discovered with nowhere to run?

The blood oozing from the bite marks was already starting to slow, but the ache hadn't let up yet.

Great.

In pain. Right next to deltas that had no problem eating a dog alive.

It was going to be a long night.

45

MASON shoveled up one last scoop of dirt and tossed it onto the mound. He slapped the flat of the shovel all over the bulge in the ground. His back ached from the hours of concerted effort. He wiped sweat from his brow and flung it onto the freshly tilled dirt. The dim light of the LED lantern cast soft shadows on the grass.

The dead man didn't get a casket and he wasn't more than four feet under, but it would have to do. Paying due respect had to be balanced against what was physically possible. There was no one to whisk away the cold body. No one to drain the fluids in preparation for viewing. No backhoe to dig out a proper grave.

Improvise. Adapt. Overcome.

The Marines drilled that maxim into every jarhead's brain. It had long since burrowed into the fabric of Mason's being.

He leaned on the shovel and glanced up into the dark sky. Where was Beth? She should've been home by now.

Ahmed leaned over with his hands on his knees. "Should we say something?"

"Not my area of expertise," Mason replied. "Go ahead if you want to."

Ahmed nodded and then stared at the darker soil of the mound. "May his eternal soul find forgiveness and may he find in the next world the peace he sought in this one."

Mason nodded. "Well said. Are you a religious man?"

Ahmed turned to him. His eyes focused somewhere a million miles in the distance. "I once was, a long time ago."

Mason didn't know how to respond to such a cryptic answer. So he didn't. "We've done the best we can for him." He picked up a bottle of water and took a long drink. "Let's head back to see how everybody is doing."

Ahmed nodded and dabbed his forehead with a mostly white handkerchief. He accepted the offered bottle and guzzled the remaining half.

Mason shouldered the shovel and grabbed the lantern. He held it between them for a moment and thought he saw something unspoken in Ahmed's eyes before his neighbor turned away. He was a strange fellow.

There were times when the silence between them felt frigid with underlying currents. Maybe it was a cultural thing. His daughter Noor had clearly become Americanized and so had no accent. Ahmed's accent was subtle but Mason still detected it. Unless he was way off base, he placed the origin as being from Iraq. He'd spent enough time there to develop an ear for the peculiar singsong pitch that typified an Iraqi's flavor of Arabic.

He didn't ask about it.

He didn't ask because it didn't matter. If they'd shared a Sunday night dinner together before the outbreak, then he would've asked. It would've been part of the get-to-know-you process. But he didn't need to know this man in this new reality. He just needed to work with him until he could formulate the next best step for his family.

Ahmed unlocked the gate and pushed it open enough for them both to slip through. He made certain it was shut behind them as Mason continued on to the front door. He pushed it open and immediately noticed the prevailing silence.

Noor ran out from the kitchen. "Baba! I took care of Clyde!" She saw it was Mason and stumbled to a stop, staring at the ground shyly.

"He's right behind me," Mason said. "Where is everyone?"

Noor pointed toward the staircase. "Iridia is upstairs. Theresa and Elio—"

"Noor, my dear," Ahmed said as he entered and secured the door. "Have you been helping out?"

"Yes, Baba. I took care of Clyde. He's so cute. And I finished organizing all the food in the kitchen cabinets. Come! Let me show you!"

Ahmed gave her a proud hug and followed as she dragged him into the kitchen to show off her achievement.

Mason carried the lantern upstairs to check on the kids. They were probably ready for bed. Strange that Noor wasn't with them though. He knocked on the bedroom door to the left. "Theresa? Elio?"

Iridia opened the door... naked. Really? She belonged in a nudist colony. A small furry face appeared at the door. It looked up at Mason and hissed.

Where was Max when he needed him? Their old bullmastiff would've run that cat off in no time. A gang leader had killed their dog over a week ago and yet, every morning Mason caught himself waiting for Max to jump on the bed for a wrestle play session.

Mr. Piddles had adopted Iridia for some reason. Maybe it was because they were both so irritating.

"Do you need something?" Iridia asked, standing there completely naked.

Mason forced his eyes to stay level with her own. "You can't walk around like that. It wasn't okay in our house, and it's even less so here."

"Who's walking around? I'm hanging out in my room."

"Your room?"

She nodded like he'd just said the most obvious thing in the world. Parts of her just below his eyeline jiggled. The movement dragged like a weight on his attention. Fortunately, irritation proved stronger than curiosity.

"One, this is not your personal room. Two, put some clothes on! You'll give Ahmed a heart attack like that."

"Fine!" she said and slammed the door shut.

Really? Like a clueless teenager? This is what he had to deal with?

He pounded on the door, doing his best not to punch a hole through it.

It opened a sliver.

A whiskered face appeared in the crack and hissed.

"I'm not dressed yet!"

Mason pinched his eyes shut and did his best to breathe. One. Two. Three. Four. Five. He exhaled.

"Where are Elio and Theresa?"

"How should I know?" she said and then slammed the door shut.

Panic stabbed at Mason's heart. His frustration with Iridia completely swept away by the surging anxiety.

"Theresa! Elio! Where are you guys?" he yelled to nowhere in particular.

Ahmed appeared at the bottom of the stairs. "What's going on?"

"Are Theresa and Elio downstairs?"

"I don't think so."

Noor appeared at her father's side and looked up the stairs at Mason. "They haven't come back yet."

Come back yet?

"Where did they go?" he asked.

"They went on a neighborhood patrol like you wanted them to. But I haven't seen them come back yet."

Mason leaped down the stairs so fast he almost ran over both of them. He stopped abruptly. "Tell me what happened. When did they leave?"

Noor's eyes opened wide. She jumped behind her father and peeked out from behind his back.

Ahmed wrapped his arm around her and patted her head reassuringly. "It's okay, dear. Please tell us."

"It was a while ago. They were on a bike together when I saw them. I asked them where they were going and they said you wanted them to do a neighborhood patrol. You know, to look around and see how things are. For situational squareness, I think."

Cold sweat dripped down Mason's back. In a flash, he knew what had happened.

Theresa and Elio had left to go get his mother.

How could they be so foolish?

They had no idea how dangerous it could be out there. And Beth should've been back by now as well. The father part of Mason's brain urged him toward blind panic. The soldier and close protection officer part of his brain prevailed. He started mentally assembling a plan of action when a familiar sound intruded on his thoughts.

"Noor, get to the bathroom," Ahmed said as he hurried her upstairs.

Mason recognized the rhythmic thump of a helicopter approaching. He ran upstairs and barged into Iridia's room.

"Hey! A knock would be appreciated," she said.

The state of her undress was the last thing on Mason's mind. He inched the heavy curtain to the side and peeked down on his house next door. A Sikorsky SH-3 Sea King hovered a hundred feet in the air. A red glow reflected off the pilot's visor. All of its nav lights were shut off. This wasn't a diplomatic mission.

The side door rolled open and two black ropes tumbled out. A red light stick dropped and bounced on the grass. Two men fast-roped down and landed on their feet in his front yard. They pulled night vision goggles down over their eyes and then grabbed the suppressed HK MP7 submachine guns slung to their chests. They pushed out to establish security while two more pairs zipped down.

An assault team.

"What's going on?" Iridia asked.

"Shhh. Quiet."

46

The six men in black tactical gear and body armor signaled each other as they headed toward his home. Two went for the side gate and circled around to the backyard. The other four stacked up on the front door. Mason watched with grim fascination as one man kicked the door in and the other three rushed in to secure the room.

He and his men had used the same tactics countless times in Fallujah.

What did they want? Had the officer they'd killed alerted a SWAT team that the supposed cop-killer was still alive? Had they come to finish the job?

A few minutes later, the pitch of the spinning blades changed. The chopper descended and landed in the street. The six men filed out and hustled toward it, making sure to cover their assigned fields of fire as they went. The last man covering their six hopped in as the chopper nosed up and lifted into the air.

They were professionals.

The chopper whined as it clawed for altitude. Another minute and the thumping faded into the dark sky.

What was that about?

Mason thought he was just thinking to himself, but then his handheld radio repeated the words.

"Seriously, what was that about?"

Beth!

"Where are you? Over."

"Parked behind a house at the end of our block. I heard that helicopter flying in and hid. Is everyone okay?"

"Shut your bike off and stay put. I'll be there in a minute. Which house? Over."

"The hideously lavender one at the south end of the block."

"On my way. Over." He released the transmitter as he headed downstairs. "Ahmed, be ready to open the gate."

"Of course."

As much as Mason's body protested, the elation of having one of the women in his life out of harm's way overrode the twinges, aches, and outright pain. He jogged down the street with his Glock in the low-ready position, scanning for threats. Half-expecting the inky forms of the assault team to bleed out of the shadows.

He arrived at the hideously lavender house at the end of the block. In the darkness, it wasn't half as ugly as in the light.

Beth ran into his arms as he approached.

He kept the muzzle pointed in a safe direction while also wrapping her in a hug that was only matched by the strength of her returned embrace. Her hair smelled musky and fresh at the same time. Her body molded into his.

She was home.

A tear rolled down her cheek.

"Honey, are you okay?" he asked.

"I am now."

"I'd love to hug you for hours, but we need to get back to safety. I'll cover us while you push Spock."

They made it back in short order and stowed the bike in the courtyard. He noticed the busted two-way radio and realized why Beth hadn't been in communication for the larger part of her journey. At least the walkie-talkie had worked while she hid at the end of the street. Whatever the case, she was home and more important matters required attention.

They secured the house and gathered in the kitchen. Beth took a long drink of water and then splashed a handful on her face. She dried herself and then stared at Mason in silence.

"What happened?" he asked.

"I'll tell you later. Where are the kids?"

Kids.

She'd already emotionally adopted Elio as a family member.

It was Mason's turn to stare in silence.

"What?" Beth asked.

"Theresa and Elio left."

"Left where?" Beth said as her voice jumped up a key. "Why did you let them leave?"

"I didn't. They snuck away. I assume to go check on Maria."

"They're out there alone, Mason!"

"I know. I just found out when that chopper arrived."

"What was that all about?"

"I don't know. They came in hard and fast. Heavily armed. Very professional. They busted into our house, didn't find whatever they were looking for, and took off."

"Where are you going to look for the kids?"

"I didn't have a good route put together yet. They're likely somewhere between here and Inglewood."

"There are a thousand different ways they could've gone. You'd be wandering around hoping to get lucky. There has to be a better option."

Mason calmed the urgency pulsing in his brain and tried to come up with even one alternative. The walkie-talkie at his hip squawked.

"Did you find Theresa and Elio?"

Iridia. Upstairs. Even her concern was lazy.

Mason clicked off the power with an agitated flick.

Wait a second.

He considered the possibility. Maybe. Juice would know for sure.

"What are you thinking?" Beth asked.

"Theresa has one of these walkie-talkies. Maybe we could get through to her."

"We have a pair like those," Ahmed said. "You'd be lucky to get reception a couple streets over."

"As they are, you're right," Mason answered. "But what if we could boost the transmission? If it's possible, we could at least communicate one way. If we could tell them where we were as we searched, they could move toward that spot. Then, like you said, within a few blocks range, we could pick up two-way communication."

"How do you do that?" Ahmed asked.

Mason pressed the transmit button on the two-way handheld radio. "Juice. This is Mason. You still monitoring this frequency? Over."

"You bet, Sarge. What was that about a chopper? Over."

"I'll tell you later. Question for you. Over."

"Shoot. Over."

"I've got a set of consumer-grade walkie-talkies and one

of them is definitely beyond transmission range. Would it be possible to patch my walkie-talkie over to your system and then have you transmit to the same frequency with the amplified power of your radio? Over."

"Standby."

They all waited until Mason began to wonder if the connection had died.

"Mason. This is Juice. I think I could work up a solution for that. How far away do you think this other walkie-talkie is? Over."

"No more than ten miles. Over."

"It should be possible. How fast do you need it? Over."

"Yesterday. Over."

"It's going to take a minute. But I'll get on it. Over."

"How long do you think? Over."

"A few hours, at least."

He couldn't wait a few hours.

"Copy that. I owe you one, bro. Over."

"Negative on that, Sarge. Sit tight and I'll put it together as fast as I can. Over and out."

Beth turned to Mason. "We can't wait that long. What if it ends up not working?"

Mason nodded. He understood the danger. The only problem was that heading out into the night with zero idea of where the kids were was a recipe for disaster. He wasn't especially concerned for his own life, except that losing it would leave Beth to fend for herself.

And an untimely end would do nothing to help his daughter and Elio either.

So what, then?

47

ELIO scratched at the crud gluing his eyelids together. He managed to pry them apart and blinked a few times wondering where he was. A Ford logo on the glovebox a foot in front of his face hinted at things he didn't want to remember. The group of deltas had departed in the middle of the night. They'd decided to sleep in the truck rather than venture out into the darkness.

He simultaneously registered an aching hip from laying on one side all night long and also the thrill of being so close to Theresa.

She lay pressed tight to his body as the bench seat was just deep enough for both of them on their sides.

The dim light outside told him the sun was coming up. He wondered when they'd finally gone to sleep. There was only so long they could lay absolutely still and silent waiting for the deltas to leave. And then, when they did, waiting for them to return. Waiting in paused terror for one of the deltas to realize they were trapped inside.

He wanted to get up and check the area but, more than

that, he didn't want to disturb Theresa. Her body melded to his in a way that made him uncomfortable and excited all at once.

Speaking of excited, he realized with horror that he was sporting a raging boner. And that his fully-at-attention manhood was pressed firmly into Theresa's backside. Thinking about her sent a pulse of excitement through it.

Oh God, no.

How horrifying. She'd wake up and feel it jabbing her in the butt cheek.

Humiliating.

He had to move, but couldn't. If he tried to adjust to get a little pocket of air between his eagerness and her body, she'd wake up and feel it.

Maybe he could stay still and just let it relax away. Then there wouldn't be any evidence when she woke up.

That could work.

Elio took a slow breath and let it ease out. He consciously tried to relax the straining tension in his underwear. He tried that for a number of breaths and then realized with a shock that it wasn't helping at all. In fact, he was even harder.

Maybe he could think of Algebra class. That class was enough to put anything to sleep. It was like getting hit with a tranq dart. He squeezed his eyes shut, ignored his aching hip, and tried to focus on x's and y's and equal signs and how they related to each other in the most boring way possible.

The images in his mind dissolved into Theresa's gorgeous smile. She really was gorgeous. He throbbed involuntarily.

This was *not* working.

He needed something simpler. Counting. That could work.

One. Two. Three. Four.

He focused as hard as he could on the numbers. And not on the softness of her body.

Five. Six. Seven.

"Are you awake?" Theresa whispered.

His hardness twitched in response. Whether from the shock of knowing he was busted or at the anticipation of what might happen next, Elio wasn't sure.

No. No. No.

The more he tried to relax, the more it twitched.

"Why are you tapping me?" Theresa asked as she glanced back and realized his hands were nowhere near her backside. Her eyes opened wide.

Elio closed his and wished lightning would tear through the inevitably cloudless sky and blast him into little bits of charred, embarrassed dust.

Could it get any worse?

"Your little friend seems to be wide awake."

She called it his *little* friend. Okay, it just got worse.

"Sorry," Elio said. "It's, uhh, like that in the mornings."

"No reason to be sorry," she said as she looked at him with barely concealed laughter. "You know, just the miracle of nature at work."

"So you think it's a miracle of nature, huh?"

Theresa's cheeks burned pink and she covered her face. "That's not what I meant. I was just... I mean..."

Her awkward discomfort made her more gorgeous than ever. Her long brown hair fell in waves off the edge of the seat. The heat of her body still formed to his own made his heart race and palms sweat.

Kiss her.

What if she didn't want him to?

Do it!

What if she didn't like it? Or thought he was being too forward?

Kiss her!

Now!

48

Elio propped himself up on an elbow and dipped his head. With her hand still over her eyes, he kissed her. Her hand fell away revealing gorgeous brown eyes. A smoldering heat reflected in their depths. She closed them again and slipped a tentative tongue between his lips.

According to all reasonable logic, they should've both recoiled at a deep kiss flavored with morning breath. But neither did. The shared heat burned away all conscious thought. Burned away all observation that didn't involve the magnetic pull between their bellies, and lower.

Theresa shifted onto her back as Elio scooted on top of her. Her legs parted wider as he settled his weight between them.

A squirming coil sizzled in Elio's gut. The pressure of their connection blasted electric waves down to the tips of his toes and up to the top of his scalp. He was fully clothed, and yet he'd never felt such overwhelming arousal.

He lowered his full weight on top of her and kissed her again. This time there was no hesitation on either side. He probed and she parted to accept him.

The outside world slipped away. The dangers. The concerns. The struggle. All of it simply faded. Their connection melted away all that was secondary and no longer meaningful.

Elio's stomach clenched and his hips thrust forward. He didn't do it on purpose. He would've been too embarrassed to be so forward. His brain was like a backseat driver shouting to be heard while his body raced forward, oblivious to everything but its own desired destination.

Theresa's hips rolled back accepting his advance.

What was happening?

Was *it* happening?

What about his mother? The Wests? The world outside?

Whatever. It could wait. The softness of Theresa's lips and skin was all that mattered.

Elio pulled back to catch a breath. He held himself up a bit so he wouldn't crush her, even though that was what he wanted to do most.

To be so close to her that their bodies merged. To be so connected that the math that started with two variables combined into one solution.

The tips of their noses touched as they stared into each other's eyes. Her eyes spoke a wordless invitation. He couldn't understand why she'd chosen him for such a heavenly offering. He was no god. He was barely a worthwhile human being. He'd been nothing but a failure at both being a student and a wannabe gangster.

And yet she'd chosen him.

"You're so beautiful," he said.

Her amber eyes sparkled with a light that took his breath away.

"Kiss me," she said.

He lowered his lips to hers when the walkie-talkie on the floorboard sputtered to life.

Theresa and Elio. This is Mason. You need to stop what you're doing. It's dangerous and you don't understand the possible consequences...

A jolt of cold reality crashed like an icy wave over the heat in Elio's belly. He grabbed at the walkie-talkie and flipped the knob until it clicked into the off position.

They both froze, knowing the moment had shifted. Been cut short. They looked at each other.

Theresa nodded toward the passenger door. "Peek out and see what's going on," she whispered.

He slid over and lifted up slowly, ever so slowly, until his left eye could see out the corner of the window. The deltas had not returned. All that remained were irregular patches of red staining the concrete below.

He moved sideways to get a better view.

Still no one.

He looked around in all directions.

"Looks clear," he said.

Theresa pushed herself up and glanced around to verify his conclusion. She picked up the walkie-talkie and turned it back on, still making sure to keep the volume low.

...can help you. Please come home and we can help you. We're worried sick about you both.

Theresa clicked the transmit button. "Dad! It's me, Theresa. Can you hear me?"

It was silent a moment and then continued.

Theresa and Elio. This is Mason. Please stop what you're doing. You don't know how unsafe it is. Please come home. I—

"Dad! It's Theresa! Can you hear me?"

...a smart way to do this.

Theresa tried again and got no response.

"He can't hear us," she said looking at the walkie-talkie like it had personally betrayed her.

"We can't go back yet," Elio said. "We're only a couple of miles from my apartment. Let's get my mother and then head back."

Theresa bit her lip and stared at the walkie-talkie as Mason continued asking them and then telling them to go home. She clicked it off. "Okay."

They gathered up their belongings and then scanned the area again before unlocking the door.

Elio opened the door and hopped down. He offered a hand and helped Theresa down.

She landed lightly and smiled. "Sir, you are too kind."

Elio attempted an awkward bow with a sweep of his hand across his waist. He didn't attempt to make it awkward. That was just how it turned out.

Whatever. He didn't care. His own shortcomings couldn't be all that horrible if someone like Theresa could see beyond them.

"And you, Madam, are too beautiful."

49

The remaining miles to Elio's apartment passed uneventfully, on the outside at least. The inside was another matter. His thoughts soared to the heights and plummeted to the depths with dizzying speed. It was enough to make him want to barf.

As they turned left on Sixth Street and Elio saw his apartment building down the street, his stomach jumped. He couldn't wait to run up the stairs to their one-bedroom fourth floor apartment. To throw the door open and find his mother safe and sound.

But the nagging doubt in his gut tempered the excitement.

She could be gone, either from the apartment or from the world altogether. The closer they got, the greater the contrast of his thoughts. One second joyous anticipation and the next wretched resignation.

"See the faded blue building down on the left?"

"Yep," Theresa replied.

"That's it. There's an alley on the near side. Let's take it and we can park in back."

"Got it."

As much as his sense of machismo was offended by riding on the back of the cargo bike while Theresa pedaled up front, he didn't mind having to hold her hips to steady himself. And he enjoyed the smell of her hair as it drifted back over him.

Theresa carefully steered them around a patch of shattered glass. She turned left and took them around to the back of the apartment building.

Elio couldn't believe it. After waiting so long, he was home. "I'll stash the bike behind the dumpster."

Theresa nodded and hopped off.

Elio hid it as best he could and then turned to the rear door. A large red triangle was spray-painted on it. The symbol of the sickness was pretty much everywhere. It had begun to merge into the background noise. Like billboards on the freeway.

He opened the rear door. A wave of stink billowed out. Rotten, stifling air that made them both gag. Dim light from the window on the front face filtered down the long hall. He led them in and then tried the door to the stairs. It opened half an inch and then clanged to a stop. Looking through the sliver, he saw something barring it shut. He tried to get his fingers through the crack but there wasn't enough room.

"There's another stairwell at the other end of the building," he said quietly. He held a finger to his lips and then motioned for her to follow.

They tiptoed down the hallway, doing their best to step over the bottles and cans and trash that littered the floor. Why did people have to throw their junk everywhere the minute things went south? Did they all do it? Or did just a few do it but enough for everyone?

Whoever did it, it covered the threadbare carpet like an extra layer. And it reeked. Stank so bad their eyes watered.

Thinking more about the disgusting taste in his mouth and less about where he was going, Elio planted his foot on a soda can. It crunched flat. The sound echoed up and down the corridor. He froze, waiting for the consequence.

A door ahead creaked open.

Elio pulled Theresa into the slightly recessed space of someone's front door. He flattened into the door as much as he could.

Further down the hall, stubborn hinges whined in protest.

A barrel appeared. Black, long, cylindrical.

A shotgun.

No. He'd come too far to get killed now. Could life be so cruel?

The shotgun extended into the hall and then turned in their direction.

An old lady stepped into the hallway. A black hairnet covered large, bright purple rollers. A cigarette dangled from her lips like she'd forgotten it was there. She turned to him. She wielded a broom in her hands like she was ready to beat the stuffing out of whoever was responsible for the mess.

Ms. Kaminsky. He'd seen her many times in the past but had never stopped to say hello.

"Young man, why are you hiding over there? Did you make this mess?"

The words were more an accusation than a question.

Elio peeled off the door and sucked air to catch his breath. "No ma'am. I didn't do this." He approached her and she raised the broomstick at him.

"I'm not afraid of you." She thwacked the wall.

Elio almost laughed. "Ma'am, you should go back inside and lock the door."

"You think I'm afraid? I heard the ruckus. Even with my hearing aid turned down."

Ruckus?

"It's dangerous out here," he said. "It's safer inside your apartment."

"It's always dangerous these days. Used to be a good place for working families. Not anymore."

"Do you have somewhere you can go?"

"What? And leave my home? I've lived in this apartment for thirty-eight years. I'm too old to move."

He took another step forward.

She waved the broomstick. "That's close enough!"

He didn't think her old bones could do much damage, but he didn't want her to have a heart attack trying.

She adjusted her thick glasses. "Hold on a second. Aren't you Maria Lopez's boy?"

"Yes, ma'am, I am."

"And who is that hiding behind you?"

Elio stepped to the side. Theresa wasn't necessarily hiding. "This is my friend, Theresa West."

"Hello," Theresa said.

"Come over here, the both of you."

They walked over and stopped in front of her.

"Friend, huh? You two weren't getting fresh outside my door, were you?"

Elio looked around at the piles of filth. He couldn't imagine anyone ever feeling fresh in these conditions. "No, ma'am."

"Is he telling the truth, young lady?"

"Yes, ma'am."

"Well, you keep a watchful eye on him. Boys his age have

only one thing on their hormone-addled minds. They may talk up your pretty eyes or sweet smile, but their depravities are aimed much lower."

She pointed the end of the broomstick at Elio's chest.

"They want what's in your bloomers. Trust me. I remember."

Theresa choked and coughed and only partially succeeded in concealing her laughter. "I'll keep that in mind, ma'am."

"Mind that you do." She turned back to Elio. "Haven't seen you around since these shenanigans began. Do you think it's right to abandon your mother in such times?"

"I was injured. I came back as soon as I could. Have you seen her?"

"Not for a week or so now. It wasn't safe to walk out my own front door." She bristled and her old, curved spine strained to straighten. It didn't, and she collapsed back into the pronounced hunch that afflicts the elderly after so many years battling gravity. "Well, I apologize for being such an ungracious host."

Host? Was she the unelected, post-apocalyptic hall host?

"Do you like chocolate chip cookies?"

Elio must not have heard her right. "What?"

"Young man, I am too old to waste time repeating myself."

"Yes," Theresa said from behind him.

She beamed and tapped the broomstick on his chest.

"Splendid. You go check on your mother and I'll bake up a fresh batch of cookies. Come by when you're finished, and I promise you won't be disappointed."

Elio didn't know what to say. So he was polite.

"Thank you, Ms. Kaminsky. We will."

50

They continued down the hall and found the other stairwell door unlocked. They were about to head up when the old lady shouted from down the hall.

"Walnuts or pecans?"

"What?" he asked.

"In the cookies. Which do you prefer?"

"Pecans."

It seemed ridiculous, but if he had a choice, he'd choose pecans any day. Walnuts didn't have much flavor.

"I'll have to see if I have any. I know I had some last week when I baked that pecan pie. But I might've used them all up. Maybe I could go around—"

"No!" Elio shouted. "Walnuts are fine!"

"Well, if you really don't mind. I guess—"

"Thanks," Elio said. "I have to get upstairs to check on my mother."

She waved them on. "Well, why didn't you say so? Get along now. Tell your mother I said hello and I hope she is well."

Elio raced up the stairs doing his best not to slap the

concrete with every step. He didn't want to attract any more attention. The next person to hear them might not be so harmless. He rounded the second, third, and made it to the fourth floor. Breathing hard, he darted out of the stairwell, no longer able to control himself. No longer caring if anyone heard his pounding footsteps. He made it to their apartment, number 407, and tried jamming his key into the keyhole. His shaking hands kept missing.

Theresa came to his side and wrapped her hands around his and calmly guided them forward. The lock clicked and he threw open the door. "Mom! It's me, Elio! I'm home!"

He rushed through their tiny living room. The futon couch that also served as his bed at night was in the upright position. He glanced at the kitchen to the left and there wasn't enough room to miss her. He ran into her bedroom and then into the single bathroom.

That's all there was. It wasn't like you could miss another person in less than five hundred square feet of space.

Elio sat on her bed as his shoulders crumpled forward. "She's not here. I should've come sooner." A hollow ache in his chest reminded him of the place where his heart had once lived.

"Maybe she left a note or something to tell you where she went."

Hope sparked in his chest once again. Maybe she wasn't gone forever. That single candle of burning possibility was everything. But he hesitated getting up from the bed to go check. Because what if there was no note? What if she really was gone forever?

He wanted to stay seated forever so that the possibility of seeing her again couldn't be extinguished.

As he set there paralyzed with hope and fear, a scream from outside the window jolted him to his feet.

"Help! Help me! Help!"

He jumped to the window and looked out at the street four floors below.

Halfway down the block, an overweight man wearing only one sneaker fled down the middle of the street. A short sleeve button up shirt clung to his shoulders and trailed out behind as he ran. The grubby white wifebeater stretched around his belly flopped up and down with the rhythmic motion of his legs pumping on the pavement.

"Help me!" he screamed as he ran.

Behind him, several deltas pursued. All men. They shouted meaningless gibberish, only the sounds didn't need to form words for the communication to be clear.

Theresa joined him by the window, and they watched in grim horror.

The deltas caught the doomed man less than twenty yards from Elio's apartment building. They pulled him down and attacked without hesitation. One bit into his neck and tore out a chunk of flesh. Blood spurted out and arced over splashing little puddles on the pavement.

"No! No!"

Another bite and the man's struggling limbs went limp. His resistance weakened as the deltas began to devour him. They each took their share of the prize with a quiet cooperation that was unsettling.

Elio turned away and pulled Theresa with him as the beasts began to tear the body apart.

They hunted, killed, and ate human beings.

Elio realized they weren't zombies like you always read about. They weren't one giant, homogenous mass of flesh-eating idiots. They were smarter than that. The incident on the highway yesterday meant they had tribes or groups that stuck together and were willing to battle outsiders for resources.

They were like cavemen. Or monkeys or something.

Human, but not quite human.

Elio held his arm around Theresa's shoulder as he walked them both back into the living room. "We couldn't have done anything for him."

Theresa stared at the floor in silence.

Elio squeezed her in a side hug. "Are you okay?"

She didn't blink. "They eat people."

He didn't know what to say. What could he say?

Yeah, no big deal. Or yeah, that's so messed up.

He didn't know what to think about it himself, and so he had nothing to offer for support. He was grateful to have his attention drawn away as he spotted a piece of paper on the kitchen counter with a can of his favorite soup, chunky clam chowder, anchoring it down. He picked it up.

"Theresa! Look!" He flapped the sheet of paper wildly in the air. "Come on!"

Theresa stared at him blankly, still overwhelmed at what they'd just seen.

Elio grabbed her hand and dragged her toward the door. "The note says my mom is on the third floor at Ms. Garcia's!"

Hope once again flared in his chest. He raced down the hall dragging Theresa along. He took the stairs two at a time and got to Ms. Garcia's door in record time. He pounded on it yelling for his mother, utterly oblivious to the danger so much noise created.

"Mama! It's me! Open the door!"

The door swung open and there she was. Looking skinnier and dirtier than he'd ever seen. But she was alive!

"Mijo," she said as he collapsed into her open arms.

51

When Elio finally stopped crying, his mother's shirt was as soaked as his own. Part of him had never believed he would see her again. That the odds were too long and his hope a childish rejection of cold reality. Like closing his eyes would make the bad things disappear.

But she was alive!

She kissed his forehead and then turned away as another coughing spell quaked through her small frame. After it subsided, she drew the handkerchief away from her mouth. Bright red speckles dotted the white cloth.

He listened and finally tuned in to the rattling sound her lungs made as she breathed in and out. "Are you sick?"

Maria shook her head and smiled as if his concern for her was foolish. "I'll be fine, Mijo. Don't you worry about me."

Ms. Garcia brought a plate of saltines and hard cheese from the kitchen. "You are sick, Maria Lopez. Don't try to play your boy the fool."

Maria raised her eyebrow at their neighbor. "I don't recall asking your opinion on the matter, Isabella."

Ms. Garcia placed the tray on the small coffee table in front of them and wagged a finger at his mother. "Good friends don't require permission to speak the truth."

Elio clasped his mother's hands in his. "Mama, you have to come back with us. Theresa's family has a secure house and plenty of food and water. They're even getting medicine."

His mother's lips pursed together and curled into a grimace. Elio was well aware of her resentment towards Mason and the blame she laid at his feet for not bringing his father home from the war in Iraq. But she didn't know the whole story. Not the truth that Mason had spoken while he thought Elio was sleeping.

Did Mason kill his father? Yes. But did that make him a murderer? His heart told him no. He'd never personally been in a war, but he was old enough to realize that mistakes could happen when death lurked around every corner.

Elio hadn't tried to discuss it with Mason since the night of the revelation. He wasn't sure he ever wanted to discuss it again. And yet, he knew that someday they would. And maybe that someday would be a chance at healing for them both.

As ill-defined as his own feelings were, he knew without a doubt how his mother would take it. It would only confirm the grudge she'd nursed for so long. And it would only make it worse.

"You have to come with us, mama. It's the only chance we have."

His mother shook her head. "No, I can't go. I can't leave Ms. Garcia alone."

"She can come too," Elio said, without knowing how all of them would get back on the bike or whether inviting another person was a decision he could make on his own. It didn't matter. He'd say whatever he had to say to get his mother to a safer place.

Ms. Garcia folded her arms over her ample chest and shook her head. "I will be going nowhere. This has been my home for many years, and it will be my home to the day that I die."

"Isabella," his mom said, "you can't stay here alone."

Ms. Garcia looked at her like she was crazy. "If I remember correctly, it was I who knocked on your door bringing frijoles and tea. I've got quite enough stored up to outlast this little spell of confusion."

"Mama," Elio said, "you need medicine and Theresa's mother has it."

Theresa nodded. "It's true. My mom is the chief veterinarian at the Los Angeles zoo. Or at least she was. She brought home enough medicine for any of us that need it."

"I'll pack you some food for the trip," Ms. Garcia said.

Maria stood up and swayed a little bit until she rested her hand on Elio's shoulder for support.

Ms. Garcia wagged a finger in her direction. "Don't make me kick you out of my home. I would prefer we part on good terms." With that, she turned back into the kitchen as if the matter was settled.

Maria stared into the air and then nodded. "Okay. I'll go. Let me gather up a few things."

A few things.

It wasn't a figure of speech. His mother had always spent every extra dime on him. His needs came first and even his wants when there were enough dimes to cover them. But for herself, there was never more than a little.

As Elio had grown older, he'd noticed the disparity more and more and he burned with guilt that she'd sacrificed so much for him while he'd always demanded more.

He would change that. He didn't know how exactly, but he would. It was a promise he'd made to himself and one he meant to keep.

Ten minutes later, the three stood at the open door and each exchanged a warm hug with Ms. Garcia. His mother trembled as she thanked the older woman for everything. Her fingers shook as they pulled away and they all said goodbye.

As dangerous as the outside world could be, Elio longed to get back on the road. The sun was climbing into the sky and more than anything Elio didn't want to spend another night outside.

He considered dropping by Ms. Kaminsky's to see if she really did make cookies. The thought of a freshly baked cookie, even one with walnuts, made his mouth water. But in the end, he decided that if they did get made, the elderly woman needed them more than he did.

He guided his mother down the stairs and stopped at the back door to the building.

"Wait here," he whispered. He turned and eased the door open, peeking through the widening crack for any sign of danger. He slowly emerged and looked around.

Nothing to worry about.

He opened the door and helped his mother outside. They crowded onto the cargo bike with Maria sandwiched between them. Theresa thumbed on the battery lever and the bike lumbered forward with noticeably less pace than before. He kept his feet down on both sides letting the pavement skid under the rubber soles of his sneakers while Theresa worked to get the pedals going.

They came to the end of the alley, turned right, and

headed back in the direction from which they'd come. With the help of Theresa's constant pedaling, they picked up speed. Not as fast as before, but decent nonetheless.

Elio tried to judge if they were going fast enough to outpace a pack of deltas.

It didn't feel like it.

52

November 2004
Fallujah, Iraq

MASON rolled to the side and the body tumbled off. The head smacked the floor next to his own. The face of a dying man inches away.

"Remember your promise, Sarge."

David Lopez blew a last breath across Mason's face and his eyes went dim.

Mason swiped at the gunk clouding his left eye. The right eye was swollen shut and useless. His vision cleared somewhat and he stared into the lifeless face inches away from his own. His best friend in the world.

David Lopez.

Everyone called him Lopes because he was the fastest boot in the battalion. Ran like an antelope. Not anymore.

Blood spilled from the corner of Lopes' mouth like a trickle from a faucet. Grime and infected cuts covered his face. His hollow cheeks testament to the toll Operation Al-Fajr had taken on every man in third squad.

Mason knew the nightmarish truth even as he refused to accept it.

He'd shot one of his own men. He'd killed a man he'd sworn to protect.

He'd seen the soul leave the body. The instant the spark snuffed out.

It was in the eyes.

The transition from windows to the soul into glassy orbs that transmitted nothing.

Mason pulled Lopes' forehead to his own. "No! No! No!"

The screams choked out of his lungs. Sound may or may not have accompanied them. The air sirens in his head deafened all else. He rolled to his back and stared at the thick layer of roiling smoke above. It blacked out the ceiling, creeping closer and closer to the floor. Incandescent flames licked up the walls making the scene flicker like a disco party in hell.

CREAK.

KOOSH.

The center section of the ceiling collapsed. Flaming beams hit the floor exploding in bright orange embers and a searing wave of heat. He coughed out the super-heated air, but the soot coating the inside of his mouth remained.

Mason rolled to his side and pulled the lifeless body of his best friend near.

The fire swept closer, licking at his backside.

Let it all come down.

He was ready. He wanted to die. Wherever Lopes was in his journey on the other side, Mason looked forward to not being far behind. He prayed they would find each other, and that he would have a chance to explain. To accept the burden of whatever judgement this tragedy earned him.

Mason deserved the punishment.

He longed for it.

The blurred world went black as he closed his one good eye. He coughed and choked on the toxic air suffocating his lungs. He wondered in a vague way if death by smoke inhalation would be better than being burned alive.

He was about to find out.

"Sarge!"

The name sounded familiar.

"Sarge! You alive?"

The voice sounded familiar too.

Familiar, but unimportant because it belonged to *that* place. The place he no longer wished to be a part of. The place he longed to leave behind. Whoever Sarge was and whoever wanted him didn't matter.

It was all too far away to matter.

A gasp of thick smoke sent a wracking cough echoing through his chest. The pain was a reminder that some part of him remained tethered back there. Hopefully not for long.

"You are! Come on! Don't quit on me, Marine!"

Strong arms lifted him up and threw him over a shoulder. Mason's arms and legs dangled as he was hustled down the collapsing hallway. Higher up, the thicker smoke choked his lungs completely. His body tried to take a breath and then spasmed in agony at the result.

The shrinking rectangle of the hall ahead transformed into a wall of flames as the ceiling came down. The man carrying him leaped over the beams and wreckage. Another few seconds and they burst out of the flaming house and into the open courtyard beyond.

"Corpsman up! Corpsman up!" his rescuer shouted.

He was carried across the courtyard and to the perimeter

wall. Someone laid him on the ground as the doctor kicked into gear.

"Sarge, can you hear me?" the corpsman shouted above the howling of the inferno.

Another face appeared. Miro's.

"Damn, Sarge! Thought we'd lost you!"

Miro had pulled him out of that burning wreck. Mason didn't know whether to thank or condemn him.

Condemnation rang with greater truth. He'd been so close to escape. So close to surrender. To the darkness that promised an end.

Water washed over his face and into his eyes. Into the eye that wasn't swollen completely shut, at least.

The first stars glittered in the darkening sky. Incandescent yellow and orange flickered off the faces above.

His body dragged him back inside, dragged him away from the promise of release. The anchoring brought back sensation. They weren't good ones. His throat burned like he'd swallowed white-hot coals. He sucked in a breath and vomited.

"Sergeant West and several others need immediate evac," the corpsman said.

"Lucky, call in evac at extraction point Charlie one-four," Miro said.

"Copy that," Lucky said.

"Doc," Miro said, "we can't stay here. This inferno is going to draw the muj like moths to a flame."

"He's beat up pretty bad, but he'll make it. Help me get him up."

The two soldiers pulled Mason to his feet. The agony of standing made clear that no part of his body agreed with the medic's assessment. He took shallow breaths because anything more than a sip felt like a knife plunged into his chest. Burned lungs maybe. Probably a broken rib. His right foot was numb, which was probably a good thing because the shredded heel of his boot leaked blood out onto the dirt.

Miro wrapped an arm under his and took the majority of Mason's weight on his six-foot-six frame. "Sarge, you look like a cow's cornhole."

With his left eye relatively clear of blood, soot, and smoke, Mason started to take in the aftermath of the encounter. The house was in full flame mode. Even across the courtyard against the perimeter wall, the heat was almost unbearable. A part of the roof collapsed and an immense whoosh sent out a searing blast of heat.

Lopes was in there.

His skin blackening and cammies burning.

On autopilot, Mason took a step toward the collapsing house, but Miro held him back. "We can't get to him, Sarge. Not through that and not in our current condition."

Mason looked around. Third squad was in bad shape. Nearly every surviving soldier required some kind of medical attention. Miro winced as he touched a gaping gash running across his forehead. He wiped at the blood trickling down into his eyes.

Slowly, the crushing weight of responsibility resumed its position on his shoulders. These were his men. They needed his leadership now more than ever. Now was not the time to quit. To surrender to selfish anguish.

Mason nodded. He took a huge gulp of offered water and sputtered and coughed as the icy liquid washed down his burning throat. He took another gulp and it went down like gravel.

"Doc, go help the others. Lucky, you're on point. Miro, I'm going to need help walking."

Doc and Lucky nodded and set to their tasks. Mason looked up at the column of black smoke drifting ever higher into the sky. They had to get moving. The smoke would be a giant beacon for the enemy. They were surely already on the way to investigate, and he didn't want his banged up squad to be around when they arrived.

"Marines!" Mason shouted as loud as his voice allowed. "Let's form up and move out!"

53

The extraction point was less than three blocks away—an intersection on a main road wide enough for the Humvees to maneuver. Many of the smaller streets and alleys simply didn't have sufficient width for the oversized vehicles. Three blocks shouldn't have been too much of a hump.

But what should be and what is rarely come together in war.

Mason limped along with Miro at his side practically carrying him. They had all lost a lot of weight since that first assault on Fallujah. At least twenty-five pounds had melted off Mason's six foot frame. But the fifty pounds of full battle rattle combined with his gaunt form made him a heavy load nonetheless.

"Sarge," Miro said, "you're heavier than a pregnant heifer."

"Like your mama," Lucky said as he and another marine continued up the road in a bounding overwatch. Two men advanced while two men provided cover for possible contact.

They hadn't encountered anything since leaving the

burning house, but they were under no illusion that they were safe. Every building could hold a sniper in the dark depths of the blown out windows. Every structure could have a muj machine gun waiting around the corner. Every inch of the road itself could have a buried IED waiting to be detonated.

No. They were anything but safe. And they were in no condition to engage the enemy. With their bodies beat up and their ammo depleted, running into a sustained firefight was not something they needed right now. Besides, they had to get the computers back to the CP for analysis. One of the men had managed to snatch them from the house before it became a death trap. Who knew how valuable the intel might be? How many lives it might save?

Mason didn't know, but he did know there were some lives it couldn't save. He hoped the intel was worth something considering the sacrifice to get it.

Still, Mason wished his men had grabbed some ammo along with the heavy and immediately worthless machines. Because the possibility of useful intel wouldn't matter if they couldn't survive long enough to deliver it.

Up ahead, Lucky approached an intersection. He hugged the wall of a building on the corner as he scooted forward. He peeked around the corner and then dropped back into cover. He and another marine ran across the open space to cover across the intersection.

Crossing big open spaces like that was nervy business. There were just too many things that could go wrong during the interval of exposure.

Another pair of marines made it across. The squad proceeded in twos to cover the deadly ground. They'd all made it across without incident when Miro and Mason pulled up to make their crossing. With two more marines guarding their six, it was just the four of them left. If their luck held for another couple of minutes, they'd have one block left to cover to get to the extraction point.

It was dangerous to start feeling lucky. For everyone but Private Benjamin Hicks, the minute you started feeling lucky usually coincided with the minute the bottom fell out.

Not that Mason felt lucky in the least. He'd just accidentally killed a fellow marine. His best friend. He'd thrown up thick walls around that horror show. Compartmentalized the hell out of it because to crack the lid on that would invite utter ruin to him and his remaining men.

They needed a leader right now. Not a raving lunatic.

He knew he didn't deserve their trust, but what else could he do? Squad morale tiptoed on a razor edge. He could see in their faces how tightly wound each man was. They needed rest. Hot chow, a hot shower, and a few hours of uninterrupted sleep to strengthen their precarious hold on sanity.

And as worthless a leader as he was, Mason wasn't going to fail them if he could help it.

"Sarge?" Miro said. "You ready?"

Mason looked up at the taller man. His normally prominent cheekbones looked absolutely skeletal with the weight loss and the coating of white dust that clung to his skin.

"Admiring my handsome mug again?" Miro said with a smirk.

"Admiring how much it resembles a donkey's butt."

"So you have a thing for donkey butts, huh?"

Mason wanted to laugh but the sensation didn't make it out of his chest. There was too much weight to allow the levity to bleed through.

"Stop trying to flirt with me," Mason said, "and get us to the other side."

"Hee-haw hee-haw," Miro said with a grin.

They took two steps into the intersection when the keening whistle of incoming indirect fire stopped them cold.

"Get back!" Mason shouted.

They stumbled back out of the intersection.

The unique pitch of danger close incoming fire ended with an explosion that knocked them off their feet. The explosion was the first of many. Steel rain came down hard and fast.

Mason crawled into cover behind a nearby burned out vehicle. Miro joined him a moment later. They crouched behind the charred metal as more artillery fire plastered the intersection. The muj had clearly sighted the space and had been waiting to unload on it.

The air filled with dust and smoke. They couldn't see across to the rest of third squad through the wall of billowing particulate matter.

CRACK. CRACK. CRACK.

Gunfire erupted behind them. M16s banging away.

Mason glanced back and saw his two men on rear guard behind cover and firing at several tangos that had arrived further back down the street. One went down as his men hit their mark.

An enemy round snapped by Mason's face and punched a hole in the metal next to his head. Sparks showered onto his ear singeing the skin. He dove away to the ground.

Miro grabbed his vest and dragged him into a nearby alley.

"Help me up!" Mason shouted. He hobbled to the corner and looked out at the two marines pinned down by enemy fire. RPGs whistled down the street impacting around their position. They weren't going to last long out there. More mujahideen flooded into the street beyond. A few of the more doped up ones stood in the middle of the street like they were impervious to bullets.

One collapsed in a heap. But the objective proof didn't seem to deter the others because several more took his place.

"Get fire on those assholes!"

Miro leaned out around him and went cyclic with his M16.

Mason screamed for his men to retreat but his voice was smothered by the report of small arms fire and exploding RPGs. He sighted the M203 grenade launcher attached to his rifle and launched a grenade.

It exploded in a building facing right of their position.

He was about to adjust aim when he noticed a mortar team setup behind the enemy lines. A moment later a round exploded between their position in the alley and the two marines pinned down in the street.

They glanced back and Mason waved frantically for them to get back to safety. He and Miro laid on the suppressive fire as the men scrambled into a crouched run. They made it halfway when another mortar round whistled in and impacted in the middle of the street. The explosion killed both marines instantly.

The muj further down the street cheered wildly and broke into a run. All their firepower now directed to the corner of the alley. Bits of concrete blasted off the walls nearby as the enemy drew near.

"Sarge!" Miro shouted, "We've gotta beat feet!"

And leave the bodies of marines behind? Where the muj could recover them?

Never.

Miro pulled him deeper into the alley. "Us dying ain't gonna help those two!"

Mason felt madness clawing at his brain. The unreasoning fury that could make a man strap a bomb to his chest and blow himself up if it meant he could take out a few of the enemy too.

In that sickening second, he understood the other side like never before. And he didn't like the newfound knowledge.

He wrapped his arm over Miro's shoulder. "Let's go."

54

The Present Day
Venice, California

MASON ended another transmission and squeezed the handheld radio so hard the tendons in his fingers creaked. While he was grateful it didn't crumple into a useless hunk of plastic, crushing it to bits would've been so satisfying. And besides, the worthless thing wasn't making any difference. It was one-way communication. That wasn't even communication. That was broadcasting.

And broadcasting wasn't doing a thing.

"That's it," he said to Beth at his side. "I'm finished waiting."

Beth squeezed his arm as if that might offer some measure of reassurance. It was a thoughtful gesture, but it achieved no more than the radio.

"Honey," she said, "I know—"

"Stop. We've been through this and I get it. There are hundreds of ways they could've taken and we don't even know for sure where they were headed. But I'm not sitting around here wasting more time droning on when we don't even know they're receiving the transmissions."

Beth stared into his eyes and nodded. "I agree. It's time."

The handheld squawked.

"Mason, this is Juice. Come in."

"Juice, this is Mason. Go ahead."

"I'm picking up a weak signal on the walkie-talkie frequency. Give me a minute to dial it in and I'll get it patched over to you. Over."

"Roger that. Over."

Mason's heart jumped into his throat. Could it be them? Or was it another set of walkie-talkies using the same frequency? It was a generic set of walkie-talkies. Something anyone could've bought and received two days later.

It wasn't unthinkable that someone else in a city of millions was using the same model. Still, it was the first ray of hope he'd felt since discovering Theresa and Elio had left last night.

The key, he found, was to put a lid on your expectations. It was too easy to allow your spirits to soar at the possibility. And he knew all too well that flying so high could result in a spectacular crash if things didn't turn out like he hoped. It was how the mind worked. Sanity and stability required him to keep his hopes firmly tethered to the ground.

"... about a mile away."

It was Elio!

"We should be home soon. Say something if you heard this."

Mason mashed the transmit button and spoke in even words as his body spiked with joy and fury in equal measures. "Elio, this is Mason. We received your message. Is everyone okay? Over."

"Daddy!"

Beth squeezed Mason and burst into tears. "Thank God, she's safe."

Mason winced at the pressure constricting his ribs.

"Theresa, baby! Are you okay?"

"Yes, we're," she began and then her voice faded out.

"Theresa, hold it closer."

"Sorry," she replied, coming through clear again. "I'm a little out of breath. We're fine. Maria is with us. We're about a mile away. We'll be home soon."

There was zero chance Mason was going to sit on his hands waiting for them to cross that last span of distance. Not when any terrible thing under the glaring sun could happen.

"Theresa, give me the road you're on and what intersection is ahead."

"We're on Lincoln coming up to Sepulveda."

Mason jumped up and grabbed the keys to the Bronco.

"Theresa, did you see that?" It was Elio again.

"What?"

"Go! Go faster! There are deltas coming out! Go right—"

The walkie-talkie crackled and then cut out.

No. Please no.

"Mason, this is Juice. Something's going on upstairs. The relay will stay open, but I'll be away from comms for a minute. Over."

A familiar rhythmic thump echoed faintly from the handheld. Mason recognized it immediately. Just like the chopper that had dropped the assault team on his house.

A loud explosion crackled and sounded like the little speaker had blown.

SHUCK-SHUCK.

"Mason, I've got company here."

"Get out of there, Juice!"

"I'm not going anywhere. It's a—"

A series of explosions drowned out his voice. Then the report of the shotgun firing.

BOOM.

BOOM. BOOM.

Mason watched the breach play out in his head. The assault team dropping flashbangs down into the secret basement. Juice firing the shotgun as targets exposed themselves coming down.

CRACK. CRACK.

CRACK.

CRACK. CRACK.

The report of the assault team's MP7s as they attempted to suppress the target.

"Come and get some!"

BOOM.

BOOM.

CRACK. CRACK. CRACK.

A new voice spoke. One Mason didn't recognize.

"Tango down. Room clear." The tone was cool and collected. Mason recognized a professional when he heard one. "Sir? Sir, you should get back upstairs. The other rooms are not secure."

"Shut up," another voice screamed. "Where is my daughter? Find her! And I want the Bili chimpanzee! Find them both!"

Someone screamed. A female.

"Sir, we found this woman in the bedroom. Looks like a delta."

"Give me your pistol!"

"Sir?"

"Give it to me!"

Another scream, female again. Linda.

"Where is my daughter? Where is the chimp?" the voice shouted.

"Sir, she can't understand you."

"Shut up! You're a hired gun, nothing more!"

Linda moaned and wailed.

"Tell me where!"

CRACK.

Jesus. What happened?

CRACK. CRACK. CRACK.

"Sir, she's dead."

"Tell me something I don't know! Like where my daughter is! Where the chimpanzee is!"

Another operator continued, "Sir, this floor is clear. No sign of Iridia."

Iridia? What did she have to do with this?

"Then where is she? You said the transmissions came from this location."

"Sir, over here. A comms station. Looks like this was set up as a relay."

"A relay from where?" the voice screamed almost incoherently.

The voice. Anton Reshenko. Iridia's father.

"Sir, what should we do with the bodies?"

"Why would I care? Get us back to Milagro Tower! Now!"

"Yes, sir. Alpha Team, let's go!"

The voices faded as they moved away from the open mic.

Mason sat down hard in a chair. He pinched his eyes shut and squeezed his temples attempting to subdue the pounding in his head.

Juice and Linda were gone.

And it was his fault for getting them involved.

All of this because of Iridia and her insane father. He knew he never should've accepted the job. He wouldn't have if anybody but Miro had asked. And even then only because of the debt he owed. When someone risks their own life to save yours, can that ever be repaid?

Even more, when someone knowingly throws themselves into a situation that isn't just a risk but is a living hell where their own death is virtually guaranteed, and then somehow manages to pull both of you out of the fire, how can that scale ever be balanced?

It couldn't.

But that didn't mean that Juice and Linda deserved to be pulled into that unequal equation. And worse, that they paid for it with their lives.

Mason's teeth squeaked as his jaws ground together. A fire burned in his chest. A fury that demanded one thing and one thing only.

Justice.

Revenge. Whatever the word, the result was the same.

The death of Anton Reshenko.

But first, his daughter was in danger. She was the priority.

Mason ran outside and threw the metal gate open. He was about to run to his backyard when movement several blocks down caught his eye.

It was them!

And they were not alone.

55

THERESA pedaled as hard as she could. She turned right onto her street. Three blocks down on the left was Ahmed's house and safety. She flicked the battery accelerator lever all the way right but the bike continued to slow. The charge indicator was a hair above zero. Her thighs and calves burned as she struggled to crank the pedals around and around.

Sweat dripped into her eyes blurring her vision. She swiped at an eye and nearly lost control of the bike. The exertion had her dizzy and lightheaded.

"They're catching up!" Elio yelled.

Theresa glanced back and a jolt of terror spasmed through her body. A dozen or more deltas were a couple hundred feet behind and gaining fast. She gritted her teeth and struggled to get the pedals moving faster, but it was no use. Without the electric assist, she didn't have the strength to move all three of them.

"We're going to have to run for it!" she shouted. "The bike is done."

Maria was in no shape to run anywhere but there was no

other choice. They could coast to a stop as both the battery and her legs gave out, or they could run for it and have a better chance than none at all.

"Now!" Theresa shouted as she slammed on the brakes. They all jumped off and let the bike tumble over. She wrapped one of Maria's arms over her shoulder while Elio did the same on the other side.

"Go!" Elio shouted.

They lumbered forward and managed a stumbling, clumsy movement that turned out little faster than a slow jog.

Theresa glanced back and wished she hadn't. "Faster! Faster!" She tried to run faster but the failing strength in her legs more than balanced the adrenaline urging them onward.

Elio on the other side wasn't doing any better. His healing injuries made it so that he couldn't move much faster than Maria.

The screaming behind grew louder as their pursuers drew closer. Their voices took on an unhinged edge as they realized their prey had no escape. It was only a matter of time.

And that was only a matter of seconds.

"Leave me," Maria said as she wriggled to pull free. "You two go!"

Elio held her tight and struggled to drag her forward. Just a block and a half away. So close.

They'd almost made it.

"I love you, son," Maria said as they all stumbled to a stop. With one of them no longer trying, they had no chance at continuing forward. "Now, run!"

Elio shook his head. "Theresa, go!"

The deltas roared seeing their prey surrender.

"I won't leave you, Elio," Theresa said.

It wasn't just that she didn't want to leave his side. It was also that she couldn't. She had nothing left. Her forehead burned and her head spun. She glanced at the scratch on her wrist. It had gotten worse. Purple and red splotches surrounded the inflamed scratch. White gunk oozed from blistering pustules. Black veins zigzagged up to her elbow.

They turned around and watched in horror as the deltas drew near. Their inhuman eyes burned with excitement.

Theresa glanced at Elio. He faced the deltas with a twisted grimace on his face. He knew it was over, too. They'd come so close to having a future together.

She closed her eyes, and hoped it would be quick. Not like the man that had been eaten alive.

"Get down!" a voice shouted from behind. "Get on the ground!"

Her father!

Theresa tugged the other two to the pavement as the first few deltas crashed into them.

Gunshots split the air.

A huge male pinned Theresa down. His naked chest streaked with the caked blood of previous victims. His eyes blazed with the thrill of the kill. He bared his teeth and lunged for her throat.

His head snapped back as a fountain of red exploded from behind. He landed like a brick on top of her, knocking the wind out of her lungs.

She shoved him off and gasped for breath. She rolled and looked back down the street toward her house. Her dad sprinted toward them. A pistol in each hand kicked repeatedly as a continuous barrage of gunfire thundered in her ears. Her mother and Ahmed ran along behind.

Theresa curled up tight gasping for breath.

Delta bodies fell around her.

The next thing she knew, her father ran past them into the broken wave of deltas. His right hand now held a fully extended baton. He tore into them breaking limbs and splitting skulls. Blows and bullets rained down on the frenzied horde.

"Get up!" her mother shouted as she hauled Theresa to her feet. Ahmed helped Maria up. Elio pushed himself up and they all scrambled toward safety.

BANG.

BANG. BANG.

BANG.

She glanced over her shoulder and saw her father holding off the attackers as he retreated. He held his own, but barely. Their numbers threatened to overwhelm him again and again.

Further down the street, another pack of deltas were running in their direction. This one larger, two dozen maybe. Too many definitely. A hunting party drawn to the sounds of struggle.

Elio's foot landed wrong and he crashed to the ground.

"Elio!" Maria shouted as Ahmed continued dragging her along.

A female delta broke off from those attacking Mason and darted at Elio. She landed on his legs and bit at them.

Mason swung the baton at the nearest delta hitting it in the temple, knocking it out cold. He raised the pistol in his left hand.

BANG.

The female attacking Elio collapsed as blood geysered from her neck splattering onto the pavement.

Mason dragged Elio up and pushed him back before shooting another delta in the face. Yet another got a baton blow to the collarbone crumpling it into a groaning heap of flesh. He slowed the advance while everyone made it to the open gate and shuffled through.

"Get everyone inside!" Beth shouted. She looked at Theresa. "Go!" She turned back and drew a pistol from the holster at her hip. She slipped out the open gate and disappeared.

The front door swung open and Noor stood there with wide eyes. Ahmed hurried Maria and Elio inside.

BANG. BANG. BANG.

Theresa ran for the gate. She couldn't let her mother and father be killed. She wouldn't. She stumbled toward the gate as the ground tilted back and forth.

She got to the gate as her mom jumped through.

"Get inside!" Beth shouted.

Mason wedged through the opening. Clenched hands grabbed at his shirt. Strips tore free as they tried to pull him back toward death. He slammed the baton down again and again but more and more hands grasped for him.

Beth shoved her shoulder into the metal gate and slammed it forward.

Deltas screamed in pain as their limbs crunched between colliding metal.

Mason broke free and slammed the door shut. He threw the lock and then stuttered a step when he saw the horrific infection on Theresa's arm. He wrapped an arm around her shoulder and pulled her toward the front door.

"Come on!"

Mason was the last to enter. He slammed the door shut and locked it.

"Everyone upstairs!" Mason shouted.

Theresa stumbled upstairs and into Noor's room. She

looked out the front window and watched in horror as the first of the deltas pulled himself up to the top of the wall.

BANG.

Theresa's right ear stabbed into her brain.

The delta's head jerked back and he tumbled off the wall.

Her father pushed her back with his left hand while the pistol in his right waited for another target. "Get away from the window!"

She stumbled back into Elio's waiting arms.

"Ahmed! Get to the window in your room! Don't let any of them over the perimeter wall!"

Ahmed sprinted out of the room.

The next several minutes were a blur of yelling and gunshots. Some of the vocalizations were words and many were not. The volume outside grew louder.

"They've breached the wall," Mason shouted over the noise.

Theresa noticed the angle of his pistol aiming much lower now.

Glass shattered downstairs. Fists pounded on the plywood sheets covering the windows.

They were trying to get into the house.

Wood creaked and splintered apart.

"Fall back to the hall bathroom!" Mason shouted. He herded everyone out into the hallway. "Go!"

A groaning wail echoed up the stairway.

The voice wasn't muffled like it would've been coming from the outside.

56

AHMED lined up a shot on the beast that was once a man. The tragic creature sat atop the perimeter wall trying to figure out a way to get down into the courtyard. He had never killed a man, though it had been his primary goal for many years. And now that his wife's murderer was in his grasp, he'd done nothing. Whether the inaction stemmed from fear or reason, the result was the same.

He'd never taken a life.

And so he wondered if he could do so now.

He curled his finger around the trigger of the old Beretta M1951. The pistol's worn condition spoke to an active history spent with its previous owner. He had no illusions. He knew the gun had killed before. Likely many times. Black market weapons in Fallujah all came with histories better left unquestioned.

The gun had undoubtedly killed and it would do so again without remorse.

The delta slipped down hanging from the wall. Its feet dangling above the ground. The thing came for his daughter. Killing it was all that stood between Noor and a grisly demise.

His finger tightened on the trigger. He squinted his eyes desperately trying to keep the front sight lined up on the target. His mind screamed, waiting for the gun to fire while also dreading it.

This was it. The final instant of commitment. A commitment he feared would banish him from the grace of Allah.

Islam forbade murder.

Despite what the cursed radicals of his faith spouted to the uneducated masses. They lied to themselves and worse to others that killing in the name of Allah was righteous.

Ahmed held no such delusion.

To take another's life was wrong.

But what about a human that perhaps was no longer human? And what if this not-quite-human threatened his life? What if it threatened his daughter's life?

He glanced back and saw Noor cowering by the door. The naked fear in her eyes hammered him in the gut.

He turned back to the nightmare outside. His left hand cupped his shaking right. Fighting through the quaking, he re-centered his aim and squeezed the trigger.

A cloud puffed off the exterior wall.

He took a breath and squeezed again. The delta at the other end of the sights dropped to the courtyard as the bullet hit him in the hip.

Ahmed fired again, a little higher this time.

The delta fell to the ground and clutched at the leaking hole in its chest. Red bubbles spilled out onto the ground.

Ahmed fired another bullet to end the being's suffering. It did. He lined up another shot on a woman.

No, not a woman. A beast that threatened his daughter.

His eternal soul be damned.

He would never allow these wretches to claim his daughter. May Allah judge him in the light of this terrible end.

The shaking in his hands steadied as he pulled the trigger. A miss. He fired again and hit the delta in the stomach. It dropped to the ground cradling the red spilling from its belly.

With the decision made, the action came quicker.

BANG.

BANG.

Another delta fell. Ahmed emptied the magazine on another and fumbled to replace it with a full one.

More deltas came over the wall. The courtyard below littered with their dead and dying bodies.

There were too many. Or they were too few.

Ahmed spent another three bullets taking down another delta, but he saw the futility of it.

Glass shattered downstairs. He looked down and saw one battering at the plywood covering the first floor window. Two more beat on the front door. More glass shattered as a few others flowed around the house looking for the easiest way in.

Ahmed's legs went numb as he heard the sound of wood tearing apart.

"Fall back to the hall bathroom," Mason shouted from the other bedroom. "Go!"

Ahmed raced to the door and guided Noor into the hall.

A loud groan made Ahmed jump. It was too loud.

And too clear.

"Baba! I left mama's necklace in the kitchen!"

"Forget it," Ahmed shouted as he grabbed her hand to

pull her to the bathroom at the end of the hall. It was their final defensive position.

"I have to get it!" Noor shouted as she wiggled free of his grasp.

Her small, fragile form slipped down the stairway.

"Noor!" Ahmed shouted. "Noor!"

Someone grabbed his shoulder and spun him roughly around.

In a fog, Ahmed reacted without thinking. He raised the Beretta and fired.

Mason grabbed his wrist and cranked it over as the gun fired. A bullet punched a hole in the ceiling.

Ahmed stared at the man he'd nearly killed.

Mason stared back with cold, hard eyes. The eyes of a killer. The same eyes his wife must've seen before bullets tore through her body.

Ahmed wondered at the cruelty of it all. To be killed by this man. The same devil that had killed his wife. His precious daughter lost to the savages.

What was the point of life when such cruelty prevailed?

"Get everyone into the bathroom!"

Mason shoved Ahmed away and then bounded down the stairs. Roaring fury with a raised pistol in each hand, he looked like the coming of death itself.

Perhaps he was.

57

They hurried to the bathroom and crowded in. Ahmed closed the door so that only his arm with the Beretta extended stuck out. He cursed himself.

Why had he let his wife's murderer run after his daughter?

Why had he not done it himself?

Confusion, rage, and shame bubbled like acid in his stomach.

Mason had saved his daughter from the deranged police officer. Ahmed could not deny that truth. Did perhaps some part of his rational mind understand that only Mason could save her, if anyone could?

Ahmed couldn't recall consciously engaging in that train of thought. Had it been too fast to remember?

Or was the reason much worse?

Was he too cowardly to leap into the jaws of death to save his own daughter, just as he had been too weak to save his wife?

Was his cowardice to doom the two most important people in his life?

He cursed himself silently. He didn't deserve Allah's grace. He deserved an eternity of misery, of punishment, of pain. May Iblis take his soul.

The chattering of the others behind was a distant hum to the volume of the accusations in his heart.

He had tried to be strong. To protect his family from harm. He had failed. Failed in every meaningful way. And so his life was worthless. Worth nothing and so could be spent without regret. If Noor was to die, the decision was easy to follow.

He wondered if throwing himself into the arms of the deltas was spiritually no different than suicide.

He wondered why he even bothered wondering.

Because it didn't matter. Not if Noor was taken.

If that happened, nothing mattered forever more.

Gunfire erupted downstairs and the wailing and screaming intensified.

Ahmed threw the bathroom door open.

She would not die alone!

He ran down the hall screaming at the top of his lungs, "Ana aasifah! Ana aasifah!"

He slammed into a body flying up the stairs. The impact sent the Beretta skittering down the stairs. It no longer mattered. He welcomed death.

"Go! Go! Go!" Mason shouted in his face.

Ahmed blinked hard and realized it wasn't a delta come to claim him.

Mason carried Noor over one shoulder. He spun Ahmed around and shoved him down the hall. Feet thumped the stairs behind them.

They all piled inside and slammed the door shut just as clenching hands arrived.

Mason lowered Noor to her feet. She clutched Nalasif's

necklace tightly in her hand. Though not worth his daughter's life, it was as precious as a material possession could be. The golden Farvahar pendant was a symbol of ancient Iran. The flat, stylized rendering of spread wings and tail feathers with a robed man in the center spoke to Zoroastrian roots and the Persian empire that spread its beliefs. Though born in Iran, his wife had always rejected the modern Islam of her homeland and clung to the deeper traditions that ran in her blood.

Her rejection of his faith had always been an uneasy truce between them.

Though the necklace represented an ancient religion he thought blasphemous, it also carried his wife's blood and ancestry. And for that, it was precious.

Noor burst into tears as Ahmed wrapped her in a suffocating hug. "I'm sorry, Baba. I'm so sorry."

"Innah bikhayr, qalbi. Innah bikhayr."

"Back away from the door!" Mason shouted.

Ahmed stared at him in a haze of confusion and wonder. Mason had saved his daughter a second time. Did such a man deserve to die for a sin committed long ago? Could the present cancel out the past?

He didn't know. He kissed Noor's forehead and wiped away the tears streaming down her cheeks.

They all pressed together toward the opposite end of the bathroom. The little chimp leaned out of Beth's arms and reached for his daughter. Beth let Noor take him. The chimp touched a trail of wetness on her cheek and then put the finger into his mouth. He snuggled up into Noor's neck and her tears turned to a smile as she stroked his back.

The bathroom was not large. Not large for the number of people packed inside. Mason's family. Elio and his mother. Iridia holding Mr. Piddles. Himself and Noor.

Mr. Piddles yowled nervously in Iridia's arms. She held him close, whispering assurances in his ear. She stepped into the shower and helped Maria in after her. Elio and Theresa pulled tight together. Beth backed up with all of them behind. Ahmed guided Noor to Beth who helped her into the shower.

Mason stood at the front, only a couple of feet from the door as it shuddered and shook from the impacts on the other side. He held two pistols forward waiting for the first brute to break through.

Ahmed had thought nailing a second bedroom door to the inside of the bathroom door had seemed silly. He didn't think so now.

The pounding outside shook the walls. Dust billowed out of cracks forming around the door frame.

Mason handed him one of the pistols. "Take it. Make every shot count. I've got one extra magazine for you."

Ahmed accepted the weapon and lined it up on the door. He was stupid to have lost the Beretta, but he would give a good account of himself before the darkness claimed him.

He stepped forward to join Mason. Their shoulders touched and Mason glanced at him for an instant.

Wood splintered as the first door started to give way.

"Beth! Don't let them take the kids!" Mason shouted.

Beth drew her pistol and turned toward those behind her. "I won't."

Mason looked at Ahmed with eyes that could've cut throats. His jaw hard and unyielding. The smallest nod of his head said it all.

Ahmed returned the acknowledgement.

There was no escape.

They would die.

They both knew it.

But they would not die quietly. And they would not allow these fiends to take their children.

Ahmed said a silent prayer. He didn't know how Allah could judge the righteousness of their actions in such a situation. He did know one thing.

He wouldn't have to wait long to find out.

58

MASON's heart thudded in his ears. The pounding in his chest was like a beast trying to break out of a bony cage. The surge of adrenaline threatened to swamp his reason. He took a deep breath and held it, fighting to maintain his reason. To hold on to the steady voice in his head rather than succumb to the chemical madness urging him to survive.

The screaming and yelling outside the bathroom door projected a physical tension. Their madness broke like towering waves on his drowning resolve.

A thunderous crash sounded and the door shook. Another crash and the interior door, the last layer of defense, splintered in the center.

Mason aimed the Glock at the crack. It would soon give way and whatever appeared in its place was going to eat a few hollow points.

Ahmed shouted something but it didn't register. He bumped Mason's shoulder.

"What?"

"Did you hear that?"

With his eyes still focused on the growing fissure in the door, Mason broadened his awareness. He heard it.

Another thunderous impact and the crack tore open with a fist smashing through it. The fist pulled back and then an eyeball appeared. It glared at them with hungry intent.

BANG. BANG.

Two rounds punctured the eyeball sending the body thudding to the floor. The remaining deltas screamed in rage. Numerous hands grabbed the edges of the splintered hole and yanked it open wider.

BANG. BANG.

BANG. BANG.

Mason fired into the hole knowing he was doing heavy damage, and also knowing it wouldn't be enough. He counted off rounds and replaced a spent magazine before the last one cleared the chamber.

At his shoulder, Ahmed banged away until the slide locked back. Mason grabbed the spent pistol and gave Ahmed his replenished one. He slammed in another magazine and got back in the fight.

The slide locked back on Ahmed's pistol. Eight rounds later, Mason's did as well. He dropped the Glock and whipped out his folding knife and expandable baton. The center panel of the door was almost completely ripped out. The only reason they weren't getting through was that a large delta had been halfway through when Mason had put a bullet in his brain. Grimy hands and ragged fingernails ripped through the man's flesh trying to yank him back and out of the way.

The delta's body broke loose and disappeared beyond the door. A delta with a matted beard of dirt and blood jumped through the opening reaching for Mason. His outstretched hand came within a few inches before the whistle of the baton shattered the bones in his wrist. He screamed and Mason thrust the baton forward, shoving him back into the chaos of bodies behind. Another leaped through before Mason could raise the baton. The momentum slammed them both into the bathroom wall.

Mason shoved the knife up into its belly and twisted. The attacker crumpled to the tile floor as yet another took its place. Ahmed wrestled with another that hadn't yet gotten all the way through.

"Beth! Do it now!" His own voice sounded far away, buried beneath the keening whine in his ears.

Beth pointed her pistol at Theresa. Tears raced down her cheeks even as her hand held steady. "I'm so sorry, baby." She shook her head. "So sorry."

Theresa cowered away in the corner of the shower. Elio stepped in front of her. "Don't do it!" he shouted.

BOOM.

A massive concussion outside blew the door off its hinges. It knocked Mason and Ahmed down like blades of grass in a hurricane. Smoke and particulate matter swirled in the air.

Mason lay on the floor trying to catch his breath. He wiped debris out of his eyes. Through the hazy blur, he saw deltas falling left and right. The hallway flashed with gunfire, but all he could hear was the high-pitched whining. He touched his ear and felt the warm slick blood before he saw it.

A blur of fur swept by as Mr. Piddles streaked out into the hallway.

The last of the deltas fell and the blinding flashes in the hallway subsided. A large figure in black tactical gear appeared in the doorway. A black mask and goggles hid his face.

Mason tried to rise.

"Stay down!" the operator yelled as he pointed a submachine gun at his chest.

59

Mason slumped to the floor looking for his weapons as he did so. The knife wasn't in view. It was likely buried under one of the delta bodies wedged in around them. He looked back and saw everyone on the floor, inside the shower and out, slowly recovering from the grenade blast.

The operator looked back down the doorway. "Clear!"

Another man appeared in the doorway. A thick fur-like sideburn clung to one of his cheeks. The other cheek had a patch of raw, red skin where a sideburn used to be. A substantial paunch hung over the belt line of his pants.

The operator grabbed the man's shoulder. "Sir, we need to restrain these people first."

The man flung off the restraining hand. "Iridia! My darling daughter!" He clumsily stepped through the bodies on the floor and grabbed Iridia's hand.

"Daddy!" Iridia said as she held to the side and hugged him.

So this was Anton Reshenko. The man that had unleashed an assault team on his home. The man that had killed Juice and Linda.

He was going to pay.

"You must come with me, dear," Anton said. He passed her into the protective arms of the man in black. "Let nothing happen to her!"

He turned and spotted Clyde in Noor's arms. His eyes lit up spotlights. "Give me the chimp!"

Noor cowered in the corner and turned to shield Clyde.

Anton lurched over and yanked the little chimp out of Noor's arms. He held it by the arm like a dirty rag. Clyde howled and cried trying to reach Noor.

Beth screamed. "No! Don't take him!" She lunged for Clyde but tripped over one of the bodies on the floor.

Anton stepped around her and passed it to an operator waiting at the door. "Secure the primate!"

"Yes, sir," the man nodded and disappeared down the hall.

Beth screamed and struggled to rise. She was going to try something stupid.

Not before he did, though.

Mason spotted the baton partially buried in bits of wood. He slowly reached for it, wrapping his fingers around the handle.

Anton turned to him. "I am Dr. Anton Reshenko. You are Mr. West, I presume?"

Mason wasn't in a chatty mood. He swung the baton up at the forearm of the operator. The end of the metal shaft connected with a satisfying crunch. He scrambled to his feet and drove a shoulder into the injured man's sternum and drove him backwards out into the hall.

He raised the baton and chopped down at Anton's head but stumbled mid-swing. The angle changed and caught him on the shoulder. Anton crumpled to the ground like his bones had turned to jelly. The baton rose for the death blow.

SHUCK-SHUCK.

"Drop it!" Another operator appeared at the door pointing a Mossberg 500 at Mason's chest.

A baton versus a shotgun might've been a fair fight under the right circumstances. But the operator had the drop on him. It would punch a hole in his chest before the baton moved an inch.

"Okay," Mason said as he opened his fingers and let the baton fall to the floor.

"Step back!" the operator yelled.

Mason did as ordered while also scanning the room for an opportunity to turn the tables. Nothing came to mind. There just weren't a lot of options when a professional had a shotgun pointed at you.

The operator helped Anton to his feet and pulled him into the hallway.

Anton cradled his left arm in his right. He groaned and cursed. He stared at Mason with murderous eyes. "Take them with us. All of them. Except that one."

Another operator appeared and dragged Ahmed into the hall. He returned and grabbed Beth. "Let's go!" He dragged Beth out of the shower and passed her to another operator standing in the hallway.

"No!" she shouted and struggled to break free of an unyielding grip. "Don't leave him!"

They were *not* going to take his family. Mason lunged for the rifle hanging from the man's chest when the butt of another rifle smashed into his cheek.

The impact torqued his head to the side and dropped him to the floor in a heap.

The muzzle of the rifle pointed at his forehead as a black boot doubled him up with a kick to the stomach.

"Don't kill him!" Anton yelled from the hallway.

The operator pressed the muzzle hard into Mason's forehead. It felt like the man was trying to dig a hole through his skull with a blunt stick.

"Why not?"

"Let the deltas find him," Anton replied.

A voice echoed in from the hallway. "Sir, we've got incoming contact outside. We need to get moving."

"Get everyone on the chopper!" Anton shouted. He looked at Mason as he rubbed his injured shoulder. He grinned wickedly. "I might've thanked you for keeping my daughter safe, Mr. West."

The operator flipped around the rifle pinned to his head and then slammed the butt into his face.

The world winked out.

60

ELIO grunted as one of the soldiers in black shoved him into a seat. The same man pushed Maria down next to him.

"Buckle up!" the soldier shouted to be heard above the roar of the helicopter's spinning blades.

Elio clicked his lap belt and helped his mother with hers. He wrapped his arm around her and pulled her close. She said something but he couldn't make out the words.

CRACK. CRACK.

The gunshots punched through the blanket of sound buffeting the cabin. Two soldiers sat on the lip of the doorway with their feet braced on the skids below. They picked off the faster deltas that broke free from a pack approaching from down the street.

CRACK.

"We need to get this bird in the sky!" one of the soldiers shouted as he pulled Ahmed into the cabin and shoved him toward a seat. They were all inside. All except Mason.

Elio stared at the group of hunters closing in. They would find Mason sooner or later. And there was nothing any of them could do to change that.

"Hold tight!" the pilot shouted.

The whine of the engine increased. The helicopter lurched to the side as it broke contact with the street and jumped up into the air. Elio gasped as the lap belt dug into his waist. One of the soldiers on the skids lost his balance and tumbled forward. He fell ten feet and smacked into the pavement.

CRACK.

A bullet punched through the metal skin of the helicopter. Elio couldn't tell where it ended up.

The man howled in pain as the first delta reached him. The others piled on.

"Leave him!" Anton shouted.

"But, sir. He's got no chance on his own."

"Then he shouldn't have fallen out. Take us up!"

"Yes, sir," the pilot said.

The helicopter lifted into the air and the screams of the dying man quickly faded away. A soldier slammed the door shut and then dropped into an empty seat.

Elio's stomach rolled over as the chopper clawed for altitude. It slid sideways through the air in a sickening way that reminded him that he never wanted to ride a helicopter again. He turned to Theresa and saw the tears in her eyes. He touched her forehead. The skin burned his fingertips. The fever was getting worse.

Beth sat on the opposite side of Theresa. Their eyes met as his hand drew away. The hollow look in her eyes told him she knew what was happening. Theresa was infected and there were only two possible outcomes.

Bleeding to death as her body broke down, or worse, changing into a delta.

She held Theresa tight and looked away, staring blankly at nothing in particular. He recognized the emptiness in her eyes because he'd seen it many times in his own mother's. As much as Elio wanted to fight his way free to help Theresa and rescue Mason, he wasn't stupid enough to believe it would do any good. He wasn't a scientist or a soldier. He was a kid.

And he wasn't even that great at that job either.

Iridia sat at the front of the cabin with her father. Anton was his name. The man definitely wasn't what he'd pictured for a super smart scientist guy. He looked more like Elvis past his prime. A used car salesman with a splash of crazy.

Anton glanced at Elio and his eyes narrowed as he studied him.

Elio squirmed in the seat and wanted to look away. Anton regarded him with a cold calculating gaze. As if Elio were bacteria mashed between two glass plates and being studied under a microscope.

No. As unimpressive as Anton appeared on the outside, Elio could tell he was a dangerous man.

His eyes watered and yet they could not blink. Anton's gaze hypnotized and dissected him.

Iridia pulled her father's attention back to whatever it was she was shouting in his ear.

The mind control ended and Elio's eyes dropped. He took a big breath after realizing he'd stopped breathing. There was something dangerous, something mesmerizing about her father. He projected the self-assured mania of a false prophet. His absolute expectation of your obedience almost ensured it.

One of the soldiers sat near the front with Clyde in his lap. The poor little guy tried to escape toward Noor but the soldier held him tight.

The helicopter lifted higher and Elio gasped as he stared into the distance.

Los Angeles was destroyed.

Smoke billowed into the air from innumerable fires below. A solid, frozen river of cars choked every highway. The unbroken mass disappeared into the distance in every direction. Freeway ten to the east. The four-oh-five to the north and south. Millions of people in millions of cars all trying to escape at once. It was never going to work. It was like trying to push a watermelon through a water hose. The roads simply weren't made to move that volume of traffic.

They only kind of worked on regular days because everyone didn't want the same thing at the same time.

They crossed over the ten and headed toward the towering skyscrapers of downtown Los Angeles. In the mid-day sun, the air hanging above the city looked darker than usual. He would've thought that without all the millions of cars spewing noxious chemicals into the air every day that the smog would've cleared out in no time. And maybe it would have. But the hundreds of fires around the city spewing dark smoke more than made up for the decrease in emissions.

Elio's stomach jumped into his throat as the chopper jerked to the side and dropped altitude. He gritted his teeth to keep from puking, and then they stabilized. He squeezed his mother tight as much to reassure her as himself.

A beeping alarm pierced the noise of the blades chopping through the air. A red light in the ceiling of the cockpit flashed on and off. The pilot checked gauges and flipped switches trying to handle whatever the problem was.

Anton grabbed a headset clipped to the wall and slipped them over his head. He yelled into the mouthpiece as if that might help the situation.

The helicopter bucked again and Elio barfed into his mouth when it rolled over onto its side. He doubled over the seatbelt with his arms and legs dangling freely. He looked through the closed side door at the ground some two hundred feet below. His back slammed into the metal wall as the chopper rolled and righted itself.

The piercing alarm continued to whine as the pilot wrestled with the controls. The nose dipped forward and they plunged downward like the big drop on a roller coaster.

Only they weren't on rails and Elio didn't expect to make it off this ride.

61

His mother screamed and her vice grip around his hand tightened further. He realized it would've hurt if his brain had the extra bandwidth to process the sensation. But it didn't. It was fully occupied with the certainty that he was about to die.

The ground rushed up to meet them.

Elio's head swam. The weirdest sensation assured him that he was stationary and that it was the world falling toward him. Cars that had moments ago looked like children's toys grew larger as they plummeted.

The chopper bucked forward and a large, yellow school bus came into view. It rushed at them at a dizzying speed.

Elio pinched his eyes shut. He held his mother's hand with all the strength left in his body.

The chopper jerked up at the last second. His stomach bombed out of his throat. His hip bones dug painfully into the thinly padded seat. He blinked his eyes open as the front of the school bus disappeared underneath the front of the chopper.

And then it crashed.

His head slammed into the metal wall as everything jerked to the right.

A terrifying screech stabbed the air as the blades dug channels into the pavement before shearing off completely. Sparks flew and the side door peeled away as they skidded over the concrete. The cabin rolled several times and then slammed to a stop into the side of a building.

Elio sat motionless wondering if he was dead. A thought dimly occurred to him. He couldn't be dead if his whole body hurt this badly. Right?

He licked his lips and tasted the salty metallic bite of blood. He squeezed his eyes open and realized they were upright. He checked on his mother. She had a gash on her cheek dripping down onto her chest. She moaned, which meant she was alive. On the other side, Theresa slumped in the seat blinking slowly as Beth ran her hands over her daughter's body.

Across the cabin, the soldier sitting next to the missing door had a fragment of metal protruding from his chest. Blood poured from his mouth. He stared at the jagged tip. A shaky hand touched it and then he passed out. Or died. Elio wasn't a doctor, but the injury didn't look like something you could survive.

The remaining four soldiers hurried out of their harnesses. Two climbed out of the twisted wreck, one of them had Clyde wrapped under an arm. Another helped Anton and Iridia out of their seat belts. The others climbed into the cockpit to check on the motionless pilot.

Elio looked across the cabin. Noor had already gotten free of her belt and was trying to help Ahmed do the same. His right leg was bent at an impossible angle. A stick stuck out of his torn pant leg. The jagged end was pale and white.

Not a stick. A bone.

Ahmed screamed as he tried to move that leg.

One of the men from outside returned.

"We have to beat feet, sir. We've got tangos gathering to investigate the crash site."

Anton nodded and wobbled before catching himself. "How's the pilot?"

The soldier in the cockpit shook his head. He glanced toward the back of the cabin. "What do you want to do with them?"

"Bring them. They might be useful."

A soldier reached for Beth's seatbelt, but she swatted his hand away.

CRACK. CRACK.

A voice yelled from outside. "We've got contact!"

"Sir, we have to move out!" another yelled.

Anton glared at Beth. "Get them out of the helicopter!"

"Get up, now!" the soldier shouted.

Elio didn't require encouragement. He flung off his seatbelt and helped his mother to her feet. The soldier shoved them toward the missing door. Elio stumbled forward and would've landed face first outside if the cabin floor hadn't been flush with the ground.

He stumbled out and caught Maria before they both ate asphalt.

Theresa and Beth came out next with the pushy soldier roughly urging them on. He turned back and saw Ahmed's leg. "Can you walk?"

"I will try. Help me out and give me the dead man's rifle."

Ahmed screamed as the soldier helped him out onto the street. He accepted the black rifle and flipped the barrel to the ground. Leaning on it like a cane to keep weight off his right leg, he managed a few steps. He looked down at Noor at his side and forced a weak smile. The source of his remaining strength was no secret.

Elio would've taken the work of the cane, but he was already struggling to help his mother along. Her already weakened state wasn't improved by the crash.

Theresa was in no shape to run for several blocks either. The fever burned through her like a flame through a snowflake. Beth had Theresa's arm wrapped over her shoulder. She urged her daughter along even as she bore most of her weight.

Anton huffed and puffed alongside Iridia. Their levels of physical fitness couldn't have been further apart. They appeared to have escaped relatively unscathed.

And yet, as battered as some of them were, they still had a chance. Mason didn't even have that. Theresa's father had become something like a father to him since the outbreak. Maybe finding out the truth behind his own father's death in Fallujah had dissolved an invisible barrier between them.

It would do no such thing for his mother if she ever found out.

The lead soldier pointed at two of his men. "You two cover our six. I'm on point. Move out!" The three soldiers surrounded their small group and guided them away from the crash site and out into the middle of the street.

Up ahead, about four blocks away, was the Milagro Tower.

That was the good news. Unfortunately, there was also bad news. Very bad news.

Numerous packs of deltas emerged from side streets, all heading in their direction. The closest group was no more than a hundred yards away and closing.

A soldier grabbed Elio's shirt and shoved him forward. "Run!"

62

They hobbled along as fast as they could. They would've already been run down, but the closest group of deltas paused at the crash site. Perhaps drawn by the scent of fresh meat. Whatever the reason, the delay didn't last. Still a couple of blocks from the building, and another group was on their tail and catching up.

Elio had his arm wrapped under his mother's and helped her along as fast as he could. As slow as they moved, Ahmed moved slower still. He hopped along using the rifle for support. His mangled right leg dragged along the ground leaving a continuous trail of blood.

The screeching and howling from behind echoed through the canyon of tall buildings.

CRACK. CRACK.

The two soldiers guarding the rear followed about twenty yards behind, stopping now and again to pick off faster deltas that charged ahead of the others.

The lead soldier halted mid-stride and waved the group on. "Keep moving!"

Elio glanced back. The nearest hunters swept over the

two trailing soldiers. One soldier disappeared beneath the frenzy of limbs. The other soldier turned the gun on himself and the back of his head exploded.

"No!" the lead soldier yelled.

The body collapsed and a delta was on it before it hit the ground.

Elio's limbs felt like lead. His life was in danger and he knew he'd never run faster. At the same time, it felt like he'd never run slower either. He urged his mother on with all the strength left in his body.

Two more blocks to safety.

Ahmed tripped and crashed to the pavement. He rolled over and the palms of his hands bled from where the skin had been shredded away. Noor tugged at his shirt to get him to stand up. He tried and then collapsed again. He shook his head.

"I can go no farther. You must go, my dear."

"No, Baba! No!" Tears streamed down Noor's cheeks.

Ahmed wiped her face leaving trails of smudged dirt. "Habib Albi," he said and then kissed her forehead. "I'm so sorry."

Beth wrapped her arm around Noor's shoulder. "We'll take care of her. I promise."

A single tear welled in the corner of Ahmed's eye. It broke free and raced down his colorless cheek, disappearing into the thick beard. "Thank you."

Beth pulled Noor away while the hysterical girl fought to stay with her father.

The remaining soldier retrieved Ahmed's fallen rifle and placed it in his hands. He pulled a baseball-like grenade off his vest and placed it on the ground. "Yank the pin and release the spoon."

Ahmed nodded. He rolled over into a seated position

and brought the rifle up into his shoulder. He watched Noor and the rest of the group continue down the street.

Elio choked back tears. For Ahmed. For Noor. For Mason. For Theresa. For his mother. For the world of suffering.

A torrent of gunfire cut loose. Several deltas fell and then the rifle went silent.

"Don't look back!" Beth yelled as they made it to a half a block from safety.

"Allahu Akbar!"

BOOM.

The exploding grenade echoed down the street like rolling thunder.

"No! Baba! No!" Noor yelled as Beth pulled her onward.

Elio glanced over his shoulder. Ahmed's sacrifice slowed down their pursuers. But it didn't stop them. Several lay dead on the street. Several more staggered around screaming. Another pack appeared from between two buildings and closed in. Now, less than twenty yards back.

The lead soldier carrying Clyde sprinted to the entrance area of Milagro tower.

Elio marveled at the odd destiny that connected him to this building. Less than two weeks ago, it held the promise of his death. Now, it held the promise of his life.

What had once been an elegant entrance of all glass and shining metal was now a patchwork of plywood and security fencing. The soldier kicked open a makeshift door and waited at the entrance, waving them forward.

Elio and his mother lagged a little behind the others. He'd practically carried her the last block and his strength was failing. Failing fast. He didn't look back. He didn't need to.

The cries of the hunters were right behind them. Their

nearness threatened to drown his reason, subdue his will to survive.

He knew their hands would pull him down at any second.

Theresa, Beth, and Noor made it inside first. At least they would live. Iridia pulling her father along made it through next.

If only he'd been stronger. It was the story of his life. Forever coming up short. Forever one step behind the pace. He regretted the failure more for his mother than himself. She'd suffered so much over the years. She deserved better than to die like this.

A hand grabbed his shirt and tugged backward. The fabric ripped and Elio broke free.

The soldier waiting at the door fired.

A bullet snapped by Elio's head and a body thumped the ground.

The gun fired again as Elio rushed his mother through the door.

The soldier slammed the door shut and barred it from the inside with a couple of two by fours.

"Get to the elevators!" he shouted.

Elio pulled his mother across the wide expanse of marble floor and into the open elevator where the others waited. The soldier joined them and Anton flashed a keycard over the black pad protruding from the mirrored wall. A vaguely robotic female voice responded.

"Hello, Dr. Reshenko. Where do you wish to go?"

"My office."

"Descending to the basement laboratory."

Anton growled. "No. Go to Mr. Cruz's office."

"Ascending to the seventy-third floor. Please stay clear of the doors." The elevator dinged and the doors slid shut.

They started up. Elio supported Maria. The crash and subsequent escape had taken it out of her. She trembled in his arms and, for the first time in his life, he realized that meant they'd switched roles for good. Going forward, maybe it was now his job to be the strong one. The one that wouldn't allow them to give up or surrender. She'd been strong for so long that seeing her so weak was almost more than he could bear. But it was also precisely why he alone absolutely had to bear it.

Anton doubled over holding his knees for support. He coughed and wheezed. Thick tendrils of saliva dripped out of his mouth and swayed in the air.

The elevator stopped. "Seventy-third floor." The door dinged open. Another soldier dressed in all black like the others waited outside the door.

"Where's the rest of the team?" he asked.

Anton pushed his way out of the elevator waving the guy off like an annoying fly buzzing around his ears.

"Escort Iridia to my quarters." He turned to his daughter and cupped his hand against her cheek. "Go have a hot shower, my precious. You will find a dresser in the bedroom full of your clothes."

Her face brightened with a million dollar smile. What used to be a million dollar smile, at least. She started to walk off with the soldier, but then stopped and turned. "Papa, my friend is sick. Can you help her?"

Anton held his arms wide. "She will be taken care of," he said with a smile.

She nodded and left with her escort.

Anton's smile vanished. He marched over to an office door and threw it open. "Put them in here and post a guard. No one is to go in or out unless I say so. Do you understand?"

"Yes, sir."

The soldier in the elevator herded them out and toward the open door. As they walked by, Anton pointed at Theresa. "That one is infected. Put her and the chimp in secure cells in the lab."

One of the soldiers grabbed Theresa's arm and pulled her to the side. He and the soldier holding Clyde started back for the elevator.

Beth lunged for her daughter but their escorts intervened and dragged her away.

"Don't touch them!" Beth screamed. She fought to break free, but the soldiers were too strong. "No! No!"

Elio watched Theresa. Her eyes rolled around not comprehending what was happening. Her skin glistened with sweat. An intricate maze of black veins covered her left arm.

"Don't do it, hero," the soldier behind said as he rammed the butt of his rifle into Elio's back.

If it weren't for his mother at his side and him bearing most of her weight, Elio would've thrown his life away to help Theresa. But he couldn't bring himself to leave his mother. Not after he'd taken so long to find her after the outbreak. He was the only one his mother could count on.

Elio caught Anton's gaze before being forced into the room. "I'll kill you if you hurt her."

Anton chuckled and his jowls jiggled with the effort. He shook his head disdainfully. "Hurt her? Look at her. She's already dead."

63

November 2004
Fallujah, Iraq

MASON put one foot in front of the other. The limping cadence had become a meditation that kept him going. The simple mechanics of walking had become anything but. Each step was a struggle of the will against an unrelenting foe—the body's physical limits.

Or the mind's perception of them.

Whatever was at fault, the results were the same. Every step was an all out battle between total collapse and one more fight.

Another foot forward and the rhythm continued.

Had the rest of third squad already made it to the extraction point?

They'd only been a couple of blocks away when they ran into the ambush. As much as he wanted to get there himself, he also dreaded the thought of arriving. Evac meant time to think. Time to register losses. Time to think about the families back home that would never be the same.

And time to remember Lopes.

Sharp pain radiated up his right leg. He stumbled and Miro took on the additional load.

Mason gritted his teeth and refocused on the steps. Thankfully, the immediate needs of survival kept his brain busy. The priorities of the present kept a comfortable distance between the now and thoughts of anything in the past or future.

The sounds of active fighting died away as they continued twisting through back alleys doing their best to continue heading west in the general direction of the extraction point. They came to the end of an alley and stopped.

Mason tugged a laminated map out of a vest pocket and a flashlight from another pocket. He wrapped his fingers around the lens and clicked it on. Dim light escaped from the slits between his fingers. He rotated the map, orienting to it as best he could. They weren't exactly lost, but they weren't exactly not lost either. The rat's maze of alleys they'd traversed over the last hour didn't have a single street sign. One presumably didn't move through this section of the city without local knowledge. Most of the alleys didn't even show up on the map.

"What do you reckon, Sarge?" Miro said, leaning over his shoulder and tracing a finger across the map.

"I think we're somewhere in this area," he said pointing to the northern edge of the Old Fallujah district. The absence of any major roadways made it likely. "I think we drifted too far south. We gotta backtrack a ways."

"Wonderful," Miro said before cramming a wad of Red Man Golden Blend inside his cheek. He worked the loose leaf chew to get the juices going. "Chaw?"

Mason dug out a wad and began working it in his

mouth. The sharp tobacco tang managed to cut through the ash flavor in his mouth. It was a welcome change. Spit juice dribbled down his throat stinging it like liquid fire. That was less welcome.

On the upside, it was a reminder that he was still alive. The challenge now was staying that way.

They both considered the map, and what it would mean to head back in the direction from which they'd come.

The air temperature was dropping fast. They were in for a real freezer. Each night when the sun dipped below the horizon, the desert city plummeted into a fierce cold.

Suffice to say, neither man relished the idea of spending the night alone in a city crawling with people that wanted to kill them. Not to mention the fact that they'd assuredly freeze their butts off. And nobody would be getting any much-needed sleep for the exact same reasons.

That was the thing about life. It could always get worse.

Mason was thinking through the options when a sound caught his attention. A distinct sound. One that sent a jolt up his spine. Thankfully, a spasm of excitement and not dread as was the usual case.

"Hear that?" he asked Miro.

Miro tilted his head like a dog trying to understand a spoken word.

The sound grew louder.

"Hot damn, Sarge! That's gotta be one of ours!"

Mason stashed the map and flashlight, and then shouldered his rifle. He edged up to the corner of the alley and peeked around. About a block and a half down the street, a Humvee sped in their direction.

What was a single Humvee doing out on its own?

They waited as it approached. When it closed to within a hundred feet, they stepped out waving their arms wildly.

The vehicle skidded to a stop and the driver door flew open. A marine popped up above the door and waved them over.

Mason had seen him before but couldn't recall his name. Ramirez, maybe.

Miro wrapped an arm around Mason. The two stumbled like a pair of drunks in a three-legged race. They made it to the vehicle and piled in.

"Ramirez, right?" Mason said.

"Yep."

"What are you doing out here by yourself, Corporal?"

"We were on an evac mission to get you boys and got ambushed. Shit went sideways and I got separated from the rest of the unit."

"We know the feeling," Miro said.

"Where were you headed?" Mason asked.

Ramirez pointed down the road. "To Phase Line Fran, I think."

Sounded like as good a plan as any. In the opening days of the attack, the Army TF 2-7 had secured the highway that bisected Fallujah into northern and southern halves. If they could make it there, they'd be home free.

"Sounds like a plan," Mason said.

A bullet pinged off the hood grabbing all of their attentions.

Ramirez hit the gas and the four ton vehicle lurched forward. "Overstayed our welcome!"

They roared down the street. Headlights swerved over the dark scene as Ramirez jerked the steering wheel back and forth to avoid obstructions dotting the street. The last thing they wanted was to hit a chunk of concrete, snap a tie rod, and end up plowing into a building. Buildings in Fallujah weren't the framed drywall constructions common in California. They were thick concrete and smashing into one would more likely end up with you through the windshield than the vehicle through the building.

Ramirez navigated the dangers with skill honed in combat. Mason gripped the seat in front as the Hummer went up on two wheels skidding around a huge crater in the center of the road.

The Hummer came back around to the center of the street. The headlights lit up a man further down the way. He looked up and froze. Flowing black garments covered him from head to toe. He knelt by the curb on the left side of the road, fiddling with something. Something wasn't nothing in Fallujah.

Not good.

At all.

"Get up in the turret and light him up!" Mason shouted.

Miro climbed up behind the fifty cal and tried to get into the fight. "It's jammed up!"

Mason passed Miro's rifle up to him. He then dropped the window on the driver's side and got his M16 into the fight. Both of them banged away as they approached but the bouncing, jarring movements of the vehicle threw off their aims again and again.

Now less than a hundred feet away, the man stood and faced them. He held something in his hand.

Mason didn't have to see it clearly to know that it was a detonator. He lined up a shot and fired just as the Hummer bounced to the side.

Miss.

They hit a patch of smooth pavement and Mason zeroed the front sight.

CRACK. CRACK.

The muj dropped to the ground.

The sides and roof of the Hummer pinged with incoming rounds. Mason scanned the buildings as they blurred by but found no targets.

"Slam that pedal down!" he shouted.

Ramirez nodded and the metal beast jerked forward throwing Mason over into the passenger's side door.

He righted himself and watched in horror as the man he'd dropped rolled over and looked their way just as they passed.

BOOM.

64

The taste was the weird thing. He took another sip. It burned like vodka but with a harsher bite. Gutter cheap vodka stank to high heaven, but even that swill made this stuff smell like lavender and roses. He should've sprung for the good stuff, and anything would've been the good stuff relatively speaking. Beth would be back from the bathroom any minute. He had to come up with what to talk about next. First dates sucked as a rule. But this one felt different.

This one felt like forever. To think it would be crazy. To say it would be dating suicide.

Was she feeling the same way?

How could he ask, but not really ask?

Mason hated the artifice of the dating game. That every date was another hand of poker where what you had and what you bluffed were equally important.

He took another sip of the gut-burning swill and then lay back on the sand. The roar of the crashing surf drowned out the throngs of people crowding the beachside restaurants.

Another taste of vodka touched his lips... but the bottle was still in the sand next to him.

How?

Pain jolted through Mason's chest.

Blinking his eyes open was an impossible task. He did it anyway.

The hazy dream dissipated like smoke in the wind. Another hazy dream replaced it. This one immeasurably worse.

The circumstances of the dream crashed together like a falling Jenga tower in reverse. And the result was just as stable. A drop landed on his lips and slipped into his mouth.

He spat out the nasty taste of diesel fuel and blood. Noxious fumes permeated the interior of the Humvee. Mason swiped at his eyes and the left one came away clear. Clearer.

The dream of their first date was better.

Their Humvee had been hit by an IED at point blank range.

Mason oriented himself and realized the vehicle was upside down and he was laying on the roof. He turned and found Ramirez in the front seat. The half of his head that remained wasn't enough by half.

Where was Miro? He'd been up in the turret from what he could remember.

A drop of diesel hit a gash on his cheek. He winced at the sting.

He had to get out of there. If the fuel didn't catch and toast him, muj would show up any minute to pick the carcass clean. Gritting through the pain, he turned around and tried to open the passenger door.

Jammed.

He rotated a little further and then slammed a boot into

it. The impact sent a thousand stinging ants echoing through his limbs. At least that meant he was alive. The entire concept was beginning to feel less and less like a blessing, and more and more like a curse.

He kicked again and the door creaked open.

After scrambling out, he pulled himself to his feet and shouldered his M16. He stumbled around the wrecked vehicle and found Miro lying on the street. The Texan didn't appear as beat up as Mason expected.

Then again, he wasn't moving.

Mason knelt down and dug a finger down into Miro's neck. He felt the carotid still pulsing with its life-sustaining delivery of oxygenated blood.

"Got a dip?"

Mason flinched involuntarily at the unexpected sound. "Miro, you scared the piss out of me!"

"Not my fault you're so jumpy."

Mason continued checking him over and, although he found any number of things that would've made your average worker skip work and rush to the ER, he didn't see anything that was going to kill him in the next five minutes.

Anything but staying where they were.

"How do you feel?" he asked.

"Like a turd sandwich."

"With dijon mustard?"

"We don't eat that fancy crap in Texas. With barbecue sauce."

"We have to beat feet, bro. We're lucky the place isn't crawling already."

"Help me up, Sarge."

Mason wasn't sure he could get himself back up, much less help someone else. But that wasn't going to stop him.

He ignored the agony and got them both on their feet.

They steadied each other as the street momentarily rolled like the surface of the ocean.

"How's Ramirez?" Miro asked.

Mason shook his head.

"Damn," Miro said in anger before spitting a glob of blood onto the pavement.

They gathered up their gear. Miro took the driver's service rifle because his was nowhere to be seen. They took a last look at the ruined vehicle and the dead Marine inside.

"We'll come back for you," Mason said through gritted teeth. The tension in his jaws was just as much a response from the pain as the rage. He grabbed Miro's vest and pulled him away from the grisly scene. "We have to get down to Phase Line Fran. It shouldn't be more than a klick away."

Mason started off walking—limping was more accurate—keeping the rifle butt seated in the hollow of his shoulder. He swept the street and buildings for targets. It was quiet. Too quiet. He glanced up as movement caught his attention. The curtains in a window on the second floor of the building to their right fluttered closed.

They made it another fifty feet and again his attention focused on another darkened window. A silhouette disappeared inside.

"Sarge, you get the feeling we're being watched?"

"Yep."

"What do we do?"

"Keep moving."

65

The Present Day
Los Angeles, California

ANTON verified his instructions were being carried out and then went looking for Mr. Pike. He'd told his bodyguard to wait outside his office. And yet, he was nowhere to be seen. He scratched at the bald, raw patch of skin where a luxurious sideburn used to be. Scratching it sent a shiver of pleasure down his spine. And yet it also made it more maddeningly itchy.

Where was Mr. Pike?

He passed one of the faceless, imbecilic hired brutes in the hallway. Anton stopped the man. "You. Find Mr. Pike and send him to my quarters. Remind him that I am not accustomed to waiting."

"Yes, sir," the hired hand said and then strode off with purpose.

Anton strode to his chambers, doing his best to remain calm. The events of the day had his already taut nerves overstretched and ready to snap. His daughter thoroughly deserved to be the recipient of his agitation, yet he couldn't bring himself to take it out on her. For all her faults, she was all that remained in the world of his beloved Katerina. And for that alone, she deserved forgiveness where others would merit punishment.

He opened the door and smiled upon seeing her discarded clothes on the floor leading to the bathroom. She needn't worry about picking them up herself, after all. They had a maid for that. Even in the new beginning, it was important to remain civilized. The remaining help lived in the lower floors, where the tawdry details of their personal lives were appropriately hidden from view.

As much as Anton abhorred their breathing the same air, he also understood they occupied a necessary position in the scheme of things.

He kicked the garments aside and plopped down on the plush red couch. He stared at the enormous canvas on the wall. An abstract piece of swirling, brushed purples and gold hues.

Garish. Whimsical.

Repulsive.

His former employer, Gabriel Cruz, may have been the wealthiest man alive, but his tastes were pedestrian. His vision limited. His life meaningless.

Anton was far more inclined towards the classical. The ageless. The profound. He hadn't yet had an opportunity to remodel the space to his liking. There would be time for that now that Iridia was safe.

Had Gabriel died in the aftermath of the outbreak?

No one in the company had heard from him for over a week. And with Milagro Tower being the corporate headquarters, it stood to reason that its owner had either died or been stranded in some backwater from which he would never emerge.

Either scenario was pleasing.

Anton had kowtowed at the foot of his master's throne for far too long. For as far back as he could remember. The time for his own rule had arrived. Like the great Genghis Khan, whose visage graced the silver Dirham in his pocket, his destiny had arrived. All the years of unheralded toil had paid off.

Mankind would survive. Now there would be time for its wisdom to catch up with its technology. Soon they would have the mindless muscle to build a better future. The deltas, as the common folk had taken to calling them, would become the necessary labor of a sustainable future.

Their brutish might had yet to be productively harnessed, but that was to be expected. Evolution required time. Time to adjust to the new paradigm.

A master race and a subservient one.

Each assigned by their capabilities and potential.

His research hadn't had time to gather results on the potential offspring of delta reproduction. The crisis of concurrent peak events had made a certain degree of prognostication necessary. Would children born to the brutes retake the intellect of their ancestors? Or would the virus pass in-utero damaging the fetus' prefrontal cortex just as it had the mother's?

The uncertainty of that question had led him to create an MT-1 variant. MT-1 itself had been an unqualified success. Per the design, it had killed off the vast majority of humanity while leaving a small percentage changed. A smaller percentage yet were likely resistant or had somehow managed to avoid infection.

The variant, once perfected, would reliably cause the

change while not killing the subject. The variant would be as critical to the new world as MT-I itself was to the old one.

The variant would need to reliably create the *right* delta as well. One of the weaknesses of MT-I had been that, while it produced deltas, it didn't do so with any degree of exactitude. It had to do with the varying efficiency with which it burned out the prefrontal cortex.

It changed some into servile beasts. Others into raving lunatics. And yet others, a fleeting few in his research, it left some spark of intellect. Some hint at what the person used to be.

Nature was a complex phenomenon. And the human brain its highest achievement. So perhaps the variability was to be expected. Yet it was also a failure. One Anton intended to rectify in the development of the variant.

There would be time.

Mankind now had a generation or more to address the burdens brought on by overpopulation and the rapacious use of technology. The world had time to recover. Humanity had time to forge a new path to prosperity.

His beloved Katerina would be proud. If only she were alive to witness his magnificent achievement. While small minds might besmirch his actions, history would someday reveal the evident truth.

One man had saved humanity from extinction.

Anton wasn't a greedy man. One overly longing for adulation. But it would be just for that truth to be universally accepted within his lifetime. He didn't require an award, only acknowledgement.

The shower water cut off and he listened with contentment to Iridia shuffling through the well-appointed bathroom.

How she must've suffered out there in the darkness, in the dirt.

She deserved to be here in the light, in the heavens.

A knock at the apartment's front door startled him.

"Come," Anton said.

The door opened and Mr. Pike stepped in. His hair was gelled and swept to the side. His jaw was smoothly shaven and his dark suit pressed. Anton hadn't seen him so presentable since before the outbreak.

Why now?

"Sir," Mr. Pike said as he stepped in and closed the door. "It's good to see you. May I ask where the others are?"

It wasn't like his bodyguard to be so inquisitive.

"They are resting and recovering. As you might imagine, they were not coping well with the challenging conditions."

The bathroom door opened and Iridia stepped out wrapped in a towel. The bottom edge ended far too soon, revealing an altogether inappropriate amount of thigh and leg. Her skin glistened with moisture.

"Iridia!" Anton said. "Cover yourself!"

"Oh Papa. Don't be such a prude." She waved him off dismissively and pranced across the living room to stand in front of Mr. Pike. She held the towel in place with one hand and extended the other. "Papa never mentioned how handsome his new bodyguard was."

Mr. Pike stood there with his jaw hanging open.

Iridia smiled, obviously enjoying the effect her appearance was having.

The bodyguard took her hand and kissed it. His eyes flashed as his lips broke contact with her skin. "It's a pleasure to meet you, Iridia. I've heard so much about you."

The point to his manicured appearance no longer held mystery.

The usurper. The ingrate. As useful as he was, Anton decided his employment would end sooner than later. And his termination would likely be more complete than simply losing a job.

Iridia feigned embarrassment. She appeared that way, but Anton knew it was a ploy. His daughter didn't have a modest bone in her body. So like her mother.

"Enough!" Anton yelled. "Am I to suffer such indignity? Return to the bathroom at once!"

Iridia flinched at his harsh tone.

It broke his heart to treat her so, but he would suffer a thousand heartbreaks to preserve his daughter's dignity.

Her? With a bodyguard?

Never.

66

Iridia was destined for greater things. She would carry his genes into the future. And in no possible reality would a simple bodyguard plant her garden with such mediocre seed.

"Yes, Papa," Iridia said as she hurried back as commanded.

Anton waited for her to shut the door before unleashing a hint of his anger at this ill-suited suitor.

"Why were you not at your post when I returned, Mr. Pike? I do not employ you to disobey my instructions."

The bodyguard's eyes hadn't left the closed bathroom door. He stared in awed silence.

"Mr. Pike!"

He jerked and then turned to Anton. His eyes slowly focused.

"Did you hear me?"

"Yes, sir," he said. "I mean, no. Sorry. What did you say?"

Anton's blood boiled. He longed to kill the man where he stood. He didn't attempt it of course. He was not armed. And even if he was, he was no match for the muscled savage.

"You may leave!"

"Yes, sir."

He opened the door and was about to step outside when he paused and turned. "Sir, how is Mason?"

"Mr. West?"

"Yes."

"He did not make it back."

Mr. Pike pursed his lips together and looked at the ground. He stood there in stunned silence.

"That will be all, Mr. Pike. I'll let you know if I need anything."

"Yes, sir," he said as he closed the door.

As soon as the door shut, Iridia slipped out of the bathroom and sat next to him on the couch. Her damp towel would no doubt stain the crushed velvet fabric.

He didn't care. It was a monstrosity in the first place. He wrapped an arm around her shoulder and pulled her close.

Her eyelids lined with moisture as she buried her head in his chest. Her sandy blonde hair was so much like Katerina's. She'd been blessed with inheriting almost all of his wife's genes determining appearance. He wasn't so deluded as to not realize he was physically rather unimpressive. His physicality was severely lacking. Of that, there was no doubt.

But the strength of modern man was not determined solely by physical prowess. In fact, the further mankind travelled from its hunter-gatherer origins, the less and less important brute strength had become. By some estimations, it had taken nearly 200,000 years to escape from the servitude of simple survival. And only within the last century or two had the power of the mind assumed its rightful role at the top.

It wasn't that the brain was all of a sudden important

and never was before. Of course, it was always the key to our evolution and eventual ascension to the pinnacle of power. The evolving brain raised our ancestors from the immediate needs of scavenging food from the dirt to building a system that funneled resources from every corner of the globe directly into our ravenous mouths.

Humanity had acquired god-like powers. And life in the clouds offered a view of near limitless distance. Of where we had been and where we might go. And yet, our meteoric rise planted a seed that proved to be our undoing. Pride. Hubris, as the Greek playwrights called it.

Grounded confidence transformed into foolish arrogance. We came to believe that, as self-made gods, there were no limits. That the very discussion of exterior limits was anathema to our intrinsic character.

The very ambition that had raised us out of the primordial abyss threatened to drag us back under.

Anton had seen it all at such a young age. The city packed with people. Scurrying like rats for a bigger bite of cheese. He'd seen the inevitable downfall. The utter ruin. And he had committed his life to preventing it.

Through decades of research into viral evolution, he'd studied how the simplest life form could radically transform the most advanced.

There had once been great debate over whether a virus should be classified as a life form or simply an assemblage of building blocks such as proteins, lipids, and carbohydrates. As impassioned as many scientists had gotten in the debate, it had never elicited more than a derisive laugh from Anton.

Of course, viruses were a life form. They were a parasitic life form. But wasn't all of life?

Wasn't mankind?

We required resources to survive. To procreate. And much like a successful virus, modern man had overwhelmed its host. Its very success sowed the seeds of its eventual destruction. And, like a simple virus, mankind could not survive without the resources of its host. No matter how much we believed in the illusion of our invincibility.

It had been this realization that had long ago determined Anton's direction.

Mankind had succeeded beyond the wildest dreams of its ancient ancestors. It claimed to stand apart from the intricate system of support that made its lofty position possible. But the disconnect was never real.

People living in more marginal regions of the planet understood the truth because they were forced to bend to it despite all the eons of progress.

Over time, Anton came to understand two simple facts.

One, there were too many of us.

And two, the majority of that over-burgeoning population contributed little to the continued evolution of our species.

In fact, he came to understand that the masses actively contributed to a weakening of our genetic promise.

And so destiny called upon him to create MT-1.

The future of the human genome required only two things. It required a ruling class that aspired to the continued development of mankind's most important tool: our brains. And it required that those humans have abundant access to resources.

The Delta Virus, as they called it, was the agent of our future prosperity.

Anton winced as pain stabbed the blistered fingers of his left thumb and pointer finger. He released the coin in his pocket and withdrew his hand. The two finger pads were worn raw. Skin peeled around the edges of the wounds.

"Papa, you're bleeding!" Iridia said.

"It is of no consequence," he replied as he dabbed his fingers on the already blood-red couch. He kissed her forehead and stroked her damp hair.

His fair Iridia. As beautiful as a sunrise.

As attractive as she was, he couldn't help but wonder if she deserved to be among the fortunate few who were now tasked with carrying on with the evolution of the intellect. It wasn't that she was stupid. He didn't think that, necessarily.

Perhaps she had never been adequately challenged. Intellect didn't develop in a vacuum. It developed as a direct result of conflict and struggle. Anton himself was proof of that. His childhood years had been a constant fight for survival.

A constant engaging of the brain to solve life or death situations.

If she hadn't experienced enough struggle in her life, he had only himself to blame. After losing Katerina, Anton had wanted to do nothing more than shelter his daughter from the cruelty of the world. He'd fought to give her every opportunity, to stack the deck in her favor before every deal of the cards.

And yet, he knew she was nowhere near his intellectual equal.

But then again, he'd endured hardship he hoped she would never understand. Such was the paradox. The struggle facilitated the full expression of the brain's potential. But having achieved that potential, even Anton shielded his offspring from enduring the very same thing that had lifted him to such heights.

He kissed her forehead again and smiled.

"What's wrong, Papa?"

Anton stared into her crystal green eyes and saw the eyes of his long-dead wife. Katerina had suffered and died. He couldn't bare to see the same thing happen to Iridia.

"Nothing, my dear," he said as he stroked her hair. "Everything is fine now."

He vowed to protect her from struggle and pain. And he accepted his own hypocrisy. He was, after all, just a man... flawed and imperfect like all the others.

Well, not quite like all the others.

67

Anton held his daughter tight. So much had happened since she'd snuck away to Los Angeles to have that pointless interview with that idiot director. He wished the man was still alive so he could kill him for causing so much trouble.

"Papa?" Iridia said.

"Yes?"

"What will happen to my friends?"

My friends.

Iridia had never referred to anyone with such concern discoloring her voice. He'd been careful to protect her from the weakness that attachment engendered.

"Like you, they will have the opportunity to refresh themselves and then we will discuss how next to proceed."

"What about Theresa? She's infected. Can you help her?"

"Why do you worry for her?"

Iridia dropped her gaze. "She's my friend. I care about her."

Anton grabbed her by the shoulders and squeezed hard

enough to guarantee her undivided attention. He stared hard until she lifted her eyes.

"They are not family, moya dochka. Never trust anyone who isn't family. You know this."

Iridia shrugged. "I know. I know. But these people are nice. I'm alive because of them."

"You are alive because you are a survivor, as I am. Remember your mother. She placed her trust in others and she died for it. Never forget that."

"I understand."

She understood, but she was not convinced. And that meant these people were dangerous. He would let nothing come between them.

Nothing.

Iridia looked at him twisting her mouth to the side.

"Speak," he said.

"You didn't answer me."

She had the defiant spirit of her mother.

"Didn't I?"

"No," she said. "Can you help her?"

These people were very dangerous indeed. Anton did his best to keep the irritation from his voice as he responded. "While there is—"

"I knew it! I knew you could help!"

"Let me finish. While there is an antiviral treatment, it yet exists in vanishingly small quantities. What if you or I get sick? Should either of us die so that this girl we do not know may live?"

Iridia pulled away. "But I do know her. And she's been very nice to me. Even when I didn't deserve it."

"For you, I will consider it."

Iridia pursed her lips together. The usual curves

flattened into tight lines. She rose and retreated into the bathroom and closed the door.

Anton rose and spoke through the barrier. "Wash away the clinging dirt. It is better this way."

She didn't respond.

Her new friends would need to be dealt with, and soon.

Anton exited the apartment and found Mr. Pike at his post by the door. "Stay here and let no one enter."

"Yes, sir."

Did he have a particular glint in his eye as he responded?

Anton marched down the hall and entered the elevator. He waved his keycard over the reader.

"Hello, Dr. Reshenko. Where do you wish to go?"

"The lab."

"Descending to the basement laboratory. Please stay clear of the doors."

Anton almost snarled at the perpetually genial voice and the overly courteous programming. Artificial intelligence so terrified humanity that they demanded any incarnation of it genuflect in every interaction so that mankind could remind itself of exactly who was in charge.

But polite programming didn't change the fact that AI was doing more and more while error-prone, weak-willed humans were doing less and less. It was not unthinkable to believe that Anton had saved humanity from some impending robotic apocalypse.

"Basement Laboratory."

The elevator dinged and the doors slid open.

He stepped out and ignored the guard standing next to the security doors. He used his keycard to get through and headed straight for the detention cells. The Patient Wing, as they euphemistically named it.

It wasn't Iridia's friend he'd come to see. He couldn't care less about the girl. No, it was the esteemed Senator Rawlings that piqued his interest. Anton had inoculated him with a variant of MT-1 that was designed to guarantee the patient changed into a delta. The original had a different goal and so a different, but related, formulation.

Another swipe of the card and he was in a corridor lined with locked doors. Each door featured a large, thick glass window which made for easy viewing within the cell. He strolled down the line and stopped at the proper cell.

There on the other side of the glass was the elderly senator. The results appeared promising.

68

Anton hadn't seen him since yesterday evening. The senator had been fully engulfed in the fever at the time. The variant had proven to be a slower acting agent and he was anxious to get a definitive result either way. The critical juncture had to have passed. A continuing decline into a terminal hemorrhagic fever or a quick recovery even as the prefrontal cortex burned itself out.

The infection was too far gone for the cure to arrest its progression, assuming it even worked the same on this mutated form of MT-1. But that was also assuming Anton chose to give it to the senator in the first place, which he had no intention of doing.

Yes, the man had been instrumental in carrying out Anton's destiny. And what? Did that create some kind of reciprocal obligation?

No. It didn't. Every tool had a shelf life, a period of time after which it was discarded because it was no longer useful.

Senator Rawlings was one such tool.

The senator was to be commended for the fact that, even at the end of his utility, he was able to offer one last service to Anton, to mankind. The development of the MT-1 variant was critical to ensuring a stable work force moving into the future. The future of intellectual progress would undoubtedly require a servile work force to provide for its basic needs like food production and other manual labor.

And the man that could reliably provide such labor would be well-positioned in the new society. Anton would accept the responsibility with his usual humility and expectation.

He knew some would ignorantly call it slavery. But they would be wrong. Anton himself agreed that historical slavery was a mistake. To subjugate one intellect to the whims of an equal intellect was morally reprehensible. It was against nature.

But a delta was not of an equal intellect. A delta lacked the very thing that made us human: the higher functioning brain.

People owned apes and no reasonable person protested that it was slavery. The deltas, in general, were closer to apes than humans. There hadn't been sufficient time to perform a longitudinal study to determine exactly how their cognitive functioning compared, but the observations he had made indicated a close pairing. Taking into account the natural variability of the virus' efficacy, it was reasonable to conclude that some deltas were likely less capable than apes on the cognitive scale.

Anton stared into the brightly lit room. Curiosity at the senator's fate had his fingertips trembling on the glass.

The senator lay curled up in a corner next to a bare metal bunk. His thin arms covered his face. A white medical gown streaked with dried feces and blood draped over his wrinkled, frail body. The wheelchair used to cart him downstairs sat next to the bunk.

Anton tapped the glass.

No response.

Anton frowned.

Had he expired? Perhaps the fever had taken him. The weak sometimes expired before the change could take place. The stress on the system could simply be too much. And the senator was nowhere near in his prime.

Anton banged on the glass and the body didn't move. He removed his keycard and swiped it over the reader next to the door. A red light switched to green and the magnetic lock disengaged. He pushed the door open and quietly stepped inside.

The body flinched and Anton froze. Not because he was scared, but because he'd thought the senator had passed, which would've been a terrible indicator for the potential of the variant serum.

The old man peeked out from beneath a filthy sleeve.

Anton stepped closer while still being certain to remain out of reach.

The elderly man growled. An inhuman voice echoed in his throat.

Pride warmed Anton's chest. The variant had worked! It would take many more tests to validate its efficacy, but this result was encouraging.

"Congratulations, Senator Rawlings. You've bolstered my confidence in the variant. While I commend you for your service, I must also inform you that your utility is now at an end."

The delta didn't respond. Not that Anton expected it to. Complex verbal language was no longer within the scope of its abilities.

"Try not to worry, you will perish soon enough."

To Anton's surprise, the words sounded almost regretful.

With agitation, he examined the underlying emotion. Was it attachment? Was he breaking faith with the very rule he'd just reminded Iridia of?

No.

No, he wasn't.

He regarded the old man with the same admiration a carpenter did a trusted hammer. And so, in like manner, there was some regret in discarding it when the time came to replace it.

Anton squatted down so he could look one last time into the senator's clouded eyes.

The old man uncurled and lunged at Anton.

In fear, Anton lashed out and happened to catch his attacker on the chin. The delta's head snapped to the side and it collapsed into a heap of withered flesh.

Anton stumbled back in shock and tripped on the wheelchair. He fell into the wall and cracked his head into the concrete. His heart pounded wildly in his chest.

The changed man looked up at Anton. Blood gushed down his chin from the ragged wound created by his teeth slicing through his lower lip. The length of the lip dangled by a remaining bridge of skin.

"You idiot!" Anton screamed as he kicked the cowering delta in the side.

While the kick felt good, the insult felt better. Much like the average person might use a more mundane expletive like asshole. Only 'idiot' was far more derogatory an insult.

He never understood why a person might opt for something so perfunctory as asshole. The asshole was simply an alternative combination of letters that meant the same thing as anus. And the anus was a useful, if under-appreciated, part of the human body. Yes, there were possible allusions to filth and disease, but was there disgrace in effectively doing a dirty job?

No.

Because it was a job.

A function.

An idiot was infinitely worse. An idiot was a machine with apparently working parts but whose whole did not exceed the sum of its parts. In fact, it was quite the opposite. An idiot equaled less than the sum of its parts. And worse yet, it implied a squandering of the human potential.

And this delta who had once been Senator Charles Rawlings was truly an idiot. He had underestimated Anton from the start. His dreams had been small. His vision myopic.

And now his brain had devolved to a state that more accurately reflected his true character.

If Anton's work created the conditions in which a certain measure of poetic justice could be carried out, he was not averse to its appreciation.

69

BETH forced back the ocean of tears threatening to pour out of her eyes. Now, more than ever, she needed to keep it together. A broken, insane mind wasn't going to be much help to Theresa. And her daughter needed her.

Needed her to do what?

She didn't know how to save Theresa. She was a veterinarian, not a scientist at a pharmaceutical company. She had no idea how to create or manufacture an antiviral drug that might save Theresa's life. And even if she did, even if all of that was true, none of it would matter because there wasn't enough time.

Theresa needed immediate treatment.

The fever had already been building and the massive exertion of fleeing the deltas seemed to have accelerated her deterioration. And that wasn't the worst of it.

The worst of it was that Beth couldn't be with her.

If indeed this was an illness that couldn't be stopped, then Theresa deserved as much comfort as she could have. It tore Beth's heart out to think it, but if her baby was going to pass, she wanted to hold her head and kiss her forehead as she went.

But she couldn't be with her because she was locked up like a criminal by Iridia's insane father.

A knot in Beth's throat choked the air from her lungs. She bit down on her tongue in the hopes that the pain might keep her mind from coming undone. The bright sting and salty taste drew just enough of her attention to keep her from completely melting down.

She paced across the office interior toward the locked door. The locked door with the trained-to-kill soldier guy outside. She needed to break the door down and go find her daughter. Anton had ordered her to be taken to the lab.

She pounded on the door, not expecting any more reaction than the nothing she'd encountered already.

No response.

She tried the handle and it was still locked.

Beth needed one thing right now. She needed Mason. Always, but now more than ever. She needed the man she'd grown to trust implicitly over the years. This was his area of expertise. Beth was a healer at heart. She could be hard when the occasion required it, but she had no training in the tactics of aggression.

A whirlwind of emotion threatened to sweep her away. A wild voice begged her to surrender to the agony, to the madness where reason limped to die. Losing her husband. Losing her daughter. The voice demanded she give in.

And so much of her wanted to.

But a tiny voice somewhere in the chaos told her to be strong. To fight for her family. To rise above and act.

She reached for the voice, clung to it, coddled it so that it wouldn't be snuffed out by the riotous winds enveloping it.

Yes. She had to act.

But how?

Someone spoke.

Beth looked up and didn't recognize the face for an instant. So deep was the battle for her sanity that the words were echoes without a source. Sounds she noticed in passing and couldn't catch before they faded away.

"Are you okay?"

Elio. That's who this was.

He squeezed her shoulder and forced a smile.

Beth's conscious thought resurfaced gasping for air like a diver testing, and perhaps sinking just beyond, the limits. "I'm okay."

"How did you think Theresa was doing?"

Beth bit her tongue again to keep her mind reined in. She coughed to get the air moving in her throat.

"She's not well."

Elio pivoted on his heel and marched over to the closed door. He banged a fist on it. "Hey! Open the door! Open it!"

Again, no response.

"Elio, come sit with me," Maria said. She sat in a cushioned chair holding Noor in her arms. The poor girl hadn't said a word since her dad got left behind. She didn't speak or cry or do anything more than allow herself to be led around. It was like there was no longer a person inside.

Elio banged on the door again. "We need some help in here! Now!"

The door flew open sending Elio stumbling backwards.

"No!" Maria shouted, but it was too late.

The guard launched at Elio and smashed a fist into his cheek. Elio's head snapped around and he crumbled to the floor.

Maria set Noor in the chair and crawled to her son. She

screamed as she touched a wound on his cheek. She turned to the guard and hissed like a snake. "You sick animal!"

The guard raised his fist, preparing to do the same to her.

Maria ducked her head and curled her body over to protect her son.

The guard strutted back to the open door. "If I come in again, someone's getting their jaw broke." He grinned wickedly like he couldn't wait to come in again.

Sick animal, indeed.

He deserved to be put down like a rabid dog. If only Beth had a pentobarbital dart available. She'd spike it into his carotid artery and deal with the guilt.

He closed the door and the lock clicked into place.

Beth helped Elio to his feet. She examined the cut and wished she had some medical supplies; anything, really. The wound needed stitches but she had no way of administering that treatment.

He touched his cheek and grimaced. "I'll be fine. How are we going to get Theresa?"

Beth almost smiled.

The boy that had informally joined their household ten days ago was not the young man that faced her now. The affection he had for her daughter hadn't changed. But the way in which Beth regarded him as a potential suitor had. He had the makings of a good man. A man worthy of her daughter's future.

If she had a future.

A new voice floated in from outside the door.

"Look at this! This shirt is ruined! Soda *everywhere*! Here, hold it for me. Oh my! I should've worn a bra!"

70

A loud smash and then a thud followed. The lock clicked open. Iridia, wearing nothing up top, poked her head in as the door opened. She grinned. The door opened further to reveal the guard crumpled up on the ground. A large metal vase lay next to him. "Looks like I've still got it, even if I haven't seen my trainer in a million years."

Beth stared in shock.

"Why is everyone just standing there? I'm here to rescue you," Iridia said.

No one moved.

"There is a cure for Theresa's sickness. It's probably in the lab somewhere."

Still no one moved.

"I'm waiting," Iridia said as she slipped back into her shirt. She tapped her foot impatiently.

Now that made sense.

Beth's brain clicked into gear. She turned to Elio. "I'll go. You should stay with your mother and Noor."

Elio's brow crinkled together.

"They aren't in any condition to go. Besides, I'm the best doctor we have."

Elio's eyes dropped. "You're right. You go." He met her gaze again. "Save her."

Beth nodded and then turned to Iridia. "Let's go!"

They had to find the lab.

"Might come in handy," she said as she picked up the metal vase lying next to the unconscious guard. Though she was sorely tempted to kick him in the groin, she edged around and headed for the elevators.

They entered an elevator. Beth stared at the card reader at a loss.

Iridia grinned and pulled a keycard out of her pocket. "I stole it from my dad's desk. I'm amazing, right? You can say it."

Beth accepted the offered card and swiped it over the reader.

"Hello, Dr. Reshenko. Where do you wish to go?"

Did they have a voice scanner type thing? One that would analyze the pitch and cadence of a person's voice and identify it as uniquely as a fingerprint?

She tried to sound like Anton, which came out horribly.

"Uh, to the lab," Beth said. "Please?"

"Descending to the basement laboratory. Please stay clear of the doors." The elevator dinged and the doors slid shut.

Beth's stomach jumped into her throat, partly from the acceleration as the car started its descent and partly because she couldn't believe it worked.

The elevator went on for what felt like forever before finally easing to a stop.

"Basement Laboratory." The doors dinged and slid open.

A guard sat behind a desk with closed glass doors in the

hallway beyond. He stood and circled around to step into their path.

"Who are you?" he asked.

Iridia stomped up and stopped inches from his face. At her height, she looked down a little to meet his gaze. "*Who am I*? Are you kidding me?"

She looked back at Beth like the world had gone crazy, which it had. So Beth wasn't sure how to respond.

"I am Iridia Reshenko! Your boss' daughter! Now get out of my way!"

The imperious tone exuded from her like a birthright. It oozed the expectation of obedience.

"Sorry, ma'am," the guard replied. He checked the clipboard in his hands. "It's just that I don't see anything about you coming down. And Dr. Reshenko didn't mention it."

"My father sent me to retrieve his notes. He is too busy for such trivialities. Now, open the doors!"

The guard flinched like the lash of leather had bitten into his skin.

"Sorry, ma'am, but who is this with you? And why is she carrying a flower vase?"

"My father will have your head! Give me the phone!"

The guard's eyes opened wide.

"Did you not hear me? Give me the phone!" Iridia's tone exuded fury and entitlement. It broke the guard's will. He turned to reach for the phone on his desk.

His outstretched hand didn't arrive at its destination.

Beth raised the vase and chopped it down on the back of his head.

The guard crashed to the floor.

Iridia hopped around in little circles pumping her hands in the air. "We make a killer team!"

"Keep an eye on the guard. I'll be back as quick as I can."

Iridia nodded as Beth hurried to the glass doors and pushed. They didn't budge. She swiped her card over the reader. A red light switched to green.

"Welcome, Dr. Reshenko," the same tastefully feminine voice said.

She pushed on the door and it soundlessly eased open. Must've been magnetic.

She ran through a hallway with floor to ceiling glass panels on each side. She passed glass doors all labeled things she didn't care about.

Spectrometry. Mycology. Other departments.

There!

She spotted what she was looking for.

Patient Wing.

She swiped Anton's card and entered.

A hallway with doors on the right. Each door had a large observation window in its center.

She peeked into the first window. The room was empty. A sparkling clean white room about ten feet by eight feet with a stainless steel bunk. The next room wasn't empty.

Beth staggered to a stop and swallowed hard to keep from retching.

A human corpse lay on the floor. A rivulet of congealed blood and feces stretched from between its legs to the drain in the center of the floor. Its face was frozen in hollow-cheeked agony. The lips peeled back to reveal large teeth. Black boils dotted its skin. They left a hundred tiny trails down to the drain. The skin hung flaccidly from the bones like melted candle wax.

The walls were splattered with viscera unfit for closer inspection. A label next to the door read *MT-1 Variant 3A*.

What was MT-1?

Beth choked down the lump in her throat and continued on. The next several doors revealed revolting variations on the same scene and had the same label next to each door.

She kept moving, not lingering as soon as she could be certain the tragedy inside wasn't her daughter. She looked away and hurried to the next door.

She froze.

"Clyde!" she yelled as her heart nearly burst with joy. The little Bili chimp looked to the glass and grinned. His large brown eyes sparkled. He jumped and rolled around, screeching and hooting with pleasure.

Beth swiped the card and barely had the door open before Clyde leaped onto her leg and climbed up into her arms. He nuzzled his moist nose into her neck and cooed like a baby. He was a baby.

Her baby.

The one that lived.

She placed him on her back. He wrapped his long arms around her neck and held on as easily as a creature does that has evolved for such behavior.

She'd found one baby, but that still left another to be found.

71

Beth rushed by an empty room. The wing only had three more doors before it ended. Doubt twisted in her gut. Maybe this wasn't the right place. She was about to pass the next door when the figure inside moved. It was an elderly man wearing a filthy medical gown. He lay on the ground touching a lower lip that appeared more detached than attached. An empty wheelchair sat next to the bunk.

What misery must he have endured?

What torture at the hands of that madman Anton?

Her heart ached for the injustice, the misery. She had just about decided to check on him when a scream froze her heart.

She recognized the voice.

Theresa.

She bolted past another door with an unspeakable scene inside and arrived at the last door.

Theresa was there, huddled in the corner, shaking and screaming.

Beth swiped the card and rushed to Theresa's side and took her daughter's face in her hands.

Theresa's eyes were bloodshot and unfocused. Her skin was dotted with bruises. One arm a network of black veins.

"Baby," Beth cried out. "Oh my baby!" She stroked her hair. "It's okay, honey. I'm here. It's okay."

She said it but knew it wasn't true. It wasn't okay. The infection was getting worse. How long did Theresa have left? She had to find the serum!

Beth tried to help Theresa stand but she couldn't. The wheelchair. She sprinted back to the cell with it and the old man. She swiped the door open and grabbed the wheelchair.

"I'll come back for you if I can," she said as she wheeled it out into the hall. The elderly man didn't react.

She helped Theresa up into the chair and then wheeled her down the hall. She passed the open door with the old man and said a silent prayer for his future as she went.

An intercom hidden somewhere in the ceiling crackled to life. "Deltas have entered the building. Deltas have entered the building."

Oh no.

Beth crashed through the door to the patient wing and back into the main corridor. She raced along and found a glass door that looked promising. Unlike all the departments she'd run across thus far, this glass was tinted black and so concealed the interior.

Immunology.

She swiped through, rounded a corner, and then skidded to a stop.

A large lab of sparkling white and steel. An advanced array of imaging equipment occupied the surfaces of numerous tables. It wasn't the hi-tech look of the place that stopped her cold.

It was the large fluid-filled, clear glass cylinders lining

the far wall that did. Each held the preserved corpse of a primate.

A knot choked Beth's throat closed.

She recognized them. Each and every one.

The missing Bili chimpanzees. The ones her boss Diana had lied about saying they'd been transferred away to non-existent, third world country zoos. Lies. All lies.

She scanned down the line and almost broke down when she saw the last one. A sob spasmed in her chest but couldn't escape the blockage in her throat.

Jane.

Clyde's mother that had died on the operating table even as Beth saved one of her babies by emergency Cesarean section.

Her dear Jane.

Frozen in fluid. Her arms floating with empty eyes staring out at nothing. The incision through her abdomen still present.

Theresa coughed and a tendril of blood spilled out onto her shirt.

Black despair tried to pull Beth under. It dragged at her feet, demanding she surrender to the suffering.

But she didn't.

Because Theresa needed her.

And she'd suffer a million times over for one of her children.

Beth turned away from the display tanks. She would accept that pain, deal with it, but not right now. She ran to a line of small refrigerators along the wall to the right. The first couple didn't contain anything that might be helpful.

But the third one did.

She pulled out a rack of four vials. The front of the rack had a printed sticker attached.

MT-1 Antiviral Doses.

This had to be it!

She pocketed the vials and looked around. She found a nearby cabinet of medical supplies and tore through it until she found a sealed bag containing a sterilized syringe. She ripped it open and loaded the dose.

She hurried back to Theresa and lifted the arm of her daughter's shirt. She poked the needle in and injected the dose. Theresa didn't react.

Beth withdrew the needle and tossed the syringe on a counter.

Had the infection progressed too far for the dose to work?

If not, how long for it to take effect?

If it did work, would there be any lasting damage?

She had more questions than answers. All questions and no answers was more like it. She was about to leave when she noticed a door on the far wall.

Antiviral Serum Production.

She had to get back to Iridia, and who knew where the deltas had broken in. But this was important. It could be *the* thing to change everything. Wasn't this what the world was waiting for?

She rolled Theresa over and set the wheelchair to the side. She swiped a card reader. It blinked green and she opened the door.

This museum of horrors had a Mona Lisa.

Jack, the Bili chimps' pack leader and Jane's mate, was inside. He was alive. And that was the only good thing Beth could see about his situation.

And even that was questionable.

72

MASON pinched his eyes shut. No, that wasn't right because they were already shut. He squeezed them tighter. A sharp pain jabbing his cheek rose above the complaints emanating from numerous other places in his body. The sensation focused his mind, surprising him because it was a valid indicator that he was still alive. The memory of the final few minutes of consciousness flooded into his brain.

An uncomfortable weight pressed onto his chest. Was it the knowledge of what had happened?

His eyes snapped open.

Mr. Piddles sat on his chest staring down. So it wasn't only the knowledge.

Mason looked around the bathroom.

He was alone.

Rather, he was the only one alive.

He tried scooting the cat off, but it resisted, leaning against his hand. He picked it up and moved it, which didn't go over well.

Mr. Piddles hissed and darted out of the bathroom.

Stupid cat.

Mason pushed himself up into a seated position. His head spun and a wave of nausea clenched his gut and made his mouth water. He concentrated on simply existing. That alone was nearly impossible.

Several inert bodies lay around him. He scanned each one and was relieved to confirm that none of them were of his group. He searched the floor looking for the dropped Glocks. None were present. The assault team had scavenged the weapons. At a time when there was no obvious resupply, it was smart to grab weapons when you could. He would've done the same thing.

Unfortunately, the absence of firearms meant he was extremely vulnerable to any threats that might arise.

He found the Bonowi baton partially concealed under a delta's body. He pulled it free and snapped it to full extension. It wasn't a pistol, but it was a whole lot better than nothing. He looked around for his knife but didn't see it. Maybe it was underneath one of these bodies, but Mason didn't know if he had the strength to dig through the carnage.

First things first. He had to get up.

He gripped the vanity and pulled himself to his feet. A sharp pain flared in his cheek making his legs wobble. He sat on the vanity to stay upright. He picked up a fragment of mirror from the countertop and peered at his reflection.

He knew there wouldn't be a bright-eyed, cheery faced image staring back at him. But what he saw was almost unrecognizable. On a disturbing and profound level, his psyche refused to admit that it was him. White bone peeked out from a deep gash running diagonally down his cheek. Dark blue patches surrounded both eyes. He reached up to touch the open wound and winced as a stabbing pain in his forearm briefly rose above the other stimuli.

A three inch jagged splinter of wood protruded from the muscle. Mason gritted his teeth and yanked it out. The intensity of the wound faded leaving the gash in his cheek to once again command his attention. It needed stitches. A couple dozen by the looks of it. He spent a few seconds inventorying the countless cuts and scrapes.

He felt more dead than alive, but he'd make it. He'd been worse off before.

With the quick self-assessment complete, the next thought that jumped into his mind was how to get to his family.

The chopper had presumably returned to Milagro Tower, as Anton had mentioned in the broadcasts during the assault on Juice's bunker. But the tower in downtown Los Angeles was twenty miles away. And there was no such thing as easy-driving miles anymore.

He had the Bronco. It could handle jumping curbs and bulldozing over small piles of debris no problem. But the news reports had shown that the roads in and around downtown were jammed with abandoned vehicles. It had been nearly a week since the media went silent, but there was no reason to think the roads had magically cleared.

As heavy and strong as the Bronco was, it was no Abrams tank. He wasn't going to be able to point it at a block of densely packed cars and roll through it.

The electric cargo bike was likely still down the street, but the battery was dead. He had no doubt he could maneuver it through the maze of cars, but it might take half a day to get there. He still had Spock, Beth's Vulcan 750. It was small enough that he could probably wind his way through the jam-packed streets while also picking up speed in any open areas along the way. With a combination of speed and maneuverability, he should be able to get there in a couple of hours if things went well.

It would have to do.

He took a number of deep breaths while listening for movement or other clues about who or what might remain in the house. The only sound was the slow inhale and exhale of his own breath. There didn't appear to be any immediate threat. He nudged bodies around looking for his lost knife. The third body revealed its location. It was still stuck in the corpse's torso. Mason tugged it free and wiped the crimson stain on a fragment of clothing clinging to the delta's waist.

Mason worked his way out into the hallway, stepping over lifeless limbs. His heart wanted to grieve for them. These people likely led ordinary, comfortable lives just ten days ago. The intervening days had taken away everything, starting with the mind that made them human, and ending with the blood that kept them alive.

They didn't deserve this end.

His family had been taken by a maniac. Juice and Linda had been murdered by the same man.

Mason had only one objective, though it came in two parts.

Save his family.

And kill Anton Reshenko.

73

He crept down the hallway toward the stairs. What next? The house. Clear the house to ensure no one else got left behind. Deal with threats if any arose.

The air reeked of human excrement mixed with the sharp scent of blood. He longed for a gulp of whiskey to burn away the foul taste coating his mouth.

The rooms upstairs were empty and the rooms downstairs turned out to be the same. The front door had been blown off its hinges and lay on top of a body on the floor. The body lay perpendicular to the door underneath its center. Both ends of the door balanced in the air like some kind of twisted playground seesaw.

Was this the new world? Would children ever be free to play outside again?

Mason skirted around the macabre arrangement and stopped beside the open doorway. He listened and heard a commotion outside. He raised the baton, preparing to strike down whatever was coming.

Nothing came.

He listened again. The sounds appeared to be coming

from beyond the courtyard, out in the street. He quietly slipped outside and surveyed the bodies in the courtyard.

These used to be people. People with families and lives and dreams.

Mason threw a stick of dynamite on that train of thought. It would take him nowhere useful right now.

He saw Beth's motorcycle over by the gate where they'd left it. A tiny spark of hope flickered in his chest. Movement created optimism. If he was doing something, going somewhere, then he still had a chance. He crept over and was about to throw a leg over the seat when he stopped.

There was a puddle of shiny, black liquid below the engine. A viscous drop hit the surface as he watched. He knelt down and took a closer look.

A large caliber bullet had punched a ragged hole in the engine. Mason didn't know if the assault team had purposely spiked the vehicle or if it had been hit by a loose round, but it didn't much matter. The bike was going nowhere fast. He was tempted to try to start it anyway to see what happened but with the odds leaning toward a fiery explosion, he decided against it.

Which left the Bronco.

It could get him closer, but he'd get bogged down at some point. And he wasn't in any kind of shape to walk for miles and miles.

Anger burned in his chest. He had to get to his family and yet had no way to do it. They wouldn't survive for long. Anton had killed Juice and Linda in cold blood. He was more than capable of doing the same to Mason's family.

Juice and Linda.

They'd been murdered, and the knife that twisted in Mason's gut was that he was partly to blame. They'd gotten involved by helping him. Juice's generosity had gotten him and his wife killed. His old friend was exactly what this changed world needed most. An inventive problem solver that knew how to get things done.

Mason listened again to the movement somewhere beyond the perimeter wall. He climbed up on the bike and peeked over.

In the middle of the street, a small group of deltas surrounded the body of one of the assault team members. They'd managed to tear through his tactical gear and expose the flesh below.

Mason wondered how long he'd been out because the corpse was utterly ravaged. The leg bones looked like they'd been cleaned with a scrub brush. A large delta gnawed meat off a small bone. Maybe from the hand or foot.

The operator's HK MP7 lay a couple feet from his body. The deltas ignored it, not understanding its value. Mason knew better, but he also knew they wouldn't ignore him. And a baton wasn't enough offense to take on the eight deltas picking the corpse clean.

He dropped back down off the bike and made his way around the back of the house. He found a trashcan and used it to hike up over the wall and drop down into his own backyard. He strode toward the Bronco, still thinking about his part in Juice's death. About the injustice of cutting down a man with so much to give.

He jolted to a stop mid-stride. A memory flashed into focus. Maybe Juice wasn't done helping.

Maybe it was time to reveal his latest and greatest invention.

74

Mason shook his head. It was insanity, of course. But he couldn't think of a better option. He hopped in the Bronco and fired it up. The throaty old bruiser growled to life, the rumbling an assertion that it was ready for anything.

He pulled out on to the street and revved the engine at the group of deltas. They screamed and shouted. Half of them cowered in terror and the other half glared, ready to charge. He could run them down and try to recover the rifle, but could he live with himself having done it?

No.

These people, or creatures, or whatever, were not enemy combatants. They hadn't willingly entered a war zone to fight and possibly die if the vagaries of war turned against them. Besides, what about Linda? Was there something there that could be saved?

Mason hit the gas, weaving around bodies where he could and rolling over them where he couldn't. The wet crunch under the tires only vaguely distressed him. The weary numbness in his mind kept it somewhat at a distance. He remembered the feeling well. He and his men had felt it in Fallujah. It was a survival mechanism. The mind closing in on itself when the horrors of the outside world threatened to unravel it.

Compassion required comfort, to some degree at least. When all comfort was stripped away, when only suffering remained, it was a rare soul that could still hold onto both compassion and sanity at the same time.

Mason left the group to their grisly business and headed toward Juice's house. He turned south and headed toward the canals.

Movement up ahead caught his attention. Five people sitting in a front yard. Numerous large planters had replaced the usual turf. They sat huddled together in one of the aisles between planters.

Were they crazy?

As he got closer, he saw the truth of it. Not people. Deltas. A family with three kids. All of them either naked or wearing fragments of tattered clothing.

Mason slowed as he got closer.

The mother plucked a tomato from a tall plant and handed it to one of the young boys. The boy accepted it and popped it into his mouth. He crunched down and juice dribbled down his chin. The other two held their hands up asking for their fair share.

The father stood up and faced the Bronco as Mason stopped in the street. He stepped in between his family and stared at Mason. His eyes narrowed and his body tensed.

They seemed so normal. And yet, the differences made the scene all the more surreal.

Clearly, they weren't all aggressive. Why were some more aggressive and others, like these people, almost normal?

Mason didn't want to scare them or start a confrontation, so he eased off the brake and continued on.

He was a few blocks away when an enormous, muscled delta loped out into the street. It must've been a bodybuilder in its previous life.

It stood in the middle of the street staring at the approaching Bronco. No stitch of clothing remained. The creature didn't flinch as Mason drove closer. Did it not recognize the danger of getting run over? Did it not understand what happened when flesh collided with steel at twenty miles per hour?

Mason scanned both sides of the road and didn't see a clear path. It would've been easier to drive straight through the unfortunate creature. There was no threat of damage to his vehicle. But he couldn't bring himself to do it. With less than thirty feet remaining between them, Mason steered left and hopped over the curb. He smashed through a black wrought iron fence and demolished what had once been a meticulously manicured front yard. He stomped on the brake as the next yard had a concrete retaining wall a couple of feet high.

The Bronco could get over it but attempting the feat at speed was asking to get the front axle ripped off. The huge tires locked up and gouged trenches through the yellowing grass. In a city that required so much water and had very little supply of its own, Mason never understood why so many people had enormous green lawns.

Used to anyway.

With the constant supply of water shut off days ago, this yard, like countless others, was already starting to fade. Mason edged the Bronco up to the retaining wall until the tires touched. Movement in the corner of his eye caused him to glance to the right. The large delta in the street was no longer alone. A small pack surrounded him, all watching intently. The leader tilted his head back and shouted.

Mason looked around in alarm. More deltas streamed out from between houses and joined the growing pack in the street.

It was way past time to go.

Mason let the Bronco drift back a little and then gunned it. The front tire slammed into the retaining wall and bounced up. Unfortunately, it then crashed back to the grass. Having it in four-wheel-drive would've been a big help, but there was no chance he was gonna jump out and set about locking the hubs while deltas stared at his back.

The largest delta, the one he should've run over, screamed and the press of bodies around him, now maybe two dozen strong, broke as one for the Bronco.

Mason let the Bronco roll back a little further and then gave it more gas this time. It hit the retaining wall and bounced up, but again dropped back down before the tires could catch on the lip.

The mass of bodies smashed into his vehicle like a wave breaking on a rock. The Bronco leaned to the side before dropping back onto all four tires. The leader of the deltas scrambled up onto the hood and started pounding on the windshield.

Mason threw it in reverse and the delta slipped, crashing onto the hood like a bull with its legs cut off. He threw it in drive and floored it. The Bronco lunged forward and the hood jerked up as the tires clawed up the retaining wall. The delta on the hood launched off into the air like he was shot from a catapult.

The front tires rounded the edge and Mason hit the gas again. The rear tires bounced over and he was clear of the obstacle. He jerked the steering wheel to the right and tore through the raised yard. He didn't slow down as the Bronco flew off the elevated terrain and dropped hard to the street level. The impact shook free the last couple of deltas clinging to the side of the vehicle.

Mason gave it some gas and got back up to speed. He glanced in the rearview mirror and watched as the hunting pack reassembled. The hulk one appeared out front. He shouted in rage and then took off in pursuit. The pack followed.

With only three blocks and one turn to go, he doubted he'd be able to shake them.

75

The Bronco skidded to a stop. Mason glanced in the rearview mirror and saw the deltas about a block back. He hadn't been able to go fast enough or far enough to completely lose them. He turned to the house outside and wondered if he was in the right place.

Juice's house looked more like it belonged in Fallujah than on the once prestigious canal streets of Venice. Whereas the smooth concrete, glass, and metal construction had once looked sleek and modern, it now looked decrepit and ancient. The concrete exterior was pocked and crumbling, evidence of a chopper's M230 chain gun in action.

They'd unloaded on the place.

Leaving the keys in the ignition and the engine on, Mason eased down onto the street. His jumping days would not be back for quite some time. He made sure the door lock was up and not engaged before closing the door. If this insane idea didn't work out for whatever the million reasons were why it shouldn't, maybe he could make it back for a quick escape. He didn't think the deltas would understand how to open the door to get in and even if one did, he was absolutely certain they wouldn't know how to operate a vehicle.

He looked down the street and the approaching deltas exploded in roars and hoots, thinking they'd cornered their prey. If his escape plan worked out, they'd be in for a big surprise. He ran around to the side of the house, still in shock at the amount of damage the building had sustained. He stepped through a gaping window and crunched on the carpet of glass inside. He headed through the living room toward the back hallway with the Bonowi baton raised and ready to strike.

The hum of the deltas outside grew louder, closer. Their individual voices began to separate and become distinct.

Mason hurried to the bathroom and discovered a huge hole in the shower floor. The assault team had used explosives to breach the basement bunker.

He carefully stepped over the crumbling subfloor and held onto the sides to lower himself into the room below. Signs of the ferocious battle were everywhere. Chunks of plaster torn out of walls. White dust covered the floor. Bits and pieces of metal and plastic everywhere. Shell casings like popcorn littering a movie theater.

He turned and found Juice on the floor with his back against the wall. His head tilted to the side at a grotesque angle. His chest was a ruin of pulverized flesh and bone. The lights in the ceiling above flickered and Mason half expected the body to get up and lunge at him like a cheesy Halloween haunted house. He scanned further right and found Linda. She was no better off.

He had no idea how Juice had planned to continue a relationship with a delta, but he understood the commitment to try. He would do the same thing if Beth got infected and changed. He'd never give up on her. But now it didn't matter because Juice and Linda would never get a chance to fight for their future together.

All because of one man.

A man that needed killing.

A shriek from somewhere above cut short the eulogy in Mason's mind. It would have to wait. He hurried to the workshop wondering if it still contained Juice's latest invention.

The Personal Aerial Transport. PAT.

His friend had a thing for acronyms. He'd once claimed that the perfect acronym made an invention ten times more valuable. It was all about the branding.

He opened the door and found it in the center of the workshop just as before. Looking just as crazy and unreasonable as before. How could eight million people fly their own PAT around? The logistics of moving roadways from the 2D world up into the 3D world where things could move in all three axes seemed impossible. Mason hadn't said it to Juice earlier because there was no point in raining on his parade.

This future wouldn't have eight million PATs flying around. At this point, just one would be enough. He walked to the corner of the room and punched the button to open the bay roof. A long crack appeared in the ceiling. The two panels slid apart spilling dirt and whirling clouds of dust.

Mason stepped up into the half-cage that all too closely resembled a coffin or some kind of medieval torture device. He hoped its appearance wasn't indicative of what was about to happen. He slipped into the harness and surveyed the controls.

Not complicated. A left joystick with a white decal that

said **POWER**. A small digital screen behind that. A right joystick with a white decal that said **NAVIGATION**.

Okay.

He tapped the dark screen and it blinked to life. He zipped through a series of menus about FAA disclaimers, legal waivers, and operational instructions.

He wasn't a read-the-manual-first kind of guy, even when he had the time for it to be an option.

A crash outside in the main basement room briefly grabbed his attention. The deltas had found the way down. He turned back to the screen.

Come on.

Come on.

He tapped yet another *I AGREE* button and finally found what he was looking for.

START

A round, green button. He tapped it.

Both turbines spun up as deltas appeared in the doorway. They didn't hesitate.

The two roof panels continued to slide open. Now about three feet apart. PAT was probably six feet across at its widest point—the outside of each propeller housing. Mason took hold of the left joystick and eased it forward. The whirring rush of the propellers increased. The vehicle lifted half an inch off the ground and skidded to the left before Mason dropped it back to the floor.

The first delta jumped straight at him.

Mason caught it in the chest with a hard kick that sent it sprawling backward into the one behind.

Mason glanced up. Just one more foot of clearance.

Another delta lunged for his arm but tripped on the two hitting the floor. Its hand instead clipped the power joystick. The turbines roared and PAT jumped up a couple of feet and then dropped back to the floor. Mason's neck popped and his teeth slammed together with the impact.

Another delta grabbed Mason's leg and tried to pull him back toward the others behind. The harness securing his torso held him in place.

With the other foot, Mason landed a hard kick to the delta's temple and it stumbled back in a daze. More deltas entered the room. He kicked and kneed as many as came within range.

Enough clearance or not. It was now or never.

76

He shoved the power joystick forward and again the propellers whooshed into high gear. The PAT jumped off the ground and tilted forward as the weight of a delta clawing at Mason dragged it down. He kicked it in the solar plexus and it fell back. The vehicle righted itself and began to rise through the opening above.

Deltas surrounded the gaping hole that was once the front yard. They reached out trying to grab at him as he ascended. One reached too far and fell into the workshop and smacked the concrete floor twelve feet below.

Another leaped across the empty space. It misjudged the distance and slammed into a skid, doubling its body around the metal pole. The additional weight dragged the PAT lower. It dropped back down into the bay.

Above him, surrounding the square aperture, the frenzied deltas clawed at empty air. And now the room below held more of the same. A tall one jumped up and grabbed the feet of the one clinging to the skid.

The roof panels clanged to a stop in the fully opened position.

Mason slammed the power joystick all the way forward. The turbines howled as they blasted air over the deltas below. The cowlings shook as they edged toward the operational limits. The descent halted but full power wasn't getting it moving up again.

The delta attached to the skid popped up as the weight on his feet unwrapped him from the metal pole.

Mason kicked it square in the face. Its head snapped back and the one clinging to its feet pulled them both down.

PAT vaulted into the air. It zipped past the ring of deltas outside and rose higher until it jerked to a stop about fifteen feet in the air.

What now?

Mason looked down. A taut, thick black cord stretched from the battery compartment on the bottom of the vehicle down into the workshop below.

The power cord.

Seriously?

As brilliant as Juice was, why didn't he make it like the magnetic adapter on Apple laptops? The kind that yanked free if you pulled too hard. That would've been a really nice feature just then.

A small lever locked the adaptor in place on PAT. He stretched down with his right hand making sure to keep his left hand pouring on the power. It was just out of reach.

He scrambled to unlock the harness. As the final clasp came free, PAT lurched to the right. Mason slipped and the world seemed to click into slow-motion. He tried to grab anything that would halt the fall. His fingers slipped over the control arms. He fell away from the vehicle. A fingertip scraped the landing skid on the way down.

He was a dead man.

Only he landed on the cord, one leg straddling each side. His hands clamped down and arrested the descent.

He glanced around. What an insane situation.

Above, PAT self-stabilized doing its best to maintain position and altitude. Surrounding him on all sides with barely six feet of clearance, deltas screamed for his blood. Below, more howled and shrieked, expecting him to fall at any second.

The cable jerked in his hands as the muscled delta he'd confronted on the way over pulled himself up.

Mason scrambled up the cable and hooked a leg over a landing skid. He smacked the release lever open with the side of his hand.

The adaptor didn't break free. The thing was stuck in there due to the strain!

The delta's ripped arms bulged as it pulled higher. It glared up at Mason with burning eyes.

Mason pounded and pounded on the adaptor but it wouldn't disengage.

The delta made it up another couple of feet, now only a few feet below the skids.

Mason banged on the adaptor but, with the tension and the angle, it wasn't going to separate.

The delta grabbed hold of a skid with one hand and Mason's leg with the other. He yanked down hard and Mason grimaced as something in his knee popped. A muscled arm reached higher and grabbed a handful of his shirt.

He slipped forward until their faces were inches apart. The eyes. There was no reason in them. No pity.

Mason unclipped the Recon knife from his belt, flipped open the blade, and slammed it down into his attacker's eye socket. It reached for the knife lodged in its skull with both hands and fell like a stone.

Mason reached up and eased back the throttle. The turbines slowed and the machine drifted lower. The tension on the cable relaxed and Mason smacked the adapter as hard as he could.

The end broke free and fell away. He pushed the throttle forward and the turbines kicked into gear, lifting him clear of the threat.

Now hovering some twenty feet above yard level, Mason eased off the power and stabilized altitude. PAT hovered in place while he carefully climbed up into the usual standing position. He buckled in and only then took a big breath of relief.

The deltas below were in an absolute frenzy. Their primitive minds bewildered by having cornered prey somehow escape. They crowded in around the open bay. One was pushed by those behind and tumbled down into the workshop.

Mason turned to the west and watched the setting sun dipping into the ocean. The deep blue cut a sharp line into the pale orange sky. High above, pink clouds reflected the waning light of the half disc still above the horizon.

The view was stunning.

One of those sunsets tourists wrote home about. One of those sunsets that made you remember why you paid so much to live on the west side.

Mason stared in awed silence.

A gust of wind pushed him out over the canal before PAT automatically adjusted. The movement broke the spell. As beautiful as it was, it was nothing without his family.

He rotated the navigation joystick to the left and PAT deftly yawed left. It spun around in place and the city of Los

Angeles came into view. Hundreds of fires burned throughout. Their inky trails of smoke lifted and curled and dissipated into the sky above.

He yawed further and downtown came into view. There, reaching higher than all the others, was his destination.

Milagro Tower.

Assuming he could actually fly there.

He kicked up the throttle while easing the navigation joystick forward. PAT tilted forward and slowly picked up speed. The roar of the twin turbines drowned out the enraged deltas below. He slid over the landscape, adding more power to gain altitude while moving forward.

Mason had never been a pilot in the military. The closest he'd ever gotten to flying a plane was in a computer game. He tilted the nav joystick left and felt the machine respond. He tilted it right and got back on course. He eased forward on both joysticks and PAT tilted forward, picking up speed while maintaining altitude. It was kind of like a computer game, only a mistake would kill you instead of starting over at the last waypoint.

Now a couple hundred feet in the air, he shot toward downtown like an arrow at the target. The endless veins of unmoving cars below accentuated the sense of freedom the machine engendered. It truly was a genius invention. Part creative. Part engineering. All awesome. This was the future mankind had been dreaming about for decades. The actual arrival of the fabled flying cars that everyone had always said was right around the corner, but never was.

This was the reality that would never arrive.

Mankind had turned down a dark alley and there were no more corners ahead holding the promise of a brighter future.

77

BETH stepped into the small room. The hairs on the back of her neck stood on end. Clyde chittered in agitation.

A box framework of metal poles surrounded Jack's six and a half foot frame. Restraints bound the ape to the poles at the ankles, knees, wrists, and elbows. Poles encircled his waist and chest, leaving no room to move. Two plates of metal came together around his neck. The plates had been raised so that his neck was stretched tight. A half-sphere of tightened screws surrounded and pinned his head in place.

A truss work of torture.

IV lines trailed out of his body in several places. Red fluid coursed through the tubes. Beth didn't know the details, but clearly his blood had something to do with the cure.

That's why Anton wanted all the Bili chimps. He was harvesting them for the serum.

Jack blinked and hooted. He jerked against the restraints but they held him fast.

Disgust, pity, and rage filled Beth's heart.

Jack had never liked her. He'd even tried to kill her.

Worse, he'd played a part in Jane's death. That said, he didn't deserve such torture, such cruelty. And Beth wasn't the type to sit by while an animal suffered.

Clyde climbed down and ran over to his father. They'd never met after the birth, but the little chimp seemed to sense the connection. He scrambled up the bars and sat on the plate stretching Jack's neck. He chittered and hooted, stroking his father's face.

Jack licked him and softly hooted in return. They knew the truth about each other. Beth saw it clear as day. Anyone would have.

She set about unbuckling the restraints, unscrewing the poles and screws, and pulling out the IV needles. He held still, seemingly understanding that she was trying to help. She got the last arm free and stepped back.

Jack stepped out of the hideous box framework with Clyde in his arms. He held the little chimp at arm's length turning him over and over examining every square inch.

Hanging upside down, Clyde screeched his discomfort and Jack quickly flipped him right side up.

A terrible and familiar shriek seized their attention. Another answered it and many more joined in the chorus.

Deltas in pursuit of prey.

The noise wasn't necessarily close, but it wasn't far away either.

It was time to go.

Beth tentatively reached for Jack's hand. Part of her mind screamed to run away. This ape was far larger, stronger, and faster than she was. And he had already tried to kill her once.

Was she crazy?

Her fingers slipped into his hand. He trembled at her touch, but made no aggressive moves.

"Jack, we have to leave," she said hoping the tone of her voice would convey as much as the words. "Those things are dangerous. We can't let them catch us."

He stared at her while Clyde chewed on his chin.

"We have to keep the baby safe," she said.

She gingerly pulled his hand and he followed. They walked hand in hand into the larger Immunology lab and Jack spotted the display cases filled with his dead and preserved family.

He dropped Beth's hand and dashed directly to the cylinder holding Jane. He tapped the glass but she, of course, didn't respond. He moaned softly while trying to touch her fingers through the thick glass. He turned Clyde around and held him up to the glass.

Beth walked over and softly touched the glass. She'd raised Jane from an infant. The Bili chimp was as much a daughter as Theresa. "I'm so sorry," she said as a tear slid down her cheek. "I didn't know. I swear."

Jack turned to Beth and tilted his head. He curled a thick, black finger and scooped the tear from her cheek.

The shrieking deltas echoed through again.

"Follow me!" Beth said. She hurried back to Theresa in the wheelchair and led them out of the room and began tracing her way back to the main entrance of the basement laboratory.

The echoes of the deltas seemed to be getting louder and closer, but their luck held and they didn't run into any as they went.

Luck could be a fickle mistress.

Beth swiped them through the final glass door and saw no sign of Iridia or the knocked-out guard. That wasn't a good sign.

She hurried to the elevators thinking that maybe, just maybe, they were going to make it.

And that's when their luck changed.

Several deltas rounded a corner and stopped in their tracks some twenty feet away. They howled and shrieked but didn't come closer.

Jack jumped to the front and roared, beating his chest with one hand while holding Clyde in the other.

The deltas melted back, clearly aware of the alpha in their presence. Clearly aware of the damage he could do.

Beth smacked the elevator button and looked up at the digital display above the door.

73

It slowly began ticking down. It had a long way to go to get to the basement.

Come on.

Come on!

More deltas began arriving behind the first few. Their numbers began to swell.

Beth checked the elevator's progress.

48

As more piled in behind the first few, the group grew more aggressive. They crept closer, growling and swiping the air at Jack. Testing his resolve to defy their superior numbers.

Jack brought Clyde to his face and touched their foreheads together. Their eyes blinked in unison. He turned and passed his son to Beth. Clyde climbed up and settled around Beth's neck. Jack extended a finger and touched Clyde's chin.

He then turned back to the deltas. He opened his mouth wide revealing huge canine teeth. Four sharp daggers. Each several inches long. He roared and leaped ten feet through the air crashing into the mass of bodies.

His teeth sliced through flesh. His hands and feet tore limbs from bodies. He snapped through bones like toothpicks. The first few fell like wheat to the scythe. But there were too many.

The elevator dinged and opened.

Beth swiped the card.

As the doors closed, Jack disappeared under a blanket of bodies clawing and tearing at him.

Beth wanted to scream. She wanted to hurt something. Or someone. Someone in particular.

Anton Reshenko.

A darkness in her heart longed to kill the man that had caused so much suffering to so many.

78

November 2004
Fallujah, Iraq

MASON limped along with Miro's help. They did their best to move from cover to cover. A pile of rubble here. The burned out entryway of a building there. Every move through open space filled with tension, waiting for the first bullet to snap by. The one that would signal the start of the ambush. The ambush that would undoubtedly end their escape.

They didn't have to wait long.

They'd made it a block and a half south from where the IED had taken out Ramirez and the Humvee. He was beginning to think maybe, just maybe, they'd get down to Phase Line Fran without running into further contact.

Yeah, right.

The first bullet pinged off the pavement inches from Mason's right foot. A tiny cloud of dust poofed up. The first round didn't come to the dance alone. Gunfire echoed down the narrow street as multiple assailants hidden in windows fired on them.

Mason sprinted for the nearest doorway. It was dark inside and he had no idea if he might be running right into a nest of bad guys. But in this case, the unknown was better than the known because the known was them getting shot to pieces.

He flew through the doorway as bullets pinged the face of the building. They entered a dark hallway of what appeared to be an apartment building. Closed doors lined the hall on both sides. Night had descended on the city outside and the unlit interior offered even less visibility. Exactly the right situation for NVGs. Thank Uncle Sam for technology.

He dropped the goggles over his eyes and powered them on. Tried to power them on. No luck.

"Miro," he whispered, "try your NVGs. Mine are dead."

"Already did. Same here."

"Wonderful."

Miro tapped his shoulder to let Mason know he was ready to move. "Unflappable optimism. That's what I've always liked about you, Sarge."

"That's me," Mason said as he flicked on the Surefire flashlight attached to his rifle. Two narrow beams of light pierced the length of the corridor. They moved down the hall as fast as they could, waiting for a door to open and an AK to unload on them.

He tried not to think about how exposed they were. How stranded and outnumbered. Thinking about things too much in a life or death situation wasn't always an advantage. The clarity could paralyze you.

They got to the end and found a back door that exited to an alley. Mason chose left, hoping to continue south toward their intended destination. Gunfire echoed through the alley. From where exactly was impossible to tell.

The alley curved to the right and came to an intersection. Mason knelt at the corner and caught his breath. Tried to, at least.

More gunfire echoed down the alley. This time louder, closer.

"Move out!" Mason whispered. They dashed across the tight intersection and into the alley on the far side just as tracer rounds zipped behind their heads. A torrent of fire ripped through the intersection.

"Almawt la'amrika!"

"Sa'aqtalk!"

Numerous voices shouted threats and promises from around the corner. The volume of voices and volume of fire indicated a large enemy force. A dozen or more men. Not the kind of odds Mason wanted to face in their current condition.

They followed the alley curving to the left, skipping the first couple of doors they passed. They entered the third one and plunged into darkness. The voices of their pursuers grew louder. Mason tried a closed door on the right and found it unlocked. He and Miro spilled through it and came face to face with a middle-aged bearded man holding a child in his arms.

The child appeared to be a year old or so. A beautiful little girl with large, dark eyes. She reminded Mason of his own daughter back home. Not that they looked much alike. It was just the age. The innocence. Theresa was now four-years-old but she still retained some of the round features of her younger self. The girl stared at Mason with a curiosity that only a child could have in that situation.

The man turned to shield the baby with his body.

"Please, no hurt," he said over and over in heavily accented, broken English.

"Quiet!" Mason whisper-shouted as he locked the door.

"No hurt! Please!" the man continued on babbling in terror.

Mason closed the door and took up a position beside it. "Shut him up!"

Miro marched over and cupped a large hand over the smaller man's mouth. "Shhh!"

The muffled words stopped.

"Sit," Miro said in his ear as he grabbed the man's shoulder and shoved him down onto a couch covered with a wild assortment of cushions.

"I do. No hurt!"

Miro grabbed his mouth again. "Quiet."

The man finally got the message and stopped talking. He hugged the little girl to his chest.

Mason watched him to make sure he wasn't going to pull a gun or start yakking again. Instead, the man glanced nervously at a doorway to his left. Mason flashed his light in that direction and saw a sink and five gallon water bottles in the next room. The kitchen.

He tried to remember the rudimentary Arabic they'd been taught back at Camp Fallujah while working up to the assault. He wasn't exactly the tower of Babel with languages, but he knew enough for rudimentary communication.

"Shakhs akhr?"

He was pretty sure that meant "Someone else?"

The man quickly shook his head. "No. No. No." He continued shaking it.

Too quickly.

"Miro, check it out," he said as he pointed to the kitchen.

Miro nodded and sliced the pie into the room. He

entered and reemerged a moment later with a woman struggling and shouting at them both. Miro wrapped a hand over her mouth and pinned her to his chest. Her muffled screams dipped and rose in volume as her wild movements intermittently broke the seal over her mouth.

She was going to get them all killed if she didn't shut up.

She bit down on Miro's hand and he yelped with pain. She slipped free and cowered on the couch next to her husband. Miro raised his clenched hand to crack the woman a good one.

"No!" Mason shouted as he stumbled over to intervene. They weren't here to beat up on innocent people. But they did need to keep her quiet. He slapped a hand over her mouth and put his mouth next to her ear.

"Nahn In yadurr bik," Mason said. It was as close to "We won't hurt you" as he knew how to say.

She seemed to finally get the message as her piercing wail quieted to a sobbing murmur.

A hard pounding at the door made Mason jump. He whirled around with his rifle ready to go.

"Aftah!" a harsh voice yelled from outside. "Aftah albab!"

79

The man outside pounded on the door again. Someone yelled from farther away and the man gave a gruff reply. His footsteps receded. Perhaps they'd decided the door was locked and their quarry must've gone elsewhere.

The voices faded and it sounded like the search had moved on down the alley.

That's when the little girl shrieked. Whatever curiosity she had minutes ago had finally settled on the side of fear. Now committed, she wailed and sobbed like an alarm bell going off.

Mason turned to quiet her when bullets blew holes through the middle panel of the door. The bullets peppered the wall next to the couch. He stepped back and dropped to a knee ready to fill whoever entered full of holes. Miro dove into the kitchen and rolled into cover behind the wall.

The husband pulled his wife to the floor while still holding his daughter in one arm. The child curled into his chest bawling like a banshee.

No use in trying to quiet her now.

Men gathered outside the door. They spoke in harsh,

clipped tones. Mason didn't catch the words but he understood them well enough anyway.

The Americans are inside. Good. Let's kill them.

That was the conversation, or near enough.

The wife screamed and clutched her chest. She struggled to her feet while her husband tried to hold her down. She shook him free and yelled something Mason didn't catch before dashing into the kitchen.

"What the hell are you doing?" Miro shouted. "Get down!"

Mason ran into the kitchen and saw the woman digging through a deep drawer on the far side.

Miro had his sidearm drawn and pointed at her. "I said get on the ground!"

"Lower your weapon, Corporal Pike!" Mason shouted.

He didn't. "She's digging for a weapon! Get on the ground or I will shoot you!"

More gunfire blasted through the front door from the hallway. The muj knew they had the right door now. The husband shouted something. The wife frantically shoveled through the drawer. She latched onto something and whirled around with something black in her hand.

BANG. BANG.

Smoke wafted from the muzzle of Miro's M9.

The woman collapsed with two holes in her chest. The black thing in her hands tumbled to the ground.

"Goddammit, Corporal!" Mason said as he wrenched the pistol out of Miro's hand.

The husband appeared around the corner. He stared at his wife and then at Mason holding the smoking gun.

"Nalasif! Nalasif! No!"

He sobbed and screamed at the same time. He rushed to his wife's side and set the girl on the floor next to her.

The girl dipped a finger in the blood pooling beside her mother.

The enraged man picked up the thing she'd dropped and showed it to them while screaming wildly.

A small black, zipped bag.

He yanked open the zipper and pulled out a bottle of prescription medication.

"Heart! Heart!" he shouted. He lunged forward and began beating on Mason's chest armor.

Miro had just killed a woman for trying to get her medication. But Mason couldn't blame him, no matter how messed up the situation was because they'd both heard countless accounts of Marines that had been killed by someone who claimed to be an innocent civilian.

Nothing made sense in Fallujah. That was all there was to it.

The husband climbed Mason like a tree as he beat his fists and clawed at him.

The shock kept Mason from responding. Or maybe it was the horror. He blocked the ineffectual swings with one arm while his mind reeled. The horror of busting into this man's life and killing his wife a few minutes later. And all the while claiming to be the good guys and being there to help the very people whose lives they had just destroyed.

Mason shoved the man aside and stooped to check on his wife. She was dead.

The report of AK-47s turning the front door into toothpicks went quiet and the voices of their pursuers came through loud and clear.

"Sarge, we have to get outta here!"

Miro pulled him to his feet.

"I'm sorry," Mason said to the raving husband. "I'm so sorry."

The daughter's hands were covered with her mother's blood. She'd streaked it across her own face. She grabbed a golden pendant hanging from her mother's neck. It looked like a bird symbol of some kind. She sobbed while pulling on the pendant as if that might make her mother wake up.

The husband lunged forward and wrapped his hands around Mason's throat. His nails dug furrows into Mason's skin.

Mason's black revery snapped. He slammed a fist into the man's stomach, doubling him over. The clenched fingers hooked on the chain of his dog tags and it snapped as the man fell away.

Mason's dog tags slipped out and fell to the floor as Miro dragged him toward the open doorway at the back of the kitchen. Their flashlights bobbed and weaved as they sprinted through a plain back room with only a bed and another door. They smashed through that door and entered a small open air courtyard.

The voices behind grew louder. The enemy rushing through the small home.

Mason ran to the perimeter wall abutting the alley. Miro clasped his hands together and Mason stepped into the offered foothold. The adrenalized Texan nearly threw him over the seven foot wall. He managed to grab hold of the edge and fall down the other side. Miro was up and over an instant later.

They scanned the alley in both directions and saw no immediate threats.

"I thought she was getting a weapon, Sarge," Miro said as his voice cracked with emotion. "I swear I did."

"I know you did. I know."

Mason didn't want to think about it anymore. Right now

or ever. Besides, they didn't have the luxury of contemplation. Their survival required immediate action.

Mason looked down the dark alley to the south. It ended about a block down. It was too dark to tell for sure, but they had to be getting close to Phase Line Fran.

A Humvee screeched to a stop on the street beyond. A mounted spotlight on the roof bathed them in light, nearly blinding them as well. A soldier in the turret pointed his fifty cal down the alley, above their heads.

"That's our ride!" Mason shouted as Miro wrapped an arm around him, and they sprinted as fast as their damaged bodies allowed. They made it halfway when the fifty cal opened up.

Withering fire sliced through the air just above their heads. Tracer rounds snapped by like lasers. The concussion of the passing rounds slapped them from above.

Sporadic return fire chipped off the walls nearby as they ran for it. They were running through a meat grinder. Weapons designed to chew up flesh and spit it out.

Mason knew they had no chance. Continuing to run was merely a mechanical performance until the curtain came down.

The door to the Humvee flew open and they piled in as the turret-mounted gun continued to vaporize everything and everyone unlucky enough to be in its field of fire.

Miro slammed the door shut and the vehicle jerked forward.

The marine in the turret dropped down and stared at them both with wide eyes. "Sergeant West, third squad?"

Mason slumped into the seat and nodded with what little energy remained in his body.

"We thought we'd lost you guys!"

Mason closed his eyes and tried not to see the images forming in his mind.

Of the other men of third squad that were gone.

Of the woman with holes in her chest.

Of Lopes.

Mason had made it out alive, but he'd never felt more lost.

80

The Present Day
Los Angeles, California

MASON guided the personal aerial transport through the open expanse. The Milagro building lay a half mile straight ahead. The rush of air from the twin turbines rumbled in his chest. Wind whipped through his hair. A twisting plume of smoke curled up from the street below. He followed it to the source and saw a few deltas climbing around a downed chopper.

No.

No. No. No.

The fuselage lay on its side. Gouged tracks in the street showed where the rotor had chewed down to nubs. The tail lay a hundred feet behind the cabin.

Judging by the devastation below, the odds of survival weren't something he wanted to consider. Even if there were just bodies below, he wasn't going to let his family be...

No.

Not going to happen.

He eased back the throttle and guided PAT down towards what he knew might be the final seconds of his life. Knowing it, and accepting it. If Theresa and Beth were gone, he had no reason to live.

He'd aim the transport directly at the aft gas tanks. The darker patch of concrete underneath showed that at least one of the tanks had likely been punctured.

Not good.

One of the tanks had likely been punctured.

He was so busy visualizing how he was going to go out in a glorious fireball that he hadn't considered if they were still alive and trapped inside. If that gas caught, they'd be burned alive.

Mason yanked back on the throttle and PAT dropped toward the street below. At fifty feet to go, he slammed the throttle forward. The turbines screamed and the hull shook so hard it nearly tore apart. The transport clawed for lift even as inertia continued pulling it lower.

He stared down gritting his teeth, waiting for the bone-crunching impact to shove his pelvis up through his ribcage.

The deltas shrieked up at him like a god descending from Olympus. Terror and wonder gleamed in their eyes. They backed away, wary of getting too close.

The twisted wreck below rushed up in a blur.

He'd overreacted. The emotional response coupled with the unfamiliarity with the operational parameters of the transport combined to cause disaster. Like many catastrophic accidents, seemingly small mistakes could combine to cause unthinkable disaster.

The transport's skids crashed into the passenger cockpit door. Metal screeched against metal. Glass fragments exploded out tearing into the flesh of the nearest delta. Its screams were lost to the groaning of metal stretched beyond its tensile strength.

And then he was in the air again.

The harness straps viciously cut into his thighs as the vehicle lifted into the air. It half-bounced, half-accelerated off the crash site. The cartilage between his vertebrae flattened like jello discs smashed in a concrete accordion.

The impact jarred his hands off the control joysticks. With no direct input, PAT leveled itself out ten feet above the wreck.

Mason looked down into the crashed chopper and saw two bodies. The pilot and one of the operators in black tactical gear. He eased PAT lower and found no one else.

So everyone but these two had survived the crash. The survivors must've headed for Milagro Tower. He scanned down the street and saw another pocket of deltas, less than a dozen, gathered in the center of the street. They were bunched up around something.

They were feeding.

But on what?

Or who?

Mason worked the controls and left the chopper behind. He swooped down on the pack ahead. Some of the more timid ones scrambled away to safety, while others ignored his approach completely. At the center of their activity lay two bodies in black tactical gear.

The rear guard had been overrun. Which meant nobody was left to protect the others.

He spotted a smaller knot of deltas further on. Their filthy bodies packed so tight at the center that Mason couldn't make out the victim.

Please, God.

Please.

Mason hit the throttle. He bumped the nav joystick forward dipping the front lower. PAT flew in hard and fast. The landing skids tore into them, carving a channel through their ranks. The vehicle canted over forty-five degrees as their limbs and heads smacked off the skids.

The pack consciousness shifted. The feeding frenzy died and they turned as one to consider the new threat. Hands grasped for the skids. Several got a grip and dragged PAT, and Mason, lower.

Mason stomped on the fingers curled around the skids. Deltas howled in pain as his boots crushed slender bones. He broke free and lifted a few feet above their heads.

Numerous dead and partially dismembered deltas surrounded a body at the center. Despite its mutilated state, he recognized the beard and lanky frame.

Ahmed.

An M4 rifle and an empty magazine lay on the pavement next to him. Evidence of shrapnel hits radiated from his position. A fragmentation grenade.

He must've sacrificed himself to give the others a chance.

Mason stared at Ahmed's shredded corpse and closed his eyes. As sorry as he was for the man, he couldn't help but register elation that it hadn't been Theresa or Beth.

He lifted into the air and left the gruesome scene behind. Looking ahead, he saw a group of deltas disappear inside the tall, white cylindrical tower.

He prayed to any god that would listen that his daughter and wife were still alive.

And would remain so.

81

Skimming above the ground, Mason searched for signs that his family had come this way. He saw nothing but the occasional body of a dead delta that had likely been shot. So much death. So much darkness. All because of some virus.

The final days of news media coverage ran stories speculating that the virus had been manufactured. What if it was true?

Technology had taken mankind to unimaginable heights. Could it be that it also brought them to such depths? Irony was a concept only an advanced brain could appreciate. *Appreciate* was perhaps not quite the right word.

Would modern man die off leaving the deltas to scratch their way back to civilization or, perhaps more likely, to surrender to oblivion?

Mason cut off the morose ponderings as he neared the tower. Melancholic contemplation wasn't going to do anything to help his family.

Several deltas emerged from the building's entrance. They glared up at him some fifty feet above their heads. A few more joined them.

He wasn't going to get inside on the ground floor. Which left only one other option. He pushed the throttle forward and the transport climbed higher. Office windows slid by in a blur as he picked up speed. The roofs of surrounding buildings appeared as he neared the top.

A gust of wind hit him from behind. PAT careened toward the face of the building. Mason jerked the nav joystick back and the machine slid to a stop two feet from a huge glass window. At this close distance, the interior revealed itself. An expanse of tightly packed cubicles. Empty aisles carved channels through the ordered hive. The quintessential model of corporate productivity. But all the worker bees were gone. Surprisingly, there were no signs of the devastation that had claimed the city. Neat stacks of papers lay on desks. White boards hung on cubicle walls held grand schematics that no longer mattered.

On the desk nearest to the window, small framed pictures of loved ones sat in a neat row next to a dark flatscreen. Whoever once gazed upon those pictures to marshal the grit needed to grind out another day in the matrix was now long gone.

In all likelihood, the ones in the pictures were as well.

Mason backed away from the vertical surface and continued his ascent. Another minute and he crested the edge of the roof. A large circular helipad occupied the center. Maybe a hundred feet in diameter. In the center of it was a painted red circle with the number twelve inside. This must've been the chopper's intended destination.

Before it crashed and became a delta magnet.

A lower deck shaped like a twenty pointed star surrounded the helipad. It extended beyond the helipad on all sides, likely to catch anyone that got blown off before they pitched over the actual edge and fell a thousand feet to a conclusive end below.

Mason rose above the helipad and then slid over to line up in the center of the circle. Hovering above the painted number, he eased back on the power. A gust hammered him from the side. PAT glided toward the edge as Mason brought it down hard. The skids bounced a few times and then ground to a stop.

Los Angeles extended in all directions. He punched through the screen to initiate the shutdown sequence. The turbines spun down as Mason released the latches on the harness. He stepped down and stumbled forward, finding the solidity of the surface unfamiliar.

Another gust of wind whipped across the roof and he braced against it. It wasn't like a hurricane about to toss him off the top like a coconut from a palm tree, but it was still more than a little unsettling.

He climbed down the ladder at the east edge of the helipad onto the larger deck below. As he stepped off the final rung, muffled voices echoed through the door to his right. He couldn't make out the words above the whistling wind.

Mason posted up on the side of the door and waited.

The handle rattled but the door stayed closed. It rattled again. The door itself shook as whoever was inside tried to batter it down.

"Get that thing open!"

Mason recognized the voice. Anton's. The man that had taken his family and left him to die.

A shot fired and the lock blew outward.

Mason hugged the wall waiting for the door to open.

Another shot and then a body rammed the door open. A large figure in a dark suit fell forward.

Mason tackled him to the ground before he had a chance to recover. He caught the guy in the temple with a vicious elbow. A 1911 pistol clattered away and Mason dove for it. He recovered it and had the sights aligned and his finger inside the trigger guard even before the suit managed to lift his head. A part of his brain registered the unique filigree design along the chromed slide. A yellow rose of Texas. There was only one person in the world that carried a Dan Wesson ECO 1911 .45 with a filigreed yellow rose of Texas along the slide.

The face that looked up at him was no surprise.

"Sarge? I thought you were dead!"

82

Two more figures stumbled through the open door and Mason pivoted to line up the front site on the second one. Anton Reshenko. A man with a pot belly that extended further than his time left on earth.

Mason shoved him up against the wall and dug the muzzle of the pistol into his fleshy throat.

His eyes opened wide in a most gratifying way. He knew this was it. Good. Mason cocked the hammer and grinned wickedly when Anton flinched at the clicking sound.

"Where is my family?" Mason shouted in his face.

"Please don't hurt my papa," Iridia cried out.

Miro picked himself up and pulled Iridia away from the confrontation. He knew Mason well enough to see the danger. "Sarge! Don't do it!"

Mason dug the muzzle up under Anton's jawbone. The madman groaned in pain. Lucky for him all his suffering would soon be over. The brain can't process input when it's painting a wall in a splatter pattern. "Stay out of this, Miro!"

Iridia struggled to break free but Miro's bulky six-six frame held her fast. "Don't hurt him!" she screamed.

Mason added more pressure to the metal stabbing up under Anton's fleshy chin. "Where is my family? I won't ask again."

"Please, Sarge! We need him! He has the cure for this thing that's destroying the world!"

If his family was gone, Mason honestly didn't care what happened to the rest of the world. He'd just about decided to squeeze the trigger when voices from inside the building echoed up the stairwell. He recognized them at once. He drew back and whipped the grip into Anton's temple sending him crashing to the deck.

He ran inside just as Beth rounded the staircase with her arm under Theresa's, helping their daughter up. Elio and Noor helped Maria along behind them. Maria saw him and scowled. Her hate would have to wait. He hurried down the stairs and picked Theresa up in his arms.

"Go!" Beth shouted. "They are coming up after us!"

Mason didn't need to know who the *they* were. Their inchoate shrieking echoed up the stairwell. He carried Theresa up the last flight and out onto the roof. Iridia knelt beside her father stroking his cheek and blubbering.

"Miro, find something to barricade the door!"

"Copy that," Miro said as he cast around for something suitable.

"Are you okay?" Mason asked Theresa as he laid her gently on the deck as far from the roof access door as possible.

She stared past him with unresponsive, bloodshot eyes.

"Honey?"

She broke into a coughing fit. Blood flecked from her lips onto Mason's face. Her skin glowed with a pale sheen. Red veins traced through the whites of her eyes. He wiped away the gathering sweat above her eyebrows. Her forehead nearly burned his fingertips.

"You're evil!" Beth screamed from behind.

Mason turned to see Beth leap at Anton. Her right fist broke through his upraised arms and smashed into his nose. Red exploded down over his chin and onto a wrinkled shirt and coat. She connected with a right hook to his ear before Mason dragged her back.

Elio and Noor helped Maria out onto the deck. "They aren't far behind!" he said as he moved the trio away from the door.

A growing hum of shouting and shrieking echoed up the stairwell.

"You murderer!" Beth spat at Anton. "You did it!"

"Beth," Mason said into her ear. "What are you talking about?"

His words distracted her bloodlust and she calmed a little. She answered in words dripping with hate. "He created the Delta Virus."

"What?" Mason and Miro said in unison.

Beth stopped straining to get free. Her animal mind relinquished control back to her thinking mind. "He did it." She waved her hands around. "He did all of this. He's insane."

Anton wiped at the blood streaming out of his nose. The terror in his eyes flashed to fury. "Insane?" he shouted. "I'm insane?" He spat blood onto the deck.

"You destroyed mankind!" Beth said.

"I saved mankind! That you don't see it is no great surprise."

"Papa? What do you mean?" Iridia froze as she tried to understand his meaning.

Mason couldn't believe what he was hearing. He'd never

believed the conspiracy theories. Surely the virus had been a freak of nature? A freak of biological potential that humanity knew always existed but hoped would never arise.

Miro ran to the door with a metal pipe he'd found. He slammed the door shut and wedged it between the door handle and nearby conduit. It wasn't going to hold forever. Maybe not even for long. Miro drew his ankle pistol and covered the door. He looked over his shoulder and grinned. "Feels uncomfortably like the Alamo, huh Sarge?"

Only a dyed-in-the-wool Texan could make light of their dire situation. It was one of the things that Mason appreciated most during their tour in the sandbox.

Mason released Beth now that she appeared to be in control again. He kept the forty-five aimed at Anton's chest. "Talk."

Anton glared at him disdainfully, as if the pistol pointed at his chest didn't exist. "Your wife was partially correct. I did, in fact, create the Delta Virus, or what should more properly be called the Darwin Virus."

"Why?"

"Why?" Anton asked incredulously. "Because our wisdom had yet to catch up with our technology. We were the most successful cancer the world has ever seen. We were killing our host. And like any parasite, we would've all died when the host died."

It took every ounce of resolve for Mason not to pull the trigger until the slide locked back. "You're insane."

Anton laughed. "Every genius in history has been called insane by the mediocre minds surrounding him. Truly great men rise above the petty concerns of the merely average. Am I insane not to have wasted my life in a haze of mindless consumption?"

"No," Mason said. "You're insane because you think killing mankind is the way to save it."

Anton wiped at the blood dripping from his chin. "You're a fool to believe anything else could have. You misunderstand an evolutionary truth of our species. We choose comfort over pain. We choose the known over the unknown. These two primal urges paired together guaranteed we would never take either sufficient or timely action to save the host, and hence ourselves."

"People were starting to get it," Beth said.

Anton laughed derisively. "Changing lightbulbs and dumping Amazon boxes in recycling bins were their solutions. The ones everyone could get behind. Pathetic. It changed nothing. Worse, it made people feel effective even as humanity continued to fall."

"And so you decided to handle oblivion yourself?"

"I pre-empted the inevitable, desperate madness. The decline that would've brought mankind back to the dark ages or worse. All that we'd struggled for lost to darkness and degradation."

"How is what you did any different?"

"We now have a chance to move forward, replete with relative abundance, while still retaining our technological and intellectual achievements. The planet requires time to heal and our reduced population will offer it that respite. By the time we have regained our previous peak, we will have gained the wisdom to sustainably coexist with it."

"You're twisted."

"I'm a realist. I don't live in the fantasy that mankind can somehow live apart from the world that sustains it."

Enough. While some of what this guy said rang true, killing off most of mankind wasn't the solution.

"Where's the cure?" Mason asked. The bigger picture stuff could wait. His daughter desperately needed help.

"Here!" Beth said as she dug a vial out of her pocket.

The door shook as the first few deltas encountered the barrier between themselves and their prey. Their primal rage spilled through the door.

The faint sound of rotor blades chewing through the air drew Mason's attention. He scanned the horizon to the north and saw a huge chopper heading their way. A VH-3D Sea King by the looks of it.

"You expecting company?" he asked.

Anton grinned and nodded.

Mason's jaw tightened. Two handguns weren't going to last long against an assault team.

83

Mason grabbed Anton by the collar. He had every intention of killing the scumbag, but he didn't want to waste an advantage if the approaching chopper improved the situation from a last stand at the Alamo to a Mexican standoff.

While he knew he could count on Miro, two pistols against a team of six or more operators carrying battle rifles barely qualified as a standoff. Maybe it was just a different version of the Alamo.

The only advantage he had was the forty-five pointed at their boss's chest. Maybe he could negotiate terms.

It wasn't a great plan, but the chopper was closing in fast and Mason couldn't think of any better ideas.

"Miro, guard them!" he shouted. "Everyone else, stay down!"

"Copy that, Sarge!" Miro said as he took up a position near the others.

Mason shoved Anton forward, purposefully yanking him around to keep him stumbling and off-balance. He climbed up the ladder to the helipad, pulling Anton up after him. "Don't do anything stupid."

Anton smiled at the approaching chopper. "Put down your weapon and I won't have my men kill you and your family."

Mason slammed a clenched fist into his solar plexus. Anton dropped to his knees gasping for breath.

"Threaten my family again and you'll die first." He yanked Anton to his feet and wrapped an arm under his neck and pulled tight. He didn't have proper body armor, but this would do.

The chopper pulled in fast and flared hard to touch down soft as a feather on the helipad. Eight men in desert camo with United States flag patches on their chests filed out of the cabin and set up firing positions. The center of their perimeter had their HK 416 rifles zeroed on Mason and Anton. One of the soldiers turned and waved at the chopper. His right shoulder had an army green arrow-shaped patch with a black dagger on it.

These weren't like the others. These were Army guys. Specifically 1st Special Forces Operational Detachment - Delta. These were some serious professionals. Way beyond Mason's pay grade.

Two more soldiers jumped out of the cabin. They helped a tall, lanky man in an immaculate dark blue suit step out onto the helipad. He wore thin-framed fashionable glasses of a matching color. His bald head would've given him away if Mason hadn't already recognized him. He strode toward Mason as if he owned the world.

Which made sense because he mostly did.

Gabriel Cruz. The world's wealthiest man. The same man Mason had inadvertently saved from that mad dog gang leader.

He came to a stop ten feet away from Mason. The Delta operators stayed between the two parties with their rifles never wavering from their chosen targets. Mason had no doubt that if he turned the gun from Anton to Gabriel, his head would end up like a watermelon at a Gallagher comedy show.

"Mr. West," Gabriel said. "Let's dispense with the theatrics. We are both reasonable men." He took another few steps forward with his hands raised.

"Mr. President, please maintain a safe distance," the operator standing next to him said.

Mr. President? What was that about?

Gabriel nodded. "I'm sure you have questions about my newly appointed position, but they'll have to wait."

"Okay," Mason replied while at the same time wondering if such a thing was even possible.

"Sir, please step away from him," the operator said.

Gabriel waved him off. "I have nothing to fear from this man. He saved my life less than two weeks ago."

"All the same, sir, I'd appreciate your cooperation."

"Captain Whitaker, you will do your job and I will do mine. Am I clear?"

"Yes, sir."

Anton reached for his boss. "Thank you for coming for me! This madman wants to kill me!"

Gabriel's good humor melted away until only ice remained. "Then he and I are in agreement. You betrayed me. You overstepped your limited authority."

"I did what needed to be done," Anton replied. The imperious weight in his voice cracked mid-sentence. It rose in pitch and wavered. "Surely you of all people must see that."

"I see that you are unhinged, and that my trust in you was a grievous error in judgement. I will not repeat the mistake."

Gabriel looked at Mason. "Would you mind placing your weapon on the ground? You don't require the leverage and there would be none even if you did. Besides, I think these fellows would feel much better about it."

Mason didn't see the advantage in not complying. It sounded like Gabriel could offer them help. He lowered the pistol, making sure the muzzle didn't cover anywhere near Gabriel's direction. He released his neck lock on Anton who gasped and sputtered to get more air into his lungs.

"I've come for the serum, Anton. Where is it?" Gabriel said.

"My wife has it," Mason said. "We have people on the deck below, but we have a big problem."

"What is that?"

"Deltas are about to break through the door below and out onto the roof."

"How many?" Gabriel said.

Mason glanced at the soldiers flanking the president. "More than your firepower can handle."

Captain Whitaker narrowed his eyes at Mason. "Sir, we can handle it."

"Captain, I'm not doubting you or your men. But this isn't the safest position for the president to be in."

Mason knew as well as any soldier the drive to take it to the enemy. But he also knew the cost of losing men in the effort. And there was zero chance Captain Whitaker would put the president in danger no matter his personal feelings.

Gabriel turned to his detail's CO. "Captain, get those people aboard."

"Yes, sir!"

Before the captain could get his men in motion, gunfire erupted on the deck below.

84

Mason ran to the edge of the helipad and saw the nightmare unfolding below. Deltas dashed through the opened roof access door.

BANG. BANG.

"Get to the ladder," Miro shouted as he dropped one. He covered the rear of the group as everyone hurried to the ladder. Several deltas followed close behind.

Miro dropped another. Mason fired from above, knocking down a couple about to overwhelm his friend.

Still more bodies surged out onto the roof. There were too many, and there was no place to retreat from the top of a skyscraper.

Captain Whitaker and several operators appeared at Mason's side as the deltas below encircled the group trying to get up the ladder. Beth struggled to help Theresa up. An operator slid down the ladder and hefted Theresa over his shoulder. He headed back up and Beth followed.

"Fire for effect," the captain shouted above the thumping chopper and the screaming chaos.

Mason's ears rang with the concussion of numerous

rifles letting loose a withering barrage on the deltas below. He ran to the ladder as the operator carrying Theresa appeared on the top rung. The soldier heaved her over, knocking Mason's forty-five out of his hands. The pistol clattered to the concrete.

Mason ignored it and helped his daughter onto the helipad. He passed her off to a waiting soldier and then pulled Beth up with Clyde around her neck. He helped Noor next and then extended a hand to Maria as she made it to the top. She snarled and climbed over without his help. Elio arrived next while Miro covered their six with the help of the operators above.

The numbers coming through the door started to overwhelm the suppressive fire. A surge of bodies pushed through the steel rain. Miro jumped up the ladder as a delta leaped on his back. The two fell backwards and Miro ended up pinned underneath. The delta landed on Miro's back, straddling his waist.

Mason looked to where he thought Miro's forty-five had fallen to the ground.

It wasn't there. Where was it?

There wasn't time. He turned back and jumped off the helipad.

His foot caught the delta in the back of the neck. A satisfying crunch and it pitched to the side in a heap. Mason landed wrong and his ankle torqued to the side. Pain jolted up his right leg.

Miro pulled him up. "Damn, Sarge! You're a regular Sam Houston!"

A couple of deltas reached for them and collapsed as a fountain of blood exploded from their foreheads.

Mason glanced up and saw Captain Whitaker zero on

the next closest delta and dispatch it in like manner. Still more came. "Get up the ladder, Corporal!"

"Roger that!" Miro said as he scrambled up the rungs.

Mason followed close behind. He made it up and then jerked to a stop as the situation resolved to clarity. All of the operators stood at the edge of the helipad firing down on the deltas as they darted out onto the roof below. As many as they knocked down, more followed. They would not be held off forever.

But that wasn't the worst part.

The worst part was that he'd found Miro's forty-five.

Anton stood ten feet away with his back to Mason. He held the missing forty-five in his hands with the muzzle touching the president's chest. He whipped the pistol across Gabriel's face knocking his glasses off. A red gash lined his cheek. Anton yelled something lost in the din.

His weapon.

About to be used to assassinate the President of the United States.

No.

Not going to happen.

Not in a million years.

85

A delta appeared at the top of the ladder. The soldiers shifted to incorporate the expanded field of fire, but they still hadn't seen what was happening behind them.

The first delta got a double tap to the forehead and it pitched backward.

Captain Whitaker and his men had their hands full slowing the advance, never mind stopping it.

Mason glanced at Beth and she shook her head. Of course, she knew what he would do next. He didn't waste time responding. Instead, he hobbled toward Anton hoping the bastard didn't turn around before he got there. Anton raised the pistol to Gabriel's head just as Mason dove forward.

BANG.

The pistol fired as Mason steamrolled into Anton's ribcage. They crashed to the ground and Mason made sure his full weight came down on top of the dirtbag.

Anton landed with a grunt and the pistol clattered away. He clawed at his chest and sucked at air that wouldn't flow through a spasming diaphragm.

Mason rolled off and recovered the forty-five in one smooth maneuver. He finished the roll and came out with one knee down and a foot planted. The front sight raised to find Anton.

Only the planted foot taking his weight was the one with the busted ankle. He nearly pitched over before dropping that knee to the ground to arrest the fall.

The threat was neutralized, but the damage was done. A single bullet that he could never get back. He looked over his shoulder dreading to verify what it had done. Preparing to accept responsibility for the assassination.

Gabriel stood like a stone, clutching his chest.

Mason stood and limped over. "Are you okay, Mr. President?"

He didn't respond.

Mason brushed Gabriel's hand away and patted over his shirt. There was no hole. No blood. A miss.

Gabriel looked himself over.

Captain Whitaker appeared beside them. "Time to go, sir. Now!"

Gabriel nodded.

Captain Whitaker yelled the order and two of his men ushered the others aboard the chopper. Two other soldiers retreated from the edge of the helipad and took up defensive positions near the bird.

Miro scooped Iridia up and carried her to the chopper. She stared in shock at her fallen father before disappearing into the chopper's interior.

A roar from below momentarily rose above the thump of the rotors. The deltas must've realized the change in momentum. One appeared at the top of the ladder. It didn't get higher before a bullet punctured its head and sent it reeling backward.

Gabriel knelt beside Anton and dug a hand into his left pocket. He withdrew what looked like a small silver coin. He held the coin in front of Anton's twisted face. "I saved your life in the alley that day. I lifted you out of the gutter and gave you a future."

Anton pushed himself up on his elbows.

Gabriel curled a fist around the coin. "And you betrayed me. Unwavering loyalty. That was the only rule that can not be forgiven."

Anton snarled and spat blood onto the ground. "I saved mankind! I did what you and all the other spineless cowards could not. You should be on your knees thanking me!"

Gabriel flicked a straight right and caught Anton on the chin. His head snapped back and he collapsed on his back. "Anton Reshenko, I sentence you to death for your crimes against humanity."

Anton's eyes opened wide with fear. He reached up as a submissive animal does to an alpha.

Gabriel slapped his hand away. "Goodbye." He turned away and allowed Captain Whitaker to help him back to the chopper.

Mason followed them inside.

"Sit here," Gabriel said pointing to the seat next to him.

Mason nodded and took the offered seat.

The chopper's engine spun up and the thump of long blades slicing through the air picked up.

The four operators holding the defensive perimeter retreated into the cabin while continuously firing at the advancing deltas.

Anton struggled to his feet and stumbled toward the chopper.

While several deltas advanced on the chopper, one broke off toward Anton.

An old man. His lower lip dangled from his chin. His thin limbs moved with unexpected energy.

"Don't leave me!" Anton shouted.

Captain Whitaker tapped the pilot's shoulder and pointed his finger up and twirled it.

The chopper groaned and lurched off the roof.

Anton wrapped an arm over a landing skid and held on as the chopper lifted higher.

The old delta reached him and grabbed hold of his waist.

Anton glanced down at the delta in terror. "No, Charles! No!"

The elderly delta bit into the bulge of belly spilling out of Anton's shirt.

Anton screamed and lost his grip. He crashed down to the helipad. The delta crawled up his body and bit down on his face.

The surrounding deltas converged on the struggling pair. Anton disappeared beneath a wall of flailing flesh.

The sickening screams of his final seconds were lost as the chopper lifted higher into the air.

Mason held the overflowing trash bag open as Beth shoved another outfit of Theresa's inside. Her room looked like a poltergeist had crossed over. While she rested in the chopper out on the street, they packed up one trash bag each of personal possessions.

One bag each to contain the entirety of their lives.

That was hard enough. But the fact that they had exactly five minutes to make those decisions made it next to impossible.

How was a person supposed to look at a lifetime of accumulation and memories and decide which handful made the cut?

And how was that supposed to happen when each decision got less than a second or two of consideration?

It *was* impossible.

And so they did the best they could.

Beth dug through Theresa's sheets and fished out a prize. Lambchops. As bedraggled as ever. Both eye buttons missing and ears frayed into stringy threads. The loyal lovie looked more like garbage than something you'd want to shove into a trash bag of your dearest belongings. Despite his appearance, or maybe because of it, his inclusion was never in question.

She crammed him inside and Mason tied the top into a knot. He hefted the bag over his shoulder and was about to walk it out when Elio appeared in the doorway.

"I got it," he said as he grabbed the bag. "You need to go easy on that ankle."

"Thanks. You're a good kid, you know."

A lopsided smile spread across his face. He nodded and departed with the last bag.

Mason checked his watch.

Forty-two seconds left on the clock.

He gathered Beth in his arms. He glanced over her shoulder at the corner of the room. "I remember the night we put together Theresa's crib. In a room about half this size. How we argued if it should go by the window or in the corner."

She squeezed him tight, shaping her body into his. She rested her cheek on his chest. "And I remember how I convinced you I was right."

Images flashed through Mason's mind. Beth's bare skin moving in ways that would make the Pope blush. They'd built a life together. Much of it here.

A cat meowed in the hallway.

Mr. Piddles strolled in and wrapped his body around Beth's leg. He twisted through her legs with his long tail curling around behind.

"Looks like we're all out of trash bags," Mason said.

Beth arched a brow at him. "He's going. Iridia is going to need him now more than ever."

Iridia was in the chopper in Miro's arms. She hadn't

stopped sobbing since losing her father. Beth was right, as she usually was in matters of the heart.

Mason surveyed the overweight feline. "Well, I suppose we could eat him if food gets scarce."

Beth cuffed his shoulder. "Not funny."

Mason laughed anyway. It was an empty sound, but at least it existed for a brief span. The sadness in his heart needed whatever help it could get.

They stared at Theresa's room in silence, knowing they would never see it again.

"Hey," Mason said, "the upside is that you've always wanted to live in San Francisco. Weird that it's going to be the new capitol."

"This wasn't exactly the scenario I'd envisioned."

Mason nodded in slow motion. "I know."

"Do you think life will ever be normal again?" she asked.

"I hope so."

He knew it would never be like it was. He knew that world was gone forever. Whatever came next might aspire toward similar ends, but whatever it became, it would undoubtedly be different.

Because every result was a combination of the innumerable conditions that preceded it. And the world they now faced had been fundamentally altered. Whatever came next would grow from that changed soil.

Beth's expression darkened. Moisture welled in the corners of her eyes.

"What're you thinking about?" he asked.

"We need to check on my parents on the way north," she said. "They might still be alive."

"We will," he said, without knowing if the diversion was actually possible. He had no idea about the refueling situation or any number of other factors that might preclude another waypoint in the journey.

The not knowing didn't matter.

It was a dilemma that didn't require an immediate solution. It could wait a few minutes. And with only seconds remaining of their old lives, the future seemed far away.

Captain Whitaker appeared in the doorway.

"We've got contact outside. It's time to go. Now."

Beth scooped up Mr. Piddles.

"Ma'am, the President didn't say anything about a cat."

"He's going. It's not up for discussion."

Beth marched past the captain staring holes into him as she went.

Mason passed him with a lopsided grin. "She loves animals."

Mason followed her out of the house they'd spent so much time, money, and energy making their own. As much as his heart mourned the loss, the depths of his soul appreciated a more important truth.

He still had his family.

Billions of people had died or lost those they loved. Incalculable loss. Incalculable suffering.

And yet he still had the two things that mattered most.

His daughter and his wife.

While Theresa was still very sick, the serum was apparently working because her fever had subsided and she was again responsive.

He helped Beth into the chopper and climbed in behind. Six trash bags were crammed into the rear area. One each for Mason, Beth, Theresa, Elio, Noor, and Maria.

The President motioned for Mason to return to the empty seat next to him.

Mason sat down and secured his seat belt. He accepted the headset offered by Captain Whitaker.

"Take us back to the capital," the President said over comms.

"Yes, sir," the pilot replied.

The President turned to Mason. "Mr. West."

"Yes, Mr. President?"

Mr. President?

Too weird, but being surrounded by an elite team of special forces operators lent a certain gravitas to the claim.

"You've saved my life on two occasions. You seem to have a knack for it."

Mason had no interest in gratitude or back-patting. His daughter was still very sick and, despite receiving the serum, still had a hard recovery ahead.

"Sir, no thanks are necessary."

"I wasn't going to thank you. I was going to offer you a job."

Mason's head spun, seemingly faster than the rotors as the chopper lifted into the air. The pilot yawed to the north and picked up speed while continuing to climb. Far below, Mason watched as a pack of deltas stood in the street, looking up at the beings that, from their perspective, must've seemed like gods.

Fragile gods, to be certain.

"A job, sir?" Mason asked.

"A position in the Presidential Protective Division."

"Sir," Captain Whitaker cut in, "Alpha team is more than capable of attending to that duty."

"Captain, your skills are required for higher priority missions."

"I'm sorry, sir. But your safety is *the* highest priority."

"This isn't a discussion, Captain," the President replied

with an edge of impatience creeping into his voice. "Besides, it's high time we reconstituted the Secret Service and its mission."

The President turned back to Mason. "What do you say? Will you keep me alive while I go about the dangerous business of rebuilding civilization?"

It was insane to even consider. And yet, it made perfect sense. He'd had over a decade in the close protection business and many years in the Marine Corps before that. He knew how to save a life, and he knew how to take one.

If this man could bring mankind back from the brink, then he deserved everything Mason had to offer.

Even his own life, if it came to that.

Beth wouldn't like it, but he didn't really have a choice.

"Yes, sir, Mr. President."

THE END OF BOOK 2

Turn the page for a preview of *The Fragile Hope*, book 3 in the *Edge of Survival* series. Preview only available for ebook format.

WANT BOOKS FOR FREE?

Join the Readers Group to get a free copy of The Last Day, Sole Prey, and Saint John. One novel, one novella and one short story, all for free. You'll also receive exclusive discounts on new releases, other freebies, and lots more.

Go to WWW.WILLIAMODAY.COM to find out more.

OTHER WORKS

Extinction Crisis series
SOLE CONNECTION, a Short Story
SOLE PREY, a Prequel Novella
SOLE SURVIVOR, Book 1
SOLE CHAOS, Book 2
THE TANK MAN, a Short Story
THE PLUNGE, a Short Story

Edge of Survival series
THE LAST DAY, Book 1
THE FINAL COLLAPSE, Book 2
THE FRAGILE HOPE, Book 3
THE DESPERATE FIGHT, Book 4

The Best Adventures series
THE SLITHERING GOLIATH
THE BEEPOCALYPSE
THE PHARAOH'S CURSE

Short Stories
THE GENDER LOTTERY
SAINT JOHN
SHE'S GONE

QUESTIONS OR COMMENTS?

Have any questions or comments? I'd love to hear from you! Seriously. Voices coming from outside my head are such a relief.

Give me a shout at william@williamoday.com.

All the best,
Will

THE GOAL

I have a simple storytelling goal that can be wildly difficult to achieve. I want to entertain you with little black marks arranged on a white background. Read the marks and join me on a grand adventure. If all goes well, you'll slip under the spell and so walk alongside heroes and villains. You'll feel what they feel. You'll understand the world as they do.

My writing and your reading is a kind of mechanical telepathy. I translate my thoughts and emotions through characters and conflict in a written story. If the transmission works, your heart will pound, your heart will break, and you will care. At the very least, hopefully you'll escape your world and live in mine for a little while.

I hope to see you there!
Will

MY LIFE THUS FAR

I grew up in the red dirt of the Midwest, the center of the states. I later meandered out to the West Coast and have remained off-center ever since. Living in Los Angeles, I achieved my Career 1.0 dream by working on big-budget movies for over a decade. If you've seen a Will Smith or Tom Cruise blockbuster action movie, you've likely seen my work.

The work was challenging and fulfilling... until I got tired of telling other people's stories. I longed to tell my own. So, now I'm pursuing my Career 2.0 dream—a dream I've had since youth—to write stories that pull a reader in and make the everyday world fade away.

I've since moved to a more rural setting north of San Francisco with my lovely wife, vibrant children, and a dog that has discovered the secret to infinite energy. His name is Trip and he fits the name in four unique ways.

WILLIAMODAY.COM

Printed in Great Britain
by Amazon